BOUND

SEP7 '20

Sarah Bryant

Proudly Published by Snowbooks in 2012

Copyright © 2012 Sarah Bryant

Sarah Bryant asserts the moral right to
be identified as the author of this work.

Snowbooks Ltd.
email: info@snowbooks.com

www.snowbooks.com

British Library Cataloguing in Publication Data
A catalogue record for this book is available from the
British Library.

Paperback ISBN 978-1907777-58-5
Hardback ISBN 978-1907777-61-5

BOUND

Sarah Bryant

To Tanit Sakakini for the inspiration, and Elaine di Rollo for keeping me honest.

Acknowledgements

I'd like to thank everyone who supported me through this literary U-Turn: Clare Whittaker, Carol Christie, Elaine Di Rollo and Tanit Sakakini for reading and commenting with complete sincerity, despite thinking I'd gone mad; Elaine again for never being afraid to tell me what I've got wrong (or to like the villain better than the hero!); Tanit again for all of the hours of Dogboy scheming that somehow led to this; my husband Colin for not running screaming when I say, 'I'm stuck on a plot point, let me tell you about it…'; Laura Erel for giving me the teenage girl's perspective; and last but by no means least, the team at Snowbooks for throwing caution to the wind and giving me the chance to indulge my lifelong obsession with YA literature. I love you guys!

Pronouncing Gaelic Words & Names

Ruadhri = Rory

Each Uisge = Ach (like the composer Bach) Ishkeh

Sìth = Shee

Cait Sìth = Kite Shee

Madainneag = Matin-ag

Sláinte = Slawn-jeh

Uamh-an-Aingeal = U-ah an Ahn-jehl

I love thee to the depth and breadth and height
My soul can reach...
– Elizabeth Barrett Browning

CHAPTER 1

Sophie was the only passenger on the ferry that evening. She stood on deck for the crossing despite the low sky and lashing rain, her iPod pumping out the Lachrymosa from Mozart's "Requiem". She couldn't have planned such a perfect soundtrack if she'd tried, but as it was she hadn't tried, because she'd meant to feel elation at this point in her journey. Instead, she'd never felt so alone, so much in an alien country as she did now, in what was still a part of her own.

The feeling had begun as soon as the train pulled out of Edinburgh. By the time it reached the Highlands' brooding peaks and dim, mist-shrouded valleys, Sophie felt a million miles from home. Even the sea, when she reached it, was unfamiliar. There were no pleasure beaches here, only black mountains plunging into steely water. She had to keep reminding herself that this was what she'd chosen, what she wanted. That if it put five hundred miles between her and London, then any amount of rain and isolation was worth it.

But when Ardnasheen finally came into view, her spirits sank even further. The village was no more than a scatter of white cottages huddled between the great black mountain at its back and the opaque water in front. Her eyes traveled the shore, looking for what the pub landlord's email had called "the Big House". The Ardnasheen website referred to it as "Madainneag", which apparently meant "Morning Star" in Gaelic. But when Sophie spotted it, she couldn't think of a less likely name. There was nothing bright about it. The medieval tower, the battlements and turrets were barely distinguishable from the dark woods at its back, and the rest of the house's sprawling form blended with the murky colours of the shore. Not one window was lit.

Sophie turned away, toward something pale in her peripheral vision. She pushed back the dark hair that had blown into her eyes – and then she froze. The light-coloured patch resolved itself into a figure standing on the headland to her left, watching the boat. Watching her.

Her first, panicked thought was, *They've followed me.* But the figure didn't lurch or shift or reach out for her. It didn't move at all. Gradually, the panic drained away, allowing her to see it for what it really was: a statue, with downcast eyes and hands clasped, apparently in prayer. It was too dark to make out whether it was a Madonna or an angel, but its elaborately draped clothing suggested one or the other. She wondered whether it was a holdover from a more religious time, or if it marked something more sinister. The site of a shipwreck, perhaps, or the point where a fishing fleet, running for home in the teeth of a storm, had been dashed against the rocks.

Stop it, she told herself, as the thrum of the engine beneath her feet changed timbre. She shut off the iPod as their forward momentum slowed. She couldn't make out any kind of dock or pier. Then she spotted a man knee-deep in water a few meters ahead – a good twenty meters from the rocky beach. The deckhand coiled a rope and tossed it and the man caught it, the boat's lights reflecting off of his yellow rain slicker. Apparently the pier was submerged.

"Watch your step," the man called to Sophie as the skipper cut the engine. "It's a flood tide."

Resigning herself to a week of wet boots, she shouldered her backpack, picked up her harp case, and stepped off the boat. "You must be Ruadhri," she said as she splashed toward him along the pier.

"Aye," he answered, extending a hand, "and you'll be Sophie Creedon."

"That's me," she told him, shaking it, and trying to hide the pause it had taken her to understand him. Her own mother was Scottish by birth and had spent her childhood in the Borders, but years in London had smoothed the burr off her speech. To Sophie, Ruadhri seemed almost to be speaking a foreign language.

"Well then, welcome to Ardnasheen," he said. Glancing down at her harp case, he added, "You're no planning on surfing, are you?"

"Pardon?" Sophie asked, and then, seeing where he was looking, she said, "Oh, no. It's a harp."

Ruadhri raised his eyebrows. "Is it, now? You any good?"

"No one's ever run screaming."

He smiled. "Aye, well, maybe we'll put you on one night. Come on out of the rain for now, though. Pub's this way."

Sophie hadn't expected to be put to work on the first night, but she had little choice. Ruadhri strode toward one of the low white buildings. As they approached, Sophie could hear the murmur of conversation and snatches of music, smell the smoke of a wood fire. There was a hand-painted sign hanging outside the door reading "World's End". On the door itself, someone had painted a symbol in black paint: a circle, with three cat's-eye shapes meeting at a point in the center. It looked familiar to Sophie, though she couldn't quite place it.

Ruadhri opened the door for her, and she stepped into a small cloakroom hung with dripping waterproofs. "Leave your gear here," Ruadhri said.

Sophie took off her pack, and then stood holding onto her harp case doubtfully.

"Ach, go on and leave it," he said. "No one'd touch it even if it was the crown jewels."

"Really?"

"Aye: why bother stealing when there's nowhere to go with the goods!" Laughing, he pushed through the double doors into the room beyond.

Sophie put the harp carefully into a corner, shed her wet

12

jacket, took her phone out of the inner pocket and slipped it into the pocket of her jeans. Then she followed Ruadhri into the pub. The room was warm and humid with the gathering of damp bodies, and smelled strongly of stale beer, but Sophie felt better as soon as she was through the door. Ardnasheen might be a wild, lonely place, but its pub wasn't. Everyone seemed to know who she was, and to be happy to meet her. She was overwhelmed by greetings from every side.

Amid the blur of faces, her eyes caught on an older man perched on a stool at one end of the bar. He had a grizzled beard with traces of ginger, and wore a deerstalker cap and an old army coat. "What'll it be?" he said in a strong Irish accent, nodding to her. "First drink's on me."

"Ah…" said Sophie, eyeing the shelves of whisky dubiously. "Coke, please."

"Coke!" the man laughed, his green eyes twinkling as if it was the funniest thing he'd ever heard. "Pull her a pint o' eighty, Ailsa!"

"Oh no," Sophie said, "I can't. I mean I'm not – "

The man waved away her protests. "No police here, lass – you can do as you like."

"Michael," said Ruadhri, "stop trying to corrupt my waitresses! Ailsa, pour the girl a Coke."

"Aye aye, captain," said the girl behind the bar.

"Don't you start!" Ruadhri told her, but his heavy features pulled themselves into a smile nonetheless.

"One Coke," Ailsa said, setting the glass on a free spot on

the bar. "For our latest victim." But she smiled and winked at Sophie.

"Thanks," Sophie said, taking the drink and an empty bar stool.

Ailsa shrugged, and wiped a glass ring from the bar. Sophie took the opportunity of her diverted attention to have a good look at the other girl. She seemed older than Sophie – she'd have to be, to be running the bar – though she probably wasn't as old as her height and her expertly applied make-up made her appear. She was a good half a head taller than Sophie, with the willowy body Sophie had always longed for, a pretty oval face, wide hazel eyes, and long, red hair looped into a knot under a purple baker-boy hat.

"I'd say you picked a wild night to come in, and apologize for the weather," Ailsa said when the bar top was spotless again, "except that the weather's always like this here, and as west coast nights go, it's not particularly wild."

"Really?" Sophie asked, a cold runnel of doubt creeping back in.

"Aye," said Ailsa cheerfully, resting her elbows on the bar. "What else would you expect from a place called Ardnasheen?"

"I don't know. What does it mean?"

"Stormy headland."

"Well then, I guess I'd hope that whoever named it was exaggerating in the name of romance."

Ailsa snorted. "Gaelic place names are never romantic. My ancestors must have been the most literal people ever to walk

14

the earth. Honestly, everything up here's called something like 'Ugly House by a Bog' or 'Pond of the Dead Sheep.' So, Aird-na-Sín, Stormy Headland, *voila!*" She flicked her tea-towel in the vague direction of the windows.

Sophie sipped her drink, and glanced doubtfully at the dark glass running with rain.

"Cheer up," said Ailsa. "You'll get used to it soon enough. Still, I was gobsmacked when Ruadhri said he had an email from a London girl asking about the job advert. Most of us can't wait to get out of here."

She phrased it like a statement, but Sophie heard the question in it. "I wanted to get as far from home possible," she said. "I Googled 'ends of the earth' and this is what came up."

Ailsa laughed. "That's good! I'll have to remember that. So, what did they do to you?"

"Who?"

"Your parents, your boyfriend – whoever it was that made you want to run to the ends of the earth."

For a mad moment Sophie considered telling Ailsa the truth: she'd never believe it anyway, and it would probably earn a laugh, which, she guessed, was something Ailsa valued. After her fright on the boat, though, she didn't even want to think about why she was here, let alone speak it out loud.

"My parents," she said, falling back on the easy excuse. "They split up, asked me to choose. I told them I'd give them till Christmas to work it out, and if they didn't, I'd stay here."

Ailsa laughed again. "You and I are going to get on fine. So, I suppose you left school?"

Sophie shook her head. "I finished sixth form last summer."

"But you only turned seventeen in June!"

"How do you know that?"

"I read your application. Oh, don't look at me like that. Ruadhri gave it to me. He wanted me to have a say in who was hired. Said he couldn't face the thought of bickering barmaids. But of course, you're too young to tend the bar anyway...so, we're back to you finishing school a year early." Ailsa rested her elbows on the bar, her chin on her clasped hands and her eyes, expectantly, on Sophie.

Sophie sighed, and decided to get it over with quickly. "I did all of sixth form in one year."

Ailsa raised her eyebrows. "So, you're clever, then?"

Sophie shrugged. "I only did it because I was tired of school. Plus, it meant my parents didn't really have any choice but to let me take this...ah...sabbatical. Not if they want me to accept the place at uni, anyway."

"You have a place at uni?" Sophie nodded. "Oxford, I suppose." Ailsa said it ironically, but Sophie didn't smile back. "Holy hell – you *do* have a place at Oxford!"

"What about you?" Sophie asked to change the line of questioning. "Have you finished school?"

Ailsa nodded. "Last summer. Didn't much fancy uni – I want to travel. I came to work here to save the money for it."

"Which is never going to happen," said Ruadhri, appearing

16

behind the bar, "if you don't actually *do* some work." Ailsa rolled her eyes. "But as it's a slow night, and you're piddling the time away anyhow, why don't you take Sophie up to the house?"

"Can't we get a lift?" Ailsa asked hopefully.

Ruadhri cast a leery eye around the pub. "You mean there's someone here you'd trust behind the wheel of a car?"

"Yes," she said. "You."

"I'm running the bar."

"And there's no-one here you'd trust behind the bar, either?" Sophie suggested.

Ruadhri laughed. "Clever girl. Best watch your back, Ailsa, or you'll be out of a job."

"Funny," Ailsa said to him, and then, to Sophie, "come on – it looks like we're walking."

Sophie drained her glass. "Thanks for the drink," she said to Michael.

"My pleasure," he said, nodding to her with a vague smile.

Sophie went to the cloakroom and slid on her jacket, which was cold now as well as wet. Before picking up her pack and harp case, she checked her phone for messages. She'd promised to text her mother as soon as she arrived, but knowing her mother, there'd be five anxious messages already, asking her where she was.

"Don't bother," Ailsa said, coming into the cloakroom and pulling on a black-and-purple waterproof. "No reception out here, unless you climb the mountain." When Sophie looked at her in despair, she laughed. "Don't worry," she said, "we have

17

these amazing things called landlines, if you need to call your boyfriend."

"I don't have a boyfriend," Sophie said.

"You must be joking!" Ailsa said, pushing the door open.

"What would be the point of that?"

"I just meant it's hard to believe. You're a stunning girl."

"And *you* are very straightforward," Sophie said, feeling herself blush. Then, because Ailsa was still waiting for an explanation, she added, "I guess none of the boys I know agree with you."

Which wasn't strictly true. Sophie had had her share of offers, but all of those boys had left her cold. Or rather, they had when she'd considered that sooner or later, if she let one of them get close, he might find out her secret.

"They're probably just intimidated by a girl who can do two years' worth of school work in one," Ailsa said. Then, glancing down at the triangular case, "And also plays the harp."

"That was definitely not on my application!"

"Ruadhri told me," Ailsa said. "Just now. You know he'll have you playing here every night if you aren't careful. He loves live music."

"Maybe he'll forget about it?" Sophie asked hopefully. She loved to play, but not in front of an audience.

Ailsa just laughed and said, "It's a long walk. I'll get a wheelbarrow."

Sophie followed her out the door, wondering if she was serious about the wheelbarrow. Ailsa disappeared around the

18

side of the pub, and came back pushing a wooden hand-cart. "It's for the tourists who over-pack," she said to Sophie's questioning look. She helped her put her things in the cart, then they set off up the narrow road toward Madainneag, each pulling a side.

"Back to men," Ailsa said, "I'll warn you now, you'll be getting more attention here than you ever imagined."

"Why?" Sophie asked, wiping rain from her face and wondering whether any of her clothes would still be dry by the time they made it to the house. At least her harp case was waterproof.

"They outnumber us five to one – or something like that. Lots of work for men here in forestry or game, but not much for women. Unless you're the kind of woman who enjoys shooting half-tame birds and dragging deer carcasses off the hills."

"Ah…not so much."

"You aren't a vegetarian, are you?"

Sophie shook her head. "I'm just not into meat that's quite that…fresh."

"A few weeks of haggis and black pudding will take care of that," Ailsa said, patting Sophie's shoulder consolingly.

But Sophie wasn't listening. They'd reached the last of the village houses, and the road ahead disappeared into darkness. She stopped walking.

"Scared?" Ailsa asked.

"No," Sophie answered, too quickly. "Only – how will we find our way?"

"You'll be amazed what you can see in the dark, especially

19

when there's no choice," Ailsa said, and resumed walking. Sophie followed her, more frightened of being left alone than she was of the road through the dark woods.

"It seems strange," she said, to keep herself from thinking about what might be hiding in them, "to be staying in the laird's house."

Ailsa shrugged. "There are no cottages free, the B&Bs can't afford to give up rooms for nothing, and we can't afford to rent them on our pay. Madainneag is empty except for the laird, and he keeps himself to himself, so it makes sense in its own funny way."

"So the laird really does live in the house," Sophie said.

"Oh, aye," Ailsa said, with a clear note of disapproval in her voice. "In the tower."

"You don't like him?"

"He's…difficult," Ailsa said. "Set in his ways."

"Oh, well, that's just what old people are like, isn't it?"

To her surprise, Ailsa laughed – a throaty, infectious laugh. "Old? Who told you that the laird is old?"

"No one," Sophie admitted after a moment's consideration. "I just assumed, when I heard that he lives alone all the way out here – " She cut herself off, not wanting to offend Ailsa.

"Go on and say it: why would a young person choose to live at the back of beyond? The answer is, I have no idea – not when he's got as much money as Lucas Belial does. But he isn't old. No more than twenty, and probably not that. God, if I were him, young and rich and gorgeous, I'd fly off somewhere sunny and never come back." She paused thoughtfully, then said, "Still, his living here – it's not even close to the strangest thing about him."

"Which is what?"

Ailsa was silent for a few moments. "You can decide that for yourself," she said at last. "If he ever condescends to introduce himself to you," she added.

Sophie couldn't help wondering if there had been something between Ailsa and the laird, and that was the reason for her animosity. But she didn't know her nearly well enough to ask. Instead, she said, "Is the house haunted?"

Ailsa snorted. "Are you joking?"

"That depends on your answer."

"Well, I've never been woken in the night by anything but Michael's senile pet peacock – Christ, you should hear that bird screech! But to tell you the truth, I spend as little time at the house as possible. Haunted or not, it's a creepy place. So old and quiet. When I first came here, I had nightmares about getting lost and wandering around the corridors until I starved."

"Thanks," Sophie said dryly, "now I'll have them too. But wait – when you first came here? I thought you grew up in Ardnasheen."

"No," Ailsa said. "My mum's house is twenty miles inland. Not far as the crow flies, but it's mountains the whole way, each one higher than the last. It would take days to walk it, not to mention a better pair of boots than I can afford."

"Why would you walk it?"

"Because there's no other way to go direct."

"I read there are seven miles of road on Ardnasheen."

"Aye – but all of them lead to the sea. The only way on and off this rock is the ferry."

Sophie considered this for a long moment, feeling suddenly very ignorant, and more than a little claustrophobic. When Ruadhri had suggested she take the ferry to the village, she had assumed it was simply the more convenient route, not the only one.

"Well," she said at last, "it's a good thing I don't have anywhere to go."

Ailsa laughed, and then they walked on in silence for a few minutes, until a dim light showed through the trees. Sophie's first reaction was to panic – until she saw that it was a warm, ordinary, yellow light.

"Home sweet home," Ailsa said as they emerged from the trees onto a gravel drive. The house looked even bigger and more imposing up close – or what she could see of it, anyway. The light Sophie had spotted came from a small window at the top of the tower, and there was another one further down, by the main door. All of the windows in between were dark.

They passed the tower, and then a Gothic section of arched windows and crenellated roofs, which merged into a Georgian section, from which protruded the columned carriageway over the main door. One of the heavy outer doors was open, showing inner doors with stained glass panels, light shining through them from the room beyond.

Ailsa pushed the inner door open, and Sophie picked up her

bags and followed her inside. They stood in a wide, oak-paneled hall. A grand double stairway swept down from a shadowy gallery above. On one wall was a fireplace so vast that Sophie could have stood in it, had she been so inclined. On another was a row of curtained windows. Looking up, she saw that the light came from a chandelier made of deer antlers.

"Jacobites used to meet in this room," Ailsa informed Sophie. And then, "What did the Jacobites do again?"

Sophie shrugged. "We never really did Scottish history."

"Good. If you'd lectured me on Jacobites, I'd have got you fired immediately."

"Right," Sophie smiled. "I'll remember that: no historical lectures."

Ailsa grinned, taking off her cap and shaking water from her hair, which fell in a coppery sheet almost to her waist, Sophie noted, not without jealousy. "Come on, I'll show you your room." Ailsa flicked a switch and a light came on in the gallery above them. It barely penetrated the shadows of the stairway. "Our bedrooms are in the new wing," she said, starting up the stairs, "which means that it's only a hundred years old, instead of five."

"Hopefully it also means there're fewer ghosts," Sophie answered.

At the top of the stairs Ailsa switched on another ineffective light, and turned down a wide corridor lined with oil paintings. Sophie slowed down to study them. Some of them were so darkened by time that the subjects were barely discernible.

Those that Sophie could see were all landscapes, murky and cloud-ridden, decidedly Scottish. They rounded a corner into a narrower corridor, this one painted white and decorated with elaborate plaster molding. The carpet looked less worn than the previous one, and though its background was a somber dark green, it bloomed with yellow roses.

"Bathroom," Ailsa said, opening a door near the end. Sophie saw a plush, over-decorated crimson room dwarfed by a giant clawed tub. "And toilet," she added, opening the door opposite onto a tiny violet room containing an old-fashioned, raised-tank toilet and nothing else. "Quirky, don't you think?" she asked. Sophie smiled hopefully. "My bedroom is the one at the end," Ailsa continued. "This one is yours."

She opened the door beside the red bathroom and turned on the light. Sophie put down her backpack and took a long look around. The room had two large windows, with curtains of pink brocade that looked as if it had once been red. The bed was high, with a counterpane and canopy to match the window curtains. There was a tired looking mahogany dresser with a dim, speckled mirror, a wardrobe of similar vintage and condition, and a small desk under one of the two windows. Beside the other was a fireplace, full of what might have been bricks, except that they were smoking sullenly.

"Peat," Ailsa said, answering Sophie's quizzical look. "Madainneag's answer to central heating. I tried to start them for you, see, but it's hell getting them to burn."

"Thanks anyway," Sophie said.

"Well, what do you think?" Ailsa asked, with an amused half-smile. "Is it everything you imagined?"

"Actually," said Sophie, beginning to smile herself, "it's better."

"You're joking!"

"I'm not. I'd be disappointed if it looked like a five-star hotel."

Ailsa shook her head. "Well then, you might just last here after all. I'll leave you to it, but if you need anything, just knock."

CHAPTER 2

If Ailsa had asked Sophie's opinion a week later, she might have answered differently. Throughout that week the weather never varied, except that the rain turned intermittently to hail, and the wind increased to a gale. Her harp case still sat unopened in a corner of the room. Her fingers were too cold and stiff to play, and the wind too loud.

There was little time for it even if she'd been in the mood. Ruadhri put Sophie to work right away. She didn't mind it. She'd waited tables before, and the clientele here – mostly hill-walkers and the occasional yacht crew – was generally mellower than it had been in London. But she dreaded the end of her shift, and the long walk back to Madainneag. The early autumn evenings meant that it was dark even when she managed to get off early, and more often than not her shift and Ailsa's didn't coincide, so she was walking alone.

Likewise, the bedroom that had originally charmed her with its shabby romance had come down several notches in her estimation since then. Though she'd learned how to get the peat bricks burning, the changeable wind had a way of sending acrid backdrafts down the chimney, which drove her, choking, into the corridor. Worse, the Bronte-esque bed curtains housed a colony of spiders, and Sophie spent two nights being jolted from sleep by arachnids dropping onto her forehead before she took the whole lot down and shoved it into the washing machine in the ground-floor kitchen, not caring if they came out in shreds. (The curtains emerged intact, though several shades lighter.)

Worst of all, she found that wifi connections, like phone cells, were non-existent on Ardnasheen. Her only contact with the outside world was via the newspapers the ferry brought every other day, and the crackling bakelite phone in the entry hall at Madainneag. Even that was unreliable, the line sometimes crossing so that she could hear several other ghostly conversations, and sometimes dropping the connection entirely. She'd braved it to speak to her parents once (still fighting) and to a few school acquaintances (school was exactly the same without her.) After that, it hardly seemed worth the effort.

Then, just as she was beginning to come around to her mother's view that she'd made a daft decision to come to Scotland, the weather changed. It was her first day off and she'd looked forward to sleeping in, but she was awakened early by a bright shaft of sunlight coming through a gap in the curtains. She sat up, disbelieving until she heard the silence. No howling wind, no hailstones crashing against the window glass, no icy drafts working their way through the warped old sashes. She leaped out of bed, dragged the curtains back and looked out. The sky was a clear, pale blue, the sea a smooth indigo, the trees brilliant with water droplets in the bright morning sunlight. A faint golden light lay over everything, making it look like a fairy-tale landscape.

Sophie dressed quickly, pulling on walking boots and jeans and the fleece-lined parka her mother had bought for her before she left. "Not up there, it isn't," she had said, when Sophie, looking at sleeveless tunics, had protested that it was still summer. Now she was glad that her mother had insisted.

She strapped her harp case to her back, and then went down to the kitchen. She took some fruit and a bottle of water, and then went out through the kitchen door. The kitchen itself seemed to be a new extension to the house, all stainless steel and chalky paint. However, the dooryard it let out into was paved with time-worn flagstones, covered in moss and edged with lavender and rosemary bushes which scented the chilly morning air, along with heather and bracken and pine, and the sharp scent of the sea. Sophie stood still for a moment, just breathing it in. It felt to her as if she'd been imprisoned, and this was the first fresh air she'd breathed in a week.

She had no idea of the lay of the surrounding land or, more to the point, where she might find a sheltered spot to play. But the paved road that led to Madainneag turned into a dirt track on the far side of the house, curving into the hills behind. It seemed as good a choice as any. She walked along the back of the house, studying the seams of its many renovations and extensions. After the house she passed a derelict stable yard, empty except for an incongruously brilliant peacock pecking at the cobbles. It looked up at her for a moment with beady, intelligent eyes, then fanned its tail-feathers and let out an alarming squawk. It began stalking toward her with a purpose, and Sophie hurried on.

A few minutes later she came to a paddock where two sturdy grey ponies with feathered legs stood grazing. The ponies came curiously to the fence and let her stroke their noses. She gave them each one of the apples she'd brought, and after that they followed her for the length of the paddock. Beyond it the track curved around a hill, skirting a rocky beach. Far out near the tide line, a blond woman in a bright red jacket walked slowly along, picking something from the rocks and putting it into a sack. Shellfish, Sophie guessed, or possibly seaweed. She liked the smell of the wind coming off the beach, but she wouldn't be able to hear the harp against it. She turned inland.

After following the curve of the hill, the track ran into a valley between steep mountains. Their lower slopes were covered with bracken and blooming heather, but higher up they were all jagged black rock. The wind ruffled the heather; high above, a sea eagle let out a piercing cry before diving toward a shoal of fish out in the bay. A group of black-faced sheep grazed in a hollow, and rabbits scurried away from her into the grass. Far off down the valley, she could see what might be a herd of deer. Though she had been walking no more than fifteen minutes, it felt to Sophie as if she were miles from anywhere.

She'd walked another quarter hour when the road split

around a tiny cottage. It sat in the middle of an overgrown garden, like an island in a stream. It was old and dilapidated, its garden rife with weeds, and she'd have guessed that it was abandoned, if there hadn't been a wisp of smoke curling from the chimney. A large rowan tree full of unripe berries grew by the front door, its branches overhanging the building, almost embracing it. A string of brass bells hung from one of the low branches, tinkling softly as it moved in the wind.

The place gave Sophie a strange, wary feeling, and she was about to walk away when someone called out, "Here, lass!"

She turned. On the door step, nearly hidden in the shadow of the tree, an old man sat smoking a pipe. He was bundled in a shapeless brown coat despite the warm sun, and his gaunt face was partly hidden by a tweed cap. He beckoned to her with one gnarled hand. Reluctantly, Sophie stepped toward him. "Hello," she said.

"You'll be the new lass," the man said, looking up at her with dark eyes. Sophie noticed that he was missing several teeth. Though he looked frail, his intense gaze made her uneasy.

"That's right," she said.

"Ye shouldnae hae come here," he said, pointing at her with the mouthpiece of the pipe. "Ye should gae hame now."

Sophie's mother had told her to expect prejudice against southerners in Scotland, but she hadn't expected it to be so blatant. "I'm very sorry that you think so," she said coldly, trying to sound firm and unshakable, though her feeling of dread had redoubled. "But you'll have to take it up with Ruadhri if you don't approve, as he's the one who hired me." She turned to walk away, but the man caught her firmly by the arm, his grip stronger than she would have imagined.

"Let me go!" she cried as unease blossomed into terror. She tried to pull away from him.

"Ye've nae understood me," he said, holding firm. "I mean ye nae harm."

"Then let me go," she demanded. The man's hand opened, releasing her, and Sophie backed away.

"Wait," he said, and his voice, his eyes, were pleading. The hand he extended to her shook badly. Despite herself, Sophie paused. "It isnae me you've to fear," the man said. "It's *him.*" He pointed with his pipe to the northwest.

"Who?" Sophie asked.

"The exile. He'll want wha's yours."

Sophie backed away another step. "I don't know what you mean."

He shook his head, his eyes sad. "Ken, ye don't. Ye couldnae guess. Nae one could, who hadnae lived here as laing as I hae… who hadnae seen wha' I've seen." He paused, rummaging in his pocket. "If ye won't go, then at least take this." He held out a small wooden disc. There was a symbol on it, like a capital Y with a third line between the two canted ones.

"What is that?" Sophie asked dubiously.

"Rowan wood, and the warding rune," he said. "Double protection."

"From what?"

"From *him*. Please, take it. I'll nae have ye on my conscience, if there's a way about it."

Sophie didn't want the thing, but she also didn't want the old man following her, and she suspected that he would do exactly that until she did as he asked. Gingerly, she leaned forward and took the wooden disk from his palm. He nodded as she put it in her pocket.

"Ye've my blessing, lass," he said, and then he stood up and disappeared into the house.

Sophie wasted no time in getting away from the cottage. She headed back toward home, but after ten minutes she stopped, rationality taking over the blind panic that had been driving her. What, after all, had really happened? An old man had warned her vaguely of danger, but he'd done nothing to harm her. In fact, he'd done the opposite. He might be mad, or more likely, senile, but he'd seemed to have her best interest in mind. She wasn't going to let one peculiar interlude wreck her plans.

To convince herself, Sophie unslung her harp case and sat down on a wide, smooth rock among the bracken, a little way off the road. She didn't take the instrument out immediately. Instead, she took out her last apple and ate it slowly. By the time she finished it, one corner of her mind was already choosing tunes while the rest had slipped into the meditative state that always took her before she started to play. She brought out her harp and tuned it, letting the valley's ambient sounds settle into her, become part of her. Then, tossing the apple core in the direction of a rabbit burrow, she tipped the harp onto her shoulder and began to play.

Sometimes she imagined time as a net which music allowed her to slip through. Sometimes she saw it as a wind parting around her, not quite touching her as long as her fingers touched the strings. All she knew for certain, though, was that when she played, hours slipped away as quickly as seconds did the rest of the time.

She played a set of Shetland reels, and then a slow air that melted into another. When her fingers felt supple enough she went to work on a piece she'd spent the better part of the summer arranging, and she still hadn't finished. She'd taken an ancient pipe tune, a *pibroch*, as her starting point, having read somewhere that such music actually pre-dated the bagpipe, and had first been played on harps. Among the intricate variations that made up this type of music, there was a chordal refrain that made good use of the deep, resonant bass strings.

When she played it on her bigger harp, which she'd left at home, it felt as close to perfect as any music she knew. Even here, out in the open with the smaller instrument, the close, resounding harmonies swept her up until she forgot where she was. And so she was startled, when the shadow fell over her, to find that it fell from behind her: the sun was half-way down the western sky.

Sophie clapped her hands over the strings to silence them, and looked up. A man was standing behind her, and because the sun was behind him, he was no more than a tall black silhouette.

It reminded her of something she thought she had forgotten: a night when she was very young, and awakened to see a similar black figure standing in her doorway. It had been featureless and transparent as a shadow, but she'd known that it was studying her, with a cold and certain menace. It had taken a step toward her – she had heard the floorboards creak when it moved – and then she'd hidden her head beneath the covers. She'd lain there shuddering until morning, too terrified to sleep, too terrified even to scream for her parents.

Now, looking at the man's dark figure, she felt a moment of the same mute terror. Then he stepped to the side and came into focus, and the impression vanished. He was a very young man, perhaps a few years older than Sophie was, though there was something older about his obvious, arrogant self-assurance. And aside from his clothing – dark jeans and a faded, black, long-sleeved T-shirt – there was nothing dark about him. He was very fair, his longish hair almost white under a backward-turned tweed cap, his deep-set eyes pale blue in an even-featured face. He wore heavy walking boots, which were caked with mud, as if he'd walked a long way. He stood with his hands in his pockets, his mouth quirked into a half-smile, and Sophie couldn't help but think that he was appraising her.

"What?" she asked, when his stare became too much.

"Nothing," he said, the laughter in his eyes echoed in his voice. "I was only thinking how long it's been since this glen's rung with the sound of a *pibroch*. Never mind a *pibroch* played by a girl as pretty as you."

"You know your ancient music," Sophie said, putting the harp's levers down and opening the case. "Impressive." But she made sure she didn't sound impressed. He seemed far too certain of his own charm for her liking.

"Please don't stop on my account," he said. Sophie hadn't been in Scotland anywhere near long enough to untangle its various accents and dialects, but she thought there was something more foreign than that in the way he spoke.

"Don't worry," she answered. "I don't know you well enough to do anything on your account." She shouldered the harp case and began walking toward home, though part of her was telling herself she was being an idiot. It wasn't often she met a man who looked like this one did, let alone one who flirted with her. True, he made her feel an inexplicable unease. But she also felt an undeniable attraction, and so she paused when she heard him call, "Wait!"

He ran to catch up with her, then took off his cap and bowed to her with a flourish. "Sam Eblis, at your service." He pushed back the wing of hair that had fallen across his face, replaced his cap and smiled apologetically. "Please forgive me if I offended you – as I said, it isn't often I meet anyone out here, let alone a girl of your charms."

"My charms," Sophie repeated with an ironic smile, beginning to walk again. He had to be teasing her. Nobody really spoke like that.

"Where are you going?" he asked.

"Why do you want to know?" she answered.

"So that I might have some chance of seeing you again."

Sophie rolled her eyes, stopped, and turned to him, fully prepared to tell him off. But his expression was contrite.

"I'm going home," she said, relenting.

"Which is?"

"Madainneag."

He raised his eyebrows. "Well then, I offer my condolences."

"Why do you say that?" she asked, with a sudden tinge of the chill she'd felt speaking to the old man at the cottage.

"Have you met the laird?" he asked, with an odd emphasis on "laird".

"No," Sophie answered. "Why?"

He gave her a long, searching look, and then he said, "Wait until you've met him. Then you'll see."

It was close enough to what Ailsa had said to make Sophie curious. "Does anyone actually *like* Lord Belial?"

"Not recently," Sam said grimly. "But let's not talk about him. Let's talk about you."

"What about me?"

"Oh, I don't know…where you learned to play the harp?"

"In countless weekly lessons," she said.

"Or why you're going home, when it's a beautiful day, and your first free one since you arrived?"

"How do you know that?" she asked sharply, on her guard again.

He shrugged. "This place has a population smaller than your average primary class, and a similar mentality. Everyone knows everything about everyone – even a newcomer like you, Sophie Creedon."

Sophie gave him a dubious look, but didn't rise to the bait. "Then how come I've not heard of *you*?"

He shrugged. "I don't spend much time in the village."

"You're a gamekeeper?"

"Do I look like one?" he asked, glancing down at his clothes.

"Minus the gut-stained army jacket."

He laughed. "Touché. But no – my game keeps itself, such as it is."

Sophie cocked an eyebrow. "*Your* game?"

"Aye – a few refugee deer and a flock of inbred pheasants. No one's hunted on my land in…well, longer than anyone remembers."

"You own land, too?"

Sam nodded. "Belial doesn't own all of Ardnasheen, no matter what he'd have everyone think. The northern half of the peninsula is mine."

"Do you have a house like Madainneag?" Sophie asked, hoping that she didn't sound too keen.

But Sam shook his head. "One and a half walls of one. The rest fell down about the time they stopped hunting on the land."

"Where do you live, then?"

"The gatehouse."

"Why would you have a gatehouse," Sophie asked, "when there aren't any inroads to Ardnasheen?"

He gave her another appraising look. "You don't miss a trick, do you?"

"I like to think not."

"Very well then, Sophie Creedon-who-doesn't-miss-a-trick: it's a gatehouse for sea traffic."

"You're making this up."

"I'm not!" he said with exaggerated affront. "It's right at the head of the pier, like an ordinary gatehouse on a driveway. You're welcome to come visit, if you don't believe me."

"I'll take your word for it," she said, wondering whether he really meant the invitation.

They walked for a time in silence until, looking up, Sophie realized that they were nearly back at the house. She could see Ailsa taking in laundry from the line in the kitchen dooryard, and the very homeliness of the image made her suddenly ashamed of the suspicion with which she'd treated Sam Eblis. He was certainly arrogant, and a bit too forward for her tastes, but in his way he'd been welcoming.

"Sam," she began, "I want to say – "

"No need."

"But – "

"Really." Sam picked a yellow flower and turned it thoughtfully in his fingers. "Though if you're truly worried, there's a simple way to make amends…"

"Oh?" she asked, fighting the blush that rose in response to the glint in his eye.

"Begin again," he said.

"How so?"

"I'll think of something." He tucked the flower behind her ear, turned and strode back up the path. Just before it hooked around the hill, he turned and shouted, "Lovely to have met you, Sophie Creedon!"

Sophie shook her head, but she smiled as she walked across the overgrown lawn to join Ailsa.

CHAPTER 3

"So," said Ailsa, one eyebrow raised, "I see you've met Sam."

"You have good eyes."

"Sam's hard to miss," she answered, un-pegging a pair of socks.

"Do you really wear this?" Sophie asked, plucking a purple leopard-print bra from the line.

"Don't try to change the subject," Ailsa said, whisking it away and dropping it in the basket.

"What subject?"

Ailsa rolled her eyes. "You can't possibly be as hopeless as you pretend to be."

"You'd be surprised."

"So you're telling me you've spent the afternoon with the most eligible bachelor in this whole godforsaken place, and you have absolutely *nothing* to report?"

Sophie shrugged, set down her harp and reached for a

T-shirt. "I didn't spend the afternoon with him – just walked a little way. And as for the eligible bachelor, he's good looking alright, but he knows it."

Ailsa chuckled. "He asked you out, didn't he?"

Did he? Sophie wondered, thinking back over what he'd said. It seemed that they'd discussed getting together sometime, but when she thought about it now, she couldn't remember him actually asking her. In retrospect, their whole conversation seemed made up of tangents and suggestions.

"I'm not quite sure, actually," she answered, and Ailsa laughed again.

"That's Sam, alright," she said. "Never straightforward, but always interesting."

"You sound like you know him well," Sophie said, reaching for more laundry.

Ailsa smiled wistfully. "Sadly, no. He comes into the pub sometimes, but despite my best efforts – not to mention my creative lingerie – " she plucked a violet thong from Sophie's hands " – he appears not to be interested."

"Maybe he's playing hard to get," said Sophie.

"Impossible, more like." She gave Sophie a critical glance. "Or maybe he's more a frail pixie type than a ginger-haired amazon type."

"Frail pixie!"

"Well, perhaps not 'frail'…"

Sophie shook her head. "I doubt it had anything to do with pixies or amazons. He was only teasing the new girl."

"I don't understand you. Why do you have such a low opinion of yourself?"

"I don't," Sophie said, "it's only…" She trailed off, looking at Ailsa, who looked back at her expectantly. She had no idea how to explain to Ailsa that she'd always stood a step back from the school social scene; that she preferred a night in with a good book or a new piece of music to dressing up and heading to a stranger's house to drink pilfered beer and meet boys. That though she had been respected at school, and friendly with a number of girls and boys there, Ailsa was the nearest thing to a best friend she'd ever had. Because, if she did, then Ailsa would want to know why.

Glancing inadvertently at the dark woods behind them, she concluded, "I was the school swot. I guess the others – boys in particular – saw me as a brain, rather than a girl."

It wasn't much of a justification, but it was one she'd learned people seldom argued with – including, apparently, Ailsa, who shook her head, unpinning the last of the clothing (another outrageous bra, this one in red satin and black lace.) "It's true," she said, "boys at school are hopeless. It must be the pack mentality or something – they're far too easily intimidated by girls who know their own mind. But you're not at school now. The blokes here, they might not be much older than you or me, but you're better off thinking of them as men rather than boys. They aren't faffing about with notebooks and football jerseys, they're working for a living. And for all he's well off, that applies to Sam Eblis, too."

Sophie looked over at Ailsa as she picked up the laundry basket. "Sam is rich?"

"Land rich, sure," said Ailsa, heading toward the kitchen door. "As for cash, I have to admit I really don't know. Though given the car he drives, he can't be doing too badly."

"He did say he owns half of Ardnasheen," Sophie remembered. "It's strange that both of them are so young – I mean Sam and Laird Belial."

"I agree," Ailsa said, switching on the kettle. "But then, maybe it's perfectly normal for the landed classes. I can't claim to know. Like a cuppa?"

"I'll get it," Sophie said, taking out the cups and tea bags. "What happened to the old lairds?"

Ailsa shook her head. "I don't know much about it. Sam inherited from an uncle who lived abroad all his life. I don't remember him ever coming here before that. The Eblis' big house is long gone, and even Sam's place was derelict until he moved up and renovated it."

"By himself?"

"He hired workers for some of it."

"No, I mean, he came here all by himself?"

"Yeah – apparently he fell out with his family," Ailsa said, filling the mugs. "I think it was over the inheritance, in fact – because they were passed over, or whatever. Or maybe it was because Sam changed his plans. He was at uni – Cambridge no less – but he left and came up here when he got the news. And he's been here ever since."

43

Sophie considered this. Something about it nagged at her, giving her a vague feeling that the pieces of Sam's story didn't quite add up, although she couldn't point to any one anomaly. "Where did he come from? Before uni, I mean."

Ailsa swirled the teabag in the water with a spoon. "You know, I'm not sure. I assumed he was Scottish because of the accent, but it's hard to place. Kind of generic toff-Scots."

"Don't his friends ever come visit him?" Sophie asked, not quite sure why she was pressing the point. "Or his other family?"

Ailsa shook her head, shoveling sugar into her tea. "Not that I've noticed. He seems to spend most of his time alone." *Like an exile,* Sophie thought, feeling the wooden disc in her pocket, and then wishing she hadn't. "Though maybe not for much longer?" Ailsa added with a suggestive smile.

Sophie couldn't quite smile back. To dispel the creeping unease, she asked, "So you said he works – what does he do?"

"Forestry," Ailsa said. "Mostly chopping down rhododendrons before they engulf the place. I heard he has plans to build a lodge, but that could just be gossip."

There was more that Sophie wanted to know about Sam, but she knew that to ask Ailsa any more would be to confirm all of her suspicions. Instead, she said, "So what about Laird Belial? What's his story?"

Ailsa smiled. "His story makes Sam's look like Happy Families. But if I'm going to get into that, I need biscuits."

Sophie rummaged in the cupboard and found a packet of

custard creams. She tore it open, set it down between them, and then sat down to listen.

"Okay, so," Ailsa began between bites, "this house has been continuously occupied since the Dark Ages, or the Picts pitched a wigwam here, or whatever. The last Lady Belial, the one who had the place before Lucas, she lived here alone. Had done since who knows when."

"Was she Lucas's grandmother?" Sophie asked, dunking a biscuit in her tea.

"You know, I'm not actually sure how they were related," Ailsa said, her brows drawing together. "But she couldn't have been his grandmother. In fact she wasn't even properly Lady Belial. She was engaged to the laird in the '30s, but he died in the war. I guess he really loved her, because he left her the estate and the title in his will, even though they weren't married yet. And she must have really loved him, because she stayed single. She lived in this house all alone until the day she died. Can you imagine anything creepier?"

Yes, Sophie thought, *an old man spouting dire warnings in a broken-down cottage in the middle of nowhere.* "No," she said. Then, "So Lucas came here after she died?"

Ailsa shook her head, swallowing a sip of tea. "He actually came up a few months *before* she died."

"Why?"

"Because about that time, his parents were both killed. It was a plane crash, somewhere in the Middle East. They were diplomats or something."

"God, that's terrible!"

Ailsa nodded in agreement. "I guess it also explains why he's so stand-offish. Or it would do, if he hadn't been so good to the old lady. It's funny: not many young lads would nurse some distant relation through her final illness, even if she was his last living relative, and leaving him everything."

"Really?" Sophie asked, intrigued. "He did that?"

Ailsa nodded. "I used to come in and cook for them sometimes, do a bit of cleaning. Clara – that was Lady Belial's name – she was losing it by then, if you know what I mean. Couldn't remember what decade it was, and argued about everything. But Lucas never lost the rag with her. In fact, odd as it sounds, I think he really cared about her. He even had her buried in style, with that huge great headstone."

"What huge great headstone?"

"In the cemetery, up in the clearing." Ailsa pointed out the back door. "Go and have a look sometime. It's creepy, but kind of beautiful too. There's a ruined chapel, and this really mad statue – seriously, it's right out of a horror film."

"Sounds great," Sophie said, making a mental note never to walk that way.

"So anyway, Clara died, and I thought after that Lucas might start to make more of an effort – you know, come out to the pub, mix with others his own age."

"But he didn't," Sophie said.

"Nope. He just holed up in that tower and forgot about the rest of us, I guess."

"Do you think he's upset about the old lady?"

Ailsa half-smiled. "Not unless they had some kind of Harold and Maud thing going on, that no one knew about." She paused. "Nah. I think he was just always stuck up. He was decent enough to do the right thing by the old lady, but after that..." She shrugged.

"In that case," Sophie said, "I'll do my best to avoid him."

"That's right," Ailsa agreed. "You stick to Sam Eblis: he knows how to have fun."

CHAPTER 4

Sophie wrote letters to her parents that afternoon while Ailsa was at work, sitting at her desk in the mellow autumn sunshine. Because she was still annoyed with them, she planned for them to be identical, short and to-the-point. But after she'd assured them that she was surviving in the north without them, and still planned to come home at Christmas time, she relented. For her father, she wrote a description of the scenery, the house, and the more colorful locals. For her mother, she described her new friend Ailsa – her mother had always been anxious about her lack of close friends.

As she was sealing the envelopes, Sophie wondered whether she should have told her mother about Sam as well. She knew that she'd be beyond delighted to hear that Sophie finally had some interest in a member of the opposite sex. In the end, though, she decided against it, partly because there wasn't really much to tell, but also because thinking about Sam made her feel strange. It was partly the jittery feeling of a possible crush, but there was also a sense of apprehension that she could neither pin down nor justify. It was similar to the feeling she sometimes had after waking from a dream of doing something she shouldn't have done, when a vague, drifting remorse would haunt her all day.

By the time she had addressed the letters, the sun had sunk behind the western mountains and night was falling fast, bringing a chill with it. She stirred up her fire and then lay down on her bed, watching a hesitant tongue of flame lick up around the peat squares. She thought she would just close her eyes for a moment, and then go make tea for herself and Ailsa. Within minutes, though, she was asleep.

*

When her eyes opened she was in a cemetery, lying on a high stone bench beneath an old, sprawling apple tree. She wore a long, loose, deep blue dress that left her arms bare, but though the air was cool she didn't feel cold. What she felt was alive: more so than she ever remembered feeling. The air smelled sharp and sweet and somehow ancient, like church incense. The headstones and statuary threw crisp shadows in the moonlight, the apples on the tree were dark and perfect, and the grass, when she reached down to touch it, was velvety against the tips of her fingers.

Something tapped her hand. She sat up, looked around and saw that it was a red tea-rose, from a bush that rambled over the bench. Except that it wasn't a bench, as she'd assumed, but a mausoleum so old it was breaking apart, jagged black cracks gaping on whatever it contained. But she felt no fear, no revulsion, rather a comforting familiarity.

Sophie blinked, and somewhere in between the closing and opening of her eye, a girl appeared, perched on a low branch of the tree. She wore a short, white, sleeveless dress. Her face was a pale brushstroke on the night, her hair a tumble of silvery dreadlocks that reached to her waist, dwarfing her delicate frame. Her eyes were brilliant and black as a bird's.

"Sophia!" she said in a voice like a flute, her smile warm and joyful.

"Suri," Sophie said, and then wondered how she had known the girl's name.

"I've missed you," Suri said, cocking her head wistfully. Her accent was American, her voice familiar.

"I'm sorry," Sophie said, and she meant it, though once again she didn't know where the words had come from, or what it was she regretted.

"Don't be," Suri said. "You did what you had to do." Her eyes were heavy on Sophie, as if she were willing her to know something that she couldn't say.

"I don't understand," Sophie said.

"And I can't explain it to you."

"You can try."

Suri shook her head, sighed, and said simply, "I'm bound."

"To what?"

Suri only smiled and said, "Don't look so grim! You'll have the answers, as soon as you remember the questions."

There was a flicker of recognition somewhere deep inside Sophie then, like the surfacing remnants of a long-forgotten dream. She shut her eyes, trying to concentrate. As soon as she reached for them, though, the half-recollections slipped like shadows out of her grasp. When she opened her eyes again Suri was sitting beside her on the mausoleum, holding a perfect red apple in her hand.

"Try this," she said. "I know they've got a bad reputation after the thing with the snake – not to mention that 'mirror, mirror' business – but nothing wipes the scales from a girl's eyes quite like forbidden fruit." She smiled conspiratorially.

Sophie took the apple. She turned it in her hands for a moment, wishing that Suri hadn't brought up Snow White: the film had terrified her as a child, and the queen's white face could still make her shudder. *It's only a dream,* she told herself, and bit into the apple. Its flesh was as sweet as its bright skin promised, but as soon as she swallowed it a wave of dizziness came over her. For a moment she was whirling on a dance floor, wide blue skirts fanning and strong arms around her. The next, she stood watching the flashing swords of two men fighting as a knot of black-clad figures looked on. And then they were gone, leaving a muddy field and a dark-haired man kneeling by a broken sword, his head bowed beneath a grey and empty sky.

The images dissolved, leaving her reeling. She grabbed for Suri's arm, but her hand met only cool air. Suri had slipped off of the mausoleum to stand several yards away, by a stone angel. Its back was to Sophie, and its wings were wrong: not feathered, but boned and bat-like, clawed at their joints. Suri looked into Sophie's face, her own smooth and beautiful and oddly remote, given a few steps would have closed the distance between the two of them.

"And so it begins," she said.

"What?" Sophie asked.

"The rest will come, if you let it. But opening yourself to the truth makes you vulnerable to lies." She cocked her head, birdlike. "Let your wisdom guide you – it's still there, somewhere."

"But I don't – " Sophie began.

"Listen," Suri said, "and you will. Don't dawdle, though... you don't have much time."

And then she was gone. Sophie was alone in the cemetery with no light but that of the moon and stars, which seemed suddenly cold and alien, as the gravestones had become sinister. She slid off of the mausoleum, and stood for a moment wondering what she was meant to listen to. Then she saw a dark object in the branches of the tree. Approaching it, she found an old-fashioned radio – a wireless. She recognized it from an illustration in a history book about the Second World War.

She looked at it for a moment, and then she turned the knob labeled "On". The radio crackled to life, and the silence of the cemetery was rent by a wretched cry. It went through her like fire, nearly bringing her to her knees; and then it came again.

Instinctively, she put her hands to her ears, but as she covered them she remembered what Suri had said: *Listen.*

Reluctantly, she lowered her hands. When the sound came again she let it, and this time she realized that it was music – terrible, tortured, but music nonetheless. A violin. *Listen.* She dug for it, clutched it, followed its tortuous path like a tree root through the earth –

– and then she sat up, gasping and disoriented. It seemed she lay in a crypt, hung with black crepe. Beyond her, dark shapes loomed out of shadows thrown by a murky red light. Then she heard the wind howling in the eaves, and she remembered. She was in her room in Madainneag, in Ardnasheen, and she'd just awakened from the strangest dream she ever remembered having. Then the wind screeched again, and with it she heard something else: the same agonized strain of music she'd followed out of the dream.

Listen, the dream-girl had said. Well, she was listening. She couldn't not: it was as if the music went straight to the core of her, wringing her heart. Bach, she thought, and familiar enough that it must be famous. Baroque wasn't her genre, though, and she couldn't name it. Nor did she know what the dream meant, if it meant anything at all. But she did know one thing for certain: she had to find the source of that music.

With shaking hands, Sophie pulled the chain on the bedside lamp, but nothing happened. Pushing back the bedclothes, she slid to the floor, then felt for the light switch on the wall by the door. The overhead light was out, too. She took a deep breath, refusing to lose her nerve, telling herself it was just a power cut, that it couldn't be unusual in a place like this. She should have anticipated one, in fact, by virtue of the three paraffin lamps on the mantle-piece. She took one of them down, lifted off the globe, and lit it with a stick of kindling from the fireplace.

She felt instantly better for the light. After pulling a fleece over her tee shirt, she picked up the lamp and opened the door. The hallway was damp and cold, with a draft running through it that was almost a wind in itself. Moonlight fell in intermittent flashes through the long windows, as the wind tore rents in the racing cloud. It lit the corridor in brilliant fits and starts, picking out a yellow rose on the carpet, a bunch of plaster grapes on a molding, a side table like a crouching spider in the shadows. Sophie tried to concentrate on each of them in turn, rather than on the black void ahead and what might be lurking in it.

At last she reached the stairway. Her little lamp barely penetrated the darkness there, and she descended slowly, watching each foot in turn until she was safely at the bottom. Once there, she stood for a moment, listening. The music was louder here than it had been upstairs. It flowed from a corridor that led out of the main hall to her left, black as pitch. If the corridor had windows, it seemed they were covered.

Turning the lamp wick up as high as she dared, Sophie plunged into the dark tunnel, following the tide of music. The lamp lit door after dark door, each of them firmly shut. She didn't doubt that if she tried them she would find them locked, but she didn't try. She knew that she was close now to the source of the

54

music, and it was all she could think of. It seemed the violin cried out with a human voice, lamenting a pain so wide and deep no balm could ever touch it. It held her fast in its terrible beauty.

Her heartbeat skittered, her breath grew shallow as she approached the half-open door at the end of the corridor. She stepped silently into the wedge of light it cast on the floor. If she could have seen herself, Sophie would have been disgusted at the tears gathering in her eyes; but she couldn't see herself, and in fact she wasn't even aware of them. She stood unconsciously weeping before the door as the violin went silent, the last notes dying back into the keening wind. And then she pushed it open.

The room beyond the door wasn't really large, but its wide semi-circle of windows, its black-and-white marble floor, and the light of the dozens of candles scattered across it, gave the impression of a wide-open space. That, and the fact that it was empty. Empty, that is, apart from the violinist.

He sat with his back to her in a chair near the windows, holding the instrument on his lap. He wore nothing but a pair of battered black jeans, a wide silver band on each wrist, and an intricate black symbol tattooed on the gold-brown skin between his shoulder blades. Just as Sophie opened her mouth to speak to him, a spatter of hailstones hit the window. He turned his head, revealing his face. Sophie froze, barely breathing.

It wasn't simply that he was handsome, though he was easily the handsomest man she'd ever seen. Instead, it was the overwhelming feeling that she knew him. Yet even that wasn't simple recognition. It couldn't be explained away by the

55

possibility that she had passed him once on a crowded street, or sat behind him on a train. She knew every minute facet of him, from the surprising softness of his chin-length black hair, to the inverted arch his full lips would form when he smiled, to the feel of his long-fingered hand, rough with calluses from hours of playing, against her own smooth palm. She knew that when he was angry, he was terrifying. She knew that when he smiled, his black eyes would light in a way that would make her promise him anything.

Barely aware of what she was doing, Sophie stepped into the room and walked toward him. She was only a few feet away when he heard her and turned. For a moment he just stared at her, his eyes widening with shocked recognition. "Sophia…" he said, his voice low and warm despite its unsteadiness. Sophie took another step toward him, lifting a hand as his lips began to turn upward. Then, just as quickly, his half-smile flattened, and his face darkened.

"What are you doing here?" he cried, standing up, his knuckles white around the neck of the violin. "How *dare* you come here, now, after all of this time!"

"What – what are you talking about?" Sophie stammered, even as a part of her mind was telling her that she ought to know.

"Go, Sophia," he growled, coming toward her, his face contorted by anger and pain. "Whatever you've done, undo it, and don't ever come back!"

"I don't know who you think I am – " she began, but he interrupted.

"Get out!" he cried, and she was appalled to see tears in his eyes along with the rage. "Go!"

Sophie took a step backward. Her head felt strange and fuzzy, and the room swam in front of her eyes. *He isn't meant to speak to me like this*, she thought, even as she knew that it made no sense. She didn't know him – she *couldn't* know him, nor he her, because he was Lucas Belial and they had never met before.

And still, she couldn't look away. The wiry lines of his body, the smooth, shadowed plains of his face, his wide dark eyes tore into her like grappling hooks. The vertigo was growing worse. The edges of her vision darkened, she felt sick and breathless. And then, behind him, at one of the windows, she saw a bluish glow, a nightmarish face. She shut her eyes and screamed. Distantly, she heard the crash as she dropped the lamp, and saw the flames leap up. And then darkness closed in and she was falling, through the floor, through the earth, tumbling over and over into a blind dark void.

CHAPTER 5

Sophie woke to cold and a dim, pinkish light. The fire had gone out and the wind was flinging rain against the windows again, as if the past beautiful day had never been. She had the vague feeling that something was wrong, as if she'd had a nightmare that she couldn't remember. She sat up, pulled the chain on the bedside lamp, and nothing happened. She noticed a faint, smoky smell, and looking down, she saw that the hems of her jeans were singed, her feet smudged with soot, as if she'd walked through a fire.

With that the whole night came back to her, from the strange dream to the bizarre run-in with the man who could only have been Lucas Belial, to the ghostly face she'd seen in the window. Rather than fear, though, she felt a wave of inexplicable grief. She pushed it angrily back, wondering what was wrong with her. From the moment she'd lain down the previous evening, the world seemed to have come unhinged: dream bleeding into reality and reality into madness.

Maybe, she thought, she was coming down with something. She wanted to believe it, but even if it was true, it didn't explain the man's strange behaviour toward her. Getting out of bed, she pulled the curtains open, which failed to lighten the room at all. She started rummaging in her drawers for something clean to wear, trying to push the strangeness aside by concentrating on the mundane.

Apparently, it didn't work, given that Ailsa greeted her with a knowing smile when she came into the kitchen. "Rough night?" she asked, holding a piece of bread with a fork over a gas ring, apparently trying to toast it.

"That doesn't begin to describe it."

"Sorry," Ailsa said, flinging the bread into the sink as it caught fire. "I should have warned you about the power cuts. Happens at least once a week, when the generator goes down."

"Quaint," said Sophie, turning on the tap to make certain the flaming bread was extinguished. "But the power cut was the least of my worries."

"With eye-rings like that," Ailsa said, peering at her, "there must have been a man involved. Let me guess…Sam showed up to serenade you outside your window all night?"

Sophie laughed grimly. "That would have been tame by comparison." She drew a deep breath, suddenly hesitant to tell Ailsa what had happened. But that made as little sense as anything else, and so she said: "I met Lucas Belial."

"Oh," said Ailsa, reaching for a box of cereal. She seemed unsurprised, even vaguely disappointed that Sophie's revelation hadn't been more interesting. "I thought I heard him playing last night. I guess I should have warned you about that, too."

"Yeah," Sophie said, "and about the fact that he's a psychopathic nutter!"

Ailsa smiled. "You got him in a good mood, then."

"Seriously, what's wrong with him? I went down to see what the noise was – " despite her anger, Sophie felt guilty calling that music "noise" " – and he completely freaked out, telling me I had to leave and...and..." Somehow, she couldn't get the rest of it out. "He does know that I'm living here, right?" she finished, lamely.

"Oh, aye, he knows," Ailsa said, poking at her cereal. "Which is to say that he was told. Whether he remembers..." She shrugged.

Sophie recalled something then. "He remembers. He knew my name."

"Well then, you've one up on the rest of us."

"But it was strange...he called me 'Sophia'."

"Isn't that your name?"

"Well, yeah, on my birth certificate; but nobody ever calls me that. Why would he?"

"Sophie," Ailsa said, giving her a shrewd look, "don't even think about it."

"About what?"

"He might be gorgeous, but Lucas Belial is a self-absorbed git. Stick with Sam, and save yourself a load of grief."

"Who said I wanted to stick with anyone?"

"Who wouldn't, when 'anyone' is one of those two?" Ailsa smiled, shook her head. "But believe me, chasing Lucas is beating a dead horse."

"I'm *not* chasing Lucas!"

"Good, because he's not interested in anyone but himself." Which made Sophie wonder again whether Ailsa had ever had a thing for him. "As for Sam – well, we've been over that already." She opened the milk bottle, sniffed, and then shoved it aside. "Just forget about Lucas, okay?"

"Ailsa!"

"Alright then. Come on, we might as well go to the pub. We can get breakfast there, if the backup generator's working."

*

It wasn't. The power came back on early in the afternoon, but even so, business was slow. Aside from a handful of regulars propping up the bar, Sophie had only one lunch customer. She used her idle afternoon to clean all of the tables, make sure the menu boards were current, and fill the baskets of peat and firewood. She even helped Ailsa wash a backlog of glasses and tea towels, but when all of that was done it was still only five, and her shift didn't end until six.

Ailsa had gone to move a load of towels to the dryer, and Sophie was wiping the clean bar yet again when Michael said, "Make me a pot of tea, lass?"

Sophie was surprised by the request. In the ten days she'd

been in Ardnasheen, she had never seen Michael drink anything but whisky. For that matter, she'd never seen him move from the stool at the end of the bar. As far as she knew, he might reside there permanently, living off of his steady alcoholic drip.

Nevertheless, she made the tea without comment and loaded a tray with a jug of milk, a bowl of sugar and a plate of biscuits. "Thank you," he said as she put it in front of him. "Now get a cup for yourself, and sit down with me and have a drop."

Sophie smiled, but shook her head. "No drinking on the job."

"There's no job to drink on, so far as I can see." Michael gestured to the empty room. Even the usual bar-props had abandoned him.

"Alright," Sophie said, coming around the bar to take the stool next to him. "But if Ruadhri catches me – "

Michael waved her words away. "Ruadhri went to Mallaig. He won't be back for hours. Now, milk and sugar?"

"Just milk," Sophie said, and leaned over to accept the cup he poured her. As she did so, she caught the ghost of a scent: not the damp tweed and old liquor smell she would have expected, but something surprisingly sweet. Sweet, but also sharp, vaguely exotic – and familiar. The scented air of the dream cemetery washed over her again, and for a moment she was back beneath the apple tree, in the shadow of the stone angel. Just as quickly, the flash faded, and she was sitting on a bar stool, her hands clutching a hot cup, Michael's worried eyes fixed on her.

"Are you alright, lassie?" he asked, laying a hand on her

arm. As soon as he did so, a peaceful warmth seemed to flow into her, and her whirling thoughts settled.

"Yes," she said, and then again, more forcefully, "yes. I'm fine. It's only that I didn't sleep well last night."

"You'll still be adjusting," he said, looking at her sympathetically.

"I only came from London. It's not as if I changed time zones or anything."

Michael said nothing, only sipped his tea and smiled in a way that suggested he knew better. But though Sophie was usually sensitive to condescension, she found his smile comforting.

"I suppose," he said after a moment, "you've encountered young Belial."

"You suppose correctly."

"I take it from your tone that it wasn't a pleasant meeting."

"He told me to get out of his house," Sophie said, wondering why she was telling him about it even as the words emerged. She hadn't meant to confide this humiliation to anyone, let alone an old drunk she barely knew. But something in Michael's demeanor invited confession, and she had the strong feeling that whatever she told him would go no further.

"Are you certain that's what he said?"

"I can't think of many other ways to interpret 'go and don't ever come back'."

Michael looked at her thoughtfully, and finally said, "I suppose it's only to be expected."

"Then why on earth was I sent to lodge with him?"

"There was no averting it," he said sadly.

Sophie shook her head. "So Ailsa told me. But I find it hard to believe that no one in this village has a room…an attic…hell, even a garden shed where I could have slept. Maybe I can move in here," she said, looking around the pub. "The benches at the back look comfortable enough…"

"No," said Michael wearily, "you're as well staying where you are. It'll make little enough difference now."

Sophie looked at him. He'd seemed sober enough when the conversation began – or at any rate, not irretrievably tipsy – but now she wasn't so certain. She had the odd feeling that they were having two different conversations, which coincided only incidentally.

"It makes a difference to me," she said. "Who wants a landlord that hates them?"

Peculiarly, Michael laughed, though it was humorless. "Hates you? Whatever gave you such an idea?"

"'Go and don't ever come back.'"

Michael shook his head. "I have no doubt Belial will accept the situation, given time."

"Well," she said, finishing the last of the tea, "I hope you're right. I came here for a quiet life."

Michael raised his eyebrows. "Did you, now?"

Sophie shrugged. Michael looked as if he meant to say something else, but then Ailsa came back into the room with an armful of clean dishtowels. "Chatting up the ladies, Mike?" she asked cheerfully, as she dropped them on a table and began to fold them.

"Oh, aye," he said. "But I don't think this one's biting."

"She had a bad night," Ailsa said.

"So I heard."

"Why don't you go home, Sophie? Take a nap. You won't be missing anything here, and I promise not to tell Ruadhri."

"That's silly – I'm fine – "

"Go on," said Ailsa, waving her out with a towel. "You can start the tea."

Sophie wasn't especially keen on the thought of walking home alone, but she knew that to protest further would make Ailsa suspicious, and that was something she meant to avoid at all costs.

"Thanks," she said, reluctantly untying her apron. "I'll return the favor."

"Aye, you'd better."

The cloakroom seemed colder than ever after the warm pub. Sophie pulled her coat on quickly, and then checked the batteries on her head torch. Ailsa had laughed at her when she started carrying it on her evening shifts, saying, "No self-respecting Ardnasheenian uses those!"

"But I'm a self-preserving Londoner," Sophie had told her, and then asked Ruadhri to bring a bulk-pack of batteries back from his next trip to Mallaig.

She was glad of them now as she stepped out of the pub into the murk of the rainy late afternoon. The wind had died down since the morning, for which Sophie was thankful: the only thing grimmer than endless rain was endless rain blowing straight into her face. She pulled the drawstrings of her hood tighter, and settled the torch on her head, adjusting the beam so that it threw the widest possible arc in front of her. She took out her iPod, flicked through her playlists and selected "Non-Threatening Eighties Post-Punk Pop", turned the volume down low enough to hear a car coming, but high enough to hear little else. Then, with no more excuses, she started off.

Though she suspected it was the symptom of some psychiatric disorder, Sophie had begun a ritual of counting her steps back to the house on the nights she walked alone. This, combined with the upbeat music, were the only things she'd found that would keep her eyes straight ahead, her mind from wandering too far into the dense dripping tangle of forest on either side of her. Fifty-seven steps took her from the last of the cottages to the church someone had converted into a holiday home and then, according to Ailsa, had never used since. Two hundred more brought her to the gap on the right that led down to a small, pebbly beach. One hundred and thirty seven, and she'd be at the clearing with the fallen oak tree – almost home.

By the time she reached the clearing, though, it was too dark to see it. And just beyond that, her iPod died. "This isn't happening," she said to the silence as she took it out to inspect it, but a moment's glance told her that in fact, it was. The battery was drained, though she was certain that it had been half charged when she put it in her coat pocket that morning.

Telling herself that she must have been mistaken, or that Ailsa had borrowed it without asking while she waited for the tea towels to dry, she put it back into her pocket and resumed walking. She'd lost count of her steps and so she started again, but it was difficult to concentrate without the music that had become part of the ritual. The woods around her seemed full of rustling leaves, cracking sticks and sudden spatters of rain shaken from branches juddering under the impact of who-knew-what.

There are no such things as monsters, she told herself. *No demons, no witches, no ghosts...*

The words in her mind were no more than a talisman, though, and a weak one at that. Because, while they had certainly been true over the past couple of weeks, they were essentially lies. At least one of those things did exist, or something like it.

"But not here," she told herself out loud, and then cringed at how frail her voice sounded against the dripping, breathing forest. Frail, and alone.

Except that as soon as she thought it, she knew that she wasn't. She felt the presence like a clammy wind down the back of her neck and quickened her pace, but it was too late. She could hear the wet slap of its footfalls, the susurration of decaying clothing dragging behind it. The light of her head torch began to flicker, and then it died too, but it didn't leave her in the dark. She wished that it had. The blackest void would be preferable to the eerie blue glow now illuminating the woods around her.

Sophie didn't run. There was no point, no escape from her

haunting. She knew it for certain now, and for that, though it wasn't entirely surprising, she did feel a certain despair. She had made herself believe that she could leave the Revenants behind in the city with the rest of her old life, and for a little while it had seemed to have worked. But she had been wrong, and there was nothing to do now but turn around and face it.

It was a bad one – old enough to have been battered by exposure to the elements, but not old enough yet to leave a clean skeleton. Only the pale eyes and long, red-tinged, curling hair looked remotely human anymore. The rest of it was fraying like a threadbare rag-doll, flesh crumbling off of it in translucent blue strips, clothes no more than a rent net of disintegrating fabric. Its image ran and streamed, as if seen through a rainy window.

"You don't belong here," Sophie said to it, fighting to keep her voice even.

The Revenant reached for her with a languid, fleshless hand, and a flicker in its eyes of what might have been longing.

"I can't help you!" she cried. "There's nothing here for you – leave me alone!"

Sometimes that worked. More often, though, they ignored her and continued to follow her, until their strength ran out or they lost interest or wherever it was they came from finally called them back. Without knowing what they were, Sophie couldn't begin to guess. The only thing she knew for certain – or what passed for certain in this private, lawless hell of hers – was that they couldn't actually harm her. They could follow her; keep her awake with their ghostly light, sitting at the end of her bed; dog her until she thought she would go mad trying to pretend she didn't see them; but none of them had ever been able to touch her.

Until now. For even as she thought it, this one reached out its hand and laid it on her arm. The tattered fingers were a searing cold vice around her wrist, far stronger than the creature's dejected image would suggest. As a scream built in her, the Revenant raised its other hand and laid it on her cheek. And though its face was mostly bone, she was certain that it smiled.

The scream burst out of her, though she knew that it was pointless, that it made no difference to the Revenant, and no one else could possibly hear her out here. She screamed again and again as the Revenant raised its other hand and pulled her face toward its own, as if to kiss her. She shut her eyes against it, her heart pounding so hard that she thought her chest would burst. Then, abruptly, it let go of her, uttering a catlike hiss. She opened her eyes to see it retreating, one backward step after another.

Sophie didn't have it in her to wonder why. She couldn't even catch her breath. Spangled dots crowded her vision, and she knew with utter disgust that she was going to faint. Just as her knees buckled, though, something caught her. Someone, looping strong arms under hers. She opened her mouth to scream again, but then the arms turned her around. She found herself looking into a bright light, and beneath it, Sam Eblis's perfect face.

His eyes flickered for a moment to a spot over her shoulder, and narrowed. She turned just in time to see the monster disappear back into the woods. Sam seemed to recall himself then. He shifted the head torch away from Sophie's face and looked down at her, asking, "Are you alright?"

Sophie didn't know. She couldn't think how to answer, or consider how he happened to be in a position to come to her rescue. A single thought ran through her head, drowning out everything else.

Letting go of him, looking straight into his face, she said, "You saw it too."

CHAPTER 6

"Saw what?" Sam asked.

Sophie looked at him in disbelief, but his blue eyes were ingenuous, his face showing only concern. "The Rev – " she began, and then corrected, "I mean, that *thing* that was holding onto me. I saw you looking at it!"

He looked down at her for a moment longer, eyes calm and expression unruffled. Then he shook his head. "I was looking for whatever it was that frightened you – and I didn't see anything."

"But…but I saw you…"

"I didn't see it, Sophie," he repeated. He sounded sincere, though given his guarded expression, it was difficult to tell. "What is it that you thought *you* saw?"

"Maybe it really was nothing…" Sophie answered, trying to buy time to think. She knew what she'd seen, and she was still half convinced that Sam had seen it too; but on the other hand, what reason would he have to deny it?

More to the point, his denial meant that she'd broken her

own golden rule regarding the Revenants: never admit to seeing them, to anyone, ever. She'd come to that conclusion after three years of psychiatric evaluation, which had been her reward for finally telling her parents about her "hallucinations". She'd spent the first year-and-a-half trying to convince them and the doctor that the Revenants were real. When it became clear that they couldn't see them and would never believe her, she'd spent the rest of the time madly backtracking. Telling them that she'd been mistaken, hysterical, looking for attention – anything to stave off medication and endless years of therapy.

She even, eventually, conceded to the doctor's theory that the Revenants were a combination of her high intelligence and the deep-seated abandonment issues he insisted she must have, because she'd been adopted. Though she hated him for making her do it to her parents, in the end she'd realized that it was easier for them to believe that they'd somehow failed her, than to believe that she was mad. The possibility that she could actually see something that other people couldn't had never been part of the discussion.

So she'd researched abandonment issues and played her "recovery" to perfection. Meanwhile, she didn't go out at night if she could help it, because that was when they usually appeared. When she did have to venture out after dark, she did her best to ignore them. She learned to look at them head-on and smile, or carry on a conversation as if there were nothing there. She'd even half-convinced herself that they *were* purely psychological, that if she denied them long enough, they'd go away. And now she'd undone all of it, for a man she didn't even know. Sophie dropped her face into her hands in despair.

And then Sam's hand came to rest on her shoulder. She looked up at him in surprise. "It's easy to imagine things on this road, in the dark," he said gently – kindly. "We should have lights put in."

"I…suppose that would help," Sophie said, trying to sound sincere – trying to sound anything but deranged. But as her heart rate returned to normal, what she felt was drained and dejected. For one golden moment, she'd known what it would be like not to have to suffer her haunting alone, and though it had been brief, it made the burden that much harder to bear. "What are you doing out here, anyway?" she asked, to fill the silence.

"I was going to the pub," he answered, "to look for you."

"Why?" she asked bluntly.

"To ask you to dinner."

"Really?" Somehow she couldn't quite make herself believe this.

But he nodded, nothing in his face anything less than sincere. "I told you the other day, I wanted to start again. I thought we could eat at the pub. But something tells me you'd rather not walk back to the village now."

Sophie shuddered. "Definitely not."

"In which case, I'll cook."

"Look, Sam, that's really sweet, but I'm tired, and your house must be miles away…"

"I'll cook at yours," he said, as if there were nothing strange about this, and no chance that she might not agree.

Though his arrogance irritated her, she couldn't deny that a part of her was flattered. Besides that, she had no desire to remain in the dark woods, and she was more than glad to have company on the rest of the walk home. "Okay," she said. "But I hope you can work wonders with half a box of Alpen and three apples."

Sam smiled, with what looked a bit too much like triumph. *Benefit of the doubt,* Sophie insisted to herself, and turned with him back toward the house. It was only a few minutes before Madainneag's lights showed through the trees. Sophie let out a sigh of relief. As they passed the tower, she noticed that there was a light on in the upper window again. The bizarre interlude with Lucas Belial came flooding back to her, and with it the confused torrent of longing and pain and despair that had overwhelmed her the first time she looked at his face.

Sam must have seen some of it, because he said, "Are you alright?"

"Yes, of course," Sophie said, looking quickly away from the window. She gave him a smile she hoped was convincing. Sam looked on the brink of saying something else, then he shook his head and smiled back.

"Let's get inside – you look half frozen," he said. Sophie started for the door, but Sam said, "Not that way."

"What?" Sophie asked, turning back to him. "Why?"

A flicker of intense emotion crossed his face, then he smiled.

74

"Muddy boots," he said. "I wouldn't want to track up Belial's floors."

"Um…okay," Sophie said. "You can leave them by the kitchen door." She led him around the back of the house, turned on the kitchen light and shed her wet jacket onto a chair back. As she did so, something dropped out of the pocket and onto the floor. Sam bent to pick it up, and once again, the strange look crossed his features. It wasn't quite angry, but there was an intensity to it that put Sophie on guard.

Sam turned to her, holding out the little wooden disc that the old man in the cottage had given to her. "Where did you get this?" he asked, his voice as strange as his look.

"From an old man in a cottage in the valley. The house is right in the middle of the path."

"Niall Aiken," Sam said grimly. "You should be careful of him."

"He seemed harmless enough."

"He's not right in the head. Full of strange ideas and old superstitions. That can be dangerous."

"Honestly? He looked like I could have knocked him over with a toothpick."

Sam looked at her, his eyes intent and unblinking. "Why did he give this to you?"

"I don't know…he was going on about protection, something about an exile. I thought maybe there was some incomer here he didn't like. Especially since he told me to go home."

Sam raised his eyebrows. "How rude."

Sophie nodded. "But it seems to be a popular sentiment."

"What do you mean?"

"Lucas Belial said the same thing."

"Did he, now?" Sam said, a faint smile curling his lips.

"What?" Sophie demanded.

"Nothing – only I *did* warn you."

"Yes, I suppose you did. Anyway, let's not talk about him."

"Too right." He seemed about to say something else, and then he thought better of it. Giving her a brilliant smile, he held out the disc. "So, do you want this back?"

"Not especially," Sophie answered. Sam shrugged and pocketed it, his smile back in place. "Have a seat," he said, pulling out a chair for her with a flourish.

"But you don't know where to find anything," Sophie protested.

"A kitchen's a kitchen," Sam said, nodding again to the chair. Feeling silly, and painfully exposed with no job to occupy her, Sophie sat. Sam opened the refrigerator and began poking around. He emerged a moment later with a bottle of wine, three-quarters full.

"That's Ailsa's," Sophie said.

"I'll get her another one," Sam said, hooking two glasses from the hanging rack and filling them. He handed one to Sophie.

"I don't really drink," she said.

His eyes twinkled at her, so blue they were almost violet. "You're in Ardnasheen now," he said. "It's the local activity of choice, so you'd better learn. *Sláinte.*" He tapped the rim of his glass to hers, offered her a conspiratorial smile, and took a sip, then made a face as he swallowed. "God – that's awful!"

Sophie sipped. It tasted like wine. "Is it?"

"Be glad you don't know any better."

Sophie smiled, and took another sip as Sam returned to the refrigerator and began taking things out. Sophie watched the growing pile in confusion – that morning there'd been nothing in the fridge but milk, the wine bottle and three apples. Ailsa must have sent a grocery order on yesterday's ferry, and forgotten to tell her about it.

"Can I help?" she asked.

"That would defeat the purpose," he said, reaching for a knife and a cutting board, and then laying into a green pepper.

"Of what?"

"Of convincing you that I'm really not the terrible bloke I probably seemed the other day."

"I never thought you were terrible."

He smiled, sweeping the pepper into a roasting tin. "Of course you did."

"How would you know that?"

"Your face is like an open book."

"Wow, you really know how to flatter a girl."

He looked up, surprised. "I meant it as a compliment. Ingenuousness is a rare bird these days."

"Um…well…thanks, then."

He put more chopped vegetables into the roasting tin. "So

what made you come up here, Sophie? It isn't really the obvious place for a city girl to spend her gap year."

"You'd laugh if I told you."

"Probably. But there's only one way to know for certain." One side of his mouth was quirked up, his eyes were dancing. *God*, she thought, *he's gorgeous*. But it wasn't just that that made him so appealing. There was something in his face that suggested conspiracy, and she had no doubt that she wasn't the first girl to find it intoxicating.

Which didn't change the fact that it was. She smiled. "Alright. I came here partly to avoid the fallout from my parents' divorce, partly because I've never actually been to the country where most of my music comes from, but mostly because I read 'Kidnapped' when I was twelve years old, and fell in love with Davie Balfour."

Sam stopped chopping and looked up at her incredulously. "You're joking, right?"

Sophie realized she'd been gazing at him far too long, and shook her head, then sipped her wine, which was going straight to her head. "One bout of Robert Louis Stevenson, and I was hooked. But it took me this long to actually make it up here."

"To Ardnasheen?"

"To Scotland."

"Honestly? But you play the *clarsach* – and your mother's Scottish."

"Which you know how, exactly?"

He shrugged. "Word travels in a small town."

"Well, word's right – Mum's Scottish. That's the problem, actually. She grew up on a hill farm, and hated it. She couldn't wait to get to the city. She says that once she finally made it to London, she wasn't going to let anything drag her back. Besides, Londoners tend to forget there's anything to the north of us."

Sam smiled, and once again Sophie had to slap herself mentally to tear her eyes away from the collarbones sweeping like wings into the neckline of his black jumper. "So you came for Davie Balfour," he said, "and ended up waiting tables at World's End. I'm sure there's a moral in that somewhere."

"Like 'look before you leap'? Or maybe 'be careful what you wish for'?"

"Having that much fun, are you?"

Sophie licked her finger and ran it around the rim of the glass, letting out a single clear note. "It's alright, actually. Not quite what I was expecting, but then, what ever is?"

"Very little, in my experience," he said. There was a bitterness in his voice that made Sophie's eyes snap back up to his face, but the darkness there was fleeting.

"My turn now," Sophie said, before he could ask anything else.

"Fair enough," he answered, putting the tin in the oven and coming to sit down across from her.

"Do you honestly like it here?"

He gave her a quizzical look. "Why wouldn't I?"

"I don't know…it's just that I heard you were at Cambridge, before…it must have been a big change."

Sam considered this for a moment, sipping his wine. "It was something I had to do," he said at last, his face momentarily serious.

"Do you think you'll stay?"

He shrugged, draining his glass and reaching for the bottle to refill it. "For the moment. My turn again," he said, pinning her with his brilliant eyes.

"Okay," Sophie said, suddenly apprehensive, because she knew exactly what he was going to say.

"What was it you saw on the road tonight?"

Sophie looked into the yellow depths of her glass. She could feel the liquor working its way into her limbs, relaxing her. It made her want to tell him. Still, a lifetime's habit was a hard thing to break.

"Why does it matter?" she asked. "You think I didn't see anything."

"I never said that. I only said that *I* didn't see anything."

She looked for dissimulation in his eyes. They were bright and unreadable as sea glass. "You'll think I'm mad."

"Why would I think that," he asked, "when we've had two perfectly normal conversations?"

She held his eyes for a moment, and then she looked away. "Because it *is* mad." He said nothing, only watched her, waiting. Sophie knew that it would be futile to try to deflect him. "Alright. Just remember that I warned you." He gave a slight nod, and she said, "I saw one of the Revenants."

"Revenant...isn't that a kind of ghost?"

"More of an intelligent zombie. The definition doesn't quite fit, but it's as near as I've been able to come to figuring out what they are."

"I don't understand," he said.

Sophie sighed. "Neither do I. When I was little, I thought they were ghosts, but the more I saw them, the more wrong that seemed. There's something too…solid about them. I've been through all the possibilities – vampires, zombies, wood sprites, you name it. None of the descriptions fit. They're human, but not. Dead, but alive. Looking for something I can't figure out. And as far as I know, nobody can see them but me."

Sam was gazing at her, unblinking. She looked away, furious to feel tears filling her eyes. She didn't know what they were for; she just wished she hadn't told him. It had been stupid, because now he *did* think that she was crazy.

And then he said, "I'm not sure that that's true."

She looked up at him. "But…you said you didn't see it."

"That doesn't mean anything. You've heard of the second sight, haven't you?"

"What – like seeing the future?"

"Among other things. On this coast, it's epidemic. If you took a poll in the pub, no doubt more than half of them would claim to have seen ghosts, or dreamed things before they happened, or something similar. So no, Sophie, I don't think that you're mad."

"But I don't come from here," she said, wondering why she

was arguing when he was willing to accept her bizarre confession, "and I've seen these things for as long as I can remember."

He smiled, but shook his head. "Why do you always have to argue?"

"Always? How do you know that I always argue?"

There was the slightest pause; his eyes flickered away from hers. Then he recovered, saying, "The point is, there are things in this world that aren't easy to explain. Only fools believe that we know everything there is to know. If you say you saw something," he shrugged, "who am I to say you didn't?"

Sophie searched his face, looking for a sign that these were platitudes. But his eyes were sincere. At last, she nodded. "Thank you," she said, and she meant it. In fact, she was overwhelmed with gratitude. Sam's eyes clung to hers; the faint smile was back. She didn't know how it happened, but suddenly he was holding her hand, leaning across the table.

Oh my God, he's going to –

"Hello!" a girl's cheery voice called, shattering the moment. Sophie snatched her hand back as Ailsa's footsteps sounded in the corridor outside. For a split second, Sam's face changed, darkening with what looked like fury as he turned toward the sound. Sophie shrank back instinctively. Then she blinked, and when she looked again his face wore the usual conspiratorial smile.

"Rain check?" he said to her with a wink, as Ailsa came into the kitchen.

CHAPTER 7

"Oh my God, I am *so sorry!*" Ailsa said for at least the fifteenth time.

"Will you stop!" Sophie said from the sink, where she was washing up the dinner dishes.

"Honestly," Ailsa continued as if she hadn't heard, flailing a tea towel, "Sam bloody Eblis comes to make you tea, and you end up with me as the third wheel! Could there be anything worse?"

"Yes," Sophie said, tipping a wine glass upside down to dry in the rack, "you going on about it endlessly, as if it mattered."

Ailsa shook her head. "As if it *mattered?* Sophie, are you blind?"

Sophie smiled. "No, Ailsa, I'm well aware that he's a hottie. But the dinner thing was only to apologize for having got off on the wrong foot."

"Oh, right," Ailsa scoffed, finishing the last of Sophie's glass of wine before putting the glass into the soapy water. "So you're asking me to believe that there was absolutely no flirtatious undercurrent or bodily contact when the two most gorgeous people in this swamp get together for *diner-aux-deux*?"

"That's about it," Sophie said, trying not to think of Sam's fingers around hers, and the way he'd leaned toward her just before Ailsa came in. She doubted that that was the kind of detail Ailsa was looking for – nothing had actually happened, after all – and either way, she didn't want to share it.

"You're not even a *tiny bit* attracted to him?"

"I didn't say that," Sophie answered, putting the last glass up to dry and letting the water out of the sink.

"Aha!"

"But there's a big difference between attraction and…well, anything else, really."

"Give it time," Ailsa said pragmatically. "You can't expect the strong, solitary type to offer his heart on a platter on the first date."

Sophie shook her head. "Will you stop? It was *not* a date – well, not a real one anyway – and no one is offering hearts on platters. It didn't mean anything."

Ailsa raised her eyebrows. "Okay…if you say so."

"I say so."

*

Except that that night, she couldn't sleep. She couldn't stop thinking of Sam. She turned over the things he'd said and how he'd said them, wondering if Ailsa was right. She wondered if he really had meant to kiss her, or if she'd only imagined it, along with the conspiratorial glint in his eyes. Even when she finally shut her eyes, she found his brilliant smile etched in her mind.

When she opened them, though, she wasn't looking at Sam's face, but a sky she could only think of as transcendent. It was the clear, bright lavender of the few moments before a summer sunrise, broken by the budding branches of a tree into patterns like a church window. A gentle breeze washed through the branches, carrying the faint incense smell of the dream cemetery, and rocking the bed on which she lay.

Rocking the bed? she thought, suddenly wide awake. She sat up, shedding a layer of soft white feathers that had covered her, and looked around. There were no walls to her strange bed, only golden bars that curved upward and met at a common point above her head. A birdcage.

"Sophia!" someone called from below. Sophie looked down, and saw Suri sitting on the mausoleum beneath her, wearing a pair of black cat-eye glasses and balancing a white laptop computer on her knees. She still wore the white dress, but now she had a pair of laceless black combat boots on her feet. She grinned and waved up at Sophie.

"Suri! What am I doing up here?"

Suri shrugged. "Only you know that."

Of course, Sophie thought, despite the fact that it clarified nothing. "Well, how do I get down?"

"Likewise." Seeing Sophie's irritation, she added, "I can do a search for you, if you think it'll help."

"A search?"

Suri nodded, and typed something into the computer. She considered the screen that came up, typed some more, considered some more, and finally said, "Unipedia suggests that you consider your options."

"Right. I'd have never thought of that one on my own." She looked around her, but there was no apparent door in the barred walls. She'd never had a pet bird, so she was hazy on how their cages functioned. She was fairly certain, however, that some of them had detachable bottoms to make them easier to clean.

As soon as she'd thought it she was falling, somersaulting languidly through the air like a diver, before she landed beside Suri in a pile of feathers.

"Ouch," she said, rubbing the elbow on which she'd landed.

"What were you doing up there?" Suri asked, putting the computer aside to help her brush the feathers off of her blue nightdress.

"I don't know," Sophie said, peering up into the branches of the tree. The birdcage was gone.

"Whatever. You're here now." Suri smiled and patted her consolingly on the shoulder. Like the last time, Sophie found her mesmerizingly beautiful. It puzzled her. Of course Suri's platinum ropes of hair, smooth white skin and dark, glittering eyes were striking. But she also seemed to shimmer slightly, as if she radiated a light that was just beyond the visible spectrum.

"Why do I keep dreaming about this place, and about you?" Sophie asked her. "I'm quite sure I've never been here in real life."

"That depends on what you consider 'real', and how you define 'life'."

"Pardon?"

"Sorry," Suri answered. "Clarification is off-limits."

"Whose limits?"

"Yours."

Sophie wondered if she were losing her mind. She didn't think it should be possible for her own brain to manufacture such a conundrum, sleeping or otherwise. She said, "I suppose I ought to wake up, then."

"No no no!" Suri cried, waving her hands. "If you're here, it's because you're meant to be."

"Frankly, I can't see the logic."

"Logic," Suri repeated, wrinkling her nose. "No point bothering with that." Her computer pinged, and they both looked down at the screen. It showed a picture of an envelope, with "Sophia" written on it in bold calligraphy. "You've got mail!" Suri cried gleefully.

"How is that possible?"

Suri only shrugged, and handed Sophie the laptop. "I'll give you some privacy to read it," she said, leaping up and grabbing a branch of the tree. She kicked off her boots, swung herself onto the branch and then began climbing. In moments, she was out of sight, although Sophie didn't remember the tree being so tall. She also recalled its branches being bare, but now they were festooned with leaves and fat acorns. Except that she had a recollection of apples...

Dreaming, she reminded herself, and clicked the cursor on the envelope. It split open into four points, which grew until they filled the screen and then kept growing, blotting out the computer, the mausoleum, and everything around her until the cemetery was gone. Now Sophie was standing on a black-and-white marble floor, like the one in the room where she'd seen Lucas Belial. But this wasn't a room: there were no walls or ceiling, only a shifting, deep blue mist encompassing the floor's edges.

Something touched her shoulder – a man's hand. She turned, expecting Sam's perfect face, but to her surprise it was Lucas standing behind her, wearing an old-fashioned tail suit in somber black. There was no anger on his face now; no pain. It was radiant as the sun as he smiled down at her, and she thought, *He's more beautiful than any human being has a right to be.*

Then he held out his hand. Sophie took a step forward and heard a soft rustle. Looking down, she realized that it came from her own long skirt. She was wearing the most beautiful dress she had ever seen: a ball-gown the color of the sky in Suri's cemetery, its tight bodice embroidered with tiny forget-me-nots, its skirt billowing out in silky folds, with tiny lace sleeves resting just off her shoulders.

She closed the distance between herself and Lucas, placed her hand on his shoulder as his arm came around her waist,

88

and clasped his own with her other one. There was music then, though she was certain that there hadn't been before. It was beautiful, and hauntingly familiar, but she couldn't place it, or even say what kind of instrument made it. Nor did she particularly care, because, a moment later, Lucas began to move in a dance, pulling her along with him. She wanted to tell him that she didn't know how to dance – not like this, anyway – but just as she drew a breath to say it she realized that it wasn't true. She was mirroring his complex steps without even thinking about it, as if she'd done it all of her life.

When the music ended, Lucas dropped her hand and wrapped his other arm around her, as she clasped her hands behind his neck. Like the music and the steps of the dance, it felt familiar and right – as if she'd always been meant to stand like this, in his arms. He looked down at her, and she looked back. She couldn't have torn herself away from the love and warmth she saw in his eyes for anything.

"Sophia," he said, his hands sliding to her waist as he leaned down.

She closed her eyes. His lips touched hers gently, but she didn't want him to be gentle. She thrust her fingers into his hair and pulled him closer, crushing her mouth to his, sliding her tongue past his teeth as he opened himself up to her. A few moments later he pulled away, and she moaned in disappointment. But then he began kissing her neck, his lips sending fire running through her, his tongue in the hollow of her throat like a drug. They slipped together to the floor – except that it wasn't a floor any longer. It had become a field of indigo grass, and the purple mist had cleared to a navy blue sky, blazing with more stars than Sophie had ever seen.

Lucas pulled back again, resting his head on one extended arm. "Promise you'll love me always," he said, running a finger down her breastbone, sending chills through her, until it rested over her heart.

"There's no need," she answered, even as she wondered where the words were coming from. "I couldn't be, and not love you."

His smile faltered, then flattened. He looked at her for a moment in wide-eyed fear, and then he was retreating, fading like a photograph left too long in the light.

"Lucas!" she cried as pain tore through her; but he was gone. So were the night sky and the dark blue field; the beautiful dress was reduced to a few dirty rags. Sophie sat alone in the cemetery under the tree, now a peeling paper birch with winter-bare branches, weeping her heart out into the dry brown grass, under a sky full of charcoal cloud. She knew that she mourned Lucas, but she didn't know why. She hardly cared. It felt as if her heart had been ground to sand that scoured the rest of her raw.

She wept until she had no tears left, and then she looked up. Her eyes fell on the statue of the angel with demon's wings. For the first time, she really looked at it. It was carved from what she guessed was white marble, but beyond that it was completely unlike the angels she had seen in other cemeteries. There was no halo over the angel's tousled hair. He wore no flowing robes

– instead, his spare, muscled frame was barely covered by a draped cloth. He sat slumped in the cup of his folded wings, his head bowed toward the clenched fist resting on his knee, obscuring his face.

Following a sick premonition, Sophie moved still closer. She felt sicker, but not surprised when she finally looked into the statue's face. It was Lucas's, grim and bitter as it had been the night she met him. Filled with a sudden horror, she dropped to her knees and began to dig. The earth was dry and crumbly, coming away easily. She threw herself into the work, needing to know what the statue marked; praying that it wasn't what she feared.

When her fingers reached wood, though, she hesitated. She took her time clearing the dust from the coffin's top, trying to steel herself for the sight of whatever was within. But when she finally pulled the rotted wood away, she found no body, no bones or ashes. The only things lying in that grave were the rusty pieces of what seemed once to have been plate armor, along with the blackened hilt of a sword. And though Sophie had thought that no sight could have been more devastating than Lucas's dead body, she knew in that moment that she had been wrong.

CHAPTER 8

"Sophie, you aren't even listening!" Ailsa cried, startling Sophie back into the here-and-now.

Ailsa had been describing the trials and tribulations of a romantically challenged friend from home as they walked to work, but hard as she tried to concentrate on what Ailsa was saying, Sophie's mind kept drifting back to the unsettling dream.

"Sorry," she said. "So what did Rona say to Craig?"

Ailsa smiled and shook her head. "We were *way* past Craig."

"Sorry," Sophie repeated.

"It's alright. I don't know why you'd want to hear about these people you don't even know, when you've got Sam to think about."

Sophie smiled – she hoped convincingly – and didn't contradict Ailsa. She couldn't untangle the feelings the dream had awakened in her, let alone try to explain them to somebody else. Most of all, she didn't want another lecture about Lucas Belial.

"Did you make plans to see him again?" Ailsa asked.

"Who?" Sophie asked distractedly.

"Michael the bar-prop." Sophie looked blankly at Ailsa, who rolled her eyes. "Truly, terrifyingly hopeless! I meant Sam, you dingbat!"

"Oh. No – nothing specific." He'd talked about showing her his side of Ardnasheen, but they hadn't made any firm plans.

"Well, I'm sure he's just trying not to seem too keen and scare you off," she said.

This time, Sophie couldn't make herself smile. They had reached the spot where the Revenant had approached her the night before. Her breath came shallow and her heart beat hard. She scanned the beach and woods for any sign that the creature had been there, but there wasn't so much as a footprint or ribbon of rotting cloth. She hadn't really expected one. They never left a trace. Then again, they never touched her, either. *Perhaps Scottish Revenants are a different breed...*

"Sophie – are you alright?"

"Yes, I'm fine, I...I just thought I saw something in the woods."

"Ah, that'll be the Gray Lady."

Sophie's eyes snapped to Ailsa's face. "What did you say?"

Ailsa smiled. "The Gray Lady. What self-respecting ancient estate doesn't have a Gray Lady? Ours is a long-lost Lady Something-or-Other, who died of a broken heart...or was it a stab wound? Anyway, she appears here on dark nights, when someone's walking alone."

"Are you making this up?" Sophie asked, struggling to keep her voice steady.

Ailsa rolled her eyes. "If I wanted to scare you, I could do a lot better than some daft ghost story!"

"So you don't believe it," Sophie said, breathing a little bit easier.

Ailsa shrugged. "I can't say I've ever seen anything out here myself – more's the pity. But there are plenty who'll tell you they have. Then again, that's usually at the end of a particularly good night in the pub."

Sophie turned this information over in her mind as they walked. The Revenant she'd seen would certainly fit the Gray Lady description, but as far as she knew, no one else ever saw them – except, possibly, Sam. Maybe last night's apparition had been something else? Yet it had looked and behaved like all the other Revenants she'd seen. Until it reached out and touched her.

"Oi, Sophie," Ailsa said, grabbing her arm suddenly and pointing toward the water, "look at that!"

Sophie followed her finger. The tide was out, and beyond the screen of trees lay an expanse of greenish, rocky shore. The blonde woman in the red jacket who Sophie had noticed the day she walked inland was standing there, the same sack lying at her feet. And standing with her was Lucas Belial. He wore a long, dark coat that flapped in the wind, and a serious expression on his face. The woman's face was also serious. She was near enough now that Sophie could also see that she was very young, and very pretty. A ferocious wave of jealousy blindsided her.

"Who is she?" she asked, trying and failing to make her tone light and off-handed.

"I don't know her name," Ailsa said. "She's one of the winkle pickers."

"The what?"

"People who pick periwinkles off the rocks to sell them. It's hard work, but it pays well. They travel around to different beaches depending on the tides and the weather, or whatever. That girl comes here a lot." She cocked her head with a speculative smile. "I guess she comes for more than the winkles."

Once again, the jealous rage engulfed Sophie. *What the hell is wrong with you?* she asked herself, but it made no difference. She couldn't bear to watch Lucas and the girl standing so close together, talking so seriously. When he reached out and laid a hand on her arm, Sophie turned away.

"I guess so," she mumbled, barely aware of what she was saying.

"Maybe a girlfriend will put him in a better mood," Ailsa said as they resumed walking.

"Maybe," Sophie said faintly, trying not to think about the word "girlfriend".

Ailsa sighed wistfully. "It seems everyone here can find someone except me – even grumpy old Lucas Belial."

"Give it time," Sophie said. "And anyway, we don't really know what that was we saw, do we?"

Ailsa only laughed, and a few moments later they arrived at the village. A big group of hill walkers was trailing into the pub, no doubt looking for breakfast before bagging a Munro. Sophie put on her cheerful waitress face and followed Ailsa inside.

*

By afternoon, the pub was dead. "Bloody hill walkers," Ruadhri grumbled, as he polished the bar's counter top. Sophie had grown used to this type of complaint – Ruadhri welcomed the droves of visiting hill walkers that kept his pub going, but hated their habit of drinking sensibly and going to bed early. "They're too damned healthy for their own good."

"For *your* own good, you mean," Ailsa said.

"Watch that tongue, lass, or I'll see if Sophie has a friend to replace you!"

"Right," Ailsa said, rolling her eyes. "Because pretty girls from London are just *dying* for jobs at World's End."

"Aye, they are – eh, Sophie?"

Sophie smiled. "Beating the door down. I had to leave under cover of darkness to make sure none of them followed me."

Ruadhri laughed. "Alright, lassies – have the afternoon off."

"Really?" Ailsa asked, brightening.

"Aye," he said. "Make sure you're back well before the dinner rush, though."

Sophie and Ailsa put away their aprons and headed for the door. Sophie's head had mostly cleared of the strange dream, and they chatted about mundane things on the way home. By the time they reached the house the drizzle had stopped, and there were even a few blue patches between the clouds that suggested they might clear by evening.

"I think I'll walk a bit," Ailsa said. "Want to come?"

Sophie shook her head. "I haven't practiced in days," she said. "The harp will be feeling neglected."

"Okay, then. I'll be back in an hour or so."

Sophie went into the house, hung up her jacket and climbed the stairs. She was trying to decide whether to work on the *pibroch* or something easier, so it didn't register that the door to her bedroom, which she'd closed behind her that morning as usual, was standing ajar. She pushed inside, mentally notating the *pibroch's* next section, and then stopped in shock. Lucas Belial was sitting at her desk, rifling through her composition notebook.

They stared at each other for a speechless moment, equally stunned, before Lucas's face colored and Sophie's surprise turned into anger. "What do you think you're doing!" she cried.

"I…was looking for something," he said, his expression a strange mixture of anger and wonder.

"In my things?" She snatched the notebook away from him, held it protectively against her chest.

"No…something I thought I'd left behind, before you came…" He stood up, facing her. He wasn't overly tall, but there was something about his bearing, about the burning intensity with which he regarded her, that drew her focus, making it seem as if he filled the room. Part of her wanted to shrink back from his nearly-palpable anger; but to her annoyance, another part of her longed to touch him. The images from the dream came flooding back, making her heart beat hard and her face burn.

Then he said, "Why are you still here? I thought I told you to go."

Desire flared to fury. "And what gives you the right to order me around?" she snapped. "You think because you're the laird of some godforsaken estate in the middle of nowhere, you can just tell people what to do?"

"I can when they're in my house," he said, his face and voice grim and menacing.

"Well that's easily taken care of," Sophie said, pulling her backpack out of the wardrobe and beginning to toss things into it.

"What are you doing?" he asked, watching her as if she were some kind of exotic animal he couldn't quite believe was real, and had no idea how to deal with.

"Leaving your house," she snapped, "just like you said."

"You're going home?"

His voice was so hopeful it made Sophie pause. Then she laughed incredulously. "Going home? Ruadhri hired me, and as far as I know you have no jurisdiction in the pub. I'm keeping the job. I'll just find somewhere else to live."

"Sophia, you can't!"

"Watch me."

"You have to leave Ardnasheen! You don't understand!"

She dropped the backpack, crossed her arms over her chest. "Then explain."

He wouldn't meet her eyes, and there was misery on his face now, clouding the anger. "I can't."

"Then I can't help you."

"God, you never listen to reason, do you?"

Sophie stared at him, the words clanging in her mind, reminding her of something else, though she couldn't quite place it. "Don't I?" she asked. "And how would you know that?"

He looked back at her, his face momentarily blank with surprise. Or nearly blank. There was something else in his dark eyes, now that the anger was gone. Something that she hadn't expected to see, but of which she was absolutely certain in those few moments of silence before he answered: longing.

Lucas opened his mouth to reply, but he never made it further than that, because a sudden, strange noise interrupted him. It was faint, as if echoing down a long corridor, but distinct: high, women's voices singing a strange, wavering tune, almost a chant, in a language that Sophie didn't recognize. Though there was a certain beauty to it, it filled Sophie with a cold foreboding. When Lucas looked at her again, his face mirrored the feeling, pale and pinched with fear.

"What – what is that?" Sophie asked.

"It's something bad," he answered. "Something very bad…I have to go. Stay here."

"What! But you've just been telling me to go home!"

"And I meant it. But for the moment, you must stay here, in the house. It isn't safe for you out there."

"Where, outside? Because of some weird Highland choir practice?"

"Please, Sophia. Just promise me you'll stay here."

"Until when? And what about Ailsa? She's out walking alone. If there's something out there – "

"Ailsa is fine," he said shortly. "That is, she is physically unharmed. But in a moment, she's going to need you. Wait for her here."

"Wait – how do you – " Sophie began, but he was already gone, running from the room as the women's voices faded into a silence that suddenly seemed full of menace. And despite everything telling her otherwise, Sophie sat down on the bed to wait.

CHAPTER 9

"I just can't believe it!" Ailsa said, swiping with a tissue at the tears streaming down her face. "I'm never going to get it out of my head as long as I live."

Sophie handed her another tissue. It was very late – hours had passed since the police had brought Ailsa home from the pub, after questioning her about the circumstances under which she'd found Niall Aiken dead in his cottage.

"God, his face, Sophie," she said, pulling her duvet more tightly around her shoulders. "I know they said it was a heart attack, but he looked afraid. Like he was staring at something awful when he…when he…"

Sophie looked into the smoldering fire, trying not to think of the ghostly chorus; trying not to remember the look on Lucas's face before he'd fled from her room. She had no intention of telling Ailsa about that. It was the last thing her friend needed to hear after the shock she'd had, but more to the point, speaking the words would add fuel to Ailsa's suspicions, which in turn would make it all more real than Sophie wanted it to be. It was far easier to call Niall's death a heart attack, and Lucas simply mad.

"Not that I know much about it," she said at last, looking back at Ailsa, "but maybe it's just something that happens, when you die. I mean, it had been a while before you found him… maybe it was rigor mortis or something."

Ailsa considered this for a moment, and then she shook her head. "It was more than that. Something about it all just seemed *wrong*. I mean, the door was open – why would the door be open? And all of those creepy runes spilled over the floor?"

"Maybe he was holding them when he died. Maybe he knew something was wrong, and he picked them up because…I don't know…maybe because of some weird old superstition. He was into all of that, wasn't he?"

Ailsa frowned. "I suppose he was…but no more so than most of the other old people around here. There are still a lot of them who keep to the old beliefs – corn dollies and smooring the fire and bells on the door to keep the faeries away."

"But Sam thought it was more than that, with Niall," Sophie said pensively. "He told me to be careful of him."

"Niall Aiken?" Ailsa shook her head. "He must have had it wrong. Niall was quite a sweet old man. Came to the pub sometimes for a whisky, but only ever one. Everyone says he's kept himself to himself since his wife died a while back."

"Oh," Sophie said, still trying – and failing – to make all of the pieces line up. "Well, I guess Sam's not been here very long. Those superstitions do seem strange to an outsider."

"No doubt," Ailsa said.

"Look, you've had a shock – you should really get some sleep."

Ailsa gave her a plaintive look. "Sophie...will you stay with me? I just don't think I can face the dark on my own tonight."

"I'll only be next door."

"Please? Just for tonight. I promise not to kick you or steal the covers. Or grab your bum."

Sophie laughed, relenting. "Alright. But I'll hold you to the bum thing."

Ailsa laughed too, and Sophie was so glad to see it that she didn't mind staying, although she'd badly wanted to escape to her room and consider all that had happened. That, and pack – there was no way she was going to stay in that house after the second run-in with Lucas. But Ailsa didn't need to know that yet.

Sophie turned off the bedside light. Ailsa fell asleep quickly, exhausted no doubt by her ordeal. Sophie lay staring into the darkness, convinced that she would never fall asleep that night, but when she opened her eyes again, she saw by Ailsa's bedside clock that several hours had passed.

At first she was disoriented, but slowly, the events of the past day began to filter back in. She was wide awake now, her mind buzzing, and this time she knew that she really wouldn't fall asleep again. Carefully, she peeled back the duvet and slipped out of the bed. She tiptoed to the door, planning to go to her room and play her harp until she was sleepy again, or morning came – whichever happened first.

As soon as she stepped into the hallway, though, she knew that something was wrong. It wasn't dark as it should have been, but dim with a faint, blue-grey light that came from the open door of her room. With a cold and sinking feeling, Sophie crept up to the door, and peered inside.

The Revenant wasn't the one she'd seen the night Sam came to her rescue. It was far older – ancient, she guessed, by its grinning, glowing, fleshless face, and battered, gold-chased helmet. Somehow, though, it had retained its eyes and a few long strands of yellow hair. Three gold armlets clattered around its skeletal elbow as it moved, rifling the bedclothes with the tip of a tarnished knife.

At that moment, it seemed to become aware of her. Sophie didn't try to hide; she knew too well that there was no point. The creature looked at her for a moment, and then it began to walk toward her, the knife pointed at her heart. Sophie backed away in sudden panic. For all their persistence, none of the Revenants had ever tried to attack her; none had ever carried a weapon. But there was no mistaking the intent of this ancient warrior.

Sophie backed out into the hallway, heart pounding, wondering whether she could outrun it. There wasn't really any other choice, unless she went back into Ailsa's room and tried to barricade the door against it. But she dismissed that idea even as it came to her. She couldn't put Ailsa in that kind of danger.

Taking a deep breath, Sophie turned slowly to look down the corridor, not wanting to startle the Revenant into any action before she had the chance to bolt. As she turned, however, something materialized out of the shadows: a man, wearing something long and dark, holding something that looked very like a sword, though in the dim light it was difficult to tell. He strode toward them, and half-disbelieving, Sophie realized she was looking at Lucas Belial. His face was furious, as it always seemed to be, but this time the fury wasn't directed at her.

Pointing the sword straight at the Revenant, he said, "Leave my house, now."

The creature looked at him for a long moment, and then it lowered the hand with the knife, and lurched off in the direction of the stairway. Sophie watched it, dumbfounded, until it turned the corner and was lost from sight. Then she looked at Lucas.

His eyes were there, black and unblinking, waiting for hers. Neither of them said anything. There was no need, at least for Sophie. His eyes said it all. She nodded to him once, the only thank-you she could muster. And, just before she turned back toward Ailsa's room, he nodded back.

CHAPTER 10

"Last orders!" Ailsa shouted across the packed room, to no discernible effect. The queue at the bar didn't decrease, and few of the customers even looked up, let alone made any attempt to finish their drinks. They knew that the call was only a technicality. In a village where the nearest police were an hour's boat ride away, there was nothing to stop the pub staying open all night – and sometimes it did. It was one of the perks of World's End, if you were a customer; the curse, if you were a waitress.

Sighing, Sophie collected another tower of pint glasses and took it into the kitchen for washing. This was one night when she just couldn't face overtime. She'd never slept after finding the Revenant in her room, and despite three early nights since then, she still felt drained. She'd spent the first day half-wishing, half-dreading that she'd run into Lucas again. All she could think about was the fact that he, too had seen the Revenant. Not only that, he'd commanded it. She desperately wanted to ask him about it, but she didn't want to provoke another bout of ranting.

She wavered for another day before curiosity won out. But when she finally knocked on his door, there was no answer. The tower was dark and silent. And so, when she couldn't stand her own obsessive thoughts any longer, she asked Ailsa about it.

"Oh, he went away," she said.

"Away?" Sophie repeated dumbly.

"Aye. I saw him get on the morning ferry the day after I found Niall."

"Oh," Sophie said, trying not to sound as dejected as she felt.

"Why?" Ailsa asked.

"I was just wondering…" Sophie answered lamely, and tried her best to ignore Ailsa's curious look.

Now, after several more days of obsessive thinking – this time about where Lucas could have gone, and what it had to do with the Revenant, and more to the point, why he'd so suddenly given up his campaign to get her to leave – she was exhausted. All she wanted was a hot bath and eight hours of unbroken, dreamless sleep. Given the pile of dishes in the kitchen and the queue at the bar, though, neither looked likely.

Ailsa came into the kitchen just as she'd started filling the sink with soapy water. Sophie watched as she put a Mars Bar in a bowl, the bowl in the microwave and set it for thirty seconds. When the time was up, she took it out and began to eat the resulting goo with a soupspoon.

"Don't you ever eat anything like a sane person?" Sophie asked.

107

"Now what would be the fun in that?" Ailsa answered, offering the bowl and spoon to Sophie. When she declined, Ailsa sat down on the worktop and said, "You'll never guess who just came in."

"Okay. Who just came in?"

"Your man."

"Sam?" she said, looking up sharply.

"No flirtatious undercurrents, eh?" Ailsa said with a throaty laugh.

"Why am I the only one doing anything work-like here?" Ruadhri grumbled, coming into the kitchen.

"Because I'm on break," Ailsa told him cheerfully.

"Sophie isn't."

"Aye, but Sophie was just about to clear tables up the front." Ailsa shoved a tray into Sophie's hands and added with a meaningful smile, "By the door."

"What're you up to?" Ruadhri asked, looking from one girl to the other suspiciously.

"Why is it you always assume I'm up to something?" Ailsa asked, licking her spoon. Ruadhri just shook his head. While he turned to look for something else to complain about, Ailsa leaned toward Sophie and whispered, "Go get him, tiger!"

Sophie left Ailsa and Ruadhri bickering and pushed her way through the crowd, toward the front of the pub. She looked around, but she didn't see any sign of Sam. She turned back to the bar to see Ailsa gesturing wildly, pointing toward the far end of the room. Sophie turned, working her way through the crowd, and at last she spotted Sam's bright head, at the very back of the room.

Sophie wasn't bold enough to march right up to the table and say hello, so she looked around for a way to orchestrate a "chance" meeting. Her eyes fell on the log basket by the fire. It was only half empty, but that was good enough for her. She tried not to stare at Sam as she wove her way toward it, but it was difficult. He seemed to glow in the firelight, his skin luminous, his face more handsome even than she'd remembered. She couldn't help thinking about the way he had almost kissed her; and then she wished she hadn't, as her cheeks flamed.

She was only a few feet away from him now, but he hadn't seen her. He was talking intently with someone she couldn't see through the jostling crowd. He was wearing a jacket that was spotted with rain, as if he'd just come in from outside. Then he laughed, and reached forward, and took hold of something. A hand, small and white, at the end of a red-jacketed arm. A red jacket that was also spotted with rain.

Sophie's guts froze. She picked up a fire iron and started poking at the burning logs. Half-disgusted with herself, she turned around, keeping her face to the shadows. There was no denying it: Sam sat at the table with the beautiful blonde girl in the red jacket, the winkle-picker she'd seen speaking to Lucas. They were talking and laughing as if they knew each other well, and though it appeared he had let her hand go as soon as he'd clasped it, from time to time he touched it lightly, as if staking a claim.

Sophie turned back to the fire, biting her lip to keep from crying. She clutched the mantle-piece with shaking hands, torn by a feeling of betrayal that she couldn't quite justify. After all, Sam had made her no promises. He hadn't even kissed her, and now she had no doubt that he'd never meant to. She'd imagined it all. He'd flirted with her, but it was nothing more than that. She could never compete with a woman like the one he was with now, older and wiser and nothing short of stunning.

Get it together, she told herself angrily, and taking a deep breath, she turned around. She'd steeled herself to see them holding hands, kissing – anything but gone. They'd left together. All at once, nausea overwhelmed her. She fled to the back door, shoved out into the dark blowing rain, gasping as if she could never get enough air. She stood there for a long time, leaning against the wall, letting the rain fall onto her face, willing herself to be calm.

She was just beginning to feel steadier when she heard a voice, as if someone was speaking while coming around from the front of the pub. A moment later her direst suspicion was confirmed: it was Sam's voice. He and the girl were coming back here, to…well, she didn't want to think about that. She reached for the door handle and pulled, but it seemed to have locked when it slammed shut. She couldn't just go around the other side and back in at the front, since an old wall of the house the pub had once been still enclosed the dooryard on two sides. It formed a kind of courtyard where Ruadhri stored empty kegs, and the firewood and peat in an old shed.

Normally, Sophie avoided the shed at night. The faint light from the back door reached only a few inches into it, and she had no problem imagining a Revenant waiting in one of the shadowy corners for her. Now, though, anything seemed better than meeting Sam and the blonde goddess. She wrestled with the rusty latch, managing to cut her thumb on it before she got it open. Then she crouched down in the back of the shed, sucking on her bleeding thumb and cursing Sam so roundly that it took her a moment to realize that it wasn't Sam speaking at all, but Lucas.

His voice steely as he asked, "What do you think you're doing?"

"You dragged me out here to ask me that?" Sam's voice was strange, coldly ironic.

"I dragged you out here to stop you making a very big mistake."

"Don't pretend to know my business."

"Don't prevaricate, Eblis. Your intentions are obvious."

"Then accept them, and leave me to them."

Of course – they're fighting over her, Sophie thought, feeling even sadder.

"She's not who you think she is," Lucas said, his voice ominous. "She won't give you what you want."

"I don't think she'll grudge me a bit on fun," Sam said.

"Honestly – don't tell me you're only in this to get a leg over."

"Actually, I wouldn't mind," Sam said, in a calmly mocking

tone. "But the two ends aren't mutually exclusive, which is to say that there ought to be time enough for pleasure before business – "

There was a sound then that could only be a fist connecting with flesh. Sophie flinched, and then edged closer to the door, trying to see outside. She found a crack big enough to give her a glimpse of two hooded figures streaming with rain, one shaking his hand, the other holding his face; but she couldn't tell which was which.

"You're an idiot," said the one with the hand to his face – Sam.

"Meaning what?"

"Meaning, that right hook told me all I need to know."

"Leave her alone," Lucas said, and this time there was a sincerity to the plea that melted Sophie's heart, blonde girl or not. "She's just an innocent girl." And she found herself banishing the idiotic wish that it was *her* honor Lucas was defending.

"And that, ironically, is why she's also so much more," Sam answered. "Don't tell me you haven't thought about it," he continued, his voice turning low and persuasive. "There might even be enough of her for two – "

"You are vile," Lucas spat.

"And you're better?"

"I've never crossed that line."

"Correction: you've never *yet* crossed it. But you can't tell me that you've never been tempted. You can't tell me you aren't tempted now – I mean, if she isn't the one, then who is?"

"Maybe no one," Lucas said, with chilling despair.

"I don't believe that, and I don't think you do either. So what's the point in sparing her? Piety won't get you where you want to go, and either way you'll lose her."

There was a pause. The rain dripped audibly through the holes in the woodshed roof; a frigid drop ran down Sophie's back. She realized that she was trembling, desperately waiting for Lucas's answer. She was certain that more rested on it than she could imagine, though she had no idea anymore what they were talking about.

"No," Lucas said, so softly that Sophie barely heard him. "I won't lose her again."

Sam gave a low chuckle. "Which would be touching," he said, "if it was actually within your power to stop it. But since it isn't, you might as well live for the moment. I certainly intend to. Game on, Morningstar. Good luck."

*

"You do know that you're sounding like a stalker," Ailsa said, offering Sophie a custard cream as she licked the center out of her own.

Sophie declined the biscuit and flopped back on Ailsa's bed, her head on a furry purple pillow. "Can you honestly tell me you don't think that conversation was beyond weird?"

"A fair few conversations would sound weird, out of context."

"And then calling him 'Morningstar'? How bizarre is that?"

"Well, it *is* the name of the house. Maybe it's a toff thing."

Sophie sighed. "Maybe. But then there was the *way* they were talking about this girl. It was just so…sinister."

Ailsa swirled her tea ruminatively. "How do you know they were talking about that girl? Or even any girl at all? They could have been discussing whether to put Sam's old granny in a home, for all you know."

"They weren't," Sophie said.

"Stalker."

"Stop!" Sophie cried, throwing another fluffy pillow at her friend. "You didn't hear it. It was creepy."

"Are you sure you aren't just jealous?"

"No!"

"I mean, she is very pretty. But for what it's worth, I don't think she and Sam have hooked up yet. Not even close."

"I really don't think that's what they were talking about."

"They're guys, Sophie. Of course it's what they were talking about."

Sophie didn't say anything. She was certain that Ailsa was wrong, but most of the reasons behind it were things she'd long since decided not to tell her.

"But anyway," Ailsa continued, "I wouldn't assume it means Sam's not just as interested in you."

"Um…yuck."

"Oh, come on, Sophie. You can't expect him to act like you're a sure thing after only one date – at which I was present,

114

I ought to remind you, which means it barely qualifies. He's just keeping his options open."

"Men are revolting."

Ailsa shrugged, dismembering another biscuit. "I'd have said, pragmatic."

"I guess…"

"Besides, there's another possibility you don't seem to have considered."

"What's that?"

"Couldn't they have been talking about you?"

That surprised Sophie into silence for a few moments. But then she shook her head. "I don't think so. I mean, Sam had just been with that girl. And the way she was with Lucas, when we saw them on the beach…it must be her. Do you think we should try to warn her? She might be in danger."

Ailsa laughed. "In danger of Lucas and Sam squabbling over her? That's a dream come true!"

"Ailsa."

"Okay," Ailsa sighed, putting down the packet of biscuits, "since you're clearly not going to forget about this, and I'm going to go out of my mind listening to your endless speculation, I think we should just move straight on to plan C."

"Which is what?"

"Find out the truth. Or at least prove to you that the blonde winkle-picker isn't in grave peril from Sam and Lucas."

"How?" Sophie asked, ignoring the sarcasm.

"The old fashioned way: snooping."

"I didn't know snooping was old fashioned."

"It is when you don't have broadband. Come on."

"What, now?"

Ailsa grinned. "No time like the present."

CHAPTER 11

"Where will we even begin?" Sophie said as they crept down the corridor arm-in-arm by the light of her head torch. Though they'd never actually been forbidden to wander the house, and it was unlikely that anybody would be around to notice, it seemed better not to call attention to themselves. That meant not turning on any lights.

"No worries," Ailsa said. "All we have to do is find the room with the code lock."

"There's a room with a code lock?" Sophie asked incredulously. Somehow she didn't picture Lucas as the code lock type. Rusty keys on an iron ring, perhaps.

Ailsa nodded. "Straight out of James Bond."

"Still, how do you know that's where to look?"

Ailsa shrugged. "I don't. But you asked where we should *begin*, and in my snooping experience a locked door is always an excellent place to begin. Besides, what would you put in a locked room other than dire secrets?"

"I suppose. So, do you know the code?"

"If I knew the code, I'd have poked around in there already."

"Well then how are we going to get in?"

"That's your job," Ailsa said, patting her hand. "You're the clever one."

"Yeah – at things like maths and chemistry. My college didn't exactly run evening courses in cryptography."

"In what?"

Sophie sighed. "Never mind. So, where is this locked room?"

"Now that's the tricky part. I know that it's on the second floor, and you turn right from the stairway, but after that…well, no doubt I'll remember when I see it."

Sophie was beginning to feel that this had been a very bad idea, but Ailsa was pulling her along, clearly thrilled by the adventure. Sophie followed her down the corridor with the oil paintings and into the gallery above the grand stairway. Two more stairways led up to the floor above. She'd never climbed either of them, but given their angle, Sophie assumed that the left-hand one would lead to the Gothic section of the house, the right-hand one to the turreted Victorian extension behind the Georgian New Wing.

"That one, I think," Ailsa said, pointing to the left.

The stairway pitched precipitously upward into perfect darkness, and Sophie held on tightly to Ailsa, who in turn held on to the banister. They emerged into a hallway lined with arched windows, but it was too dark to make out any more detail than that. Sophie turned the beam of the head torch to the opposite wall, which was lined with dark wooden doors, all of them shut.

"No code locks," she said, keeping her voice low. "Now what?"

Ailsa looked around and said doubtfully, "I don't know. I think there was a painting of a dog nearby…"

"Right. A locked door by a dog painting…that should be easy to spot."

"No need for sarcasm!"

Sophie smiled grimly. "Any idea which direction?"

"That way," Ailsa said, pointing away from Lucas's tower. Sophie was grateful for that. If they ran into him now, she knew that she'd never be able to think of an excuse.

"I hope this place isn't haunted," Ailsa said as the headlamp's beam flickered over dark paneling and faded furniture. Sophie thought of the Revenant in her room, and then wished that she hadn't. But there were no pale figures waiting in the shadows, only a kind of T-junction, with a short flight of steps leading downward to the left. To the right, the corridor sloped briefly upward until it hooked around a corner, apparently running into the Victorian section.

"I definitely don't remember steps," Ailsa said, heading to the right.

The corridor beyond was narrow and musty, with closed doors lining both walls, and another hallway branching off it at the far end. Sophie tried to concentrate on the doors rather than the darkness ahead. She stopped to shine the light on each handle in turn, but none of them had a code lock. They wandered like that for what seemed a very long time. Then, turning to ask Ailsa a question, Sophie came face-to-face with a crackling painting of a toy spaniel with a blue bow around its neck.

"That's it!" Ailsa cried, forgetting to be quiet in her excitement and relief. "I told you there was a painting of a dog! Turn the light around."

Sophie turned until the light cast back a dull reflection. She stepped toward it, and found a modern, brushed-steel code lock where the door's original handle must have been. But her excitement didn't last long. The mechanism had a small digital display, currently reading "Locked". She fingered the number keys, choosing a few random combinations that, predictably, had no effect.

"Did Lucas say anything on the night you met him that might give us a clue about the code?" Ailsa asked.

"No, he pretty much stuck to the 'get out of my house' theme." She gazed at the lock, running that night over in her memory, along with the argument they'd had when she caught him in her room. She tried to think of anything involving numbers. There was the date on the tower door, 1452. She typed that in, but the lock stayed locked. What else was there? Had Sam said anything that might help her? She thought back to their first conversation, to the things he'd said about Lucas. And then she thought back a little further, and a chill went down her spine.

There were no letters on the keypad, so she punched in the corresponding numbers – the place each letter fell in the alphabet. E-X-I-L-E. The display flashed up the message "Entry Authorized".

Ailsa clapped her hands and kissed Sophie on the cheek. "See? I knew you'd crack it!"

Sophie smiled, but inside she was cold. She didn't feel as if she'd cracked anything. She had the strong, disturbing sensation that something beyond her had just used her, guiding her as it must have guided her to Niall's house, and guided him to speak the word, in order for her to remember it now. *Stop it*, she told herself, and drawing a deep breath, she followed Ailsa into the room.

It wasn't large, but it was full of things: loaded bookcases, a wall covered entirely with framed pictures, a cluttered desk with a lot of computer equipment…far too much to examine by the paltry light of the head torch. She looked around for windows. There was only one, with heavy velvet drapes hanging open. She pulled them together, shut the door, and then turned on the desk lamp, facing it toward the wall to keep the light low.

"Holy hell!" Ailsa said, turning in a slow circle.

"My sentiments exactly," Sophie said.

"I *never* thought we'd find all this! What is this place, anyway?"

"His study, I suppose," Sophie said, inspecting the desk. But though the papers on the desk were concerned with estate business, she knew that the room was more than just a study. The books, the paintings, the cases full of bizarre objects gave the impression of a collection. A collection that somebody had been working on for a very long time.

She peered into one of the cases, which held a series of ancient-looking knives. On the wall above it, a sword with an intricately-wrought hilt in the shape of a mermaid hung in a scabbard. She was measuring it mentally against the one Lucas had held on the night he chased the Revenant away, when Ailsa said, "Sophie, you'd better come look at this."

There was an uncharacteristic tremor of uncertainty in her voice. It sent a shiver down Sophie's spine, and for a moment she had the overwhelming urge to turn and run from the room before she had to know what had upset Ailsa. *Stop being an idiot,* she told herself, and turned to find Ailsa staring at the wall of pictures. Every inch of available space was covered with them. Every artistic style she could imagine was represented, from fragmentary Egyptian papyrus paintings sealed under glass, to Renaissance oils, to cubist collages. And every single subject was a young woman with dark hair, a pale, heart-shaped face and luminous eyes.

"They're you, Sophie," Ailsa said.

Sophie's heart pounded erratically and she couldn't seem to draw a normal breath. Nevertheless, she stepped closer, making herself look at the pictures critically. There was no denying that the girls in the paintings resembled her. Then again, none of them was a perfect likeness. In one the eyes were blue rather than grey; in another the hair was curly rather than straight.

Whatever they meant, she was certain that none of them were actually pictures of her.

More to the point, if they were originals, they couldn't be. Many of them were unsigned, others credited to artists she'd never heard of, but a few bore famous names. Historical names. A fragile red chalk sketch – one of the closer likenesses – had "Leonardo" scrawled across the bottom corner. An oil painting of a woman in a white Dutch cap leaning out of a window was signed by Rembrandt. Another, an Impressionist group of girls seated in a café, was a Monet.

"So," Ailsa said with a shaky smile, "I guess now we know it wasn't the blonde winkle-picker they were fighting over."

Sophie shook her head. "We don't know anything, except that Lucas has a lot of pictures of girls who look a bit like me." But she didn't even sound convincing to herself.

"A bit!" Ailsa cried. "They're the spit of you, Sophie. Psychopathic nutter is right!"

"I don't think so," Sophie answered slowly.

"Christ, Sophie – in what way is this not completely deranged?"

"It's weird, yeah – but I don't think it's Lucas who's weird. I mean, he can't have made this collection. I've only just met him, and even if he had the inclination – which I doubt, given that I seem to bring out the Mr. Rochester in him – he hasn't had the time, never mind the money, to buy all of these."

"But he's rich," Ailsa said.

"Rich enough to buy a wall full of old masters, in the few weeks since he met me?"

"I suppose it's not very likely…" Ailsa said grudgingly, clearly disappointed.

"But I do think," Sophie continued as Ailsa sat down on the desk chair and began swinging it back and forth, "that this explains his reaction to me the night of the power cut. I mean, imagine he's been looking at these pictures, and then I show up out of nowhere. I'd have freaked out, too."

Ailsa stopped swinging and rolled her eyes. "Sophie, you really are a killjoy."

Sophie smiled ruefully. "So I've been told. If it makes you feel any better, none of that explains why they're here in the first place – which is, frankly, beyond bizarre."

"Do you think there's an answer in here somewhere?"

Sophie shrugged. "We can but look. Bookshelves or desk?"

Ailsa wrinkled her nose. "Books are studying, not snooping." She spun the chair around a final time and then began rummaging in the desk drawers.

Sophie smiled and moved to the bookcases. Like the pictures, the books were an apparently haphazard mixture of new and old: cheap, crease-spined paperbacks shoved in beside tooled leather in no discernible order. One thing was clear very quickly, however: the books were all about religion. She wondered whether Lucas was some kind of religious nut. It would certainly explain a few things.

Despite reading carefully through all of the titles, though, she found nothing related to art, let alone any kind of catalogue of the paintings on the wall. Before long she felt tired and dejected, and more than ready to give up. She'd come here looking to learn the identity of the blonde girl, and possibly find some kind of correspondence between her and Lucas, not to read up on world religion.

And then her eye caught on something that wasn't a book; not a book like the others, anyway. It seemed to be a ream of black paper, shoved into the top corner of the final bookcase. Sophie pulled it out, and found herself holding two home-made photo albums, the pages held together by loops of black string. On the front of the first one was a small white plate that read "1939". She flipped it open.

The first page had a fading black-and-white photograph of Madainneag, held in place by little paper corners. She turned through the book quickly. Many of the pages had only the photo corners, as if the pictures themselves had been taken out or lost. The others weren't especially exciting: just pictures of the estate and village and people carrying shotguns or grinning over deer carcasses. A dark-haired woman showed up in many of the photos. She, too, might have resembled Sophie, but the poor picture quality made it difficult to be certain.

Sophie put the book aside. The second one had no plate on the front, and when she opened it she found not photographs, but newspaper clippings pasted to the black backing paper. There were no dates on them, but by the wording and typeset and the frail yellow paper, Sophie guessed that they were very old. The first clipping was a short article about the disappearance of a London socialite just days before her debut. The girl was described as "saint like", having spent a good deal of time and money ministering to the children in the local poorhouses.

The other clippings were also about missing persons: a milliner's wife from Bath and a schoolmaster from Liverpool. If the epitaphs were to be believed, they had been as exemplary as the debutante. A quick look through the rest of the album revealed that it was full of similar clippings. By the few dates Sophie found, they appeared to be arranged in chronological order, spanning the latter half of the nineteenth century to the beginning of the twenty-first. The last entry was only a year and a half old, which meant that it had been added after Lucas took over Madainneag.

However, it wasn't the one that leapt out at her. Instead, it was one that had been cut from the local Mallaig paper in the late nineteen-seventies. It described the disappearance of a university student named Jenny MacCrae, who had been in the area on a research trip, studying sea birds. She smiled out at Sophie from the fading newsprint: a pretty girl with pale eyes and long, curling hair that might well have been red. The type of hair that's so unusual, it's impossible to forget.

With shaking hands, she peeled the clipping off of the backing paper. The paste was dry and brittle, and it came away easily. She folded it carefully and put it in the pocket of her fleece, and then jumped as Ailsa said, "Found anything interesting?"

At first, she thought that Ailsa had seen her take the clipping, but her look was genuinely curious. "No racy pictures of blonde girls? Perhaps a ransom note or two?"

Feeling guilty, Sophie forced a smile. She hoped she sounded sincere when she said, "No. Just some boring old mug-shots of posh people and dead things. Anyway," she continued, putting the albums back on the shelf, "it's getting late. We should probably go."

"But we haven't even begun looking for anything about the winkle girl. Maybe there are emails," she said, looking hopefully at the computer.

"There's no point trying that, at least not tonight," Sophie said quickly. "It'll be password-protected, and I'm code-cracked out for now." She knew that it was a lame excuse, but the last thing she wanted was for Ailsa to find anything that might relate to the album of missing-persons notices. If her hunch was right, then the less Ailsa knew about it, the better.

But Ailsa looked dubious. "What about your wall of shame?" She gestured to the paintings. "Don't you want to find an explanation for that?"

Sophie shrugged. "Maybe there isn't one. Maybe it's just a freaky coincidence. Obviously Lucas thought so, given how he reacted to me that night."

"That's a point: what *about* Lucas? We've found out absolutely nothing about him."

"To be honest," Sophie sighed, willing her face to stay straight, "I'm not sure I really want to know any more about him anyway. He seems like kind of a nutcase."

Ailsa shook her head. "Seriously? After all that angst, you've lost interest just like that?"

Sophie looked at the wall of pictures. "Obviously, he has baggage. That's the last thing I want to get involved with. He can keep the blonde girl – Sam too."

Ailsa sighed. "Okay – if you say so."

"I say so," Sophie said. *If only I believed it.*

CHAPTER 12

"Jesus, you look as bad as I feel!" Ailsa said when Sophie came into the kitchen the next morning.

"Thanks," Sophie said, pouring hot water over a tea bag.

"Sorry, I didn't mean that like it sounded."

"It's alright. I do look awful. I didn't sleep well."

"Nor me. Midnight snooping is as bad as midnight caffeine, when it comes to sleeping afterward." Sophie smiled, sipping her tea. "Anyway, this might cheer you up." Ailsa pushed an envelope across the table to her.

"What's this?" she asked, picking it up. The cream paper was heavy, good quality, and her name was written on the front in a calligraphy.

"I don't know. It was sitting under the mail slot this morning. Go on – open it!"

With a vague feeling of antipathy, Sophie sat down and ran her finger under the seal. Inside was a card, with writing on the front in the same archaic, beautiful style as the envelope. It read:

"Sam Eblis requests the pleasure of your company at Pier House for dinner tonight. The car will collect you at 7:00."

After the events of the last day, Sophie didn't know what to think. More than that, she didn't entirely like the invitation's tone. Sam seemed to assume not only that she would have done enough research on him since their meeting to know what he meant by "Pier House", and also that her acceptance was a foregone conclusion. There wasn't even an RSVP number. She put the card down, sipped her tea.

Ailsa snatched it up immediately. "Well that's dead posh, isn't it? I bet you never thought you'd end up dating the local gentry when you sent Ruadhri that application."

"No," said Sophie, "but anyway, I'm not."

"You cannot possibly try to tell me that *this* isn't a date." She waved the card in the air.

Sophie shrugged. "I guess it would be, if I were to go."

"If? Sophie, you're hopeless!"

"Why would I go out with him after everything that's happened?"

"Most of what's happened has been about Lucas. The worst Sam's done is talk to another girl."

Sophie chewed on her lip. What Ailsa was saying seemed sensible, and yet... "Doesn't it seem a little odd," she said, "him inviting me to dinner at his place, alone? I mean, I barely even know him."

"That's the point of a date, last I checked," Ailsa said. "To get to know someone, and see if you fancy another one. Anyway, you didn't seem to think it was odd having dinner alone with him here the other night." She raised her eyebrows pointedly.

Sophie shook her head. "That was different. It just sort of… happened."

"Okay. But you also have to remember, there's not much to do around here on a date, other than go to someone's house. He's not very well going to ask you out to the pub where you work, is he?"

"I suppose not…"

"Come on, Sophie," Ailsa said, "live a little!"

"I'll think about it." But even as she said it, she knew she had no intention of going. "You don't know Sam's number, do you?"

"Not off hand. But it'll be in the book. It's by the phone."

The book, when Sophie dug it out of the detritus in the phone table's drawer, turned out to be two sheets of typewritten A4, stapled down the middle. She located Sam's phone number and dialed it, but it rang out. Apparently he didn't have voice mail, and if he had a mobile that worked in the area, the number wasn't listed in the book. She sat for a few moments staring at the silent phone, wondering what to do. She didn't want to offend him by not showing up, but then again, he hadn't given her much choice. Maybe, she thought, she'd be able to track down a mobile number in the pub.

Sophie went back to her room and dressed for work. When she heard Ailsa coming out of her room, she grabbed her things to follow. She had no intention of walking the road alone. The

Revenants had never showed themselves in daylight, but then none had ever touched her or brandished a weapon before, either. Pushing the thought of the Revenant warrior's fleshless hands out of her head, she caught up with Ailsa.

"What is Pier House, anyway?" she asked.

"Didn't take you long to come around!"

"It's just a question," Sophie said defensively.

"It's Sam's house," Ailsa relented. "It's just above the pier on the other estate – hence the name."

"He said he lived in the old gatehouse."

"Is that what he called it?" Ailsa laughed.

"Yes. Why?"

"You'll see."

"Ailsa."

"I'll put it this way: if Sam's house is a gatehouse, then this place is an attractive detached villa." She hooked a thumb at Madainneag.

Great, Sophie thought, and then wondered why she cared whether or not Sam undersold his house to her, when she wasn't even planning on going there.

The wind had died down sometime during the night, but there was still a fine, steady drizzle that seemed to hang in the air without quite falling. Sophie couldn't help glancing at the tower as they passed it, but all of the windows were dark. She didn't know what she'd expected to see, but she sighed nevertheless as she turned away.

There was a good turnover in the restaurant right up through lunchtime, when a new ferry full of tourists arrived. By mid-afternoon, though, there was no one left but the usual suspects at the bar. Sophie had just begun washing dishes in the back when she heard the door open, and Ailsa greeting someone. When she heard him reply, her stomach tightened, though whether it was in anxiety or anticipation was difficult to determine.

"Sam's here to see you," Ailsa said with a smirk, coming into the kitchen.

"Okay," Sophie said, and turned toward the door.

"Wait!" Ailsa called. When Sophie turned back, Ailsa fluffed her hair and wiped a mascara smudge from under her eye with a damp dishtowel. "Alright, now you're good."

Sophie rolled her eyes, and pushed through the swinging door into the bar. Sam was leaning on the counter, talking with the bar-props. When he saw her, he said, "Good to catch up with you, gentlemen," and moved off toward the fireplace, beckoning to her to follow. Douglas and Iain nodded to him as he walked away, but Michael only gave him an inscrutable look over the top of his whisky glass.

"So," Sam said, before Sophie could get a word in, "You got the invitation?"

"Yes," she answered, "but Sam – "

"Seven's alright, isn't it?" he cut in. "I thought that would give you time to get ready, since your shift ends at six."

Wondering how he knew that, Sophie said, "Listen, Sam, that's why I'm glad you came. I'm afraid I won't be able to make it tonight."

He didn't seem angry, or upset. In fact, his confident half-smile never changed. "Surely you can't have had a better offer?"

"Of course not," Sophie said, "it's just that I'm tired...I couldn't sleep last night and – " She stopped, wondering why she was trying to justify herself when "no" should have been enough. "Actually," she began again, "I'm not so sure that it's a good idea for us to get together."

"It's only dinner, Sophie," he said, his voice warm and persuasive.

"It's a date," she replied, trying to sound firm, "and I don't really want to get involved with anyone up here, as I won't be staying long."

Except that she was suddenly uncertain whether she really meant that. Her head felt fuzzy and strange as it had on the night she'd met Lucas, making it difficult to hold onto a train of thought. She wondered if she was coming down with something, or whether it was possible to develop vertigo at age seventeen.

"Is that all?" he asked. "Because you don't have to think of it that way." His smile held no trace of the arrogance now. If anything, it was vaguely pleading. She wondered whether she was being too hard on him. "I had a lovely time with you and Ailsa the other night, but I'd really like to get to know you better. I thought we could do that now."

Mustering her courage and her remaining composure,

Sophie said, "Sam – I saw you talking to that girl in here last night. The pretty blonde one."

To her surprise, he laughed. "Mairi? I've known her for ages – as a friend. She picks winkles sometimes on the beach in front of my house."

"So you aren't...you know...seeing her?"

Still smiling, he shook his head. His eyes were wide and earnest. "Mairi's a lovely girl, but she's not the one I'm interested in seeing."

Sophie couldn't take her eyes off of his face; it was almost luminous. "That's sweet, really," she said, "and maybe sometime..." She trailed off again, this time because she had no idea what she had meant to say when she began the sentence. The words were simply gone, as if his brilliant smile had burned them away. "I mean, I'd really love to come, but..." she began again, and got no further.

He waited a moment for her to say something else, and when she didn't, he said, "If that's all cleared up, then I'll come for you at seven?"

"I...I suppose it would be alright..."

"Good," said Sam, with a nod.

Sophie nodded back, wondering what had just happened.

CHAPTER 13

Sophie had been in Ardnasheen long enough that when someone said "car" she understood "Land Rover." And that didn't mean one of the new, silver, plush-seated Land Rovers that gridlocked the streets of London's better neighbourhoods, but the green kind with shot suspension and rusting bumpers. That was what everyone drove in Ardnasheen, if they drove at all. So when she saw the little black car pull up under the carriageway, she didn't process that it was Sam's until he stepped out. He was wearing a black shirt and jacket, dark jeans, and black boots. He could have stepped straight out of a glossy magazine advert. In fact, standing by that car, he could easily have passed for a film star.

"Nice car," she said, trying not to stare at him.

He laughed. "Lovely to see you, too."

"Sorry," Sophie said.

"Don't be. It *is* a nice car. It's an – "

"Austin-Healey Sprite, Mark IV," she finished for him.

Sam raised his eyebrows. "Year?"

Sophie studied it for another moment. "Nineteen seventy?"

"I'm impressed. But actually, it's a seventy-one – one of the last few made before BL dropped Healey. Now tell me how you knew that," he said, opening the passenger door for her.

Sophie swept up her blue skirt – the only one she'd brought with her – and folded herself into the low seat. "My dad has one."

"Ah. So you aren't really a closet classic-car nut." He got in, turned on the ignition and the engine rumbled to life. It made Sophie smile with nostalgia.

"I suppose I am by association," she said. "He's been collecting them as long as I can remember, and I've been helping him fix them almost as long. As soon as he's got one up and running, he sells it on and buys another wreck. I've got to know a fair bit about them over the years."

Sam smiled, turned the car in a smooth arc and started back toward the village. "He sounds like my kind of man."

"Yeah, he's great."

"But?"

"I didn't say but."

"You thought it."

Sophie smiled ruefully. "Okay…but, the cars are one of the things he and Mum fought over the worst. She said he spent more time with them than he did with her."

"If she looks anything like you, then that is a true travesty."

"Actually, she's tall and blonde. But let's not talk about my parents. It's too depressing."

"Alright. Why don't we talk about what you're looking for in the woods?"

Sophie opened her mouth to deny it, but then she realized that it was true. They were passing the spot where the Revenant had approached her and Sam had come to her rescue, and her eyes had traveled involuntarily into the trees, searching for a pale form among the shadows.

"Force of habit."

"Have you seen it again? Whatever it was that frightened you that night?"

"No," she answered, glad that she didn't have to lie. After all, the warrior wasn't the same Revenant she'd seen the first time, and she didn't want to tell Sam about it. Or about Lucas driving it away.

Sam gave her a half-smile and an incisive look, but he didn't push the topic. He shifted down a gear as they approached the village. The rain had stopped, the clouds broken up enough to reveal a moody, mauve-and-orange sunset. A lot of the pub's customers had moved outside to watch it, and as Sam slowed down to maneuver among them, Sophie saw Ailsa carrying a tower of empty pint glasses inside. She winked at Sophie as they passed.

"So, you and Ailsa have hit it off."

"She's a laugh," Sophie said.

"And it's a good thing," he said as they left the village

behind and drove west along the bay, "since your other flatmate's anything but."

Sophie looked at him, but he was looking intently at the road. "You mean Lucas?"

He glanced at her, and she was certain she saw annoyance cloud his face for a moment before he hid it. It made her wary of saying too much about her exchanges with Lucas, so when he said, "You're on first-name terms with Lord Belial?" Sophie shrugged, hoping it looked nonchalant.

"I've got to know him a bit," she said.

"You mean he was actually civil to you?"

She looked straight ahead, afraid of what he might see in her face if she looked at him. "Why wouldn't he be?" Sam shrugged, his smile gone. Momentarily boldened by this, Sophie said, "What is it with you and him? I mean, is the animosity all about having to share a piece of land?"

"Not exactly," Sam answered slowly, "although I can see why you'd ask. Our argument goes back much further than that."

"What, like, to nursery?"

Sam laughed. "You don't let a bloke away with anything, do you?"

"Why should I?"

"Alright," he sighed. "Lucas and I...we went to school together, and believe it or not, we started out friends. Then we had a disagreement."

"Over a girl?"

"Over several." Sophie turned sharply to look at him, and

he laughed again. "It wasn't what you're thinking. Some friends and I had a plan to sneak out and meet up at a pub with some girls from the town. Oh honestly, don't look like that – everyone gets to be young and stupid once!" Sophie didn't comment. "Anyhow, Lucas was invited, but he thought it was a bad idea."

"I have to say, I'd have agreed with him."

Sam shrugged. "Fair enough. But I doubt you'd have narked on us."

"Is that what he did?"

Sam nodded. "Got us expelled. That was the beginning of our philosophical differences."

"Please tell me you don't consider yourself a philosopher."

"Oh aye," he smiled, "an agnostic too, not to mention a cynic. And just for the record, I believe in a fixed state of earthly chaos and an ungoverned universe. But at least I've never been a pessimist." It was clearly a dig at Lucas, and once again, Sophie chose not to respond, wondering simultaneously why she wanted to protect him.

The road pitched gradually upward through dense woods and then, at the top, the view opened up again. Sam paused for a moment; purposely, Sophie had no doubt. Still, it was undeniably a beautiful scene. The downward slope of the hill was unforested, sweeping down toward a small bay that glowed in the last of the light between two headlands, which curved around the silvery water like protective arms. On the higher headland, the one to the left, Sophie saw the jagged outline of what must once have been a castle, and was now no more than a ruin.

Below that, a long wooden pier stretched out into the water with a sailboat tied up at the end. She looked for the house, and found it tucked into a hollow just above the pier. She could see now what Ailsa had meant: it was a perfect miniature castle, complete with a conical turret. She relented a little in her judgment of Sam: anyone who lived in a house that whimsical couldn't take himself too seriously.

When they reached the house, though, and Sophie saw the candles burning in glass lanterns leading up the steps, she had another pang of uncertainty.

"Something wrong?" Sam asked, opening her door and offering his hand. There was really no choice but to take it. It was warm and solid, and it made her feel foolish for her hesitation. What, after all, did she expect? He'd asked her on a date, she'd accepted. Candles were fair game.

"I'm fine," she said.

"Cold?" he asked.

"A bit." She pulled her coat closer around her.

"Come inside. The fire's on."

She followed him up the steps and into a tiny porch, where he hung up her coat and his own jacket. Beyond that was a sitting room decorated in dark reds and blues, with a row of windows overlooking the water. Sam stirred up the fire smoldering in the grate, and then added a few bricks of peat.

"What would you like to drink?" he asked.

Sophie turned from the window. "A glass of water, please."

He laughed. "Water? Your parents are in London, Sophie. Red or white – or something stronger?"

"Well when you put it that way – water with ice."

He shook his head, but he didn't argue further. He went through a door into what she thought must be a kitchen and reappeared a few minutes later with the ice water in one hand and a glass of red wine in the other.

"If you change your mind, just say the word," he said, handing her the water glass and gesturing for her to take a chair.

She sat down, took a sip of water and then said, "Ailsa told me you were at university when you inherited this place." He nodded, and took a seat across from her. "So you really packed in Cambridge to come cut trees in the middle of nowhere?"

Sam sipped his wine, looking into the fire, which was actually showing some signs of life. Sophie made a mental note to ask him what trick he'd used to get the peat to burn so well. "I was never entirely convinced by university," he said.

"Convinced?"

He nodded. "It's all well and good if you're an academic – I mean, the type of person who really wants to know about the kinds of things you read in books."

"And you aren't?"

He set his glass down and looked at her. He had that gift, she thought, of looking at a person as if they were the only thing of any interest for miles around. "I am, to an extent. But only to an extent. Too many books, and I get restless."

"What were you studying?"

The self-deprecating half-smile reappeared. "Theology."

Sophie nearly choked on a mouthful of water. "You're joking."

"What would be the point of that? But if you don't believe me, come and look."

"At what?"

"My library."

Curiosity got the better of her. She stood up, and Sam took her hand. This time, when his fingers closed around hers, there was a charged warmth in the contact. She looked up at him in surprise. Sam looked back, holding her eyes for a moment longer than was necessary before he turned and led her toward the only other door in the room. He opened it and flicked a light-switch on the other side, illuminating a stairwell with a flight of steps leading upward. The walls were lined floor to ceiling with bookshelves, every inch of them crammed full of books.

"Wow," Sophie said softly, disengaging her hand in order to walk along a shelf of leather-bound volumes. They looked very old. She pulled one out at random and opened it. It was in Latin. "Don't tell me you've read them all," she said, putting it back again.

He shrugged. "Some of them I only skimmed – but mostly I've read them, yes."

Sophie couldn't contain an incredulous laugh. "So what – you meant to be a bishop and then thought better of it?"

"I was never planning to go into the church," he said,

stepping closer to her, though his eyes were on the books. "To tell you the truth, I don't much like organized religion."

"The why study it?"

"Because it fascinates me, the way it dominates human life. People found cultures and countries on it; they go to war for its sake. It's been the inspiration for the most beautiful artworks, and the worst atrocities. Even when people claim not to believe in it, it forms the very basis of their ideas of right and wrong."

He'd moved still closer as he spoke; there were only inches between them now. Sophie hadn't realized how tall he was until he stood over her, and she had to tip her head back to face him. She wasn't comfortable with that, or his nearness, but at the same time it made her feel wide awake and alive, her skin tingling where his soft breath fell. *Be careful,* she told herself.

To him, she said, "You say that as if you're above all of it."

"You have no idea," he said, his voice low and full of some emotion she couldn't decipher. Sophie tried to focus on him, but her head swam, and her breath came in shallow gasps. Although she'd drunk nothing but a few sips of water, she felt distinctly tipsy. Shutting her eyes, she tried to regain control of herself.

"Sam," she said.

"Just go with it," he answered, his lips brushing hers. She was torn, half of her longing for him to kiss her, the other half screaming that something was wrong. His body pressed against hers, pinning her to the bookcase. *Oh God*, she thought, *what am I doing?* His lips met hers again, a proper kiss this time. She tried to push him away, but she felt strangely weak and ineffective, like a netted butterfly. His image swam before her eyes, so she shut them.

A moment later, a loud buzzing broke the silence. Sophie's eyes snapped open. She saw Sam's arms on either side of her, caging her in. The cuffs of his shirt had fallen back, revealing a silver band circling each wrist, engraved with symbols, perhaps the letters of a language she didn't recognize. She had seen bands like those before. The chill that went through her now had nothing vague about it. The buzzer sounded again: the doorbell, she realized.

"Ignore it," Sam said, his voice a low growl.

"No," she said, ducking out from under his arms. "You'd better get it."

Sam turned without a word and went back through the sitting room, but not before she saw the bitter fury on his face. It was too extreme a reaction for an interrupted kiss, and with that realization, Sophie began to shake. There were spangles at the edges of her vision, like the ones that preceded her occasional migraines. Despite having no clear idea of why, she was nevertheless certain that she needed to get away from that place – from him. She wondered whether he would believe her if she said she was ill. She wondered how she would get home, if he didn't drive her. And so she was overjoyed when Sam opened the door and she saw Michael on the step, dressed in a dusty overcoat covered in tarnished war medals, and holding a book.

"Oh dear," the old man said. "I do hope I'm not interrupting anything."

"As a matter of fact – " Sam began coldly.

"Not at all," Sophie cut in, taking her coat from the hook. "Perhaps I could catch a lift back to the village?"

"What?" cried Sam. "You've just got here!"

"I'm sorry," Sophie said, not feeling remotely sorry, "but I've a migraine coming on. I'd be terrible company if I stayed. So," she turned back to Michael, "if it's no trouble…" *Please,* she prayed, *say yes.*

Michael gave her his vague, sweet smile. "Of course, my dear. I only came to return this book. I borrowed it ages ago, you see, and I forgot all about it until tonight, when I decided to clean out the stair cupboard. You wouldn't believe the things I unearthed – like my old army coat," he gestured to his clothing. "Then there was a chafing dish that must go back to my grandmother, and a basket full of – "

"Fine," Sam interrupted, taking the book. Sophie caught a glimpse of the worn leather cover: it was *Paradise Lost.* For some reason, that made her shudder again.

"Oh dear, you're chilly," Michael said, removing his coat and holding it toward Sophie. "Take this – I'll start the car." He moved down the steps and walked toward a blocky shape behind Sam's sports car. All of the candles on the steps had blown out.

With shaking hands, Sophie pulled the coat around her. It let out a waft of the incense smell she'd noticed around Michael before, and suddenly she felt better; stronger. Her vision cleared and her hands steadied.

"Sophie," Sam said, "I'm sorry if I moved too fast for you,

146

but really, you don't have to go. I promise to be on my best behaviour if you stay."

Sophie looked at him, trying to read him. His eyes were ingenuous, his smile warm, but she couldn't forget how easily he'd taken her in. Though she couldn't deny that she was attracted to him, and was still uncertain whether she liked him, she knew that she didn't trust him. More to the point, she didn't trust herself around him.

"At least let me drive you," Sam pleaded. "Michael'll be loaded this time of night."

Just then, the lights on Michael's car came on and the engine growled to life. Sophie glanced toward it, expecting a particularly dilapidated version of the ubiquitous Land Rover, and then looked again in surprise. Hulking behind Sam's sports car was a shiny yellow Hummer. Though it wasn't really her father's niche, and therefore not her own, Sophie would have bet that it was the latest model. Michael rolled down the tinted window and waved to her.

"Even if he is," she said to Sam, "not much is going to happen to me in that thing." Sam opened his mouth to argue further, but Sophie was already at the bottom of the steps. "Good night, Sam," she said, and she didn't look back.

*

"Are you alright?" Michael asked as he turned the truck and started up the winding track. Truthfully, Sophie had been more than a little worried about Michael's ability to drive after a full day in the pub, but to her surprise he guided the ungainly vehicle with perfect precision. For the first time all day, she began to relax.

"I am now," she said.

Michael glanced at her, but the dashboard lights weren't strong enough for her to read his expression. "Your date didn't go as planned?"

Sophie smiled wryly. "Beginning with the fact that it wasn't supposed to *be* a date."

Michael considered this. "Forgive me if I'm hopelessly behind the times," he said, "but when a girl and a boy meet alone for dinner, what is it, if not a date?"

"Okay, you're right," she said ruefully. "And the thing is, I knew that. In fact I fully intended not to go – or at least not to go *there*. But somehow, he talked me into it…" She shook her head, which felt clear for the first time all day.

"Don't be too hard on yourself," Michael said, shifting up a gear as they reached the end of the switchback and the road straightened. "Sam Eblis is nothing if not charismatic. He's also very determined, when he sees something he wants."

There was a bitterness to Michael's words that gave Sophie the same feeling as the last time they talked – that those words worked on more than one level. "But why me?"

He glanced at her. "I'd have thought that would be obvious. You're a lovely specimen of a female human."

"Um…thank you? Only what I meant was, why push so

hard? I've only just got here. He could take a bit of time to get to know me, before rushing me into a romantic evening."

Michael was silent for a long time. "No doubt he has his reasons," he said at last, and this time Sophie was certain that he was keeping something back.

"Well," she said, "hopefully he'll get the message after this."

"I wouldn't assume anything," Michael said, in a tone so ominous that Sophie looked at him sharply. Then he smiled. "I only mean that you shouldn't underestimate your own charms, Sophie." She looked out the window, troubled. "Here," Michael said, "have a biscuit."

Sophie opened the tin that Michael handed to her. It was full of shortbread stars, irregular enough that they had to be homemade. She took one and bit into it, then quickly finished it. Although it hadn't been offered, she took another before putting the lid back on. She couldn't help it: there was something compulsive about the biscuits that went beyond expert baking. The taste reminded her of early childhood days in the kitchen with her mother, a feeling of perfect safety and warmth. For a few moments, as she chewed, she felt it again.

"These are amazing!" she said when the biscuit was gone.

"I'm glad that you approve. Take the tin home with you."

"Oh no, I couldn't – "

"Of course you could," he said. "I can always make more."

"Well then, thank you," Sophie said, setting the tin on her lap. She looked out for a moment at the trees flashing past in the Hummer's bright headlights. "So why the tank?" she asked. "Surely the winters don't get *that* bad up here."

"You'd be surprised," Michael said. "Besides, I live in a cottage away out in the hills." He gestured vaguely to the left, though Sophie could see nothing but densely-packed trees. "You never know what you'll run into on the way home."

"Right," Sophie said, thinking of the Revenants. She wished she had a Hummer to take her to and from work. She wished she had anything more substantial than her own two feet.

They sat in easy silence as they drove through the village, past the bright lights of the pub, and then along the road to Madainneag, which, thankfully, was empty of Revenants. As Michael pulled up under the carriageway, he said, "Are you certain you're alright? Would you like me to come inside with you?"

She smiled. "No – I'm fine now. Ailsa will be home soon, and this way I'll have the bathroom to myself."

"Very well," Michael said as Sophie opened the door. "But be careful, Sophie. And if you are in need of help, don't hesitate to ask. Here – this is my phone number." He handed Sophie a card printed with the name "Michael Halyrude" and a landline phone number. She smiled as she put it in her pocket, wondering if all of the drunks in Ardnasheen had their own business cards.

"Thank you for the lift," she said. "And the biscuits."

"You are most welcome. Safe home, Sophie."

Sophie watched as he turned the car and drove off. Then she

shut the door, and for the first time since she'd moved in, she locked it.

Chapter 14

Sophie slept for only an hour or two that night, and it was a fitful sleep, plagued by anxious dreams she couldn't remember when the alarm went off. It was all she could do to drag herself out of bed. She stumbled to the bathroom and splashed her face with cold water, hoping that it would make her feel better. But when she looked in the mirror she still looked tired and colorless, unless she counted the blue circles beneath her eyes. Sighing, she went hunting for her concealer.

She found it in the top drawer of her desk, though she didn't remember leaving it there, weighing down a folded bit of old newspaper. Her spirits sank even further. She'd almost managed to put the clipping she'd found in Lucas's study out of her mind, but now the reality of it flooded back in, with all of its sinister implications.

Sophie took out the clipping and smoothed it on the desk, scrutinizing it in the stark morning light. A part of her hoped she'd been mistaken the other night, that the bad light had made her see what wasn't there. Instead, the likeness was clearer now than it had been then. There was no avoiding the truth she'd known all along: if the Revenant that had approached her that night on the road had ever been human, then it had been the missing student, Jenny MacCrae.

Sophie looked around for a safe place to stash the clipping, but nowhere felt secure enough. In the end she slipped it into the pocket of her jeans. Then she went to wait for Ailsa.

*

All morning at the pub Sophie had to concentrate to keep herself from dozing, and Ruadhri told her off three times for mixing up orders. She had the afternoon off, and she longed for the moment when she could go home and collapse into bed. But when it finally came, she found that she was too wound up to sleep. Every time she closed her eyes the picture of the missing girl was there, waiting.

She got up again, tuned her harp, and began running through scales and arpeggios in every key: an exercise that usually calmed her down. But she kept losing her place, her fingers stumbling and tangling on what usually came easily. She couldn't focus when her mind was a storm of unanswered questions.

Beginning with, what did Lucas know about the Revenants? Aside from the momentous fact that he could see them, and apparently command them, there was the subtler problem of the book of clippings. Because some of them had clearly been added after Lucas inherited Madainneag. That meant he must have been responsible for putting them there. It also meant he'd seen the others. More to the point, he must know how the Revenants and the clippings were connected. The answer was obvious even without the proof of Jenny MacCrae: those missing people had all become Revenants.

What did it mean that he could see them, too? Did it somehow explain his violent reaction to her? More puzzling – she tottered on the word "sinister" – if she was right, and Sam could also see them, then why had he denied it? How could he have listened to her confession, understood what her haunting had cost her, and still allow her to think that it was all in her own mind?

Sophie tried to imagine herself confronting Lucas or Sam, asking them point-blank what it was all about, but she knew that she couldn't do it. Part of her was afraid that they'd deny all knowledge of Revenants. The other part feared that they wouldn't. Absurd as it was, she didn't know whether she was ready to hear the explanation.

Sophie set the harp aside and walked to the window. The sky was grey, but it wasn't raining. If she couldn't lose herself in sleep or music, maybe hard exercise would help. She hadn't yet attempted to climb any of the mountains in Ardnasheen, but now seemed as good a time as any.

She got dressed, putting on her walking boots and fleece-lined rain jacket. She'd decided on the mountain directly behind the village, simply because it was the closest. She had no idea whether or not there was a designated path, so she plunged straight into the woods behind the house and started walking upward. Before long she was breathing hard and her calves were aching, but it was having the desired effect: the worries she'd begun with felt less immediate, less threatening.

The forest was damp, but not quite to the point of dripping down her neck, for which she was thankful. There was even something soothing about its silence and somber colours, the dull green and grey-brown of the pine trees broken only occasionally by the burnt-orange of drying bracken, or the falling yellow leaves of a beech or oak. She knew that it was prime Revenant territory, but somehow this didn't worry her. Maybe, she thought, because she had more disturbing things to worry about now.

She ran over the facts in her head, beginning with what she knew for certain. First, Lucas had seemed to know her the very first moment that they met, when he'd called her by the given name nobody used. Also, he seemed determined to get rid of her, for no apparent reason. Yet he'd come to her rescue with the warrior Revenant. He had a locked room with a wall full of pictures of women who looked like her. He had a long-standing feud with Sam, although they wore weird, matching bracelets. And finally – though she hesitated to include this, because she couldn't quite decide whether it was only a product of her own imagination – Suri from her dreams seemed to be pushing her toward the conclusion that once, she and Lucas had been lovers.

He's up to something, she told herself, though a deeper part of her couldn't quite believe it. Lucas didn't act like someone who had a grand plan. That was more Sam's style. And yet, he had a room full of evidence to the contrary. It seemed to her now that everything she'd ever thought she'd known about herself was up for revision.

At last the woods thinned, and the steep yellow grass slope of the mountain rose above her. She'd been climbing for a good hour, but it seemed to her that the black rocky peak was farther away than it had been when she started. She looked up at it dejectedly, as white veils of cloud whipped around it in the wind. She looked down at the village, which seemed as precarious from this vantage point as it had from the pitching deck of the ferry – like a frail strand of beads strung along the margin between the impervious mountain and implacable sea.

She began to walk again, following a sheep path that curved gently upward along the mountain's face. The wind seemed to grow stronger with every step, and she began to wonder whether it was a good idea to continue. She felt tiny, exposed, as if a strong gust of wind could pick her up and send her plummeting into the cruel green waters of the bay below. So when she spotted an outcropping of rock a little way down the slope she headed for it, hoping to shelter from the wind while she decided what to do.

It seemed to take her forever to reach it, and all the while the clouds above her darkened. *Great,* she thought, *now I'll get soaked, too.* When at least she rounded the stand of rock, though, she forgot her grim thoughts. The ground gave way beyond it, funneling into a little hollow with a dark blue pond at its center.

The wind didn't reach into the depression, and the water was smooth as a mirror. Nothing but grass grew around it, although there was the odd outcropping of black rock.

There was a peculiar beauty in its austerity that drew Sophie downward for a closer look. She was half way to the water when the ground gave way beneath one of her feet. She lost her balance and went sprawling, bashing her knee against a rock in the process. Pain exploded through her leg and it was several moments before she'd recovered herself enough to assess the damage.

The knee of her jeans was ripped, and blood was seeping through the dark fabric. Gingerly, she rolled up the trouser leg and looked at her knee. There was a deep gash, and the unbroken skin around the sides was already turning purple. *Terrific*, she thought, and slowly pushed herself to her feet. Pain stabbed through her as she tried to put weight on her leg.

She sat back down again, and pulled her mobile out of her pocket. She hadn't used it since she'd come to Ardnasheen, but she still carried it out of habit. She remembered Ailsa telling her that it was possible to get reception on the mountain; hopefully, she turned it on. The screen lit up, and then the words she'd dreaded appeared: "No Service."

She choked on a sob, wondering how she was ever going to get home, cursing herself for not telling anybody where she was going. Surely, she thought, they'd come looking when they realized she was missing? Her jacket was bright blue, it would stand out on the drab hillside…except that she doubted anybody would see her in this hollow. She hadn't even seen the hollow herself until she stood on its rim.

Taking a shuddering breath, Sophie rolled her trouser leg down again and stood up. She limped down to the water, thinking that maybe, if she soaked her knee for a little while, the pain would lessen enough for her to make it home. She was just lowering herself down when she saw movement out of the corner of her eye.

Standing on the far side of the pond was a pony – one of the grey ponies from the paddock near the house, she thought. It had to be: they were the only horses she'd seen in the area. Its chin and the tips of its long mane dripped water, as if it had just been drinking. It acknowledged her with a little, low whinny.

Sophie had been pony-mad as a child, and although she hadn't ridden in several years, she was sure that she remembered enough to guide the pony home, if it was willing. It was a mad idea, she knew – the pony might not even be broken to ride. But she could try. It was preferable to spending a night on the mountain, waiting for someone to come and rescue her.

The pony watched her with curious dark eyes as she hobbled around the pond toward it. As she approached, she noticed that it was muddy to the knees, with pond weed tangled in its wet mane and tail. She wondered what it was doing so far from the paddock. Perhaps it had escaped, then spooked and run and lost its way. She might even be doing the owner a favour by bringing it back.

She approached carefully, letting it sniff her hand for a few moments before she reached up and stroked its neck. It didn't seem remotely frightened; in fact, it took a step toward her. Carefully, she put her arms across its back and leaned her weight on it. It looked around at her, but it didn't try to move away. Clearly it was used to carrying weight. *Here we go*, she thought, and stepping onto a stone, she grabbed a handful of mane and shimmied her way onto the horse's back.

Just as she sat up, she heard something – a cry from above. She looked up. To her astonishment, Lucas was standing at the top of the rise, screaming her name. She had a moment to wonder why, and then the pony uttered a piercing scream of its own, utterly unlike any sound she'd ever heard a horse make. Sophie froze, her heart slamming against her chest as the pony reared up on its hind legs, screaming again, and then plunged into the water.

"Stop!" Sophie shrieked, trying to throw herself free as the pony plunged toward the dark center of the pond. But she couldn't. She was stuck fast to its back, unable to move her legs at all. It turned around to look at her, its eyes no longer gentle and curious but coldly intelligent, with a reddish tinge. It leered at her, pulling lips back from long, sharp, carnivorous teeth. A sob of fear escaped her throat, even as she thought, *This cannot be happening.*

"Sophie!"

She turned. Lucas was standing knee-deep in the water, a climbing rope slung over his shoulder, his eyes wide and face pinched. When the creature saw him it screamed again, gnashing its teeth.

"Lucas!" she sobbed. "I can't get off – "

"I know! Catch!" He took the rope off of his shoulder and hurled it at her. She thought that it wouldn't reach her, but his aim was perfect. It fell straight across the horse's neck.

The horse snorted, reached for it with its teeth. "Wrap the chain around it!" Lucas called. "Quickly!"

Chain? Sophie thought, reaching automatically for the rope. As she brought it up out of the water, she found that it was tied to a length of heavy iron chain. She passed it around the horse's neck as it bucked and thrashed, glad now that it couldn't unseat her. It went wild as she closed the circle of iron with the hook at its end, and at last, she felt herself sliding free.

The icy water closed over her head. She couldn't feel the pond's bottom, and the horse's thrashing disoriented her. She pulled off her jacket and dragged herself to the surface for a breath, and then sank again as something caught her foot, dragging her down. She twisted around, saw the pony's teeth sunk into her ankle, its face fixed in a kind of leer.

Hungry. The cold, deep voice washed through her mind. *Come to me.*

She fought harder and broke the surface for a moment, catching a fractured glimpse of Lucas's horrified face. He stood up to his thighs in the water, a dark-coloured sword in his hand. When he saw her he plunged toward her, caught her under the arms as the monster tried to drag her deeper. She saw the dark blade come down on the pony's white neck, heard it scream as black blood began to flow, and it let her go.

Lucas dragged her to the shore, and said, "Get away from the water," as he turned back to face the monster, now thrashing toward him. Sophie tried to stand, forgetting her injured knee and ankle in her terror. Her legs gave way beneath her. She crawled up the slope of the hollow until she was fully on dry land, and then she turned back to the fight, gasping and shaking.

The monster no longer looked anything like the pony she'd climbed onto. It reared up, twice as tall as Lucas, black blood making a lacework on its white neck. Its long teeth were bared, its eyes burned red as Lucas thrust upward with the sword. The creature twisted away at the last minute, then lunged for Lucas as it came down onto all four feet. The chain had slipped from its neck, but Lucas was swinging it, and as the monster reared again, he flicked it outward, so that it wrapped around its churning legs.

The horse lost its balance and fell backward, crashing into the water. Before it could disentangle its legs or right itself, Lucas drove the dark sword into its chest, right up to the hilt. The thing screamed again as black blood poured over Lucas's arms. He wrenched the sword free and the blood poured more thickly still. The monster fell back into the water, twitching. It seemed to shrink then, growing smaller and less solid, until at last it disappeared, leaving no trace but a dark, viscous film on the water's surface.

For a moment, Lucas looked down at the place where it had been. Then he wiped the blade of the sword on the cleaner of his sleeves, and sheathed it in the scabbard slung across his back. Sophie tried to stand as he splashed back toward her. When he reached her, he scooped her up as if she weighed no more than a bird, and took her to a sheltered spot at the base of the rise. He took off his coat – a heavy grey woolen one that looked vaguely military – and wrapped it around her, then handed her a flask.

Sophie took it with hands that shook so hard she could barely hold it. She needed both of them to bring it to her lips, and she spilled more of the whisky than she swallowed, but it jolted a bit of sense back into her. She took one more sip and then handed it back.

"So," she said, trying to keep her voice even, "are you planning to tell me what just happened? Or are you just going to yell at me again?"

Lucas looked at her for a moment, and then out across the water, with a sigh that seemed to deflate him. He sat down beside her. "I suppose I deserve that."

"I'm not looking for retribution," she said. "I just want someone to tell me what the hell is going on around here."

He looked at her, his eyes sad and defeated. "And I think you need to know," he said. "Let's get you home, and warm. And then…" He paused, studying her, as if he expected her to argue. When she said nothing, he concluded, "…then, if I can, I'll answer your questions."

CHAPTER 15

For a long time, they walked in silence. Sophie had flat-out refused to let Lucas carry her, though that was more or less what ended up happening anyway: with one of her arms slung over his shoulders, and one of his under her arms, he took most of her weight. The necessity of watching their feet made conversation difficult. But once they were in the woods and the incline wasn't as steep, Sophie turned to Lucas.

"Well?" she said.

Reluctantly, he met her eyes. "You want to know about the horse."

"Yes. But mostly I want to know who you think I am?"

"I know who you are. You're Sophie Creedon, Ruadhri's new waitress."

"But that's not what you thought when you first saw me."

"I…mistook you for someone else."

"Clearly. Who is she, some sociopathic ex-girlfriend?"

"Something like that," he said, with a wry smile. "But it

doesn't excuse how I've treated you. I can only apologize…I can't imagine what you must have thought, and I don't know what *I* was thinking. I mean, I knew that there was a new girl living in the house. I should have guessed who you were. It's just that you look so much like her…" He trailed off, scrutinizing her, as if he still wasn't entirely convinced.

"So what convinced you I'm *not* her?"

"Your room," he admitted, and he had the good grace to look sheepish. "Or more to the point, you catching me in your room. It was a bit of a slap in the face. It made me realize how mad I was acting. I mean, of course you weren't her. You couldn't be. Anyway, I hope…well, could we begin again?"

Sophie gave him a wry smile. "Seeing as you just saved my life, I suppose it would be churlish of me to say no."

"Very well, then." He held out his hand, half-covered in a black fingerless glove. "Lucas Belial."

"Sophie Creedon," she said, accepting it. As his fingers closed around hers, a jolt went through her, turning into a shivery warmth that spread through her body. She looked up at him involuntarily. His eyes were there already, waiting for hers, wide with shock, and something else – something very like the delighted recognition she'd read in his face that first night, before it turned to anger.

She opened her mouth to say something, just as he snatched his hand away and shoved it into his pocket, turning his eyes to the ground, and leaving Sophie with an overpowering feeling of loss. But he couldn't hide the flush creeping across his cheeks, confirming that something profound had happened to him, too, in that moment when they touched. Just as the silence between them was beginning to be awkward, grey stone showed through the trees.

"Home sweet home," Lucas said, in a tone that was distinctly ironic, causing Sophie to look up at him again.

"Isn't it?" she asked.

He offered her another cheerless smile. "How are you holding up?" he asked instead of answering, steering her toward the tower.

"Okay," she answered, wondering why his arm wrapped around her didn't have the same effect as their hands meeting. *Maybe it's only skin-to-skin*, she thought; and then flushed even deeper.

Lucas pushed the tower door open. Sophie expected it to creak on rusty hinges like any self-respecting castle door, but instead it swung silently inward. Likewise, there were no wall sconces with flaming torches or suits of armor beyond it, only an Ikea coat rack, a potted palm, and a very modern set of halogen track lights.

"Not very Goth, is it?" Sophie commented, limping inside.

Lucas raised his eyebrows. "Do I look like a Goth?"

Sophie looked him over. Aside from the gloves, he wore a dark red jumper that was fraying in places, black jeans, and black boots. His dark hair was tousled in a careless, rather than an artistic way, though the dousing in the pond probably would have taken care of any effort he'd spent on it. But then there was the long, dark coat she was still wearing.

"Not so much, now," she said, shedding the coat and handing it to him. "I mean, with the coat, you could still pass as an extra in an Anne Rice novel. But with the whole violin-and-candles thing, never mind that," she pointed to the mermaid-shaped hilt of the sword, still protruding above his shoulder, "you could pull off the lead."

Lucas gave a mellow laugh, and hung up the coat. "I play at night because there are fewer distractions. The candles were a direct result of the power cut. The sword…well, I assume you'd agree that was a necessary prop on today's outing."

"Well, that's me told."

His smile widened, though his eyes remained unaccountably sad. "Are you always like this?"

"Like what?"

"Stroppy."

"Only when I'm nervous."

"I make you nervous?" His look was direct, curious, not remotely flirtatious. Sophie forbade herself to blush again.

"I'm waiting for you to start yelling at me again," she said.

"I already apologized for that."

"What about snooping in my room?"

He sighed. "We'll get to that. Come on." He held out his hand, but just as Sophie reached for it, he dropped it again. *Ouch,* she thought. But then he threaded his arm under hers to help her up the stairs.

At every turn she expected to see cracks, cobwebs, crumbling plaster – anything that belied the tower's age. At every turn she was disappointed. Everything was clean and new, from the plain white plaster walls to the double-glazed window slits (how, she wondered, did he find a company willing to do that?) – clean and new to the point of austerity.

The same was true of the room at the top of the stairs. It was an open-plan living room and kitchen, which could have come straight out of a style magazine. The furniture was upholstered in pale, muted colours that reminded Sophie of Ardnasheen's stony beaches. The kitchen units were made of birch and stainless steel. Even the pictures on the walls – in styles varying from cubism to high Renaissance – seemed to settle into their understated surroundings. In short, it was nothing like a typical single man's messy, cluttered space.

"So this is where you live?" Sophie said.

"Is it not what you'd pictured?" Lucas asked.

"I hadn't pictured anything," Sophie answered, her eyes on the canvas over the sofa. In it, an armored angel stood on a gloomy beach, driving a spear through a writhing sea monster. Thinking of the horse, she felt sick.

"There's a bathroom there," he said, pointing to a door in the far wall. "You should get your wet things off. There's a dressing gown on the back of the door."

Sophie limped over to the bathroom, which was as pristine as the rest of the tower, and shed her wet clothes. Her knee seemed to have stopped bleeding, although it had swollen and

167

turned a livid shade of purple. The marks of the horse's teeth ringed her ankle like a bracelet. She wiped away the worst of the dried blood with wet tissues, and then, tying the dressing gown over her underwear, she went back out into the sitting room.

Lucas was waiting for her with a bag of frozen peas and a roll of bandages. "Give those to me," he said, indicating her wet clothes, and she handed them over. He gave her the bag of peas in exchange. "Sit," he said, indicating the sofa, "and drink this." He handed her a steaming cup. She was hoping for more whisky, but it turned out to be black, sugary tea. As she sipped it, Lucas hung her clothes over chairs he arranged in front of the radiator. Sophie watched him, feeling strange, as if she were hovering slightly to the side of herself. She assumed it was shock.

When he'd finished hanging up her clothes, Lucas said, "Can I look at the bite?" Sophie nodded. He examined her ankle closely and then, apparently satisfied, he began to wrap it with the bandage. Sophie couldn't help but notice that he was careful not to touch her skin directly. "How are you feeling?" he asked when he was finished.

Sophie smiled grimly. "Well let's see: I was just saved from a horrible death at the hands of what I'm fairly certain was an unclassified species, by a bloke who blows at least as hot and cold as the local weather, but appears miraculously when I'm in distress, which by the way is happening with alarming frequency of late. I suppose you could say that I'm just a *bit* disgruntled."

Lucas passed a hand over his eyes, and laughed humourlessly. "Where do you want me to begin?"

"Oh, hell…the vampire horse?"

"No such thing, unfortunately: it would probably be easier to kill than what we were dealing with."

"Which was…?"

"It's called an *Each Uisge*. Water horse, in English." Seeing Sophie's blank look, he elaborated: "It's a close cousin of the Kelpie, only it haunts still water instead of rivers. It lures in its prey by looking like a lost pony."

"I thought it was one of the ponies from the paddock over there." She waved vaguely toward the far side of the house.

Lucas shook his head. "Those ponies are mine, and they're completely harmless. But no doubt the *Each Uisge* wanted you to think it was one of them. They're clever that way."

Sophie considered this information, then asked, "So how did it make me stick?"

He shrugged. "That's just part of its *modus operandi*. Once it lures you onto its back, you stick fast, and it dives to the deepest part of the pool with you, where it…" He glanced up at her, uncertain.

"Come on, I'm a big girl."

"It drowns you, and then it eats you. All except for the liver – it leaves that behind. I don't know why."

Sophie looked at him incredulously, but his eyes were steady and sincere. She drew a breath, and let it out slowly. "Okay," she said. "So I'm guessing that this ech…ach…"

"*Each Uisge.*"

"Right…I'm assuming I'm not going to find it in my guide to Scottish flora and fauna."

"A guide to Celtic mythology, maybe."

"Of course. I'll pick one up next time I go to Mallaig."

He looked at her, clearly puzzled. "Why are you taking this so well?"

"I'm not. I'm using sarcasm as a shield…at least that's what Mum calls it."

"Still, most girls would be screaming or calling me mad right now."

Sophie shrugged. "Most girls haven't spent their lives pretending not to see things that shouldn't exist." She watched carefully for his reaction, and sure enough, his eyes flickered away. *Gotcha*, she thought – but that could wait for the moment. "Still, my experience with supernatural creatures is fairly limited, as these things go. So how did a mythical monster come to be living on your mountain?"

Lucas looked at his hands for a few moments, then back at her. "Sophie, mythical monsters live *everywhere*, along with a whole lot of other things that – as you put it – shouldn't exist."

"If that's true, then why aren't they common knowledge?"

"Because, as you appear to have learned the hard way, most people can't see them."

"But I can."

"Clearly."

"And you can."

"Yes."

"Lucky us," she sighed. "Any idea why?"

When he answered, it was the last thing she'd expected him to say, "Are you religious, Sophie?"

"Um…as far as it was required in school."

"That's enough to know that the basis of any faith is belief."

"I suppose so," Sophie said, inadvertently thinking about Sam, and the way her last metaphysical discussion had ended.

"The thing is," Lucas continued, "most people in the modern Western world have lost that belief; the literal part of it anyway. I mean, no one thinks that God throws thunderbolts to strike down sinners. More to the point, no one thinks that He ever really did.

"But what if that's not quite the whole story? What if the only thing standing between a literal thunderbolt and a figurative one *is* belief? What if, once upon a time, an angry God really did strike people down with thunderbolts? And the only reason he doesn't do it anymore is because no one believes that Hhe will?"

Lucas was looking at her with such earnest entreaty that Sophie had to nod, though she was beginning to wonder if she'd been right at the beginning, and he was unhinged.

"But if you found a place where people did still believe those things," he continued, "then maybe you'd find thunderbolts too. Well, Ardnasheen is one of those places."

"So I should start watching out for flying thunderbolts?" Sophie asked, cocking an eyebrow.

"Not thunderbolts, no. They aren't a part of this place's religion."

"And water horses are?"

"Yes. Because water horses belong to the *sìth,* and around here, the *sìth* have been the prevailing deities for longer than anyone can remember."

"*Sìth?*" Sophie repeated. "Am I supposed to know what that is?"

"Faeries."

"*Faeries?*"

"In the Celtic sense," he said, "which is very different from the Disney sense. Most of them aren't pretty, and even fewer are benevolent. In fact, the majority of them are what you'd call monsters."

Sophie studied him for a long moment, trying to pick the most relevant question from the swarm in her head. "How did you know to come, today? And the other night, with the Revenant?"

"Revenant?" he asked.

"That skeleton warrior thing that came to my room."

Lucas hesitated, clearly choosing his words carefully. "I had…a feeling about them. I get them sometimes."

Sophie waited for him to elaborate. When he didn't, she prompted, "But you knew exactly what you were doing. I mean, you didn't just show up, you showed up with everything you needed to fight those monsters and win. Have you killed one of them before?"

He shook his head. "Not a…a Revenant. And not a water horse, either. But other *sìth,*" he shrugged, "once or twice."

"Then how did you know what to do?"

172

He raised his eyes to hers. She could read nothing in them. "With the *sìth,* it's simple. All of them are vulnerable to iron. It's one of the few things that can kill them. It's part of the mythology…the rules of the religion, if you like."

Sophie shut her eyes and rubbed them. Her head was beginning to ache. "So basically," she said, "you're telling me that simply believing in something can make it real."

"No," he answered, as calm and patient as if they'd been discussing the weather, "I'm saying that if something is real, then believing in it allows you to see it. And the more people who believe in it, the more power it has. I know it sounds like splitting hairs, but the distinction is important, because otherwise we'd be overrun with everyone's nightmares and fantasies." He paused. "You think I'm mad, don't you."

"Not unless I think that I'm mad, too. It all makes sense, actually, in its own messed-up way." She looked at him. "The problem is, *I* don't believe in water horses. I'd never even heard of them until today. So why did I see one?"

"I don't know," he answered, with a slight hesitation that made her wonder if this wasn't the whole truth. "But I imagine it's for the same reason you can see the – what did you call them? Revenants?"

"What are they really called?"

He shook his head, and said, "Revenants is as good a name as any."

"Are they faeries too?"

"No," he said, sounding suddenly tired. "They're something quite different."

Sophie tried to keep her voice calm, but it betrayed her with a shrill note as she asked, "Because they used to be human?"

Lucas gave her a long, hard look, and then he said, "What makes you say that?"

She didn't even consider denying it; she knew that they were long past any kind of coyness. Instead she said, "Hand me my jeans, please." When he gave them to her, she took the newspaper clipping from the pocket. It was in bad shape after its dousing in the pond, but not so bad that the picture was obliterated. She handed it to Lucas.

"This girl looks just like a Revenant I saw on the road the other night," she said as he studied it. "Or she would, if the Revenant had still had its skin fully attached. But there's no mistaking that hair. I'm sure she became that Revenant."

Lucas offered no excuse or explanation. He simply said, "You're right. She did."

"Then please tell me what she is," Sophie said, wondering how he could be so exasperating while ostensibly answering all of her questions, "because I've spent most of my life trying to pretend that I don't see them, so that I don't get tranquilized or locked in an asylum or whatever they do these days to psychotics."

Lucas tossed the clipping aside and looked up at her, his face finally betraying emotion. "Don't say that!" he said, surprising her with his vehemence. "There's nothing wrong with you, Sophie – far from it."

"Then why can I see these things?"

"I don't know. I've never met a – that is, I've never met anyone who could."

"So if they aren't *sìth*, then what are they?"

"Are you sure you want to know that?"

"Positive."

He drew a deep breath, and looking like he'd rather not, he said, "They're people who've lost their souls."

Though she felt it should have done, this explanation barely fazed Sophie. "How?"

"There are certain…creatures…that can steal them."

"More faeries?"

He paused again. "No…not faeries. Something else."

What aren't you telling me? Sophie wanted to scream, but she was afraid that if she called attention to his evasions, he'd shut down altogether. Instead she said, "So what does one do with a spare soul?"

"That…gets a little weird."

"Weirder than being attacked by a pony with shark teeth that doesn't like liver?"

Lucas laughed. It brightened his face, made it come alive in a way that gave her a strange, squeezed feeling in her chest. "Point taken," he said. "Okay, remember that this is mostly speculation…but it seems there's this theory that a soulless creature might be able to pass a stolen soul off as it's own."

"Why would it want to do that?"

"To gain salvation," he said, as if it should have been obvious.

"So the other night," Sophie said slowly, "when that Revenant pulled the knife on me, was it trying to steal my soul?"

"I don't know," Lucas admitted. "It certainly seemed to want something from you, and I suppose your soul is the obvious choice."

"Has it happened before? A Revenant stealing someone's soul?"

Lucas shook his head. "I don't know."

Sophie considered this for a moment. "Have any ever tried it with you?"

His mouth turned in a brief, bitter smile. "No."

There was a long silence. When Lucas finally broke it, his question stunned her: "Why haven't you asked me about the pictures?"

"Pardon?" Sophie said – not because she didn't know what he meant, but to buy time to prepare herself for what he might say.

He smiled. "Come on, Sophie: you're far too clever to pretend to be daft. You were in my study, so you can't have failed to notice them."

"You're right," she said. "I was there, and I did notice them." She paused, then said, "I suppose I haven't asked you about them because I assumed that they weren't yours." Involuntarily, she glanced at him, looking for affirmation. His eyes were steady, but unreadable. "I mean," she continued, "how could they be? It would take a lifetime to gather a collection like that."

"Several," Lucas murmured.

"Never mind the small fortune you'd need to pay for it – assuming they're authentic."

"They're authentic," he said, once again with inexplicable bitterness.

"But since we're on the subject – why exactly *is* there a wall of pictures of women who look like me?"

He smiled without humor. "They come with the house."

"So it's really just a bizarre coincidence, then…"

"What else could it be?"

You're dodging me again, she thought. She said, "Do you know who they're *supposed* to look like?"

"Yes, actually. There's a family legend about a pair of star-crossed lovers from warring families, all very Romeo and Juliet. They were found out, and the boy was banished here. He spent the rest of his life pining for the girl. The collection was his. The women all look like his lost love. It was the only way he could keep a piece of her – of what he'd lost."

"I guess that's romantic…in a creepy kind of a way," Sophie said, thinking about the word that had unlocked the room, and how very similar it was to "banished". But something more about the story bothered her. "You tell it as if it's lost in the mists of time or something."

"That's because it is."

"But some of those pictures aren't very old."

He nodded. "It's become a bit of a tradition to add to the collection. The last Lady Belial bought a few of them. I bought a couple too, after I moved in here."

"I guess that makes sense…as much as any of this does."

All at once Lucas smiled, its beauty making her forget everything she'd still meant to ask him.

"What?" she asked.

"Nothing," he said, dropping his eyes in a way that made her chest tighten again. "I just…I have to thank you, Sophie."

"For what? Making you risk your life to save me from a horse monster?"

He shook his head. "For hearing me out, even though I was so awful to you. And for making me feel normal for the first time in – well, longer than you can imagine."

"Oh," she said. "Well, that's ironic. I've never felt normal in my entire life."

"Not even now that you know I'm as mad as you are?"

"Well, it's a start," she admitted. "But it will take some getting used to."

His smile faded a bit, but his eyes remained hopeful. "I'd ask you to stay for tea," he said, "but I imagine you're tired after today."

No! she thought. *I've never been less tired in my life!* But she knew that he was tactfully telling her that he needed time alone, and so she said, "A bit."

"I'll walk you back to your room now." Sophie tried to hide her disappointment with a smile. Then he said, "But would you go for a walk with me tomorrow? If your war wounds aren't too sore, that is. I promise we'll stay away from dark woods and isolated mountain pools."

Sophie smiled. "I'd like that," she said. "But won't Mairi mind?"

"Who?" Lucas asked.

"That blonde girl who picks shellfish. I got the impression you were seeing her."

Lucas shook his head. "Who told you that? I barely know her."

Sophie had to work to hide her sudden elation. "It's just something I overheard…"

"You shouldn't listen to the gossip around here. Most of it's absurd, the rest is nasty."

"Right. Thanks for the warning."

"You're welcome," he answered, reaching to brush a strand of hair out of her face. It seemed such a natural gesture: the type of little, throwaway kindness old lovers would exchange, like the hand that he'd offered her on the stairs, before he snatched it back. He recalled himself this time, too, the moment before he touched her. Now, though, he didn't pull back. He held her eyes, questioning. She didn't move, or look away. And then, quite deliberately, he lowered his fingers to her cheek.

The tingling warmth went through her again, and this time, in the good light, there was no denying that he had felt it too. He let his fingers trace delicately down her cheek. Sophie shut her eyes, praying that he wouldn't stop. But when his fingers reached her throat, he withdrew them. She opened her eyes, and for a moment they looked at each other, full of wonder.

And then he stood up, breaking their linked gaze. "It's been a long day. Let's get you home."

CHAPTER 16

"If I didn't know better, I'd think you were making this up,"
Ailsa said, spooning beans onto a piece of toast and putting it
down in front of Sophie.

Sophie shrugged, trying to look honest. There'd been no
avoiding telling Ailsa about Lucas rescuing her on the hill –
Ailsa had already missed her, and been waiting anxiously when
he brought her home. He'd handled most of it, smoothly talking
around the incident with the water horse to produce a convincing
enough story. But once he'd gone, Ailsa had pounced on Sophie
for the details, which she was having trouble filling in.

"Why?" Sophie asked. "You don't think I'm the mountain
climbing type?"

"No – I just can't believe that Lucas came to your rescue.
I mean, I'd have thought he'd see a damsel in distress and just
leave her to it."

Sophie laughed. "He's not really like that. At least, not now
he's decided I'm not his evil ex. He was quite nice, actually."

"Quite nice!" Ailsa cried, sitting down across from Sophie at the kitchen table with her own plate of beans on toast. "Have you forgotten that he told you to get out of his house on the night you met?"

"He apologized for that."

"And don't you think there's something odd about his explanation? I mean, an ex who looks so much like you he couldn't tell the difference? And didn't he call you by name?"

"There must be more to that story. For the moment, though, I'm willing to give him the benefit of the doubt. I mean, maybe he just doesn't want to start dissecting his past relationships with someone he's only just met."

"And what about those pictures?" Ailsa persisted. "You just happen to look like the long lost lady of Ardnasheen, too?"

Sophie had been successfully avoiding thinking about these things. Now she pushed her plate away and looked at Ailsa. "Okay, I know, there are a lot of unanswered questions. I'm sure he'll tell me more about it when he knows me better."

"Aha!"

"Aha what?"

"Aha, you like him." Ailsa gave her a knowing smirk.

"Well, I suppose…I mean I don't *dis*like him. He did save me on the mountain today."

"Too true – and how do you think he managed that?"

"Coincidence?" Sophie asked uncomfortably.

"Maybe he was following you."

Sophie smiled. "Now *that's* just plain melodrama. Anyway, I'm sure I'll find out more tomorrow."

"What's tomorrow?"

"Lucas asked me to go for a walk with him."

Ailsa raised her eyebrows, the smirk returning. "I see. A date."

"It's not a date."

"Kind of like dinner with Sam wasn't a date?"

"Ugh…don't remind me."

"Ach, Sophie, you're a hard-hearted woman! You're really going to stonewall Sam because he found you irresistible?"

"I told you, it was more than that. I think he put something in my drink, and then, well…" She trailed off, not wanting to think about what might have happened then.

Ailsa scrutinized her. "If you say so. But I don't think he's given up. He was in the pub just this afternoon, asking for you."

"Well, I imagine he'll get the picture soon enough."

"Oh, to have the luxury of blowing off gorgeous men…" Ailsa sighed.

Sophie smiled and shook her head. "I think I'll go to bed. It's been a long day."

Ailsa waved good-bye. "Sweet dreams of your rival lovers."

*

Lucas came into the pub a few minutes before the end of Sophie's shift the following day, dressed for walking and holding a tiny bunch of forget-me-nots. Michael eyed them over the rim of his glass as Lucas handed them to Sophie. Ailsa rolled her eyes as she went for an order in the kitchen, but she did give Sophie a covert wink.

All of Sophie's resolutions about being cool and not too eager dissolved into a beaming smile. "They're my favorite!" she said, breathing the flowers' sweet, delicate scent. "How did you know?"

Lucas smiled back, clearly pleased with her reaction. "Lucky guess?"

"And where did you find them this time of year?"

Lucas shrugged. "Lots of plants bloom out of season here. Must be the Gulf Stream."

Sophie filled a whisky glass with water and put the flowers in it. Then she put the glass up on the shelf with the expensive bottles so that no one would tip it over. "Thank you, Lucas," she said, suddenly shy of his steady gaze.

"Are you ready to go?" he asked.

Sophie was about to answer when Ailsa came out of the kitchen with a plate of spiral chilli chips and set it down in front of Michael. "Not so fast," she said, and Sophie groaned inwardly. Ailsa had teased her all day about her impending date. Apparently she wasn't finished yet. "Where exactly are you planning to take the young lady?" she asked Lucas.

"Ailsa!" Sophie groaned.

But Lucas smiled. "It's alright. I'm glad you have friends looking out for you." To Ailsa he said, "For a walk. I've got a picnic if it stays dry. Otherwise, we'll be back here, so make sure Michael doesn't eat all of the chilli chips."

Michael grinned, popping a whole spiral into his mouth. Ailsa drummed her fingers on the bar. "Alright. But you'd best have her back by dark."

"Or I'll have you to answer to?"

"No," Ailsa said. "Him." She pointed to Michael, who raised his whisky glass. Just before he sipped, though, Sophie was certain that she saw a brief, significant glance pass between Lucas and him.

Seeing what isn't there, she told herself, *because of what Ailsa said last night.* "Good-*bye* Ailsa," she said. "I left you a nice big stack of dishes to wash. Michael, see you soon."

Michael looked up from his chips to smile at her – an indulgent, grandfatherly smile. His green eyes, though, were sharp and incisive. "Remember," he said, "I'm only a phone-call away. You still have my card?"

"I don't go anywhere without it," Sophie assured him, and then, gratefully, she followed Lucas into the cloakroom. "Well, that was weird," she said when the door shut behind them. "Sorry."

Lucas smiled and shrugged, bending to pick up a rucksack. "Don't be. I meant that, about you being lucky to have friends here who care about you. It means I don't have to worry so much."

Before she could think better of it, Sophie said, "You worry about me?"

Lucas straightened up, tightening the pack's straps. He looked down at her, his dark eyes direct. "Well, you do seem to be a magnet for dangerous supernatural creatures."

Sophie wasn't sure what to make of this answer. "So," she said, pulling on her jacket as he held the door for her, "this get-together is only altruism? Your way to keep me from spending my free time monster hunting?"

He smiled, shook his head. "If I didn't think you're rather above all that, I'd say you were fishing."

"For what?"

"Compliments."

"Oh no!" Sophie said, horrified. "I absolutely *loathe* fishing." Lucas was laughing now, to Sophie's irritation. "If you can spare the breath," she said, "perhaps you could tell me where exactly we're going?"

Lucas sobered, though his eyes still glinted suspiciously. "I thought we should try another mountain," he said, "seeing as you never got to the top of the last one. I brought a good selection of iron weapons, just in case." Sophie stopped, crossing her arms over her chest. "Sorry," he said, "couldn't resist. But seriously, is your leg up for a walk?"

"It barely hurts anymore."

"Really? It was a nasty cut even before the *Each Uisge* bit you."

She shrugged. "I heal fast."

"Okay – if you're sure. Because I really want to show you *Uamh-an-Aingeal.*"

"I'm not so good with the Gaelic."

"Ah – cave of the angel? Angel's cavern? That general idea."

Sophie glanced at him dubiously. "A cave? As in, deep and dark and subterranean?"

He smiled "You forgot watery. It's a sea cave. But don't worry," he added quickly, seeing the look on her face. "There's a dry path all the way in, and I have lamps."

"Alright," Sophie said dubiously. "So what is it that makes this cave angelic?"

He looked at her, his eyes bright with anticipation. "I don't think that I should tell you that. It'll ruin the surprise."

"Well, now I *have* to see it. Let's go!"

They walked away from the village in the direction of Sam's house, but they passed by the turn-off into the woods and kept following the shore. The sky was a pale, pearly grey, the wind was low and it wasn't too cold. It was, in other words, what Sophie was beginning to think of as a beautiful day.

"So, Sophie Creedon, tell me about yourself," Lucas said after a moment.

Sophie glanced at Lucas. "What do you want to know? I mean, aside from the fact that I attract evil faeries and zombies."

He shrugged. "The mundane things. Favorite color…where you were born…most embarrassing childhood memory…"

She laughed. "Alright. Favorite colour would have to be red. Dark red, not pillar-box. Where I was born – London, I think."

"You think?"

"I'm adopted. I was found on the steps of an East End

church when I was a few days old, with no accompanying info. So barring my birth mother, it's anybody's guess where I actually came into the world."

He looked stricken. "God, Sophie – I'm sorry. I didn't mean to pry."

She smiled at him. "You weren't prying – it was a perfectly innocent question. And it's okay. Nobody ever believes me when I say so, but really, it is. My parents have always been open about it, so it's not as if I ever had to find out in some horrible way and come to terms with it. And even though I might moan about them, they're really very good parents. Actually, separation aside, I can't imagine better ones. So please, don't pity me."

"Of course I won't," he said, but he still looked unhappy and also, somehow, distant, as if Sophie's revelation had touched some raw nerve.

"Anyhow, I'm not finished," she said, to break the tension. "Since you asked, my most embarrassing childhood memory is writing a love letter to my teacher when I was nine – in which I proposed, no less."

Lucas smiled. "What did he do?"

"Corrected my spelling and gave it back."

"Ouch."

"Yeah. But it was better than if he'd made a big deal out of it. I think that a sensitive discussion about appropriate teacher-student relationships would have finished me. Now, what about you?"

"Ah…favorite colour…blue."

"Baby blue? Navy blue?"

He thought about that for a moment, and then he said, "The inside of a mussel shell."

"And you were born…?"

"To tell you the truth, I'd have to look it up. We moved around so much…"

"Embarrassing childhood memories?"

"My childhood was…regimented. Not much room for doing anything embarrassing."

"That's convenient." Sophie paused, wondering whether she should ask the next question, and then decided that she might as well. "I can't help wondering, how come you live here all alone? I mean, I know about your parents, I can't imagine anything more terrible…but you must have other friends, or family. Or you could have gone to university or something."

Lucas sighed. "I could have, I suppose. But I've already spent so much time studying, I just couldn't quite stomach any more. Not yet, anyway. So when Lady Belial fell ill, and I was contacted about the inheritance – well, coming here just seemed the right thing to do."

"Ailsa told me about that – how you came to nurse the old lady before she died."

"Is that what she said?" he asked with a self-deprecating half-smile. "Well, I hope that I was a help to her, although I doubt it." He sighed, shaking his head. "Clara was a nice lady. Deserved better from life than what she got."

"You mean her fiancé dying?"

Lucas stopped, blinked at her for a moment, and then said, "How do you know about that?"

"Ailsa."

"Is there anything Ailsa *doesn't* know?"

"Not much, apparently."

He resumed walking. "Well, you've got me – that rumor is also true. But it's more than just his dying. Losing him shaped the rest of her life, and for most of it she was lonely, which is a terrible thing."

"But I thought that she chose to stay here."

"She stayed," he shrugged, "but there wouldn't have been much of a choice involved. When she was young, women didn't have the same kind of opportunities they have now."

"Still, she could have married someone else."

"Maybe she never fell in love with anybody else."

"That's a bit melodramatic, don't you think?"

Lucas looked over at her, his eyes serious and penetrating. "Why do you say so?"

"Okay, maybe what's happening with my parents has made me cynical, but how many people really fall in love once and forever? And if something goes wrong with the first one, most people seem to find someone else, and still live happily ever after."

Lucas was silent for a moment. "I suppose that's true, a lot of the time," he said at last. "But I think there are people who are destined to love only once. They give themselves away body and soul, and after that there's nothing left for anybody else. If they lose the one they love, they'll never find another – not even if they want to." His eyes were fixed on the sky ahead, ruminative and sad. "It takes tremendous bravery to face a life like that; to hold on to that one pure thing you can never have again."

Good Lord, you're lovely, Sophie thought, trying not to gape. "Well," she said after a moment, "how can a girl argue with that?"

He turned and smiled at her. "Sorry. I didn't ask you out here to tell you sad love stories."

"It's my fault," Sophie said. "I asked. Why don't we change the subject?"

"Alright." He smiled. "How about this: you don't get seasick, do you?"

"I hardly ever get sick at all. Why?"

Lucas pointed toward the shore, which was made up of cobble-size stones. An old rowboat was resting on the dried bladderwrack, up beyond the high tide mark. Most of its paint had peeled off, leaving it a weathered grey. The only vibrant colour was the oarlocks, which were bright orange with rust. It was the kind of scene Sophie's mother would have loved to paint.

"We go the rest of the way by sea," Lucas said.

It took Sophie a moment to connect what he'd said with the ancient rowboat. "I thought we were going on a walk," she said, now eyeing it dubiously.

"Well, yes," Lucas agreed, "but if we walked the whole way, we'd have to abseil down the cliffs to reach the cave."

"I think I'll go with the boat."

"Good choice," he said.

Sophie helped Lucas carry the boat down to the water, and then stepped in. Lucas handed her the rucksack and then pushed off.

"How far is it?" she asked.

He turned and pointed to a headland at the end of the bay, a few hundred meters distant. It ended in a sheer rock face, with a dark hole at its foot. "That's the entrance, there at the bottom," he said.

Lucas was a powerful rower, and it wasn't long before they reached the cave entrance. The cliff dropped vertically into the water, which was a deep teal blue, so clear that Sophie could see individual stones on the seabed. There was a narrow platform of rock at the right side of the cave entrance, with an iron ring protruding from it. Lucas tied the boat off to the ring, shipped the oars and then leapt gracefully onto the ledge. Sophie handed him the rucksack, and then he held out his hand to her.

She felt suddenly shy, remembering the shock when their hands had touched the day before. She wondered if Lucas would pull away from her again. But his smile was unwavering, with a hint of challenge. She put her hand in his, and when his fingers closed around hers, the jolt was stronger than before, tingling right up her arm. She couldn't help looking up at him. His eyes met hers, dark and direct above his smile. He tightened his hand around hers for a moment before he released it, and Sophie had no doubt now that he'd felt it, too. More than that. He'd *wanted* to feel it.

Her cheeks burned, and she was glad that Lucas had turned his attention to his rucksack. Unzipping it, he took out two old, square miners' lamps. He handed one of them to her. "Seriously?" Sophie asked.

"Seriously," he said. "They're better than any modern head torch." He flicked the light on, and pointed it into the cave. Sophie did the same. By the lamps' light, she could see that the stone ledge on which they were standing continued on inside, widening a bit as it went.

"Scared?" he asked, with a challenging smile.

"I don't get sick *or* scared." She reconsidered this. "Except when I'm attacked by carnivorous horses."

"My kind of girl," he grinned. Holding the lamp up, he said, "After you."

CHAPTER 17

The ledge widened as they walked, until it formed a wide, sloping bank that ran along the channel of water. The rocky walls were striped with mineral deposits in ochres and browns, with the occasion flash of blue where copper ore had leached out and oxidized. The water beside them was deep, but perfectly clear and still; every detail of its rocky bed was visible.

Sophie found looking into it strangely hypnotic. "It's so perfect," she said, bending to touch the water with a fingertip. Ripples ran outward from the disturbance, as distinct as the rocks below. "So pure."

Lucas crouched beside her. "That's because there's no sunlight here, so nothing can grow. No plants, no fish, no algae to cloud it up. Nothing but stone and water."

As they moved further into the cave, the ceiling grew stalactites like long spindly teeth. Water dripped from their tips into the channel below, counting off the incalculable moments it had taken for them to form. In places the deposits were so thick they looked like frozen waterfalls running down the walls. Sophie reached out to touch one of the formations. It felt cool and damp and somehow more organic than mineral, like bone rather than rock.

"Does the channel run straight through the headland to the other side?" she asked.

"No," Lucas answered, catching her under the elbow as she slipped on a wet incline. He took her hand then, sending warmth surging through her, a gesture so unexpected that Sophie wondered how it could also feel so natural. "The cave doesn't reach all the way through – at least not as a tunnel big enough to walk in. But somewhere, a freshwater spring comes down through the hill. There's a place just up ahead where the salt water ends and the fresh water begins." He pointed to a lip of rock with water flowing over it into the channel. Beyond it, the channel narrowed to a small stream, though there was no discernible current aside from the waterfall.

"So when are you going to tell me why it's called the angel cave?" Sophie asked.

Lucas smiled, and squeezed her hand. "Almost there," he said.

They stepped through a narrow gap in between two massive stalagmites that had grown up on the shelf. Beyond them, the rocky floor gave way to packed, wet sand. It curved around the water, forming a round pool. At one end of the pool, Sophie could see the stream that fed it, snaking back into a crevice in the rock that was, as Lucas had said, far too narrow for a person to pass through.

Lucas led Sophie toward the rock wall on one side of the crevice, and then he turned his light on it. She gasped in surprise and delight: the wall was covered with drawings. Or, more accurately, with carvings: the primitive pictures seemed to have been cut into the rock. There was a fish the size of her hand, a larger form that looked like a running horse, and another that looked like a bull.

Moving her own light along the wall, she came to another set of figures. At first, she thought they were a group of dogs gathered around a man. But the man had too many appendages, the dogs too few. She looked more closely, running a finger along the arched grooves that curved up from the man's shoulders, their lower portions fringed and feather-like.

"Are these wings?" she asked. "Is this the angel?"

Lucas nodded, his eyes fixed on the drawing. "That's the popular theory. Though given that the drawings are Pictish, it's more likely a faery, or a corn god, or something else that would have made sense in their cosmology."

"And these things around him? Are they some other kind of mystery monster?"

Lucas smiled. "No. They're seals."

She turned to him. "Okay...so Pictish angels used to live here and preach to the local seals?"

This time, he laughed. "Not exactly."

"But it's something equally weird, isn't it," Sophie sighed. "The explanation, I mean."

"There is no explanation: only a handful of theories. I'll tell you mine, but first of all, are you hungry?"

"Starving, actually," said Sophie, who'd been up since six.

"Good." Lucas took off his rucksack and opened it. He pulled out a waterproof picnic blanket and laid it on the sand. "Have a seat," he said. Sophie sat, and he started taking out and opening plastic containers. There were grapes, cheese, biscuits, a bottle of water and another of juice, and various other foods that Sophie loved.

"I'm impressed," she said, popping a chilli olive into her mouth. "I didn't think these existed outside of London, never mind up here."

Lucas smiled, clearly delighted by her approval. "There are ways and means. I know it's too much, but I wasn't sure what you'd like…"

"As long as it isn't dried salt deer, I like it," Sophie said.

"No worries," Lucas said, sitting down beside her and beginning to build an oatcake sandwich. "I left the dried salt deer in the dungeon."

"Where, hopefully, it will stay," Sophie said. "So, tell me your theory."

"Well, like I said, the drawings are meant to be Pictish, though no one knows for certain. They've never really been studied or anything – in fact not many people even know that they're here."

"That seems strange. They must be important."

Lucas shrugged, pouring two cups of juice. "The Lairds of Ardnasheen never wanted them publicized. They didn't want hordes of tourists traipsing through. It's selfish, I suppose; but then look at what's happened to those painted caves in France and Spain. All those breathing people are changing the atmosphere and destroying the pictures they've come to see."

"There's an irony in there somewhere," Sophie said.

"No doubt," Lucas said, breaking off a spray of grapes for Sophie, and another for himself. "Anyway, the fish and other animals are fairly obvious. I suppose whoever drew them was just drawing what he or she saw every day, or maybe making some kind of prayer for good luck hunting or whatever. What makes the other group so interesting is that the only explanation anyone's been able to come up with that makes any sense, is also historically impossible.

"You see, there used to be seals in this cave. Grey Seals, specifically. They'd come here every year to have their babies, and then they'd leave again when the babies were old enough to survive in the sea. That could well have been happening since Pictish times."

"Right," said Sophie, "but what about the man with the wings?"

Lucas glanced up at her. "Have you ever heard of selkies?"

"No. And please don't tell me they're a seal version of the water horse."

He smiled. "Not quite, although they're *sìth,* too. They're creatures that look like Grey Seals, except that they can take off their seal skins and walk around as humans. But it's a dangerous thing to do, because if a human finds the empty skin and steals it, the selkie is trapped on land, and has to obey that person."

"So, do these selkies look like men with wings?"

"No," he smiled. "Apparently, they look like beautiful women. Hence the skin stealing. Human men wanted them as wives."

"Apparently? You mean you haven't met any?"

He shook his head. "Sadly, no. They sound fairly decent, as faeries go."

Sophie couldn't tell whether he was being serious or not. "I still don't see how the figure with the wings fits into this."

"Well, there's another myth, more obscure than the one about the selkies. It claims that the *sìth* are actually fallen angels. Those that fell on land became tree spirits and whatever, while the ones that fell into the sea became water spirits – among them, the selkies. It would make a lot of sense for the picture to refer to that story."

"Would?"

"Would, if winged angels weren't a Christian idea. The carvings in this cave predate Christ by a good thousand years."

"So whoever made them wouldn't have heard of angels."

He shrugged. "Some earlier religions had angels, but their angels didn't have wings. So even if this artist had heard of them, they wouldn't draw them this way."

Sophie considered this. "Faeries have wings, too," she said.

Lucas shook his head. "*Disney* faeries have wings. It's a modern idea, just like the wings on angels."

"Really?"

He nodded, picking up an apple and beginning to peel it. "Angel wings were invented by a fourth century artist."

Sophie accepted the slice of apple he offered. "Lucas, how do you know all of this?"

He shrugged, looking out at the dark water. "I read a lot."

"Yeah – I noticed you had quite a collection of religious books."

"They came with the house, too," he said.

"So they aren't Sam's?"

As soon as the words were out, Sophie didn't know why she'd said them. She knew that the books wouldn't be Sam's, but something still disturbed her about the animosity between him and Lucas. And when Lucas's face hardened, she was certain there was more to their history than she knew.

"You know about Sam's library?" Lucas spoke the word with an ironic emphasis that Sophie didn't quite understand, as well as an undercurrent of anger.

Still, she didn't want to lie to him. "Unfortunately," she answered. "He asked me to tea one night."

Lucas's mouth tightened to a hard line when he looked at her. "You went to his house, alone?"

She shrugged. "It seemed like a good idea at the time."

"So it didn't go well," he said, scrutinizing her. Sophie shook her head. "Did he…I mean he didn't try to…"

A chill ran down her spine. "Actually, yes. How did you know that?"

Lucas looked away, clearly troubled. "You wouldn't be the first girl he's taken advantage of." He looked back at her, reaching for her hand and clutching it tightly. "You won't go there again, will you?"

Before she could answer, Sophie's eye caught on something. Lucas's sleeve had fallen back when he reached for her hand, and now the silver cuff on his wrist caught the light. She could see that it had inscriptions on it, just like Sam's. "What is this?" she asked, touching it.

Lucas shook his sleeve back over the band. "It's…a long story," he said, his eyes on the water.

"Sam wears them, too. One on each wrist."

Still not looking at her, he said, "Yes."

"But if you hate each other, it seems strange that you'd wear matching jewellery."

Lucas smiled wryly. "It does, doesn't it? But they go back farther than our quarrel."

"Are they to do with the school you went to?"

Finally, Lucas looked at her, and she thought that she saw relief in his eyes. "He told you about that?" Sophie nodded. "Well, you're right. The…bracelets go back to our school days."

"Right."

"Listen, Sophie…I know it's really none of my business, but please promise me you'll stay away from Sam."

"Don't worry," Sophie said grimly, "I don't plan to have anything more to do with him."

"Good," Lucas said. "Because if something happened to you…" He trailed off, looking at her. Slowly, he reached up, and Sophie stopped breathing as his fingers hovered by her cheek. And then he brought them down gently, tracing a line from her cheekbone to her jaw. She caught the faint, sweet, exotic scent of the dream garden, saw a trail of stars falling through a dark sky. She remembered the feel of his lips on her throat, so real, despite being a dream. Her face flamed, and she waited for his hand to fall, so that she could turn away, compose herself.

But it didn't fall. Instead it kept moving, just as it had in her dream, his fingers trailing down her neck, stopping only when he reached the zipper of her jacket. Heat exploded through her; her heart felt like it would fly out of her chest. She felt how near he was, and unconsciously, her lips parted. He took her other hand, his fingers slipping between hers, and the dark behind her closed eyes flashed suddenly with a whirl of images. Lucas standing before her with a smile full of love and a light shining out of him, brilliant as the sun. Her white hand bound to his gold-brown one with a silver vine, as a sweet voice spoke words in an ancient tongue. The two of them twined together in sleep, in a field of indigo grass under a rosy dawn sky.

And then the pictures in her mind changed again, the images darkening as if a storm cloud eclipsed them. Through its swirling scrim she saw Lucas kneeling in the mud, his face in his hands; Suri weeping as she chiseled a symbol onto a slab of stone; and then she was tumbling through a limitless darkness that ended with her looking up at a black sky, unable to raise a hand against the rain falling in her face.

"Wait!" she cried, pulling away from Lucas as her eyes flew open. "Wait…"

Lucas's own eyes were just a few inches away, intent and unblinking. For a moment he seemed disoriented. Then he blinked, drew a shuddering breath, and sat back. "Oh God, Sophie…I'm sorry, I never meant to – "

"Don't," she interrupted, shaking her head. "It's not…I mean, it's just that…" *That what?* She took a deep breath and tried again. "I – I saw something. When you touched me."

"What did you see?" he asked, looking at her closely.

"You," she whispered, "and me. Together, but different. Lucas, you'll think I'm mad…but ever since I met you, I've had this feeling that I *know* you. I dream things…I remember things…I – I think we've…done this…before." She felt herself flushing bright red, but she held his gaze, and his fingers remained tight around hers.

He looked at her for a long moment, and then he said, "I don't think you're mad, Sophie." He brushed a strand of hair off of her face. "I think you're right."

CHAPTER 18

"Do you honestly expect me to believe," Ailsa said, dipping a piece of a chocolate bar into her cup of tea and then sucking it, "that a gorgeous guy took you on a romantic picnic out of the way of all prying eyes and nothing happened?"

Sophie willed herself not to blush, her voice not to crack as she answered, "Lots of things happened. We exchanged life stories…ate lunch…looked at ancient wall art…"

Ailsa rolled her eyes. "You are absolutely, positively hopeless." She punctuated each word with a jab of the chocolate, then popped the lot of it into her mouth.

"No," Sophie answered, "I just believe in taking things slowly." It wasn't quite a lie: she did believe it, in theory. The fact that her inexplicable hallucinations were the only thing that had stood between having very little and a whole lot to tell Ailsa about her day with Lucas was beside the point. "I suppose I'm an old fashioned kind of a girl."

Ailsa shook her head and sighed. "And the pathetic bit is,

you being old fashioned is *still* more exciting than me being up for anything! Honestly, all the single men in this place and not *one* of them is The One."

"How do you know?" Sophie asked, sipping her own tea. "Perhaps he *is* here, and you just haven't realized it yet. I mean, a few days ago I thought Lucas was far too strange…" *And now I know that we're both insane, so clearly we're meant for each other.* She couldn't help smiling wryly at the thought.

Ailsa's sharp eyes caught it. "Are you telling me the truth, Miss Creedon? There wasn't even one little kiss?"

"Not one," Sophie said. "Sorry to disappoint."

"Hm," said Ailsa. "So are you going out again?"

"Not out," Sophie answered. "In. I said I'd make him tea tomorrow."

"Oh! Adorable! I'll be sure to be nowhere in sight. Which isn't to say I don't plan to have a good view of proceedings."

Sophie rolled her eyes and got up. "Good night, Ailsa."

"Night, Sophie," Ailsa grinned.

When Sophie shut the door behind her, she let out a sigh of relief. All she'd wanted to do that evening, after saying good-bye to Lucas at the front door, was escape to her bed and think. But Ailsa had been waiting for her to come in, and dragged her into her bedroom as soon as she heard Sophie in the hallway. Usually Sophie enjoyed their late-night chats, but she didn't want to talk about Lucas with Ailsa. It was partly shyness, but mostly that she didn't understand what was going on herself, never mind trying to explain it to someone else.

She pulled the curtains across the windows, and then poked at the fire until it showed some signs of life. Nevertheless, the room was freezing. She pulled the quilt off the foot of the bed and wrapped it around her, then lay down on top of the covers. Staring into the fire, she ran through the day that had just passed.

Despite their almost-kiss and the ensuing confession in the cave, her conversation with Lucas on the way home had been basically mundane. He had seemed suddenly shy of their mutual confession after returning to the light of day, while Sophie found it simply too huge to know how to begin to attack it. Her dreams, the visions when he touched her, even her own heart might tell her that she had a connection to Lucas extending far beyond the few weeks they'd known each other. But despite all she'd learned about the vagaries of reality, things that she couldn't explain still made her uneasy.

And yet, in this case, any explanation that she came up with was worse than none. Past lives, parallel universes – faery spells, God forbid; even thinking about them made her feel ridiculous. She wondered whether the explanation wasn't far simpler: whether this was what it meant to fall in love. Because even if she'd never come closer than a vague crush before, and even if she wasn't sure that what she was beginning to feel for Lucas was love, she knew that it was different, and far more powerful than anything she'd ever felt before. Drifting on the edge of sleep, her only surprise at this realization was how little surprise she felt.

At first she thought the red light was the fire flickering beyond her closed lids. But it was too bright; the peat seldom did more than smolder. Grudgingly she opened her eyes, and then groaned as the brilliant sun seared into them. She was about to shut them again and roll away from the offending sunlight when someone said, "Oh, no! I've been waiting *ages* for you to wake up – you're not getting away with that!"

Sophie knew that voice. She sat up quickly, banging her head on the reaching arm of a Celtic cross. "What *is* it with this place?" she cried, rubbing her head as her eyes teared, blurring the view of Suri's face. "I'm always injuring myself here!"

"That's only because you've forgotten the rules," Suri said, handing her a steaming cup.

"Forgotten?" Sophie said, suddenly wide-awake. "As in, I used to know the rules? As in, I've been here before?"

"Oops," Suri said, raising a hand to her mouth. Both her fingernails and her lips were painted punk-rock black, her eyes heavily rimmed with kohl, though she still wore the innocent white slip-dress.

"What do you mean, 'oops'?" Sophie asked, taking a sip from the cup, and momentarily forgetting the question at the taste of a perfect cappuccino: the kind she'd been craving ever since she moved to Ardnasheen, where no one served anything stronger than PG Tips.

"I mean, that was one of those things I wasn't meant to say."

Suri pulled a pair of round-lensed sunglasses off of her head and settled them over her eyes with a teasing smile. "Or maybe I was. Only you would know."

Sophie put the cup aside. "This cryptic thing is getting tiresome, you know."

"Yes," Suri sighed, "I *do* know." She stood up, brushed nonexistent dirt from her dress, and unhooked a black biker jacket from the other arm of the stone cross. The same cross was stenciled in white on the back of the jacket. "Come on, or we'll miss it."

"Miss what?" Sophie asked, standing too. She realized then that she was wearing a dress like Suri's, though hers was indigo blue. There was a violet-and-black leopard-print fake fur jacket on the ground, which she'd been using as a pillow.

"Better take that," Suri said, pointing to it. "Paris can be chilly this time of year."

"Paris?" Sophie asked, pulling it on, and wondering what good jackets would do when both of them still had bare legs and feet. Suri only smiled, linked her arm through Sophie's and started walking. To Sophie's relief, they headed away from the tree and the statue of the bat-winged angel. She didn't think she could bear to look at that bizarre grave after the way the last cemetery dream had ended.

As she walked, she realized that it was the first time she'd covered any ground in the cemetery. She'd had no idea it was so vast. Graves stretched to the horizon in every direction, marked by headstones and statues and mausoleums – or so it seemed, in

Sophie's peripheral vision. When she tried to look directly at any of them, the image warped and blurred, until she couldn't tell quite what she was seeing, let alone how far away it might be.

Sometimes the sky on the horizon seemed dark, sometimes light, but never the clear, cloudless blue of the sky directly over their heads. Likewise, the landscape seemed to undulate, forming hills and valleys that were continually in motion, like waves on the sea. At times she even thought she saw figures moving among the stones. All of them disappeared when she tried to look directly at them.

"Don't," Suri said, putting a finger under Sophie's chin to turn her head back to the path in front of them. "You'll give yourself motion sickness. Besides, we're almost there."

"Are we?" Sophie asked. "This doesn't look like Paris…"

Suri lifted her sunglasses and peered around at the green grass and grey stones. "It doesn't, does it? Okay: close your eyes, click your heels together three times and say – "

"You cannot be serious!" Sophie interrupted.

"No," Suri laughed, "I really can't, can I? I think it's why I got the job."

"What job?"

"Never mind. Okay, how's this?"

She swirled a black-nailed finger in the air, and just like that, the cemetery was gone. They were standing on a littered pavement under a moody, windy, evening sky. The pavement ran along the edge of a wide street lined with antiques shops.

Though their doors were open, their wares spilling out onto the pavements, there wasn't another soul to be seen.

Nevertheless, Suri grinned. "That's more like it," she said. "Gay Paris!" She twirled on one bare foot, graceful as a ballerina, and Sophie sighed, wondering what it said about her that her dream companion was so clearly unhinged.

"*Allons!*" Suri said cheerily, and pulled Sophie along the road. They walked for a few minutes, Suri stopping now and then to look into an alley or a shop window, until she said, "Here it is," and turned down a dingy little side street. They passed a couple of padlocked doors covered in graffiti, and finally arrived at what looked like a warehouse's loading dock. Again, it was deserted, but as they stepped through its open door, Sophie saw that the warehouse itself was full of paintings. Some of them were hanging, but most just leaned against the walls, sometimes three or four deep, as if the curator had stepped out in the midst of arranging an exhibition.

"Have a good look around," Suri said, picking up a magazine from a lawn chair by the door and settling herself in it. "Take your time. I'll be right here."

"Don't you want to see the pictures?" Sophie asked.

"Nah. I've seen them before." And she buried herself in the magazine, which appeared to be printed in Arabic.

Curiouser and curiouser, Sophie thought, and moved to the first painting. It was done in a style that was vaguely Arts and Crafts, and felt familiar. Maybe, she thought, because it was a picture of Lucas. He was asleep beneath the tree in the cemetery, wrapped in a set of crimson wings. Looking at it made her wistful – nostalgic, she'd have said, if it had made any sense.

She moved to the next one, a huge canvas in moody blues and violets. It was Lucas again, standing chest-deep in water, sinewy arms outstretched and hovering just above the water's surface, like wings. The tattoo on his back wasn't black, but iridescent blue – a blue, in fact, very like the color of the inside of a mussel shell. She reached out and touched it, and was somehow surprised and disappointed to feel nothing but dry paint and canvas. She moved on to the next picture, in which Lucas was riding a grey, winged horse across a starry cobalt sky. And so on, every single painting a painting of him, in scenes that weren't quite familiar, and yet provoked no surprise. Not until the last.

It was different from the others, more formal in its composition, with many figures instead of just one. The biggest difference, though, was that its subject was Sophie. She sat on a grassy hill, dressed in a cornflower robe that looped and swirled down the dark slope. The hill was surrounded by a host of kneeling angels, with brightly colored coats and gold-washed newspaper wings. A string of words was written in a golden arc, like a halo over her head: "Her place in the midst of the angels."

A wave of dizziness passed over her. She rocked forward, and her knees buckled. She sank to the floor, and so she saw something she otherwise wouldn't have. At the bottom corner of the canvas, where an artist might put a signature, there was a symbol. It was like the symbol on Lucas's back, but also

211

different: more rounded than linear, more intricate. Though she had no idea where, or what it might mean, she knew that she'd seen it before.

Sophie stood up shakily, and made her way back along the row of paintings. Every single one of them was signed with that symbol. As she stood in front of the one with the apple tree, Suri appeared at her shoulder. She pushed her sunglasses down her nose, studying the painting over them.

"They're good, aren't they?" she said. "That's real talent, not just smoke and mirrors," she added, touching Lucas's sleeping face. "Or maybe it's love."

"Love?" Sophie asked.

Suri put a finger to her black lips. "Who said 'love'?"

"You did!"

"I did, didn't I…"

Sophie turned her back on the painting – on all of the paintings – and faced her. "Suri," she said wearily, "what the hell is going on?"

"Honey, there are only so many times I can tell you that I'm – "

"Bound," Sophie said tiredly. "Yes, I know. But you can't be bound *that* tightly, if I keep showing up here and you keep showing me…well…what, exactly? Why the paintings, and the visions, and that creepy bloody armor under the statue in the graveyard? Never mind the tree, and that psychedelic apple you made me eat…"

Suri scrutinized her for a long moment. "Clearly," she said at last, "you need an espresso and an éclair."

"Oh, good lord!" Sophie cried, twisting her hair into two bunches and pulling on them in frustration. "I don't *want* coffee or cakes, and I don't want any more cryptic half-answers. All I want is for someone to tell me who Lucas is to me, and why it seems like the whole world's gone insane since I met him!"

Suri wasn't smiling any longer. Her black eyes even seemed vaguely sympathetic. She reached out a hand and laid it on Sophie's shoulder. "That's what I'm trying to do. But I have to follow the rules."

"Whose rules?" Sophie asked, knowing that she wasn't going to like the answer.

"Yours." Suri studied her with kohl-rimmed eyes. "Look, I *really* think you need that coffee."

"Oh, what the hell," Sophie grumbled.

Suri smiled faintly and handed her a black umbrella that she was certain hadn't been there a moment before. Sophie glanced outside, and sure enough, it was raining. They stepped out onto the wet, dark street. The doors that had been closed when they first walked down it were open now, with light and music and the sound of conversation spilling out of them. Suri passed each of them by without a second glance, although many of them appeared to Sophie to be just the kind of place where one might find coffee and cake on a wet Paris evening.

And then Suri stopped short. They were standing in front of a shop whose front window was steamed up. The people behind it were indistinct blotches of color. She leaned toward the doorway and looked inside, and then, abruptly, she stepped away.

"Time to run," she said, and grabbed Sophie's hand, pulling her away from the window and back the way they'd come.

But they'd only made it a few steps before somebody called, "Suriel? And Sophia! What a lovely surprise!"

Sophie knew that voice. "Michael?" she said, turning around, although Suri still tugged at her hand. "What are you doing here? And how do you know Suri? And what are you *wearing?*" His tweeds had been replaced by a black polo-neck and beret and tiny Trotsky glasses, his whisky glass by a brandy snifter, the amber liquid glowing softly in the light from the windows.

Michael smiled. "Come inside, we'll have a chat, and a drink. It's on me."

"Okay," Sophie said, just as Suri said, "No, thank you," her voice chilly.

"It's only a drink, love," Michael said to her, with a beatific smile.

"It's never only a drink," Suri muttered, but when Sophie followed Michael inside, she followed Sophie.

"Here we are," Michael said, and sat down at a table by the window. Sophie and Suri did the same. Two more brandy snifters sat on the table, apparently waiting for them. Sophie only looked at hers – the smell of brandy alone made her feel sick. Suri downed both glasses in quick succession, glaring at Michael over the rims as she did so.

"Ah, Suriel," he said, scrutinizing her in return. "A riddle wrapped in a mystery inside an enigma…" He turned to Sophie. "Which one of you said that, again?"

"Winston Churchill," Sophie told him automatically. Then, considering the question, "One of who?"

Michael only smiled, and said, "Coffee?"

"I'd say it will keep me up all night, but I suppose that's not really possible, when it's dream coffee…"

"Anything is possible, Sophia," he said. "You're living, breathing proof of that."

Sophie felt like screaming. She had to remind herself that Michael had never been anything but kind to her, and her frustration wasn't really directed at him. Taking a deep breath, she said, "Are you going to tell me what you mean by that? Or have you taken the same vow of silence as everyone else around here?" She looked pointedly at Suri, but Suri was still glaring at Michael.

"Yeah," she said, the challenge clear in her black eyes, "are you going to tell her what you mean by that?"

Michael sighed. "There are…limitations, to what I can tell you," he said to Sophie, and then, to Suri, "just as there are for you, Suriel. But Sophia," he continued as Sophie dropped her head into her hands, "you don't need any of us to tell you the answers to your questions. You know them already."

"That's what she says, too," Sophie grumbled, pointing at

Suri. "But hard as I try, I just can't remember. I don't even know which questions I'm meant to be answering!"

Michael tilted his head to one side. "Have you considered the possibility that you aren't meant to be answering anything?"

Sophie looked up at him. "Are you serious? You really think I can just pretend that my life hasn't gone completely mental since I moved to Ardnasheen?"

Suri smirked, but Michael looked deadly serious – and oddly hopeful – as he said, "You always were an over-achiever, and everyone needs a break…"

Sophie shook her head wearily. "Sorry, Michael. There is no way I can pretend there isn't something going on."

Now Michael looked deflated, and Suri triumphant, though the triumph turned quickly to confusion when Michael said, "Well, if that's the case, then maybe what you need is a good old slap up the face."

"What?" both girls said at once.

"A clear-eyed, floodlit look at the unembellished truth."

"Ah…and how do I achieve that, exactly?" Sophie asked. "Because I doubt you're planning to just tell me."

Michael smiled sadly, shook his head. "You're right – I'm not. But don't look so crestfallen. There are endless other ways and means. Perhaps a walk might clear your head?"

"Michael…" Suri said, her tone warning.

"In Ardnasheen," Sophie told him, "you're as likely to lose your head on a walk as clear it."

"You needn't go far. Only a few steps – "

"Michael!" Suri snapped, looking daggers at him.

Michael patted her hand, which she immediately snatched away. "You don't even need to leave the grounds at Madainneag to find what you're looking for."

"Really?" Sophie asked, ignoring Suri's deadly look.

"You'll see." Michael knocked off his brandy and said, "Suri: a word." Before she could reply, he snapped his fingers, and Sophie woke up.

Chapter 19

The fire had died and the room was cold, but Sophie's head was still so full of the dream that she barely noticed. A faint light showed through the crack in the curtains. She reached for the bedside clock: it was a quarter past six. She had the breakfast shift, so there wasn't much point in going back to sleep, even if she'd been able.

Disentangling herself from the quilt, she went to the bathroom to brush her teeth and wash her face. Then she pulled on her clothes and picked up her walking boots. She was heading for the door when a thought struck her, and she turned back. There was a small set of fire irons on the hearth. She picked up the poker, looked at it for a moment, and then put it under her arm. Dream-Michael had seemed to suggest that a walk in Madainneag's grounds wouldn't be dangerous, but she had no intention of running into another one of Lucas's *sith* unarmed.

The sky, for once, was clear, but a north wind was blowing, and the puddles on the road were slicked with ice. Sophie stood for a moment looking out over the water, trying to decide where to go. She'd already covered most of what counted for "grounds" at Madainneag, and there'd been little enough to see the first time. She turned and looked at the yard to the right of the house. The empty washing line was bending and snapping in the wind. It reminded her of the day she'd helped Ailsa take in her laundry, after meeting Sam. All at once, she knew where she was going.

Ailsa hadn't given her any specific directions to the Belial burial plot, but as Sophie circled behind the house and onto a little path leading into the trees, the tingle in her spine told her that she was on the right track. The path was narrow, the bordering trees and bracken brushing against her like cold, wet fingers as she pushed her way through them. She walked for a few more minutes as the deciduous trees gave way to densely packed firs, and the pearly blue morning turned to twilight.

There's nothing here, she told herself firmly, trying not to think of Revenants, or to wonder whether fear constituted enough belief to make a monster materialize. Right on the heels of the thought, she saw something. Up ahead there was a break in the trees, and beyond it, what looked like a clearing. Within it, she could see a pale figure. Holding the poker in both hands, Sophie crept forward, keeping behind the larger trees, waiting for whatever it was to sense her and turn. But it remained absolutely still.

That was when she remembered Ailsa saying something about a statue. Feeling bolder, Sophie straightened and picked up her pace. A few moments later, she arrived at an ornate, turreted gateway in an old stone wall. The gate had once held a door of wrought-iron bars, which lay rusting now in the long grass by the wall, twisted and burst as if a giant fist had punched through it, tearing it from its hinges in the process.

Sophie stepped warily through the empty gateway. The cemetery wasn't very big: she counted perhaps a dozen stones leaning in the long grass, obscured by moss and elements until their inscriptions were unreadable. There was also a tiny chapel, its windows empty, its roof long since caved in, with an ancient yew tree sprawling over its crumbling walls. Normally it was the kind of thing that would have intrigued her, but now she barely glanced at it. Because the only thing in that forsaken place that mattered was the statue at its center: a life-sized statue of an angel, with a bat's boned wings and a head bowed in shame.

Later on, Sophie would realize that that was the moment when she knew. At the time, though, her mind simply went blank. She couldn't think past the necessity of looking into the statue's face. She felt nothing but a deep, cold trepidation as she put one foot mechanically in front of the other. And then there were no more steps to take. She looked up. Lucas's beautiful, tortured face looked back.

She knew that her world should be crumbling, but she felt nothing. Maybe, she thought vaguely, because she had known the truth all along. Maybe because, as Suri kept telling her, she remembered it.

She stood staring at the stone face for several long, numb moments before something drew her eyes down. It was a detail

220

the dream statue had lacked: a carved chain curled around the angel's feet and the rock on which he perched, running up to his wrists, connecting to the tight cuffs that circled them. Beneath the chain there were words, chipped roughly, almost violently into the otherwise carefully-cut stone. Sophie read: "On the earth He will bind you, as long as the world endures."

With that, finally, reality caught up with Sophie. She dropped the fire iron and passed trembling hands over her eyes, as if to block it all out, but the truth was still there in the darkness, bright and unavoidable. And when she opened her eyes Lucas was there too, a few yards away, watching her. His eyes were hooded and sad, but not surprised, and the sadness itself was timeless, magisterial. In that moment Sophie wondered how she could ever have thought that he was just an ordinary young man.

"Is it true?" she said in a tremulous voice. "That you're a... you're..." She choked on the word, but Lucas didn't help her, didn't fill it in. She knew that he was waiting for her to say it, to accept it. "An angel?" she grated out.

He paused for a moment, letting the word settle, and then he said, "I was, once. Now...it's complicated."

Sophie wrapped her arms around herself. "And me?" she asked. "What am I?"

"You are my one true love."

He said it simply, but at the same time, as if his entire world turned on those words. Sophie wanted to hold onto the sweetness of them, to forget the horror and the host of tormented questions they raised, but she couldn't. "So once I was...like you?"

Lucas smiled sadly, shaking his head. "You were never like me, Sophie. You were far, far better, and I ruined you. I ruined us both." His hands closed into fists by his side, mirroring the stone angel. "I was never meant to see you again."

"Then why am I here?"

"I don't know."

"Is that why you were angry at me?"

He shook his head. "I thought you were a trick. I thought they were doing it to torment me." He looked at the statue with loathing.

"So there was never another girl."

"Sophie, there's only ever been you." He looked back at her, his eyes pleading. "I'll try to explain," he said, "if you want me to. If I haven't lost you already."

She looked at him for a long moment. Though her mind told her to run, her heart wouldn't let her. Slowly, she nodded. And when he reached out his hand to her, she took it.

*

"Here," Lucas said, handing Sophie a cup of coffee. She didn't know whether to be touched or terrified that it was exactly what she would have chosen, had he asked: no sugar, a splash of milk.

"Thank you," she said, sipping it. Even the temperature was perfect. She felt dreamy, detached – shock again, no doubt.

"I phoned Ruadhri," Lucas said, pouring more coffee for himself. "He thinks you're in bed with a migraine."

"You know I get migraines?"

"Will it freak you out if I say yes?"

"Right," Sophie said, wondering what else he knew about her. Wondering whether she really wanted to know. She looked out of the picture window that framed the sea. Light and shadow ran across the water like expressions on a sleeping face.

"Why all the sneaking around?" she asked, turning back to him abruptly. "Why didn't you just tell me?"

"I couldn't." The look on his face brought her back to reality. He seemed to be waiting for her to castigate him, anticipating rejection.

"Lucas," she said, "I see Revenants and water horses. 'Your new man's an angel' is hardly even news in my world."

He smiled wryly. "I suppose it isn't, but that's not what I meant. I literally *couldn't*. When we live among humans, we're bound to silence about what we are. Though if a human manages to work it out, well, since we can't lie…" he shrugged.

"We?" she said. "There are others?" He nodded, and a jumble of clues dropped into place at once. "Michael?"

"Yes. But he's only here temporarily."

Sophie left that cryptic comment for the moment. "Sam?"

Lucas's face darkened. "Unfortunately."

"But not me."

"No. You're human."

Sophie considered her next question carefully. She knew

223

that she needed to ask it, but she dreaded the answer. "Then how can I remember the things I remember? Why do I feel like we've been together before?" A sudden, terrible thought struck her. "Unless…all those pictures you have…you're not going to tell me I'm some kind of reincarnation, are you?"

To her surprise, Lucas laughed, though it was humorless. "Sorry – it's just, there's no such thing. Every body is unique to its soul. I bought those pictures because they reminded me of you – that's all."

Sophie let out a sigh of relief she hadn't realized she was holding in. "But I still don't see how it's possible. I mean, that we were…" she waved her hand, casting about for the right words.

"It's possible because you weren't human, then."

"But I thought I wasn't an angel."

"You weren't. You were an aeon."

"A what?"

"It's one step up from an angel."

"I thought that one step up from an angel was God."

"That's because everything you think you know about angels is a product of millennia of suppression, misinformation, and overactive human imaginations."

"Like the wings and haloes."

"Exactly."

"What about harps?" she asked.

He half-smiled. "It's true we're a musical lot, but as a general rule, harps went out in the seventeenth century."

"Bows and arrows?"

"Not since the Mongols – and even then, we preferred close combat. Swords, knives, bare hands if it came to it."

"Okay," she said, "you'd better start at the beginning."

"Right, well then…have you ever read the Bible?" Sophie rolled her eyes. "Good. That's where most of the misinformation comes from. Any Gnostic philosophy?"

"I don't even know what that is."

"Dante?" She shook her head. "Milton?"

"I did an essay on *Paradise Lost* last year…. Wait – are you saying you're a *fallen* angel? Like those ones who fought God with Satan and got sent to hell?" And then, remembering the statue's bat wings, "Oh, my God – are you the *devil?*"

Lucas gave a weary laugh, rubbing his eyes. "Renaissance literature certainly has a lot to answer for. Look, do you promise to hear me out before you judge?"

"I suppose so," Sophie said warily.

"Alright then." His dark eyes looked steadily into hers. He took a deep breath, then said, "Once upon a time, I was an angel called Lucifer. Wait – " he held up a finger as Sophie opened her mouth, "you promised to listen." Reluctantly, she shut it again. "And yes," Lucas continued, "I fell. More accurately, I was thrown out."

"Exiled," Sophie said softly, thinking of poor, dead Niall Aiken.

"Yes, I suppose so. I fought Michael once, but I never fought the Keeper – "

"The Keeper?"

"Of the Balance. What you would call God. You *can't* fight the Keeper, 'devil' is only a figure of speech, and Hell is entirely subjective. Although there are demons, and arch demons – they're called daevas – and an underworld, called the Deep, which are a different matter entirely…" He paused, looked at her. "Should I slow down?"

"Maybe you should start at the beginning."

"Right, then: to understand what happened, you have to understand that first and foremost, all angels are soldiers."

"Oh. What do they fight?"

"Anything that threatens humans."

"Really?"

He nodded. "Angels were created to serve humans. All of them can fight, but they have different duties, too – they're everything from messengers to ministers to guardians. The order I belonged to was called the Watchers."

"What did you watch?"

"Everything. We were the highest order of angels: the eyes and ears of the Keeper. The arms and legs and voice, too, when we were on earth."

"Right…you know God," Sophie said, wondering whether her life could possibly become more surreal.

"Actually, I don't," he answered. "The Keeper is unknowable, at least to an angel. We got its orders, its missions, the odd revelation, but they always came via Logos."

"Who?"

"Another one of the aeons. He was the Keeper's go-between with the angels. Anyway, all of the angels you'll have heard of are Watchers – Gabriel, Raphael, Michael, and so on – because we were the only ones allowed to take human form on earth. But there were a lot of regulations that went along with that privilege. For instance, we couldn't interfere in the evolution of human civilization. We couldn't teach the secrets of Heaven. And we couldn't ever tell a human being what we were."

"Let me guess: you messed up."

He sighed. "No – Azazel messed up."

"Is he a Watcher?"

"Was."

"I haven't heard of him."

"He's gone by a number of other names," Lucas said bitterly. "Like Samael. And Iblis."

"Samael? Iblis?" she asked incredulously. "As in Sam Eblis?"

Lucas smiled faintly. "Yes, but that's jumping ahead. Back when we were Watchers, he was Azazel, and he was the favorite – the best of us in many ways. But he was arrogant, too. He thought that his privileges were no more than his due, and it wasn't a great leap from there to discontent. The longer he spent among humans, the more he began to resent things that they had, and he didn't."

"Like what?"

"Like wives. There are male and female angels, but we never form couples."

227

"Why not?"

"I don't know – it's just the way it is. Or the way it was supposed to be. But Azazel didn't like it. He became obsessed with human women, and many of the other Watchers went along with him. They realized how easy it would be to seduce humans, and convinced themselves that it was their right, as superior beings."

"That's revolting," said Sophie.

"I agree. So did the other angels. But at first, they seemed to have got away with it. They took wives and husbands, had children, and the Keeper did nothing to stop them. The children grew into monsters, made up of the worst of their two races, who caused humans endless suffering. Still, the Keeper was silent. But then Azazel's band taught their mates our secrets. Astrology, the reading of signs and symbols, sorcery – "

"Sorcery?" Sophie scoffed.

"Would you like me to make you another *Each Uisge* to prove it?"

Sophie shuddered. "Right. Go on."

"It was Azazel who revealed the darkest secrets of all: deception and war. Everything that's wrong with the world today comes from that betrayal, though at the time, the Keeper tried to fix it."

Thinking back to her conversation with Sam in the car, Sophie asked, "How did he – it – the Keeper, find out what Azazel had done?"

Lucas sighed. "We told him. Or more to the point, we told Aletheia – the aeon who was sent to question us."

"Sam blames you for what happened to him."

Lucas nodded. "I'm aware of that. And it's true, I was the first to answer Aletheia when she asked what had happened. But I was by no means the only one who corroborated the story, and the others would have told the truth with or without me. At any rate, it ended with Azazel and his followers banned from Heaven. Their armour was taken, and they were bound in the wastelands their children had made of the earth, in human form, until Judgment Day."

"Angels have armour?" Sophie asked, thinking of the grave she'd exhumed in the dream.

Lucas nodded. "An angel's armour is a bit like a human's soul: it protects us not just physically, but spiritually. And it's what keeps us whole when we move from a spiritual existence to a physical one."

"Whole, as opposed to…?"

"Have you ever dropped a mirror?"

"Right." Sophie said, feeling slightly nauseous. "So how come Azazel is still all in one piece?"

Lucas sighed. "It's a dispensation – a part of our damnation. We hold together as long as we keep to the bounds…"

"What bounds?"

"It's complicated. And not especially interesting. But their physical manifestation is these." He held up his hands so that his sleeves slipped back, showing the silver cuffs.

"So they're tracking devices, like those things they put on prisoners?"

"More or less."

Sophie considered this for a moment, then asked, "So is a fallen angel mortal?"

"No. But we aren't immortal, either. Eternal is a better word. We won't die of old age, but we can still die."

"How?"

"A number of ways. But usually by one of the Sacred Weapons."

"What are they?"

"Usually they're swords, knives and polearms, but there's the occasional throwing star or lasso or whatever. It doesn't matter, as long as they were made by a deity. Obviously, they're few and far between."

"That's…comforting." Sophie shook her head. "So anyhow, you were saying that the dodgy Watchers were exiled. What about the humans? Were they punished too?"

Lucas smiled humorlessly. "You could say so. They and every other living thing on earth were destroyed by a flood. All except for one family the Keeper considered worthy, and a few lucky animals."

"Noah's bloody ark was *real*?"

"More or less. Of course, the plan didn't really work. Humans had been corrupted, and as it turns out, that can never be undone. Plus, there were still all of those fallen angels on earth. They weren't as powerful as they once were, but they

230

were still a whole lot more powerful than humans, with a lot of time to run riot before Judgment Day."

Sophie's mind went back to the statue in the graveyard, the copy of the one in the dream cemetery. Understanding hit her with a sickening blow. "You were one of them," she said, her voice shaking. "The angels who took human women. Clara Belial...and whoever was before her...was I meant to be the next?"

"No!" he said sharply. "You've misunderstood. I wasn't exiled with Azazel. I only told you about that to give you a context for what happened to us."

"Okay," Sophie said, her voice still unsteady, "so what happened to us?"

"We fell in love," he said.

You will not blush! Sophie told herself, even as she felt the blood creeping up her neck. "But I thought that angels didn't...I mean, aside from the ones that fell..."

"They don't," Lucas said grimly. "All of those beautiful humans the others fell for, they never swayed me. But you, Sophie..." he shook his head. "The moment I set eyes on you, everything changed."

"You mean you didn't always know me?"

"Up until the flood, angels and aeons didn't have much contact. The aeons had always lived in the Garden – the place in between Heaven and the Keeper. The angels lived in Heaven, between the Garden and earth. The only aeon we ever saw was

Logos, when he came to deliver orders, and Aletheia the time she came to question us."

"So that changed after the flood?"

"No, not really."

"You're losing me."

Lucas studied her for a moment, and Sophie wished that she could read his thoughts. Finally, he said, "Do you know what your name means, Sophie?"

"It comes from the ancient Greek word *sophos,* meaning 'wise'." He raised his eyebrows, and she smiled sheepishly. "Mum's into that kind of thing. It's why she picked the name."

"Well, that's what you were: Sophia, the spirit of wisdom. After the flood, the Keeper sent you to earth. It thought that you would help humanity back onto the right path; guide them toward the best in their nature. But it didn't work. The damage had been done, and corruption came back, slowly but surely, until finally, the Keeper called you back.

"But you'd come to love the humans, despite their flaws. You saw yourself as their protector, and you couldn't bear to give up on them. You couldn't defy the Keeper's order to leave earth. But you weren't too happy about it, and I guess it wasn't so specific, because instead of returning to the Garden, you stayed in Heaven with the angels."

"Her place in the midst of the angels..." Sophie murmured.

Lucas looked startled. "Why did you say that?"

"It's something I dreamed. It was in a painting."

"A painting?" he said, his eyes suddenly intense. "What did it look like?"

Sophie shrugged. "Just like that: me, in a blue dress, sitting on a hill with a whole lot of angels kneeling around it. And just for the record, they had wings."

"That's not possible," he muttered, "I watched them burn."

"The wings?"

"The paintings."

"Why did they burn?"

His eyes flickered away, and there was anger in the set of his mouth when he answered, "Because you painted them."

"I don't paint."

"You did then. I don't think there was much of anything you couldn't do…" After a pause, he asked, "What else do you dream about?"

"All kinds of things. But there's always a girl there – Suri." There was a flicker of recognition on his face – and, strangely, of hope. "Who is she, Lucas?"

"Suriel, the angel of death. Also your best friend."

"That actually makes a messed-up kind of sense," Sophie said wearily, filing the information away with a growing list of Things to Consider Later, "but back to you meeting me in Heaven…"

Lucas shook his head, as if trying to clear it. "Right…well… those words on your painting, they're from the *Book of Enoch*. 'Wisdom returned to her place, and seated herself in the midst of the angels.' And that's what happened. You came to us, and

233

you were so good, so pure and beautiful…" He sighed. "Maybe I was always more like Azazel than I realized. All I know is that I couldn't help it."

Sophie gazed at him. His face was radiant even in its sadness. She thought of his arms around her as they danced. She thought of him wrapped in red wings, and with arms outstretched across dark water, and felt the heat rising to her cheeks.

"What couldn't you help, Lucas?" she asked.

Now it was Lucas who colored, his eyes that shifted away. "Exactly what you think."

With a boldness that didn't seem to belong to her, Sophie reached out and touched his cheek. Lucas sighed and shut his eyes. His skin was smooth as marble, but warm, alive. By now she knew to expect the charge that went through her, but not the images that filled her mind. She saw Lucas in a dark cloak, handing over a fistful of coins to a wild-haired man who gave him a chalk drawing of a girl's face. She saw him lighting candles in a darkened chapel, beneath a mosaic of a winged woman, and again in a vast marble room, sitting at a table covered in scrolls and tablets, looking through one after the next and discarding every one.

"You were exiled," she said, letting her hand drop.

Lucas caught it, held it. "Yes. After I fought for you, and lost."

"But I wasn't."

"No."

"Why were you punished, and not me?"

Love and guilt battled on Lucas's face, like the light and shadow on the sea loch. "But you *were* punished, Sophie," he said. "It was your punishment to see me stripped of my armour and cast out of Heaven, and to know that you couldn't follow. You were bound in Heaven on that day just as I was bound on earth, to live an eternity apart."

"Then what am I doing here, as a human girl?"

"I have no idea," he answered. He looked at her, his eyes suddenly uncertain. "But the real question is whether or not you want to know the answer. Because you know, Sophie, you can still walk away."

"Why would I want to walk away?"

"You're human now."

"Yes – and you must be the reason why."

He shrugged. "That may be. But it doesn't matter. Whatever reason you came for, now you're here, and you could have a simple, ordinary life. Put all of this behind you. I've caused you so much pain already, I don't want to be the cause of more."

"That isn't your decision."

"You're right," he said, his eyes direct. "It's yours. And I want you to think about it, to know what it would really mean to involve yourself with me again, before you make it."

"How am I meant to do that, when I hardly remember being with you the first time around?"

In response, Lucas got up, opened a cupboard and brought something out. He handed it to Sophie. It was a small, glass bottle

235

full of violet liquid. There was a label on it in antiquated script, reading, "Veritas. Dilute before use in non-reactive cauldron."

"What is this?" Sophie asked, wondering where one might come by a non-reactive cauldron in Ardnasheen.

"I don't know," Lucas answered. "Suri gave it to me two hundred years ago. She said if I ever saw you, to give it to you. I thought she'd been eating those apples again, but I guess she knew something I didn't."

Sophie sighed. "A riddle wrapped in a mystery inside an enigma."

"What?"

"Never mind. Okay then…I guess I'd better go find a cauldron."

"Take as long as you need," Lucas said. "I'll be here."

CHAPTER 20

The kitchen cupboards failed to produce anything that Sophie could be certain was non-reactive, so in the end she put the rubber plug in the kitchen sink and filled it with water. It was a large, rectangular Belfast sink, and Sophie had no idea whether it held more or less water than the average cauldron. In the end, though, she figured that if Suri hadn't bothered to be more specific, then it couldn't be that important.

She sat down cross-legged on the worktop beside the sink, and then she broke the seal on the bottle. The scent that came from it was nothing like the colour suggested: it was fresh and sharp, like pine and mint and spring leaves and wind over water. As she breathed it in, the room around her took on a shimmering clarity. Then she tipped the contents of the bottle into the water, where it swirled for a moment and then dispersed.

For a moment, nothing happened. Then a dark point appeared in the center of the basin, like a drop of ink, except that it widened gradually until it engulfed the surface of the water.

For a few moments it remained an opaque black. Then, like a screen flickering to life, it filled with an image.

The picture was familiar, but it took Sophie a moment to place it as the hill in the dream painting on which she'd sat, surrounded by kneeling angels. There was no kneeling host in this image, no one on top of the grassy mound. As she watched, though, the focus drew inward until she could see a figure at the base of the hill. A dark-haired girl in a silvery-blue dress, staring at the ground in front of her.

The focus drew in again, and now she could see that the girl's face was hers, although it also looked different. There was a luminosity to it like she saw sometimes in Lucas or Sam, and a subtle sense of perfection, as if nothing about her could possibly be out of place. Every fold of her silky dress, every strand of hair lay as if it had been set there by a careful hand. She saw also that the girl wasn't staring at the ground, but weeping, her tears rolling down her face and into the long grass.

There was a movement at the edge of the picture. Lucas appeared on the crest of the hill. He wore a deep red garment over dark trousers, a kind of tunic that also reminded her of a priest's robes. He didn't approach the girl by the pool, only lowered himself to the ground and sat watching her, his expression one of pity. After a few moments, the girl turned and looked at him. Their eyes met. Neither of them said anything; neither of them moved.

The picture blurred, then shifted. When it cleared again the girl was still sitting at the foot of the hill, but this time Lucas was sitting with her, a book open on his lap. Though she couldn't hear anything, Sophie could see that he was reading aloud from it. The aeon-Sophie wasn't looking at him, but she wasn't crying, either. She looked up at the horizon, her expression one of speculation.

The picture changed again. The pool and the hill were gone. Instead, the girl stood in what had once been a formal garden, but had been left untended for a long time. Flowers ran wild, roses clambering over the ragged yew hedges, stonework covered with lichen and cracks. The dress she wore now was simple, vaguely medieval in its cut, but the colour was a clear, vibrant blue. She turned, her face brightening as if someone had called to her; someone she was overjoyed to see.

Lucas stood by a door in the hedge, holding out a hand to her. She ran to him and took it, and he led her through the opening. On the other side of the door was a sea of blue, the same color as her dress. It took a moment for Sophie to see that it was made entirely of tiny blue flowers – forget-me-nots, carpeting the ground as far as she could see. Aeon-Sophie turned then, flung herself into Lucas's arms, and he caught her. They kissed like people who belong entirely to each other.

The image shifted again, and this time there was no bright garden, only rain and greyish grass beneath a cloud-ridden sky. Two figures – one in red and one in gold – fought with swords as a group of others stood watching. She recognized Suri's silvery ropes of hair, but it took her a moment longer to realize that the weeping figure Suri held in her arms was herself. The swords clashed in showers of sparks, the fighting angels skipped and whirled as if they danced a brutal ballet. And then the one in the gold tunic brought his sword down in a blow that snapped the other's sword in two.

For a moment, no one moved. And then Lucas knelt, his face bitter and defeated as he looked up at the winner. His golden tunic and long, copper-colored hair whipped like flags in the rising wind. Lucas bent his head, and the other angel raised his sword, burning now with fiery light, as aeon-Sophie broke from the knot of onlookers and flung herself toward them.

All at once, Sophie wasn't watching the scene, she was remembering it. She felt the agony of realization tearing through her, the ferocious lash of the love she was about to lose. *Take me – spare him!* The fiery angel looked at her with pitiless green eyes as she clung to Lucas. But Lucas peeled her arms back, pinned them to her sides as she fought, then pushed her into Suri's arms, which closed around her like a vice. *I love you. I'll always love you.*

The fiery angel reached again with his sword, but rather than Lucas, he slashed at the ground. A rent opened where the blade passed. Lucas looked into it for a long moment, and then he dove into the darkness.

Sophie didn't know whether she actually screamed, or simply remembered it, but she knew that she couldn't bear to watch another moment. She plunged her hand into the water and swirled it, scrambling the colours like paints on a palette until the images were gone. Then she pulled the plug and slid off the counter, shaking so hard she could barely stand. That last, awful image of Lucas, doomed, wouldn't leave her. She thought of the grave with its rusted armour, and the anguish she hadn't understood until now. She thought of herself wondering, on the brink of sleep, whether she was falling in love with Lucas.

Now it seemed absurd to her that there had ever been a question. She loved him, as she always had and always would. Her memories of that other time might still be a jumbled mess, but he was here, the still-point of her spinning world. It was like a settling, a joining of two pieces of herself she'd never known were separate. It seemed impossible that he was still in his tower, alone, wondering…

And then she was running, twisting through the corridors as if she'd known them all her life. She plunged outside, forgetting that her feet were bare, and then back in by the tower door. At the top of the stairs she stopped, breathless. Lucas sat on the sofa, putting a new string on his violin. She must have looked as wild as she felt, because his look, when he turned to her, was one of dismay.

He put the instrument aside, stood up. "Sophie? Are you alright?"

"No!" she cried. "I don't want to walk away! I don't want to be away from you, ever again!" The look he gave her then was one she knew she'd remember until the day she died. Then, somehow, the distance between them was gone, and his arms were around her, and it felt to her like coming home. His lips touched hers; she'd never tasted anything sweeter. He kissed her gently at first, and then, when she returned it, more insistently. She felt his lips under her chin, in the hollow of her throat, like the memory of the dream but a thousand times more potent.

Desire crashed inside of her. She clung to him and he lifted her as easily as if she were a child, brought her to the couch, still kissing her. She ran her hands up the smooth skin of his back, where his shirt had rucked up, and he moaned, his lips travelling down her breastbone. But when he reached the top button of her shirt, he pulled back, gasping.

"Don't – don't stop!" she said.

"Sophie," he ran a hand across his face, "we can't do this."

"Why?" she asked, her voice tremulous with the beginnings of hurt. "Did I do something wrong?"

"No!" he said, smoothing her hair back, and kissing her again, gently, on her swollen lips. "Nothing's ever seemed so right." He took a shuddering breath, and then sighed, releasing it. "But that was true the last time, too, and look what happened. I can't lose you again."

"Why would you lose me?" she asked, winding her fingers in his hair.

"Because…because this doesn't just happen. Aeons turning to humans…you finding me, against all odds, in the middle of nowhere. There must be a reason. Something's happening…"

"Well then, we'll find out what it is, and sort it out," she said. And then, pulling him against her again with a boldness that surprised her, "But for the moment, that can wait."

*

When Sophie opened her eyes, the windows were dark. At first she didn't know where she was. She sat up blearily, looking around her, and then she saw Lucas standing over one of the kitchen work tops, his back to her. The whole strange day came rushing back, and with it a surge of the love she'd carried with her out of Suri's vision. She shed the blanket Lucas must have put over her, and walked over to him. She doubted he could have heard her in her stocking feet, but when she put a hand on his shoulder he didn't seem surprised. He turned to her with a smile.

"You're awake," he said, leaning down to kiss her.

Several minutes passed before she surfaced to answer, "You shouldn't have let me fall asleep."

He smiled. "You're lovely when you sleep. Of course, you're also lovely when you're awake."

"What are you doing?" she asked, looking down at the cutting board where he'd been working. It was covered in neat stripes of chopped vegetables. Next to it was a glass of something amber-colored.

"Cooking," he said.

"You're very tidy about it."

He shrugged. "An acquired skill. It helps pass the time."

"How long has it been?" Sophie asked. "That you've been… down here."

"I don't know. I stopped counting a long time ago. There didn't seem much point."

Sophie considered this. "How do you stand it? Being stuck here, I mean?"

Lucas glanced at her, with a faint smile and a glint in his eye. "Same as the locals do. I drink."

"Seriously?

He shrugged, downed the liquid in the glass. "In moderation. Usually. Do you want something?"

"Okay. Whatever you're having."

"You sure about that?" She heard the smile in his voice, and turned to see him pouring whiskey into a cut crystal glass, before re-filling his own.

"Positive," she answered tartly, to hide the fact that she wasn't sure at all. He handed her the glass, pouring taking up his own.

"*Sláinte*," he said, and took a sip. Sophie did the same, praying that she wouldn't choke or throw up or otherwise disgrace herself. But though it was strong, she found she liked the liquor's smoky after-taste. She took another, longer sip.

"Careful," Lucas said, "it's potent stuff."

"I can handle it," she said, meeting his eye squarely. Lucas laughed. "What?" Sophie demanded.

"I'd forgotten you're so competitive," he said, tipping the vegetables into a skillet.

"Only when I know I'm better," she said, crossing her arms over her chest.

Lucas laughed again, and kissed her. "Of course you're better. There was never any question." A few more minutes passed blissfully, before he pulled away. "If you don't stop this, I'm going to burn dinner."

"Do you need help?"

"No. But you are very welcome to keep me company. Put on some music if you want." He gestured to a docked iPod on the worktop by the refrigerator.

Sophie picked up the remote, flicked through a list of albums, half of which she'd never heard of, and then through his playlists. They had strange names: "Reims 407" and "Gabe" and "Bonfire of the Vanities" and others, equally cryptic. In the end she chose the one called "Winter", simply because it meant something. The moment she heard the wailing guitar, she looked at Lucas with a cocked eyebrow.

"Not a Goth, eh?"

But he wasn't listening – or at any rate, not to her. He did seem to be listening intently to the music, his face turned toward the dark window with an unreadable expression – not unlike the way she had first encountered him, in the candlelit room, in the wake of the violin music. Then, abruptly, he shook his head, and turned back to her.

"I'm sorry," he said. "You surprised me with that one. And as for the Goth thing, I don't generally like The Cure, but this is a great song."

Sophie sipped her whisky, and answered, "Well that's funny, because I don't like them either, but I've got this song on my iPod, too."

He raised his eyebrows. "Really? Why?"

Sophie smiled, and sat down opposite him on one of the stools lining the kitchen island. "My mum, I suppose. She used to be into all of that when she was young, and she's kind of been revisiting her misspent youth since she and my dad split up. Seriously, we've listened to nothing but post-punk navel gazers all summer. I think I could recite The Cure's entire catalog of lyrics by now." She sipped, shrugged. "But once in a while, they get it right. What about you?"

Lucas said, "It always reminded me of us. Lovers who can't be together, and can't stay apart."

The words chilled her to her core, wakening a foreboding that made no sense. "That's not us, now," she said, wishing that she sounded less tremulous, more defiant.

"No," he said. "And it never will be again, if there's anything I can do about it."

"Is there?" Sophie asked. "I mean, I don't even want to think about this…but without knowing why I'm here or how it happened…" She trailed off, not wanting to speculate further.

They looked at each other for a long moment, and then Lucas said, "Well then, I guess we'd better find out."

Chapter 21

"So tell me what we're looking for again?" Sophie asked as they climbed the narrow spiral stairway from the kitchen, where they'd eaten dinner, into another round room. It was spare and white, with wide windows which, in the daytime, would frame the sea. The only furniture was a bed and a bureau made of pale blonde wood, though several towers of of books leaned against the walls. There was a door between two of the stacks, incongruously dark and archaic-looking, with an old-fashioned key sticking out of its lock.

"A book," Lucas said, turning the key and pushing the door open. Beyond it, the light from the bedroom showed the beginning of the wood-paneled corridor with the arched windows, where she and Ailsa had begun their search for the locked room. It looked like another world, compared with Lucas's modern rooms.

"And you have a copy?"

"Unfortunately, no."

"But you have read it?"

"Not exactly…it's very rare."

She stopped in the doorway. "So what's the point of going to the library?"

"We have to start somewhere. Come on." His fingers slipped between hers, and then there was no question of her not following him.

Lucas turned a switch and a row of hanging lamps came on, but it seemed to Sophie that the shadows only multiplied in their tepid light. She looked reluctantly down the corridor, and wrapped her free arm around herself.

"Are you cold?" Lucas asked.

"No," Sophie said. "Creeped out."

Lucas squeezed her hand. "There's nothing in this house to be afraid of," he said.

"How do you know that?" she asked. "Couldn't some ghost-hunting tourist materialize Lady Macbeth or something?"

He laughed. "It's a good thing you're a skeptic," he said, "or Ardnasheen would be populated entirely by your overactive imagination."

"Thanks," Sophie said. "But what about the Revenant, the other night?"

"Okay, I'll give you that. But I promise to drive them away if we see any, and other than Revenants, you'll find no monsters in this house. I put in protection against them when I built it."

"When you built it," Sophie repeated incredulously. "So what are we talking about? Garlic? Holy water?"

He smiled. "Not quite. Remember how I told you that the *sìth* are vulnerable to iron?"

"How could I forget?"

"Well, they have other weaknesses, too. Every creature does."

"What else works against the *sìth*?"

"It varies, depending on the species. Bells, running water, rowan trees, burning peat, oatmeal – "

"*Oatmeal?*"

"The Scots can use oatmeal for just about anything."

Sophie laughed, shaking her head. "So what, you used oatmeal instead of mortar between the stones?"

"Flint dust, actually," he said. "The lesser *sìth* hate it."

"Of course they do," she sighed, wondering if this kind of statement would ever seem as natural to her as it obviously did to Lucas.

They'd reached the stairway that she and Ailsa had used the other night, when she had a sudden thought. "But wait – if there are faeries and angels and Revenants, are there other things too? Ghosts, vampires, werewolves?"

"Yes and no," Lucas said. "Most myths are based in fact, but the reality generally looks very different from what you see in the cinema."

"You mean like angels not having haloes and wings?"

"That's an example," he said, slipping his hand out of Sophie's to hook a tail of cobweb that was hanging from the

249

light fixture overhead. "But only a minor one, given that reality itself is subjective."

"Subjective how?"

Lucas closed his hand over the wad of cobweb. "Easily manipulated, if you know how." He opened his hand again. Instead of the sticky wisp of spider web, he held a delicate silver filigree bracelet. Sophie gaped at him, and he smiled, his eyes warm with humor. "Don't tell me I've actually stunned you speechless."

While she was trying to think of an answer to that, he lifted her hand and slipped the bracelet onto her wrist.

"It this going to turn back to cobwebs at midnight?" she asked, holding it up to the light to study it. The individual filaments really did look as fine as spider silk, but they were very definitely made of metal now.

"Not unless you want it to." Lucas took her hand again, and started down the stairs.

"So is that how you built this place? You just sort of... prodded it into being?"

He smiled again, but shook his head. "That would have been far too conspicuous, even if I were powerful enough to do it – which, by the way, I'm not. Part of falling is having your wings clipped, so to speak. And part of that is losing the unlimited power to re-shape matter. Small things are okay," he touched the bracelet. "Houses – not so much."

They reached the landing and continued down toward the entrance hall. Sophie ran her finger along the banister, worn smooth by centuries of hands, and asked him something else that had been bothering her. "I suppose you don't age, then?"

"I age," he said after a slight pause, "but not visibly."

"So why does no one notice?" she asked. "I mean, if you're always here, and you never change?"

He smiled ruefully. "One thing I've learned about humans is that they notice very little, if it challenges what they want to believe."

"Still, in a place as small as this people *must* notice someone who never gets any older."

"That's why I take holidays. Every so often I disappear for a while."

"What's 'a while'?"

"A generation or two. Long enough for anyone who knew me to leave, or die. And of course, I don't pose for pictures, and I destroy the odd exception."

Sophie thought of the photo album in the study with all of the gaps. She guessed now who the dark-haired woman had been. She couldn't look at him when she asked the next question, but she had to ask it. "And Clara Belial? I mean, I assume you were the fiancé who was killed in the war…"

Lucas sighed. "That…should never have happened. I met her when she was here visiting family. I liked her, spent some time with her. I didn't realize she had…become attached to me, until it was too late. So yes, I orchestrated my death, to extricate myself from an impossible situation. It was cruel, but what else could I do?"

Sophie was silent for a few long moments. "Where do you go, when you disappear?"

He shrugged. "Into the hills, usually."

"You stay in Ardnasheen?" she asked and then, when he nodded, "Why?"

"Because I'm bound here. It's part of my Hell."

"I thought you said that Hell didn't exist."

"No, I said it's subjective."

"Like reality," she muttered.

"More so," he answered without missing a beat. She gave him a questioning look. "Okay, have you ever read Rimbaud?"

"I'm afraid not. I've read Rilke, if that counts. I even wrote an essay on him."

Lucas smiled. "Rilke knew all about angels. But Rimbaud knew about hell. He wrote, 'I believe that I am in hell, therefore I am there.' Impressive assessment, for a man who'd never been damned."

"How so?"

"Hell is unique and specific to every individual and his – or her – transgression. It's made of his own fears and perceptions."

"So your idea of Hell was a drafty pile in Scotland?" Sophie asked, only half facetiously.

"It's a bit more complicated than that. You see, this – I mean Ardnasheen – was originally Azazel's punishment alone. To be bound on earth in the wilderness, as long as the world endures – that was more or less the message the Keeper sent. Azazel thrived on the attention of his followers, and the power he had

252

over humans. The idea was to deprive him of that, as well as the powers and privileges he had as a Watcher."

"Then why were *you* sent here?"

He considered this for a moment before answering. "To be honest, I've never been entirely certain – and maybe that in itself is the answer. What I'd done was unprecedented. The closest crime was Azazel's, so I suppose it was logical to give me the same punishment. And then, of course, we hated each other, which was a bonus in the damnation department. The thing is, though, it wouldn't really have mattered where I was sent: being away from you was the true Hell. So perhaps they just chose at random."

"They?"

"The other angels."

Sophie felt as if she'd been slapped. "Wait – it was the *angels* who exiled you, and not the Keeper?"

"Basically. They disagreed about whether you and I were right or wrong to have…well, you know."

Sophie thought of the dream of Lucas kneeling in the rain. She thought of the vision of the dueling figures. "Is that why you fought Michael?"

He looked at her, startled. "How did you know that?"

"I saw it with Suri's truth potion."

Lucas sighed. "Yes, I fought Michael. He was our leader – our ranking officer, if you like. It was part of his job to settle disputes."

"And he does it by fighting duels?"

"I told you, we're soldiers first and foremost. But Sophie, you can't blame him for what happened. Yes, he held the sword, but there were others who felt the same way he did. A lot of them."

Sophie didn't know what to say to this. But something else was bothering her. "Michael wasn't old in the vision."

Lucas shook his head. "He makes himself look that way to blend in, here."

"Angels can change their appearance at will?"

"To an extent. Older, younger, fatter, thinner – but the basic structure stays the same. Rather like humans. And before you ask, no, I can't do it. That ability is one we lose when we fall."

Once again, Sophie saw Lucas falling into the black chasm. "But back to this whole bound in the wilderness for eternity thing – you aren't really, are you? I mean, you can leave. Didn't you just go away somewhere?"

Lucas nodded. "Edinburgh – to try to find out why you were here. Nothing can stop us leaving Ardnasheen. But if we leave, we leave behind the staves, and that's dangerous."

"Staves?"

"Difficult to explain. They're the other half of these." He held up his arms, showing the metal cuffs. "The invisible half. They act like armor, but they're fixed to a certain place – the place we're supposed to remain."

"So you aren't safe anywhere else?"

"We're safe on consecrated ground. Churches, graveyards, holy wells, whatever. But I think that was an oversight by whoever came up with the system, and anyway, it isn't much help if you have to leave your staves to get there."

"What happens when you do?"

"Our physical bodies begin to degrade. Once they fail completely – well, remember what I said about the dropped mirror?"

"Right. So how long can you stay away from these staves?"

"The longest I've pushed it is a few months."

"That's not much."

"It's a lot more than the others have. Azazel can't leave the boundaries for more than a few days."

"Why are the rules different for you and him?"

He smiled wryly. "That's one of the many things no one bothers to explain when you're exiled from Heaven."

"So basically," she said, "this is it for you, forever."

"Well, until Judgment Day."

They'd turned into another corridor. This one was very narrow, its walls made of undressed stone that seemed to radiate age, broken intermittently on one side by keyhole windows. "So what exactly is meant to happen on Judgment Day?" Sophie asked. "I mean, after the moon turns red and the sea boils?"

Lucas laughed, shaking his head. "How many times do I have to tell you that that book is nonsense?"

"So no angels slaying dragons, then?"

"Doubtful," he said.

"You don't know? Aren't angels meant to be in on that kind of thing?"

"Not really – that's aeon territory. Though we did get watered-down memos from Logos, before the Keeper stopped speaking to us."

Sophie arched an eyebrow. "You're joking, right?"

He shook his head. "After the thing with the Watchers went wrong, and then the Flood, the Keeper just sort of… withdrew. It was so gradual that at first none of us realized what was happening. But then Logos' visits got fewer and farther between, until he just stopped coming, and we were left to our own devices."

"Who's running the show now, then?"

"The Watchers – the ones who didn't fall. But they usually defer to Michael, since he's the oldest."

"Heaven's run by the guy propping up the bar?" Lucas nodded. "This is *so* not what I imagined cosmic revelations to be like!"

"Sorry."

Sophie shook her head. "So if Michael's basically in charge, can you not just, I don't know, apologize to him and go home?"

Lucas smiled ruefully. "Salvation is exclusively a human perk."

"Why?"

"Because you're fundamentally imperfect – no offense meant. You're bound to mess up a bit. As long as you realize it and repent, your soul goes to the Garden when you die. Angels, on the other hand, *are* meant to be perfect. So if we mess up, we do it consciously, or so the theory goes. And that means we can't be forgiven."

"Wow. That's harsh."

He shrugged. "I've had several thousand years to get used to it."

"But where does that leave you? I mean, after Judgment Day?"

Lucas stopped in front of a set of double doors. "Honestly, I prefer not to think about it."

Before she could respond to that, Lucas pushed the doors inward and turned on the lights. Sophie forgot then about everything but the room beyond. It was a church-like space, made of the same ancient stone as the narrow corridor. It had six tall, arched, stained-glass windows, three on each of the longer walls, though in the dark she couldn't make out their images. Six stone pillars supported the vaulted ceiling, its beams exposed like those of a half-built ship. Most amazing of all, though, were the books. Every available inch of wall space was lined in bookshelves, and every shelf was packed to overflowing with volumes.

"When you said 'library'," Sophie said, turning slowly in the center of the room, "I was thinking an empty bedroom with a few Ikea bookshelves."

"Ikea!" He shook his head in disgust. "That place is the graveyard of the modern soul."

Sophie cocked an eyebrow. "That's all very well, if you

happen to have a spare ballroom and a dungeon full of medieval furniture to decorate with."

"It's not a ballroom," he told her, "it's the old banquet hall. And I had the bookshelves built in the eighteenth century."

"Which reminds me," Sophie said, running her finger along a row of leather spines, their gold leaf titles printed in what she guessed was Hebrew. "How come you're rich? I mean, doesn't that sort of defeat the purpose of suffering in the wilderness?"

"I wasn't always rich," Lucas answered, pulling a book from the shelves. "I came here with nothing more than a loincloth, actually." Sophie feigned a sudden interest in the nearest bookcase, to hide her blush. "But one of the perks of living indefinitely is that it gives you the chance to collect some interesting relics." He took down two more books, and then pointed to a recessed glass case by the nearest window, full of rolled scrolls. "All first century. And this is a first edition," he handed her a copy of 'The Origin of Species', its pages still uncut. "And then of course there's – "

"Okay, I get it!" Sophie interrupted. "The only book you don't own is the one we need. So remind me again what we're looking for here?"

"A trail," he said, putting his books on a table and flicking on a halogen study lamp. He pulled out two ladder-back chairs, and they sat down. "One thing I love about literature is that it's an entirely derivative art form. Every great new book owes itself partly to earlier ones."

"Like how you couldn't have Aristotle without Plato?"

He raised his eyebrows. "I was going to say, like you couldn't have Harry Potter without Tolkein. But yes – it's all the same idea. Anyway," he opened one of the books he'd taken down and flipped through it, "it used to be that writers weren't as shy about lifting other writers' ideas. But they were also good about naming their sources. That's how we know about so many books that have been lost."

"Like the ones that burned in the Alexandria library?"

Lucas frowned. "That was a grim day."

"You remember it?"

"Of course I do. I was there." Lucas pointed to a glass case at the far side of the room. "Those papers are what I managed to grab before the ceiling collapsed."

"Oh my God! What do they say?"

"Nothing."

"Nothing?"

"Come look."

He took her hand and led her to the case, then flicked a switch so a light came on inside it. The case was full of miniature paintings, their paper so old the edges were crumbling. But the images were still bright and clear. They were angels, but unlike any other angel pictures Sophie had seen. These had black hair and Asian features, they wore long, bright robes and had wings painted in brilliant rainbow colours. They were all beautiful, but one in particular stood out, a kneeling figure set against an intricate background of vines and leaves and flowers. He wore an embroidered black robe, and a white cord tied around his waist, entangling his wrists; binding them. A pair of brilliant crimson wings, dotted with golden teardrops, stretched above him.

Sophie touched the glass above the painting. "That's you, isn't it?"

"It's the only picture of me that I've ever liked."

"Even though it has wings?"

"Because it has wings." There was a resigned longing in his face as he gazed down at the picture that twisted her heart. "Anyway," he said, turning off the light, "we're supposed to be finding information about you, not having a pity party for me."

"Right," Sophie said, following him back to the table, "we're looking for references to what – 'Sophia the Aeon's Trip to Earth'?"

He smiled. "Not exactly, but you're not far off." He opened one of the books and turned it toward her, indicating a passage for her to read.

"'And so sayeth Sophia in her Revelation'," Sophie read, "'the one sacrifice shall redeem the sorrows of the multitude.'" She looked up. "You're basing your whole lost book theory on *that*?"

"Of course not!" he said. "That's just evidence. I'm basing it on this."

He extracted what looked like a framed drawing from a file drawer at the bottom of the bookcase beside the table. When he put it in front of Sophie, she realized that it wasn't a picture after all, but a fragmentary page of an ancient scroll or book, painstakingly pieced together and sealed between two plates of glass. The fragment was only a little bigger than her hand.

"What is it?" she asked.

"Remember the *Book of Enoch*?" Lucas asked.

"The one with the quote from the painting."

"Right. Enoch was a prophet who was brought to Heaven. He wrote a lot about angels, including the fallen ones, and he got the facts right, more or less. That means there's nothing in his work about Satan fighting with God. Because of that, it was considered heretical in early Christian times. Most of the original copies were destroyed. For a long time, it was another lost book.

"Then, in the eighteenth century, a Scottish explorer found three copies in a church in Abyssinia. Those copies are what the modern translations are based on. But since then, far older fragments have turned up. And while they're similar to the Abyssinian copies, they're a lot more detailed."

"So you're saying that once, there was a different version of the book. A better one."

"It looks that way, though I don't know for certain. It was written long after I was exiled."

"So that's what this is?" Sophie asked, pointing to the framed scrap. "A piece of that other book?"

"No. This is something unique. You see, the Book of Enoch is actually a collection of five smaller books: the *Book of the Watchers*, the *Book of Parables,* the *Book of Luminaries*, the *Book of Dreams* and the *Epistle of Enoch*. This fragment doesn't belong to any of them, and yet the style, the names, the subject matter – even the handwriting match other ancient fragments."

"So once, there was another book in the series," Sophie said.

"No one's proven it," he said, "but I believe there was. And I think that it was about Sophia."

"Why? What does the fragment say?"

"Not much, actually. It seems to be describing the part of Heaven where Wisdom lives. The important bit is, both Enoch and 'Wisdom' – that is, Sophia – are mentioned by name."

Sophie chewed on her lip, considering this. "So why was it separated from the rest of the book?"

"Usually that kind of thing happens when a book is very valuable, very dangerous, or both."

"Valuable and dangerous to whom, though?"

"Valuable to someone who wants to help you do what you came here to do. Dangerous to someone who wants to stop you."

Their eyes met in a long look of surmise. "Alright," Sophie said at last. "So where do we find a copy of this lost book?"

"I don't know," Lucas answered, giving her a measured look. "I do know someone who might. Only he'll never give it to me."

"Sam?"

"Not Sam."

"As long as it's not Sam, I'll ask him for it. Who is it?"

Lucas answered with an apologetic smile.

CHAPTER 22

"I still don't see why Michael would help us, when he's the one who exiled you," Sophie said as Lucas parked the Land Rover in front of the pub.

"It's not that simple," Lucas answered. "Besides, it's not just me he'd be helping."

"I still feel weird about this."

"I'll talk to him first," Lucas said, and held the pub door open for her. Still uncertain, Sophie stepped inside.

"Ooh, look!" Ailsa cried. "It's Sophie and her migraine."

It was seven on a weekday, and the pub was empty except for a handful of regulars at the bar, all focused on the television. "Funny," Sophie said, climbing onto the only free stool – the one that she'd come to think of as Michael's. Looking around, she saw that he was sitting instead at a table by the fire. He and Lucas locked eyes, their gazes equally intense.

"Wait here," Lucas said and then, kissing her cheek, he went to join him.

Ailsa's eyes widened, and Sophie couldn't look at her. "Oh. My. *God!"* she said. "You ditched work to hook up with him!"

"No – I mean yes, I ditched work, and we did sort of… um…" She stopped, flustered, and tried again. "I didn't plan it. But then something came up, and – " She covered her mouth, realizing how it sounded, and then said weakly to the barflies, who were now looking at her with varying degrees of interest, "It's really not what you think."

"More's the pity," Ailsa said, pouring two Cokes. "That'll do, gentlemen," she said to Sophie's audience, who turned grudgingly back to the television. She took the drinks to a table by the window, and gestured for Sophie to follow her.

"Now," she said, sitting down, "tell me all about it – and *don't* try to tell me you spent the day in bed! Unless it was Lucas's bed…"

"Actually," Sophie said, turning the glass around in its puddle of condensation, "I spent a lot of it sleeping on his sofa, and the rest in his library."

Ailsa rolled her eyes. "Ach aye, you would."

"Anyway, I'm sorry I left you to cover for me like that. But there really was something that needed sorting – "

"Never mind," Ailsa said. "If it means you snogged Lucas Belial, it's worth back-to-back shifts." She peered into Sophie's face. "You did snog him, didn't you?"

"I might not have put it *quite* that way…"

Ailsa grinned. "A rose by any other name, and all that. And

264

don't worry about the extra shift. You can make it up to me by taking my night shift tomorrow."

"What's on tomorrow?"

For the first time since Sophie had met her, Ailsa looked abashed. "Actually I, um, kind of have a date."

"Oh?" Sophie asked. "Who with?"

Ailsa took a circumspect sip of her drink and then said, "I'll tell you all about it if it works out."

Sophie was about to prod her for more information when Lucas came back and joined them. "Michael wants to speak with you," he said.

"Alone?" Sophie asked, alarmed.

Seeing Ailsa's curious look, he added, "He said something about a biscuit recipe you wanted."

"Um…that's right. I did. Are you okay to wait for me?"

He smiled. "For as long as it takes."

Sophie pretended not to see the cheering motions that Ailsa made behind his back. She got up and walked toward Michael's table, suddenly apprehensive.

"Why the look?" he said with a kindly smile as she slid into the chair across from him. "I don't bite."

"I know," she said, not quite able to meet his eyes. "It's just that now I know that you're…well…what you are, it's strange."

Michael's eyes were as incisive as Ailsa's. Sophie wondered what he was reading on her face. "Lucifer told me that you took the news remarkably well," he said after a moment.

The name made her flinch, despite everything Lucas had

told her. "I wouldn't know. I don't imagine confessions like that happen every day."

His lips quirked upward. "You'd be surprised."

"Right," she said, unwilling to prod too far into that statement. "Anyway, what did you want to tell me? I mean, I assume Lucas asked you about the book."

"He asked," Michael said, "but I'm forbidden to speak to the fallen about Heavenly matters."

"Ah…okay," she said. Somehow the words she'd accepted from Lucas felt surreal when Michael spoke them. "But am I not just as bad?"

He gave her an inscrutable look. "Possibly. But to put it bluntly, you outranked me in Heaven, and now that you're human, I'm bound to help you."

"Really?"

"I've helped you before, haven't I?"

"You mean showing up in my dream?"

He smiled. "That…and then there was the incident with Azazel."

"You mean that night at Sam's? When you gave me a lift home?" Michael sipped, nodded. "Don't think I'm not grateful, but that was just a coincidence."

"Coincidence is far less common than most humans think."

"So you knew to come?"

He shrugged. "Of course. You called on me."

Sophie shook her head. "I know that I'd remember *that*."

"Oh God...good Lord...for Heaven's sake...ever say anything along those lines? Or even think it?"

Sophie blinked at him. "But you're not God."

"I'm as near as any human will get."

Sophie took a moment to digest this information. Then she said, "You aren't fallen."

Michael choked on a mouthful of whisky. "Good lord, no!"

"Then why are you here?"

"To talk to you about a book – or so I thought. But if you'd rather discuss my recent history..."

Sophie had to smile. "Alright, then – the book. I assume you've heard of the *Book of Enoch*?"

He groaned. "Sure, who could forget Enoch? The most tiresome little man, he was – refused to die until he was nearly four hundred years old, and kept on coming back to interrogate us – "

"Michael."

"I'm rambling?"

"A bit. What I need to know is, was there ever a part of the book that had to do with me? I mean, back when I was...um... not human?"

Michael's look turned circumspect, if no less direct. "I do recall a rumour that you gave Enoch an audience. If it's true, then no doubt he scribbled out what you told him along with all the rest."

"But you've never actually seen what he wrote about me?"

"As I told you, Sophie, it's hearsay. He may never have spoken to you at all."

"Oh," Sophie said, slumping back in her chair in disappointment.

"Is there anything else I can help with?" he asked. There was an air of elemental patience about him that made Sophie wonder, once again, how she ever could have thought that he was just a bar-prop.

"Yes, actually," she said after a moment's consideration. "Do you know why I decided to become human?"

He smiled ruefully. "If I knew that, love, I wouldn't be here."

That took her aback. "Are you saying you're here to spy on me?"

"It's not spying if I admit to it, is it?"

Sophie shook her head. "This is so weird," she muttered. Then, "Okay – if you don't know why I'm human, then do you at least know how I did it?"

"Pass again." He poured more whisky. Sophie wondered how he could hold it so well. His eyes were peculiarly lucid for a man who spent his days draining bottles of spirits.

She sighed. "Right, then, what about this: I've been down here for seventeen years. Why did you wait so long to check up on me?"

Michael shrugged. "Your transmogrification wasn't considered important until you decided to come to Ardnasheen."

"Because that meant I'd meet Lucas." He nodded. "But you

must have known I'd try to find him. What other reason would I have for…what did you call it?"

"Transmogrifying." Michael considered her question for a few moments before answering with one of his own: "*Is* that the reason why you came to Ardnasheen?"

"No," Sophie admitted. "I came to get as far away from London as I could, without being too far to go back quickly if one of my parents melted down. But of all the things I could have chosen to do, all the places I could have gone…well, I can't believe this decision was entirely down to coincidence."

"In the end, it doesn't really matter. You're here now, and until we know why, you're a potential threat."

Sophie laughed ruefully. "And here I thought you liked me."

"I do like you, Sophie," he said, with a sadness that made it impossible to doubt him. "But if you being here puts the Balance in danger, then I'm duty bound to do something about it."

"The Balance?" she repeated, wondering why it had a familiar ring.

Michael nodded. "Think of it as a universal equilibrium. Everything that is, is a part of it. But it's a delicate mechanism – easily upset."

"By what?"

"By many things. Azazel leading his angels astray, for instance – that was a bad blow. It took the Flood to set it right, and even so it's never been *quite* right since."

"And Lucas and me? I mean, what happened between us, when we were in Heaven – did that upset the Balance too?"

Michael looked troubled. "No doubt it did."

Sophie glared at him. "No doubt? You mean you don't know?"

"I'm only an angel, Sophie."

She had to laugh. "Now *that's* something I never thought I'd hear someone say!"

"But it's true. Mine's mid-level security clearance, at best. The workings of the Balance are aeon territory. Aeons, and the Keeper. Still, it doesn't take a genius to work out that your transgression had to have had an effect. And just because the effect wasn't immediately obvious, doesn't mean that it wasn't serious."

"That's only speculation!" she cried.

"Hush, Sophie," he said, glancing at the bar. Ailsa looked quickly away, pretending that she hadn't been trying to eavesdrop. Lucas didn't bother to pretend: he was half way out of his seat when Sophie shook her head at him. He sat back down, but he didn't take his eyes off of them.

Sophie took a deep breath, and turned back to Michael. "Well?" she said in a low voice.

His voice still calm, his eyes still sad, he continued, "Sophie, aligning yourself with Lucifer went against the natural order of your kind and his. Angels weren't made to love exclusively, and aeons weren't made to mix with angels – never mind, ah, cohabit with them. Tamper with those roles and the Balance *must* shift – possibly in as terrible a sense as it did with Azazel's defection. Possibly worse."

"*Possibly*," Sophie repeated pointedly.

"You must try to understand. Things were unsettled already; it was a chance we couldn't afford to take."

She considered him for a few moments. "Tell me something," she said at last. "What was Lucas like? I mean, when he was… you know…Lucifer."

Michael smiled fondly, if somewhat sadly. "Do you know what that name means?" Sophie shook her head. "Light-bringer. Morning star, by some definitions. Either way that's what he was: the shining one. The best of us."

"He told me that Azazel was the golden boy."

"Of course he did. His lack of conceit was part of what made him brilliant. As for Azazel, he put on a good show, but he was always ambitious. Always scheming." He sighed. "They were nothing alike. Complete opposites, in fact."

"Precisely," Sophie said, laying both hands flat on the table and leaning toward Michael. "Azazel did what he did out of lust and jealousy and no doubt some sort of superiority complex. Lucas and I did what *we* did out of love. I honestly can't believe that this cosmic equilibrium you're talking about could be undone because two people loved each other."

"That's just it," Michael said, his voice full of compassion. "You *weren't* two people. You were divinities. With power comes responsibility."

"But now I'm human, and he's fallen, so what does it matter what we do?"

271

Michael paused, looking into his glass as he turned it in his hands. "Do you love him now, Sophie?" he asked hesitantly.

"Yes," she answered without pause.

He looked up at her, his eyes piercing. "How much?"

"I'd die for him," she answered, surprising herself. It was exactly the kind of melodramatic line she hated in books and films, and yet she knew that it was as true as anything she'd ever said.

"In that case," Michael said wearily, "what you do matters more than you can imagine."

She stared at him, suddenly sick with foreboding. "Is that a threat?"

He smiled again, but this time there was a steely edge to it. "It's not my job to level threats. I only want to be certain you know all of the facts before you make your decision."

"What decision?" she asked, the doomed feeling deepening.

There was a long pause. "You'll know when you come to it."

"You're scaring me, Michael."

"Am I?" He patted her hand. "I don't mean to. Remember, I'm here to protect you. In the meantime, take this." He pushed a slip of paper across the table.

Sophie looked down at it blankly. "What is this?"

"The shortbread recipe. Baking always helps me to think." Another pause, this time briefer. "Biscuits or no, I've no doubt you'll do the right thing." And with that, he stood up, drained his glass and left her staring after him.

CHAPTER 23

"Well?" Lucas asked as soon as they were back in the car. "What did he tell you?"

"He told me about the Balance." She turned to him. "When were *you* going to tell me about it?"

He sighed, starting the ignition and turning up the road. "I'm working my way through all of this as fast as I can. I haven't made it as far as the Balance yet." He glanced at her. "I suppose he told you that we shot the Balance to hell."

"Well? Did we?"

Lucas was silent for a few moments. "The thing about power," he said at last, "is that it makes you afraid of what you can't control. There was no precedent for us – unless you count the Watchers who took human lovers, which I don't. It wasn't supposed to be possible for an angel and an aeon to fall in love. Could it have upset the Balance?" He shrugged. "No one knew. I suppose Michael couldn't take the chance. In his place, I might well have done the same thing."

Sophie thought about this. "Heaven sounds awfully medieval for a place that's supposed to be Paradise."

"Paradise is a human idea."

"Talk about disillusionment," Sophie sighed. "And we aren't even any closer to finding the book."

They drove for a few moments in gloomy silence. Then something hurtled across the road in front of them, all tattered edges and iridescent colours. Lucas slammed on the brakes and Sophie clutched at his arm convulsively. Then Lucas got out of the car. He peered into the darkness for a few moments, and then Sophie heard an inhuman screech. To her annoyance, Lucas returned to the car, laughing.

"It's just Michael's peacock," he said as he got back in. "And none the worse for its near-death experience."

"Oh," Sophie said, feeling like an idiot. "It's just that this bit of road – I saw a Revenant here…"

"I know," Lucas said as he began to drive again.

"How?"

"I was there."

"*What?*"

"I knew that Azazel was waiting for you. I wanted to make sure he didn't hurt you."

"I thought you hated me, then."

"I never hated you! I was only afraid of what you might be…"

"It doesn't matter now," Sophie said, slipping her hand into the crook of his elbow. But the discussion had reminded

Sophie of something that had been troubling her. "What do the Revenants have to do with all of this?"

"What makes you think they have anything to do with it?" Lucas answered.

But she had felt him stiffen for a moment when she asked the question. "How about the fact that they've been plaguing me my whole life? Not to mention that you get twitchy whenever I bring them up."

They'd reached the house. Lucas parked the car, and then, finally, he answered. "It's only a myth. Not even that. A rumour."

"If it's about the Revenants, I want to hear it."

He paused again before he said, "Alright. But let's wait until we get inside. This is no place to be telling ghost stories."

Sophie couldn't argue with that. She followed him up the tower staircase, her thoughts churning. As soon as the lights were on in the sitting room she perched on one of the kitchen stools and said, "Well?"

Lucas smiled, dropping the blinds over the dark windows. "Didn't anyone ever tell you that patience is a virtue?"

"So is sharing information," she said dryly. "All of it. At once."

"You'd have run screaming if I'd told you everything at once," he observed, flicking through menus on the iPod.

"Do I seem like the kind of girl who – " Sophie began, and then she forgot what she'd been about to say. The music he'd chosen was a solo cello, plaintive and hauntingly beautiful. "What is this?" she asked.

276

"Marin Marais," Lucas answered, pronouncing the French name perfectly. "A seventeenth-century composer who wrote for the viol – that's like a cello, but with an extra string. Do you like it?"

"It's gorgeous," Sophie breathed. Then she thought of something else. "Lucas – what is 'Reims 407'?"

He looked up at her in surprise, and then smiled, shaking his head. "You don't miss anything, do you?"

"Not if I can help it."

"407 was when the first cathedral was built at Reims. It was a Roman town then, and the bishop who founded it was a man named Nicasius. A lot of the church at that time was corrupt – as it always has been, I suppose – but Nicasius was a true holy man. He had a gift for visions."

"You knew him?" Sophie asked.

Lucas sat down beside her. "And considered him a friend."

"But how?"

"Cathedral building was new then, and it fascinated me. Whenever I heard of a new one being built, I went to see it. Sometimes I helped with the work."

"What about the staves?"

"Cathedrals are consecrated ground."

"Of course…"

"Anyway, the only time I ever saw a bishop labouring alongside the stonemasons was at Reims. It was how Nicasius and I became friends. Well, that, and he guessed what I was, and accepted it.

"After I returned here, we exchanged letters. He wrote to me about his visions. One of the last of them was of the Vandals invading France." He paused. "I only learned that it had been true long after the fact. Apparently, Nicasius warned his people, told them to prepare, but when they asked if they should fight the invaders or not, he said that they ought to pray for their enemies instead.

"When the invading army reached the gates of the city, he realized that he had made a mistake, and his people would be killed because of it. So, to allow them time to escape, he went out to face the invaders himself. They took his head at the altar of his new church. Not long after that, though, they abandoned their campaign and fled the city, leaving everything behind, including their treasure. It's said that they ran from an apparition of Nicasius, carrying his head and reciting Psalms. So: Reims, 407."

"Oh," Sophie said, feeling suddenly very young and naïve. She moved to one of the couches and pulled her legs up under her. "Now, it's time to stop stalling. What do you know about the Revenants?"

"Aren't you tired?"

"Nice try – but I slept all afternoon, remember?"

"I know very little about them, actually," he said, moving to sit beside her. "No one does, because they aren't supposed to exist."

"What do you mean?" she asked.

"Just that. They were never meant to be, in the same way

278

that angels were never meant to fall." Lucas paused, looking at the painting of the angel slaying the sea monster. "It's all part of the Balance. Some things – and some beings – are, well… sanctioned. They're meant to be, so they have their place in the Balance. Others aren't, and so they don't. But those others – they didn't exist until Azazel's betrayal. It's as if, when he went against his own nature, he changed the nature of the Balance too."

"A fixed state of chaos," Sophie murmured, remembering her conversation with Sam in the car.

"Not quite," Lucas said, "but dangerously close. Take a fallen angel, for example. On the one hand, my existence is constrained by a clear set of rules. But while many things are forbidden, others aren't, simply because when the rules of my exile were made, no one had ever thought of them."

"Kind of like no one ever thought an aeon would make herself human?"

Lucas nodded. "And because of that, the Balance is no longer stable. Ever since Azazel fell it's been swinging every which way, entirely unpredictable. I think that's part of the reason why Michael didn't approve of you and me together – he was afraid that we were a result of the imbalance. That if we stayed together, that might somehow make it worse."

Sophie considered all of it for a moment. Then she said, "So the Revenants are also connected to the messed-up Balance?"

"Not just connected – they're a direct result. It made them

279

possible, because it made way for the possibility of hitchhiking back to Heaven on a stolen soul."

A cold tremor ran through Sophie. "What are you saying?"

"Exactly what you think I'm saying," he answered, his voice calm and steady, though his eyes were troubled. "On the one hand, I'm chained to Ardnasheen like a misbehaving dog. On the other, I have the power to steal a human soul and, theoretically, get out of Hell."

Sophie thought that she was about to be sick. "It was you?" she asked, her voice wavering. "*You're* the one who made that girl into a Revenant?"

"No!" Lucas cried, his eyes wild. "I've never taken a human soul, and I never will!"

Sophie was reeling; she barely saw him. "So who – how – " And then, all at once, with crystalline certainty, she knew. "Sam made it."

Lucas nodded. "Yes, he did."

"And the others in the book of clippings?"

Lucas shrugged dejectedly. "Some of them, no doubt. Others will have been made by other fallen Watchers who believe the rumour. I used to try to stop it if I found out about it, but it's so quick…I never did anything but prolong their suffering."

"How is it done?" Sophie asked after a moment.

She was expecting a detailed archaic ritual, but Lucas answered grimly, "A kiss on the mouth."

"What?"

"It was meant to be a beautiful thing, a mercy for the holiest of humans, the prophets and the wise men and women, when their time came to die. Like Moses – the Keeper took his soul that way. But Azazel found a way to twist it to his own ends, like so many other things."

Sophie thought of Sam's lips brushing hers, and she seemed to freeze inside. "He tried to take mine," she whispered. "It was when you were away…oh my God, Lucas, he meant to make me one of them!"

Suddenly she was shuddering uncontrollably, tears spilling down her face. She was disgusted with herself, but she couldn't stop, and she was more than grateful when Lucas put his arms around her, pulled her onto his lap and held her as she wept. When she was finally cried out, she looked up at him. He looked back at her with pity, but without surprise.

"I'm sorry," she said.

"Don't be," he answered, kissing her softly on the mouth. "If you weren't horrified, I'd be worried."

She shut her eyes, breathed in his sweet incense smell. Despite everything, with his arms around her she felt that nothing could ever threaten her. "I just can't believe I ever went with him…how close I came…I was so stupid!"

"No, you weren't. How could you have known? If anyone's stupid, it's me. I never should have left you on your own here, suspecting what I did. I just couldn't make myself believe that it was really you."

"What convinced you?" she asked.

"Michael. When I couldn't find anything conclusive in

Edinburgh, I asked him flat out. He told me that he was sure you were Sophia, but that was all he knew."

Sophie traced the fingers on his hand with one of her own. "Why me?" she asked after a moment. "I mean, what's so special about my soul, that Sam would want it instead of, say, Ailsa's?"

"If you looked through that book of clippings that you found, you'll know that Revenants are always made from good people – people whose souls will almost certainly be saved. But it's never worked. That means either that it's impossible, or that no one has found the right soul yet – one pure enough to liberate a damned creature. But you aren't an ordinary human. It's no great leap to think that you might not have an ordinary soul."

Sophie shuddered again. "He isn't going to stop, is he? He's going to keep trying to take it."

"Probably. But there's something working in your favour: he can't use a soul unless it's given willingly."

Sophie was taken aback. "So the Revenants – they *chose* to become what they are?"

"In a sense, yes. But they'll have been charmed into it."

Sophie thought of the way that Sam had persuaded her to come to dinner when she was certain that she didn't want to go. She thought about how easily he had persuaded her to kiss him. In light of that, Lucas's words weren't particularly comforting.

Lucas seemed to sense this. "Besides," he said, "I'll be watching out for you. So will Michael."

"I don't think Michael trusts me, since I told him I lo – " She broke off abruptly, horrified by what she had been about to tell him. "Um…since he knows what I know."

Lucas gave her a penetrating look, but he didn't call her on the slip. "It doesn't matter," he said. "You're human, so he's bound to protect you from anything that threatens your soul." He looked down at her, holding her eyes. "Really, Sophie. It's going to be okay."

And despite everything, she believed him.

CHAPTER 24

"Are you sure about this?" Lucas asked for the fifth time, as they stood outside of Sophie's bedroom door a little while later.

"Positive," Sophie said, trying to sound as if she meant it.

"Because you can still come back with me. It would all be absolutely above board. You could have the top floor to yourself, I don't sleep anyway – "

"You don't sleep?"

He shook his head. "None of the Watchers sleep. It's part of…well…watching."

"No," she said after a moment's consideration. "Really, I'll be fine here. You told me yourself that the house is safe. Besides, if I stayed with you, you'd find out all of the tedious things about me and you wouldn't like me anymore."

"That couldn't possibly happen," he smiled, wrapping his arms around her. "But if you're sure…"

She nodded, although she wasn't sure at all. It was awfully tempting to go back with him. However, the sensible side of her knew that too much had changed in too short a space of time. As well as she might be taking it, there was still a lot to process, and she knew that she couldn't do that when Lucas was with her.

"Okay," he sighed, and then he took her face between his hands and kissed her. She was caught off guard again by the surge of longing she felt when his lips touched hers. In a dizzy rush she found herself pulled hard against him, her hands in his hair as he kissed her hungrily. It took a tremendous force of will to pull away.

"Good-night, Lucas," she said shakily, reaching for the door knob. But he caught her hand as she turned, kissed her fingers tenderly before she slipped through the door.

She shut it behind her and leaned on it, staring into the dark and trying to catch her breath. It seemed to take forever for her heart to slow to normal, and the spangled dizziness to pass. Finally, she pushed away from the door, and turned on the desk lamp.

The room she'd once thought romantic seemed shabby and diminished now. She wondered whether this was because of the contrast to Lucas's bright, modern tower, or if it was the lack of Lucas himself. Sighing, she shed her clothes and put on her pajamas and dressing gown, brushed her teeth and washed her face quickly, and then slid into bed. The sheets were freezing cold, the fire long since dead, but she didn't have the energy to try to re-light it. She thought that it would be difficult to fall asleep, but the long, strange day had finally caught up with her. Almost as soon as she'd closed her eyes, she was away.

*

Sophie didn't know how long she'd been asleep. All she knew was that it was still dark, and she had the overwhelming feeling that she wasn't alone. She clutched the covers around her and peered wide-eyed into the darkness, trying to make sense of the shadowy shapes, to account for them all. She strained to hear anything out of the ordinary, but aside from the low moan of the wind, all she could hear was her own breathing.

It's nothing, she told herself. *Shut your eyes and soon it will be morning.*

But then she heard it: the wind dropped for a moment, and in its place was a soft noise, like the fall of a slippered foot on carpet. Her eyes flew open again. She looked toward the door, which showed now as a blacker oblong against the dark: it was standing open. She was certain that it hadn't been before. As she watched, something separated from the gaping darkness. Something low to the ground, the size and shape of a dog. But there was nothing doglike in its movement. It was stealthy, even graceful, but utterly terrifying.

Sophie tried to breathe evenly, to convince whatever it was that she was still sleeping. She knew that she had only a few moments to act, but without having any idea of what was stalking her, she couldn't see what hope she had of fighting it.

The thing was beside the bed now, so close that she could feel its hot breath on her face. There was a rotten, sulfurous smell about it that made her want to gag, but she held her breath. She felt it gather itself to spring, and flung herself to the floor as it leapt with a hiss onto the bed. She pushed backward, scrabbling for the fire irons. The poker was gone, lost in the cemetery what now seemed years ago. But she doubted it would matter, if the creature was one of the *sith*: iron was iron.

Her eyes had adjusted to the dark enough now for her to see the creature's head turn toward her, its body stretch to pounce again. She swung at it with the pincers she'd grabbed, and it let out an unearthly howl as the iron connected with its head. Sophie scrambled to her feet and began to run for the door, but she stumbled over the desk chair and fell. In a moment the beast was on top of her. She felt rough fur between her fingers as she tried to fend it off, and then a clawed limb raking her shoulder. She thought, *This is how I die.*

At the same time, though, a part of her was screaming in denial. This might have been the strangest day of her life, but it had also, oddly, been the happiest. She didn't want to die when she'd only just realized what Lucas meant to her, without knowing where it would lead. *I won't,* she thought, and the air around her seemed to ripple for a moment, as if it were a cinema screen that someone had shaken.

And then a piercing scream rent the silence. She turned to the door to see Ailsa standing there, her face a rictus of horror. Worse, though, the cat had seen her too. It turned and leapt toward Ailsa, knocking her flat. She began to scream again, to beg for help. Sophie knew that she needed to kill the cat, or it would certainly kill Ailsa.

Once again her vision rippled, but this time when it stilled, she realized that she could see. The room was lit by a blue glow that seemed to come from nowhere and everywhere at once; not bright, and yet illuminating every minute detail. She got her first good look at the creature that was now pinning Ailsa: a black cat at least as big as she was, with silver-white eyes and a patch of white fur at its chest. It snarled and then lunged for Ailsa's throat, but as it did so, Sophie's arm flashed out as if it had a will of its own. She caught the creature by the neck, hauled it up and off of her friend as if it weighed nothing. With her other hand she caught the paw that rose to rake her again, and slammed the creature onto its back.

Now *she* was pinning *it*. She scanned the room for something that would act as a weapon, took in the scattered fire irons and toppled chair. None of them would help her. She needed something specific. In her mind was a half-formed image of a long, cruel knife, made of pale metal that glowed with the eerie blue-green hue of an iceberg.

Almost as she thought of it, it was real, shimmering in her free hand. Without hesitating, Sophie plunged it into the monster's breast. The cat let out a scream that pierced through her, seeming to hang in the air for many long minutes as the monster jerked and shuddered. Then it fell still, and the only sounds were the keening wind and Ailsa's terrified whimpering. Sophie pushed back from the dead thing, gasping, her heart slamming against her ribs. The blue glow was fading along with the adrenaline that had driven her, leaving her weak and shaking.

She was clammy with sweat and blood, and the shoulder where the monster had raked her had begun to burn.

She looked at Ailsa, who was kneeling now in the doorway, wide-eyed and white faced. "Ailsa – " she began, reaching a hand toward her friend. Too late, she realized that it was dark with blood. Ailsa turned from her in horror, scrambling to her feet. She turned as if to run, but Lucas appeared behind her. He caught her by the shoulders, took one look at the room beyond and blanched.

"Oh my God, Sophie – " he began.

"I'm alright," Sophie interrupted. "Just get Ailsa out of here."

Lucas looked down at the hysterical girl, as if seeing her for the first time. He nodded, and then spoke a few soft words to her, which Sophie couldn't quite make out. Ailsa slumped into his arms. He lifted her like a child.

"I'll be right back," he said.

Sophie nodded. When he was gone, she took a shuddering breath, then stood up and flicked the light switch. The room flooded with mundane yellow light, and she surveyed the damage. The place was in ruins: the bedclothes and curtains torn, the carpet covered in blood and soot, and everything smelled vaguely sulfurous. The cat itself looked like the jungle cats she'd seen in zoos, aside from the silver eyes and white patch of fur with the hilt of the dagger still protruding from the center. At the same time there was something off-kilter in its appearance, as if its proportions were skewed, but too slightly to say exactly where and how. It lay in a pool of dark, viscous fluid that looked nothing like blood, and which was blooming its way across the carpet like a poison flower.

When Lucas returned, Sophie was still staring at the creeping stain in fascinated horror. He wrapped her in his arms, and it was only then that she felt the impact of what had happened. Overwhelmed, she pulled out of his embrace and rushed to the bathroom, just in time to be sick. A moment later she felt Lucas's fingers gently pulling her straggling hair back from her neck. Even through her nausea she felt mortification that he was seeing her like this. But when she turned around to look at him at last, there was nothing but concern in his eyes. He handed her a cup of water, which she took gratefully. Unable to bear returning to her room, she slumped to the floor outside the bathroom.

Lucas sat down beside her. When she'd swallowed a few sips of water and kept them down, he said, "What happened?"

Sophie shook her head. All of it seemed jumbled now, surreal. "I don't know. I woke up and I just…knew it was there. I couldn't run away, it was too big and fast. I hit it with a fire iron." She looked at him. "I thought they were supposed to be vulnerable to iron."

"The *sìth*, yes. That," he pointed to the open door of the room, "was a *Cait Sìth*."

"Which means what, 'super-*sìth*'?"

"Literally, it means faery cat. But actually it's not a faery at all. It's a demon."

"A demon," Sophie repeated dazedly, looking up at him.

290

Then, after a moment, she said, "I thought you said the house was safe."

"Not from demons. That's beyond me. But I wasn't expecting a demon to come after you. It's been years since I've seen one at all. They're difficult to summon, even more difficult to control. As for killing them…" He gave her an incisive look. "How did you manage to summon Carnwennan?"

"Who?"

"The dagger."

"It has a name? What is this, Middle Earth?"

Lucas shrugged. "*I* didn't name it. Arthur did."

"Arthur, as in…?" Lucas nodded, and Sophie let her head fall back against the wall. "Right," she sighed. "Angels, faeries, demons, King Arthur…I have no idea, to answer your question. It all happened so quickly. One minute I was certain that cat thing was about to rip Ailsa's throat out, and then suddenly I was on top of it, and I knew what I needed to kill it, and *voila:* big scary knife."

"You summoned it," he repeated speculatively.

"Um, no. I'm quite certain I've never heard of Carnwennan until right now."

"But you must have. It's the only explanation. Normally that knife is locked in a display case in the British Museum. It's one of the Sacred Weapons I told you about. Few things other than Sacred Weapons can kill demons. You must have remembered that, and made something into the dagger, just like I manipulated cobwebs into a silver bracelet."

Sophie stared at the bracelet, still clasped around her wrist, as if it might comment on this strange new set of events.

"None of which would be particularly extraordinary if you were still an aeon," Lucas continued, "but since you're human… well, it should have been impossible."

Sophie said, "Perhaps I'm not as human as you think."

Lucas studied her for another long moment before he shook his head. "You're human enough that that must hurt." He pointed at the bloody claw-marks on her shoulder, and she flinched away. "Come on." He stood up, offered her his hand.

"Where?" she asked, getting painfully to her feet.

"My place. Unless you'd still rather stay here?" He nodded to her ruined bedroom.

Sophie shuddered. "No, thank you. But what about Ailsa?"

"She'll be fine. She'll sleep until morning, and wake up thinking it was all a bad dream."

"How did you manage that?"

"By whispering sweet nothings." He smiled at her dubious look. "Honestly – I can fade bad human memories. Another angel talent I managed to hold onto down here."

"So what happens if she opens my door and sees demon cat blood everywhere?"

"One good thing about demons is that they don't like to leave traces. The material evidence will be gone by morning. It'll be fading already."

"Honestly?"

"Have a look."

292

Reluctantly, Sophie went back toward the bedroom. When she looked inside, the *Cait Sìth*'s form had slumped and shrunken, as if the floor were absorbing it. The dark stain wasn't quite so dark, though the furniture and bedclothes were still a mess. The knife now lay on the floor beside the shriveling body, clean and shining softly. Lucas picked it up, testing its edge with a careful finger.

"You have to hand it to him," he muttered, "he makes a fine blade."

"Arthur?" Sophie asked.

Lucas gave her a strange smile. "Azazel."

"*Sam* made that?"

Lucas nodded. "He was our master smith, in Heaven."

"And he made weapons for King Arthur? Talk about disillusioned!"

"Azazel hadn't turned, then. And anyway, Arthur didn't know that he made it. It was commissioned by Merlin, millennia before Arthur was born."

"So Arthur fought demons?"

"Sometimes. And witches, and more than his share of *sìth*… anyhow, now it's yours."

"I don't want it," Sophie said.

"But you called it, and it came. That makes it yours."

"I don't plan on fighting any more demons, anytime soon. Please, Lucas, it's too creepy. You keep it."

"Well…for now." Reluctantly, he threaded the knife through his belt.

Sophie looked around the room again. "Will Ailsa be safe here, alone?" she asked. "What if something else gets in?"

Lucas shook his head. "It was after you, Sophie. Besides, whoever called up the *Cait Sìth* will be out of commission for a while. Summoning demons is exhausting." Sophie gave him a questioning look. "Or so I hear," he added quickly. "Is there anything you need from here?"

Sophie looked down at herself and sighed. "Clothes that aren't covered in demon guts," she said. "And my harp, and a toothbrush, I suppose…" She began to stuff things into her messenger bag. When she had everything she wanted, and Lucas was holding her harp case, she took one last look at the room. Then she followed Lucas out the door, shutting it behind her.

They walked for a few moments in silence, and then Sophie asked the question she'd so far avoided: "Do you know who sent it? The cat demon?"

"Theoretically, anybody – any creature – can summon a demon," Lucas said hesitantly. "But in reality, very few have the knowledge or strength to see the ritual through."

"Sam," she said bitterly.

"It's true, angels are taught to do it as a matter of course," Lucas answered. "But if Sam wants your soul, then I very much doubt he'd send a demon to kill you."

"Maybe he doesn't want my soul after all," she suggested. "Or maybe he didn't mean for it to kill me – just to drag me off to his lair, or whatever."

Lucas shook his head. "It's too risky. Demons aren't that

easy to control; nothing would guarantee that it wouldn't kill you in the process. As it very nearly did."

"Who else could it have been? Michael has to protect me since I'm human, and I haven't met any local witches."

"That doesn't mean there aren't any." Sophie gave him a sharp look, but he just said, "All I know is that you aren't safe on your own. I'm not letting you out of my sight again until we figure out what's going on."

Normally it was the kind of comment that would have made Sophie's independence prickle, but now she just felt relieved. She had no desire to meet another supernatural creature on her own.

CHAPTER 25

"Here," Lucas said when they were back in his bedroom. He pushed a door open and turned on a light, illuminating a pristine white bathroom with a deep tub. "Wash the blood off, and then we'll have a look at the war wounds."

Sophie nodded and shut the bathroom door. She took one look at herself in the mirror, and then turned away in revulsion. She looked like the victim in a bad horror film. Her aching muscles screamed for a bath, but there was no way she was going to sit in a tub of bloody water, so she turned on the shower instead. When it was as hot as she could stand it, she shed her wrecked pajamas and stepped under the stream of water.

At first her cuts stung so she thought she could barely stand it, but eventually the pain eased. For a long time she just let the water stream over her. When it finally ran clear, she washed herself all over, and her hair twice. Finally, she shut the water off and stepped out of the bath. She looked in the mirror again. There were bruises blossoming on her arms and legs, scratches on her hands and a diagonal one on her right cheek, but the only wound that looked deep was the one on her shoulder. The four parallel lines were livid on her white skin, and as she stood there a trickle of blood ran down from one of them.

Sighing, Sophie chose a towel from a heated rack. She wished that it weren't white, but there was nothing to be done about that – she wasn't going to put her bloody clothes back on. Instead she lifted them gingerly and dropped them into the bin. Then, shyly, she opened the door. Though most of her was covered by the towel, it still felt strangely intimate for Lucas to see her like that.

When she stepped into the room, however, she forgot her mortification. Lucas was rummaging in the dresser, wearing only his jeans. The black tattoo stood out on it like intricate wrought iron on the golden skin of his lean, muscled back. He chose a dark red tee shirt and pulled it over his head, leaving Sophie half relieved, half disappointed. Then he turned, and his own face flushed when he saw her.

"How long have you been standing there?" he asked.

"Long enough," she said softly, and then she shook her head, thinking, *Did I really just say that?* To hide her embarrassment, she said quickly, "Your tattoo – what does it mean?"

He half-smiled, reaching down to turn on a reading lamp by the bed. He indicated to her to sit down beside it, and went into the bathroom as he answered, "It's not a tattoo, it's my sigil. My name, in angelic script." He came back out of the bathroom, carrying a first-aid kit. He angled the light so that it shone on her

297

bleeding shoulder, and then knelt in front of her. "All of us have them. They're as much a part of us as our skin or hair."

Sophie nodded, wondering whether she'd ever had a sigil. Then she forgot about sigils and everything else, as Lucas touched the claw marks with a cloth dipped in iodine. "Ouch!" she cried.

"Sorry," he said. "I'm trying to be gentle, but these cuts are deep. The last thing you need is an infection." He studied them for a moment. "I wonder whether I ought to take you to a hospital."

"No," Sophie said emphatically. "I hate hospitals. Besides, how would you explain it? And how would we get there this time of night?"

"Okay. But if it hasn't stopped bleeding by tomorrow, we'll have to go."

"It'll stop," Sophie said. "I told you, I heal fast."

Lucas said nothing, just dabbed at the wound until all of it had been covered with the iodine. Then he cut a gauze pad and taped it down. Finally, he gave her two tablets and a glass of water.

"Paracetamol," he said. "Demon wounds hurt like hell." Sophie swallowed the tablets, thinking that "hurt like hell" was an understatement. "I'll...um...let you get dressed now," Lucas said, retreating to the bathroom with the first-aid kit.

Sophie pulled on the tracksuit bottoms she'd shoved into the bag, and then, carefully, an old tee shirt. "I'm decent," she told Lucas.

He came back out of the bathroom, picked up the bloody towel and tossed it down the stairs. "Is there anything you want?" he asked. "A cup of tea?"

Sophie shook her head. "All I really want to do is sleep."

Lucas nodded. "I'll be downstairs if you need anything." He turned to go, and a wave of desolation hit Sophie.

"No!" she cried, leaping to her feet. He turned, his eyes intent, questioning. "I…I mean…will you stay with me? Just for a little while…" She trailed off, feeling suddenly ridiculous.

But Lucas was smiling at her, and it seemed she'd never seen anything sweeter. "Of course I will," he said. "I just didn't want you to think…I mean, I would never push you…"

"It's okay," she said. "I don't think anything, except that I don't want you to go."

"Then I won't."

Lucas turned off the lamp, but there was still a soft glow from the lights downstairs. Sophie was grateful for that. She didn't think she could ever sleep in the dark again. She pulled back the covers, lay down and then looked up at Lucas, who was hovering at the far side of the bed.

"Ah…do you want me to – " he began.

"Yes," Sophie said, holding out a hand to him. He took it, and lay down carefully beside her. "I won't break," she said.

"Your shoulder…"

"It's better already." She moved closer to him, and he curled around her, solid and warm. Her heart beat against their clasped hands, and Sophie felt herself tipping toward sleep. Then she remembered. "You don't sleep," she said drowsily.

"No."

"You don't have to stay...boring..."

"Sophie," he said, "the only thing I've wanted since the day we were separated was to hold you like this again. I could lie here for a thousand years, and it wouldn't be long enough."

She smiled, and shut her eyes, and slept.

*

When Sophie awakened she was lying on something hard, and her whole body ached. "Ouch," she said.

"Well, what do you expect, taking on a demon barehanded?"

The voice was female, unapologetic, American. Sophie's eyes flew open, and she pushed herself upright to a twanging chorus of pulled muscles. She was sitting on a long wooden table. It was scuffed and stained, decorated here and there with ballpoint graffiti – and familiar. It was one of the tables from her college library.

But she wasn't at college. The table was set up under the tree in Suri's cemetery, its branches laden with blossoms that fell like snow in the gentle breaths of wind. Suri herself was seated at the head of the table in an ornate wooden chair, perusing what looked like an old-fashioned library file drawer, wearing a neat black and white hounds-tooth jacket, her hair swept into a wild beehive, topped by a pillbox hat. Sophie suspected she was aiming for Jackie Kennedy, but the effect was more 1960s airline stewardess.

It was only when she swung her legs over the side of the table that she realized she herself was dressed in nothing but a blue bath towel. "Do you pick these outfits for me?" she asked dryly.

Suri glanced up from the card drawer. "Nope. They're supplied by your subconscious."

Sophie raised an eyebrow. "My subconscious would never have chosen purple animal prints."

"What?"

"Remember Paris?"

Suri looked up at her speculatively. "Alright. Maybe I give the occasional nudge. But the bath towel is all you." She smirked. "Care to explain?"

Sophie thought back on the events preceding the dream. "Not especially," she said.

"If you're embarrassed because you're in bed with Lucifer – "

"What?" Sophie cried. "How do you know that?"

Suri took something out of her pocket and handed it to Sophie. It was an iPhone. On the screen was a streaming image: Lucas stretched on his bed, reading from a heavy leather-bound volume, while she lay curled against him, sleeping.

"Alright," Sophie said, handing the phone back. "I'm in bed with him, but obviously I'm not *in bed* with him."

Suri waved her protests aside. "You don't have to explain yourself to me. I'm on your side, remember?"

"Actually, no," Sophie sighed, "but that's hardly news." She paused, considering what Suri had just said. "You were with me when they fought – Michael and Lucas."

Suri pushed her card drawer aside and looked up at Sophie. "Of course I was with you. I couldn't let you watch that alone."

Sophie thought of the others that had stood with them in the vision. "Did the other angels really think it was wrong for Lucas and me to be together?"

Suri shook her head. "They were divided. It was why they allowed the duel. It was the only way they could think of to settle it."

"Is that why you don't like Michael? Because you were on our side?"

"What gives you the idea I don't like him?"

"The way you were in Paris, in the café."

Suri sighed. "I don't dislike Michael; I just disagree with a lot of his attitudes. And he's a stick in the mud when it comes to rules…but I really don't think you came here to talk about that."

"No," Sophie agreed. "I came here for the book." Because there was suddenly no question in her mind that this was the case. In fact, she felt a sudden, slight hope, given Suri's card catalogue, that she might actually be on her way to finding some valuable information.

"Ah. The book."

"I don't suppose you're going to just hand me a copy?"

Suri smiled faintly. "Finally, you're learning how this works."

"But you admit there *is* a book. The one I dictated to Enoch."

"Yes. But it was more of a scroll…"

Sophie pulled out a chair and sat down beside her. "You mean you've seen it?"

"Of course I've seen it! I helped you hide it."

"Where?" Suri looked at her hands. "Oh, right, you can't tell me."

"Definitely learning!" She smiled ruefully.

"I suppose it's also against the rules to tell me what it was about?"

Suri shrugged. "No doubt it would have been, if I'd read it."

"Why haven't you read it?"

"You wouldn't let me. You said that it would be too dangerous – that no one could know what you were planning. Not even me."

Seeing that Suri was still affronted by this, Sophie said, "For what it's worth, I'm sorry about that. You can read it now, if you tell me where we hid it."

Suri gave her a half-smile. "You don't think you would have made it *that* easy? Nope: you wiped that part of my memory squeaky clean."

"I can do that?"

"You *could* do that. When you were an aeon. And I did *not* appreciate it!"

"Sorry," Sophie said, and she was. But that wasn't

303

particularly relevant to the matter at hand. "There must be a reason why I keep dreaming this place, and you. Didn't I say anything to you before the mind-cleaning thing? Or maybe just after?"

"No doubt you did," Suri answered thoughtfully. "I imagine my remembering is a matter of you asking the right questions."

Sophie shook her head in frustration. "I have no idea where to begin!"

Suri studied her again. At last she said, "Okay, look: this is Suri-your-Friend talking, not Suri-the-Angel. Plain old unadulterated advice, so Views Expressed in This Soundbite Don't Necessarily Reflect Those of My Sponsors, right?"

"Um, whatever."

"What you have to remember," Suri said, leaning toward her conspiratorially, "is that you were Wisdom. Level-headed, down-to-earth, pragmatic, well informed…you get the idea. Becoming human was difficult and risky and, more to the point, way, *way* out of character. For you to try it, there must have been a pretty good reason."

"Like wanting to be with Lucas?"

"I don't think so. I mean, obviously that was part of it, but I don't think it's the whole story. You'd been apart for millennia by the time you did what you did. There must have been more to it than panting after a guy."

"Suri!"

"The point *is*, if I were you, I'd be taking a good long look

304

at the human life I'd lived so far. At the common themes and anomalies."

Sophie shook her head. "There's not much to look at. I study hard and get good marks…I play the harp pretty well…I have a spectacular lack of a social life. Aside from being certifiably scholarly, I'm really quite average."

Suri's black eyes seemed to drill into her. "Really? There's *nothing* at all extraordinary about you?"

"Not unless you count my recent talent for attracting supernatural monsters. And that all started when I came to Ardnasheen. I mean, before that I never saw – " She stopped short, wondering how she could have forgotten. "The Revenants!" she cried. "They must be the clue!"

"Interesting idea," Suri said, "if kind of morbid."

"Is there anything else you can tell me about them? Do you have any books that might help?" She indicated the card drawer.

But Suri shook her head. "It's like Lucifer told you: they were never meant to be. Besides, they're earthly creatures, not something most angels are ever likely to experience, let alone write about."

"But they're made by angels."

"*Fallen* angels. Key distinction."

Something was niggling at the back of Sophie's mind. She thought back over what Lucas had told her about the Revenants. That they'd lost their souls to fallen angels, hoping to return to Heaven. That none of the fallen had yet made it work. That her own soul might be different because she'd once been divine, but in the end it all might be no more than rumour…and yet, a rumour had to start somewhere. What had been the germ of the idea? Why would Sam think that she was a better bet than any other human? Unless –

"Sam has it," she said aloud.

"Who's Sam?" Suri asked.

"Sorry, Azazel."

For the first time ever, Suri looked stunned. "You think *Azazel* has your book?"

But Sophie was too much alight with the idea to hear the incredulity, or the indirect warning in Suri's tone. "He must! It's the only explanation that makes sense."

"Sophie," Suri said, her face serious and eyes troubled, "I know I haven't been much help to you, but please believe me when I say I think you're wrong about this. Azazel is dangerous, and more than that, he hates Lucifer. I can't think of anything that would have made you give your book to him, let alone by choice."

"But it *must* be him!" Sophie insisted. "That'll be why he wants my soul: something in the book has made him want it. He knows whatever it is that I've forgotten, and there's only one way for me to find out what that is."

"Ask him?"

"No: find his copy of the book."

"I don't like this…"

"Do you have a better suggestion?" Sophie demanded.

"Well, no, but –"

"I'm sorry, Suri. I know what I have to do."

Chapter 26

Sophie sat bolt upright in bed, and found she was alone. Panic surged through her. "Lucas!" she cried, and was both mortified and relieved to hear him bounding up the stairs.

"What is it?" he asked, rushing to her side.

"It's – it's nothing," she said sheepishly. "Only I woke up, and you weren't here…"

"I was making breakfast," he said, sitting down beside her and pulling her into his arms.

"I had a dream," Sophie blurted in her rush of relief.

"A nightmare?"

"No. It was Suri. We were talking about the book. I think Sam has it." She looked at him expectantly.

He returned with a dubious look. "I think if Sam had something like that, we'd know about it."

"Not if he had plans for using it against us. Then he'd do his best to hide it, until the right moment."

"That would be…unfortunate."

"Unfortunate! Unfortunate would be if it were in Beijing, or Vladivostok – "

"I think you underestimate Sam. Anyway, tell me what happened."

Sophie told him about her conversation with Suri, and the train of thought that had led her to her conclusion. When she was finished, Lucas said, "Okay, I suppose it's possible that Sam has it."

"But?"

"But even if he does, it's going to be next to impossible to get it from him. As Suriel told you, he hates me – very likely you, too, now you've thrown in your lot with me."

"So," Sophie argued, "we wait until the next time he goes to Mallaig, and then search his house."

"We can't do that."

"Don't tell me your conscience is troubling you."

"No, I mean we physically *can't*. Staves work for more than keeping the fallen in our place. They can also keep things out. Sam's staved his house against me, the same as I've staved mine against him."

Sophie thought about this. "What if he invites you?"

Lucas laughed wryly. "We aren't vampires, Sophie – and as it happens, the vampire invitation thing's a myth anyway. Angels, vampires – if a house is staved, it's staved."

"But Sam got in here. The night I saw the Revenant on the road, he made me dinner."

"Yes," Lucas sighed, "I remember. I hadn't got round to staving the kitchen after it was re-done. But I'll bet he didn't go into the rest of the house, did he?"

"Well, no," Sophie admitted. She thought about this, and then said, "I guess I'll have to do it. I doubt he's staved his house against me."

"Absolutely not!" Lucas cried.

"I'm a big girl, Lucas. You can come and keep watch, if it'll make you feel better."

"And how do you plan to find it? If this book's even in his house at all, I doubt he's keeping it in plain sight."

But Sophie could hear his resolve weakening. "There's only one way to find out."

"Sophie, please."

"Please, what? Pretend that none of this is happening?"

Lucas looked at her, a wild glint in his eyes. "Yes. Forget it's happening. Forget there's a world out there at all. Just stay here with me and pretend there was never anything else for us."

That startled her into silence. After a moment, though, she shook her head. "You know that I can't do that."

"I know," he said softly, sadly. After a moment, "There's no way to talk you out of this, is there?"

"No."

"Alright," he sighed, "but let me do some reconnaissance first. In the meantime, promise me you won't do anything daft."

"Like what?"

"Like go to Sam's place on your own. Or ask him questions about the book. Or go anywhere near him, for that matter. Even if he wasn't mixed up in the thing with the demon, he's still dangerous to you."

"I know that," Sophie said, "and I don't plan to do any of those things. Not without you, anyhow."

"Good," he said, and kissed her on the forehead. "Now

309

you'd better come and have something to eat. You need to be at work soon."

"Ugh," Sophie groaned, remembering. "And I'm on 'till closing."

"I thought you had the evening off?"

Sophie shook her head. "I said I'd cover for Ailsa, as she covered for me yesterday. She has a date."

"Right, then, I suppose I'll be spending the evening at the pub."

"You know, you don't have to literally watch me *all* the time."

Lucas smiled wryly. "Revenants, water horses, demon cats…care for me to continue?"

Sophie shuddered. "Okay, enough said."

*

After breakfast Lucas walked her back to her room. First she looked in on Ailsa, who was sleeping peacefully. Then, reluctantly, she faced her own door.

"I'll go first," Lucas said.

"No," she answered. "If you think it's safe, then I think it's safe."

Willing her hand not to shake, she turned the knob and pushed the door inward. Although Lucas had warned her to expect it, it was unnerving to find all traces of the *Cait Sith* erased. The bedclothes were still tumbled, the curtains torn and the fire-irons scattered, but the body and the hideous black pool of liquid in which it had lain were gone.

"I'll tidy up," Lucas said, "while you get ready."

Sophie nodded, collected her work clothes and headed to the bathroom. Inspecting herself in the mirror, she thought grimly that she'd do well to buy stock in concealer. She did the best she could to disguise the signs of the fight and yet another sleepless night. Lucas had changed the dressing on her shoulder before they left his room, and luckily her long-sleeved "World's End" tee shirt covered it completely. Sophie knew that she looked very far from her best, but at least she no longer looked like she'd been wrestling a bear.

When she returned to her room, Lucas had straightened the bedclothes and put everything else back in place, though he'd taken down the bed curtains. "They're fairly well shredded," he said, stuffing them into a bin bag. Sophie also noticed that he'd pulled her rucksack out of the wardrobe.

"Planning a trip?" she asked.

"No," he said. "You are. To my place. I can move your things after I walk you to work."

Sophie sat down on the desk and regarded him levelly. "Couldn't you ask, rather than tell?"

He flushed. "Sorry. I guess I've lived alone too long. Sophie, would you like to move in with me?"

"Really?" she asked. "Because I hear that cohabitation is the death of romance."

"That's only if you're ordinary people."

She smiled, but she said, "Honestly, Lucas – what if we drive each other mad?"

"We won't," he answered. "Remember, we've done this before."

Sophie wished that she *could* remember. Then maybe it wouldn't feel as if her world were suddenly spinning too fast. "What will I tell Ailsa?" she asked. "And will she be safe here, alone?"

"I told you, Sophie, it's *you* who're in danger, not Ailsa. She lived here alone for months with no problems. As for what to tell her…" He glanced up at her quickly, almost involuntarily. "What's wrong with the truth?"

"You mean, that I have to move in with my fallen angel boyfriend because otherwise, I might well be eaten by demons?"

He smiled. "You can tell her that if you want to. But I meant, tell her you've fallen madly in love, and you can't bear to be away from me any longer than necessary."

"Is that a sneaky way of making me declare myself?" Sophie asked, holding his eyes.

"No. It's what I plan to say to anyone who asks me what's up."

"Well," she said, smiling, "when you put it like that, what can I say but 'yes'?"

*

As soon as Sophie stepped through the door of the pub, she

knew that something was wrong. The bar props were in their usual places, but instead of chatting and bantering together, they were all staring at the television, which was tuned to a local news channel. Ruadhri and the few breakfast customers were also riveted to the screen. Michael, Sophie noticed, was absent.

"What's going on?" Sophie asked as she tied on her apron.

Ruadhri just pointed to the screen, which had flashed up an image of a pretty blonde girl, smiling into the camera. Though she'd only seen her a few times, Sophie was certain that it was the winkle picker, Mairi. The commentary confirmed it:

"…local twenty-year-old, Mairi MacIvor, who was reported missing on Wednesday. Police are now broadening the search to include all of Inverness-shire, Skye and the Outer Isles. She was last seen picking shellfish on a beach on the Morar Peninsula. Mallaig police are asking that anyone with information about her whereabouts contact them immediately. In other news…"

Ruadhri switched off the television, and the men at the bar turned morosely back to their drinks. "A bad piece of business, this," he said. "A nice lass, she was. Clever, too. You know the shellfish business was to save money for university?"

"She's not dead," Sophie said. "Not that they know of, anyway."

"Aye, but the ones who go missing here are seldom found," Donald muttered into his whisky.

"Donald," said Iain, who was sitting next to him, in a warning tone.

"It's no more than the truth, though, is it?" Ruadhri said.

Nobody answered. "You and Ailsa had best be careful," he said to Sophie. "I'll not have you walking here and back alone."

"It's Mallaig she disappeared from," Sophie said, in an attempt to assuage the chill creeping over her, "not Ardnasheen."

"Nonetheless," Ruadhri said, "you cannae be too careful. Best have your young man walk with you, or else I'll run you back and forth."

"Okay – thanks."

Ruadhri nodded, and pushed through into the kitchen. Sophie stayed behind, staring out the window at the still, grey sea. She couldn't stop thinking about Sam talking to Mairi in the pub that night. It was all too easy to imagine what had happened to her, and she knew that she needed to tell Lucas. She wished that she didn't have to make the call in front of an audience, but she also knew that there was no time to waste. She looked up the number for Madainneag on the list by the phone, and dialed, praying that Lucas was there. He picked it up on the second ring.

"Sophie?"

"Now that's just creepy!"

"Not really. You're the only one who would call me. What is it? Are you alright?"

"I'm fine, but something's happened. Mairi MacIvor has gone missing – that girl who picks shellfish on the beach."

There was a long silence, and then a dejected sigh. "I warned her," he muttered.

"So you think it's…" she glanced around at the men at the

bar, and knew that they were only pretending not to be listening intently to her conversation.

"Sam?" Lucas said. "No doubt."

Sophie felt as if she'd been punched. Somehow, the thought of someone she'd known, however vaguely, becoming a Revenant was far more terrible than seeing the ones that existed already. "Is there anything to be done?" she asked.

"Maybe," he said. "Leave it with me. And whatever you do, don't walk home alone."

"I don't intend to."

"I'll pick you up at the end of your shift."

"Okay. Thank you." Sophie put the phone down, and turned to the bar-props. None of them would quite meet her eye, but she wasn't about to be put off so easily.

"What did you mean by what you said, Donald?" she asked. "About the ones who go missing not being found?"

Donald and Iain exchanged an uncomfortable glance. Then Donald looked back at her and said, "We've had more than our share of tragedies, here. Walkers going missing in the hills, sailors falling into the sea – "

"Old folks found dead in their houses," Iain interrupted.

Sophie's chill deepened. "You mean that man, Niall? You think there was something suspicious about his death?"

Both men were silent for a moment, looking intently into their glasses. Then Donald raised his eyes and said, "All I can say for certain is that not everything here is as it seems." *No kidding,* Sophie thought. "And if it isnae too bold to say so, you'd do well to watch yourself with the laird."

"Lucas?" she asked incredulously.

"No. The other one."

"You think Sam Eblis knows something about the girl's disappearance?"

Again, the men exchanged a glance. After a moment, Donald said, "Just watch yourself, lass."

*

The mood in the pub didn't improve as the day progressed. Ruadhri was in a vile temper after finding that five kegs of beer were flat, and there was no chance of getting replacements before the weekend. Ailsa showed up for the lunch shift grumbling about the terrible night's sleep she'd had, plagued by bizarre nightmares, and Sophie could do nothing but nod and try not to look guilty. Her lunch customers seemed to complain incessantly, and they all left stingy tips. When it finally arrived, Sophie was more than ready for her afternoon break.

It was a decent day, bright in a faded, mid-autumn kind of way, with a few watery rays of sun breaking through the clouds. She pulled on her jacket and then took her tea and a handful of biscuits out back, glad to be away from the pub's morose atmosphere. She stuck a brick of peat in the doorway so that the door wouldn't shut and lock her out. Then she sat down on the large round of wood that Ruadhri used as a chopping block.

Her head was just beginning to clear when she heard voices approaching, one male and one female. They stopped on the other side of the door, apparently not noticing that it was ajar. Sophie was about to open it and let them know she was there, when she identified the male voice as Sam's.

"Can't you get off any earlier?" he asked.

"I'm sorry, but we're swamped." Sophie froze with her tea mug half-way to her lips. The answering voice was Ailsa's. "At the dot of five, though, I'm yours," she finished with a flirtatious laugh.

Sophie put the mug down, feeling suddenly ill. No wonder Ailsa hadn't wanted to tell her who she was going out with. She couldn't believe that Ailsa would even consider it, after what she'd told her about her own date with him.

"I'll hold you to that," Sam said, equally flirtatious.

"What should I wear?" Ailsa asked. "I mean, are we going somewhere?"

"Wear whatever you like," he said after a moment, "as long as it includes a good set of waterproofs."

"Waterproofs?" Ailsa asked. "Don't tell me we're climbing a mountain!"

Sam chuckled. "You'll see," at which point Sophie decided that enough was enough. She flung the door open, surprising Sam and Ailsa just as he leaned in to kiss her. She had to stifle the urge to punch him when, rather than annoyance or embarrassment, he turned to face her with a calm, cynical smile.

Ailsa, however, was livid. "Sophie!" Ailsa cried. "You've been *eavesdropping*?"

"Not intentionally." She glared at Sam, whose smile only widened. Then she looked back at Ailsa. Beneath her bluster, Sophie could see that a part of her was uncomfortable, and she appealed to this. "But why were you keeping this a secret?"

Ailsa's look turned cold. Deliberately, she took hold of Sam's hand, her eyes challenging. "Maybe because I knew that you'd be like this about it."

"Ailsa, after everything I told you – "

"As I recall," Sam interrupted, "there really wasn't much to tell."

"Only because Michael showed up," Sophie said.

"Don't flatter yourself," Sam answered, his smile unwavering, though his eyes bored into her, betraying his anger. "Ailsa, I'll see you at five." He kissed her cheek, and went back into the pub.

When he was gone, Ailsa turned on Sophie. "What is *wrong* with you? You know how long I've liked Sam, and now that he finally notices me, here you are trying to sabotage it!"

"Sabotage it?" Sophie repeated. "Ailsa, I would never do that to you. If he was anybody else, I'd be thrilled for you, but he's – "

"What?" Ailsa demanded. "What exactly is it that's so terrible about him?"

"I *told* you – "

"That he tried to kiss you," Ailsa interrupted, "which frankly shouldn't have been that surprising, given you went to his house, alone."

"Are you saying it's *my* fault, what he tried to do? Which was much more than kiss me, by the way."

Ailsa shook her head, her face flushed and eyes too bright. "That's funny, because he has quite a different memory of what happened."

"Does he?" Sophie said mechanically. She didn't want to hear Sam's version – it was easy enough to guess – but she doubted there was any way out of it now. Ailsa had clearly been saving up this resentment for a long time.

"He told me all about how you came on to him," Ailsa continued, "and how when he rejected you, you came up with this story about him attacking you, to save face."

Sophie wasn't sure whether she was more upset that Sam had said those things about her, or that Ailsa believed them. Either way, she felt betrayed, and suddenly exhausted. She thought of what Lucas had told her, about Sam charming the Revenants to their own destruction. She knew that she would never convince Ailsa that Sam had been lying, and she doubted there was any way to keep her from going out with him, either. Still, she couldn't give up on her friend without trying.

"Alright," she said, forcing herself to sound calm. "Maybe there was a misunderstanding, that night. But Ailsa, he's not all that you think he is. There are things in his past that…well, that you wouldn't like, if you knew about them."

"Oh? Then enlighten me."

"I can't," Sophie said miserably.

"Why not? I mean, if it's so very important?"

"Because I'm – " she paused, stifling an ironic smile when she realized that the word she'd been about to say was "bound". "I promised I wouldn't," she finished.

"Well, that's bloody convenient."

"Ailsa, do you know what they're saying in the bar? They think Sam had something to do with Mairi MacIvor's disappearance."

"Who thinks that?"

"Iain and Donald were talking about it this morning."

Ailsa laughed incredulously. "Iain and Donald? You might as well take advice from Dial-a-Psychic."

"Ailsa, you're my friend. Why would I try to ruin your plans without good reason?"

"I don't know," Ailsa said, scrutinizing her. "In fact, I really don't know you very well at all. What's it been – a few weeks? I've known Sam nearly a year. If it comes to credibility, you can't really compete."

Sophie tried not to show how much that hurt. "Have I ever lied to you?" she asked softly.

"Well," Ailsa said, looking at her with cold speculation, "you certainly seem to be a lot more intimate with Lucas than you've been letting on."

"*What?*"

"Or didn't you spend last night with him?"

"That has nothing to do with anything."

"Doesn't it? Who is it that's told you about Sam's deep dark past? Whose secrets are you keeping from me?"

Sophie shut her eyes, feeling like she was sliding down a muddy slope with no handhold in sight. "I'd tell you everything, if I could," she said.

"Sorry," Ailsa said, "but that isn't good enough. You know, I think I'll take off early, see if I can catch Sam." She pulled off her apron, shoved it into Sophie's hands. "After all, you owe me one." She began to walk away, but she turned back once, at the corner of the building. "And don't wait up for me."

Sophie watched her until she disappeared. In the silence that followed, all of the strangeness of the past few days finally caught up with her. She sat down on an empty keg and burst into tears, only recalling herself when she heard Ruadhri shouting for her.

She blotted her wet face with Ailsa's apron, dumped out her untouched tea and left the biscuits for the birds. It was only as she was opening the door that the full meaning of her argument with Ailsa hit her. It was true, she'd failed to stop her friend from going out with a man who might put her in very real danger. But there was one consequence of her inability to change Ailsa's mind that was, if not quite a silver lining, at least a perk. Because if Ailsa and Sam were out somewhere that night, then his house would be empty.

CHAPTER 27

"See?" Sophie said, as the Land Rover reached the top of the hill behind Sam's house. "No lights on."

Lucas said nothing, only chewed on his thumb as he let the engine idle and looked down pensively at the dark house.

"Come on, Lucas – we're here now, and we might never have another opportunity like this."

He frowned. "Still, I'd be happier if you weren't involved..."

"We've *been* through all of this. The house is staved against you; angelic staves don't work on me. There isn't any other way – unless you want to ask Michael to sneak into the house instead." Lucas sighed in resignation, pulled the Land Rover off the road and cut the engine.

The moon was full and the sky was clear, making it easy to see where they were going as they hiked down the hill toward the house. It was just as well, since they didn't dare risk turning on their head torches outside, in case Sam was still nearby.

With Ailsa. Alone. "I can't stop worrying about her," Sophie said aloud.

"Ailsa?" Sophie nodded. "It's not the ideal situation," Lucas agreed, "but on the other hand, if he'd wanted Ailsa's soul, he would have taken it long before this."

"And if he really liked her, he'd have asked her out before this," Sophie said grimly. "Why the sudden interest?"

Lucas paused, and then said hesitantly, "I know that it isn't what you want to hear, but it is possible that she's just a way to pass the time. After all, there aren't many girls in Ardnasheen, and Azazel has a weakness for women."

Sophie glanced at him. His face was ruminative rather than anxious. "You're right," she said. "I didn't want to hear that."

"But in the grand scheme, it's probably the best of the possibilities."

"Jeez, Lucas, you really know how to make a girl feel better!"

"Sorry," he said.

"Don't be," Sophie sighed. "I'm being grumpy. I've just felt all wrong since that fight with Ailsa."

"Friends fight, sometimes," Lucas said.

"This was different," Sophie said, even as she wondered how she would know, never having had a friend close enough to fight with. "*She* was different. The things she said…it was as if she thought I'd always been out to get her."

"Angels can be very persuasive. She was probably just

repeating whatever Sam said to her. She'll come around sooner or later."

And hopefully while she's still breathing. But she was exhausted with worrying about it. Besides, they'd almost reached the house. She needed to focus on the task ahead. They stopped in the driveway to look around. Everything was still and silent, the car dark, its engine cool. Sophie hung back by the Sprite while Lucas scouted the exterior.

"It really does look like he's gone," he said when he returned.

"Good. Now, let's hope he doesn't lock his doors."

"It doesn't matter if he does," Lucas said, producing a key from his pocket.

"Now why on earth would you have that," Sophie asked, "if you can't actually get inside?"

Lucas shrugged. "Just a precaution. No doubt he has keys to mine, too." Sophie held out her hand, and Lucas pressed the key into it. "Remember, no lights. Put everything back just the way you found it. And if he comes back – "

"You'll do your impression of a barn owl. All very Famous Five. Now stop worrying – I'll be as quick as I can." Sophie ran up the steps before he could think of another protest, feeling his dubious eyes on her the whole way.

It took some jiggling to make the key work, and for a moment she wondered if Sam had found a way to barricade the house against her after all. But then the bolt slid back, and the door opened into the dark porch. Sophie waved to Lucas, and then shut it behind her.

The full moon flooded the front room with blue-white light. She made her way through it with only a perfunctory glance around. The obvious place to look was the bookshelves in the stairwell. Once there, she shut the door to the living room and turned on her head-torch. The only windows were narrow ones placed high up on the stair wall. She had to hope that her light wouldn't be visible from them.

Turning to the books, she adjusted the beam until it was a narrow spotlight, and then she began to scan the spines. She took the time to check every one separately, even studying the titles in foreign languages for any word that might be discernible. Some of them looked interesting, many more of them tedious, and a few made no sense to her at all. Nothing she saw, however, seemed to relate in any way to Sophia, or even to aeons in general.

The same was true of the second bookcase. In the third, she found a copy of the Gnostic Gospels, but it was a modern paperback, and a quick flick through the pages turned up not so much as an underlined passage or scribbled margin note. She put the book back and kept looking. Some time later she found a book in French called *Pistis Sophia*. Sophie had learned Italian at school, but she kept it out anyway, thinking that Lucas might be able to read it.

She perused the rest of the bookshelves, pulling a few more volumes that looked like they might be related to Enoch or Gnostic philosophy, but she didn't hold out much hope that they'd be helpful. It seemed that Lucas had been right: if Sam had the text she was looking for, he hadn't been foolish enough to keep it in plain sight.

Sophie turned her head-torch toward the stairs. Whatever was at the top of them seemed a more likely alternative than the kitchen or sitting room, when it came to hiding a book. Turning the torch off, she began to climb by the faint moonlight sifting through the windows. At the top of the stairs there was a tiny landing with three closed doors opening off of it. She chose the nearest one, and pushed it open onto a small round room – the turret she'd seen from the outside.

The room was empty. The walls, floors and windows – even the tiny fireplace – were bare. The single ornamentation was a set of carvings built into the chimney wall, which looked as worn and battered as the gravestones in Lucas's cemetery. She ran her fingers across them, but aside from vague human figures, she couldn't make out their subject.

Leaving the turret room, she tried the middle door. It was locked. There was an old fashioned keyhole under the brass knob. She put her eye to it and peered through. Moonlight illuminated multiple dark shapes, but not enough for her to tell what they were. She turned to the final door, which opened easily. Inside was a bedroom with dark Victorian furniture, including a high four-poster bed that looked un-slept in. A single window looked out onto the sea.

Sophie pulled the curtain across it, and then turned on her head-torch. By its wan light she rummaged under the bed, taking time to feel around under the mattress and pillows. She flicked through the clothes in the wardrobe (nothing in the jacket pockets) and checked for a false back (no Narnia tunnel of trees.) Next, she looked through the dresser drawers. There were clothes, along with a variety of everyday items that were no different from what everyone kept in their dressers. She even pushed on the drawers' backs and bottoms, but they were all solid.

She hadn't really expected anything different. She'd already decided that if the manuscript was in Sam's house at all, it was in the locked room. Sophie went back to the landing and studied the door, thinking about the demon and the dagger with which she'd killed it. Though she had no real idea of how she'd managed to summon the knife, it had appeared when she most needed it. She wondered if the same could be true of a key. Telling herself that there was nothing to lose – and more to the point, no one in front of whom to look like an idiot – she put her hand over the keyhole.

"I need a key," she said into the silence. When nothing happened, she added, "Please." She waited a few more moments, but nothing changed. Glaring at the door, she said, "I, Sophia the aeon, command…" Except she had no idea who or what she was addressing with the command. "Um…a key to materialize," she finished, sounding halfhearted even to herself. She wasn't surprised when the door remained shut, her hand unencumbered by a key. "Forget it," she muttered to herself. She turned to go back downstairs – and found herself face-to-face with Sam.

She couldn't contain a gasp of horror. Sam, however,

regarded her without surprise – albeit with a cynical half-smile. She wondered where Lucas was, and what had happened to the barn owl signal.

"What are you doing here?" she demanded.

He gave her a calmly quizzical look. "This is *my* house, Sophie."

"I mean, you're meant to be out with Ailsa."

"She wasn't feeling well."

"She's at home?"

"I'll not answer any more questions," Sam said, taking a step toward her, "until you tell me what *you're* doing here. You might also enlighten me as to why Belial is skulking about in the shrubbery."

"You saw Lucas?" Sophie blurted, before she could think better of it.

Sam smiled. He stood in a patch of moonlight slanting through the narrow window. In its cold light, his skin looked like blue-white marble, his features crisply chiseled, but his eyes dissolved to black boreholes. *That's exactly how the devil would look,* Sophie thought, *if there was one.*

"Well?" he prompted.

"I was looking for something," Sophie grumbled.

"I wouldn't have taken you for a thief."

"Something that's mine."

Sam's smile broadened, but it was no less chilling. "*The Book of Sorrows.*"

The words were familiar as soon as he spoke them – so

much so that Sophie wondered how she had failed to remember them previously. She tried not to let it show in her expression, but Sam wasn't looking for affirmation. He continued just as if she'd agreed: "You won't find it in there." He indicated the locked door with his chin.

"Why are you telling me this?"

"To spare both of us a tedious round of bantering, and you some effort. Keys are notoriously difficult to summon, and even harder to summon accurately."

Once again Sophie had to force her expression to remain neutral; once again, it seemed to make no difference to Sam, who crossed the landing to the turret room without a glance at her. "The thing is, if I were you, I wouldn't put too much stock in the book." He opened the door, gestured to her to follow. "Enoch had some entertaining ideas, but in the end, he was just another religious nut." He turned back when he realized that she hadn't followed him. "Well? Do you want the scroll or not?"

Sophie stood resolutely still. "Where is Lucas?"

"Outside, watching dutifully for my return."

"Why would I believe that?"

Sam shrugged. "What does it matter? After all, he can't come in here, no matter how hard you scream."

Sophie took an inadvertent step back. Sam laughed, and grabbed her arms. He was so close to her now that she could see his eyes despite the shadows. They were glittering and strangely pale, absorbing every nuance of light and giving nothing back. He leaned toward her. Her breath came in short, sharp gasps. He might not be able to take her soul forcibly, but she didn't think this would stop him from hurting her. He pushed her up against the wall – not quite roughly, but with enough force to show her that she could never hope to fight him off. Despite promising herself not to give him the satisfaction, she could feel a scream building.

Oh God – she thought, and then she remembered that God wasn't listening. *I need you, Michael,* she thought, but half-heartedly. He could never get here fast enough to help her. There was a certain serenity in the despair that settled over her, then. . He gave her a long, probing look. And then he kissed her.

At first it was hesitant, as if he were uncertain of something, but it quickly grew more assured. Sophie's head swam as it had the first time he'd kissed her, but t time her revulsion was stronger than the confusion. She tried to pull away, wondering what had happened to the previous night's super-human strength. Then, as abruptly as he'd grabbed her, Sam let her go.

Sophie had a moment to wonder about the look of furious frustration on Sam's face before he said in a low, venomous voice, "You little bitch! You're blocking me!"

"Of course I'm bloody blocking you!" she cried, filled with a sudden, blinding fury. "Are you so used to getting what you want that you think I wouldn't fight for my soul?"

His face contorted with fury, and he raised his hand as if to strike her.

She laughed. "You think *hitting* me will convince me to hand it over?"

330

Slowly, Sam lowered his hand. Bizarrely, he'd begun once again to smile. "No. But it would be satisfying. You think you understand," he said, before she could answer, "but you don't." He turned back to the turret room and flicked a switch. It flooded with dim ochre light from a single, shadeless bulb hanging from the ceiling. "Which is why I'm going to give you what you want."

Sophie didn't follow him into the room. Every instinct told her to run for the stairs, for the relative safety of outside, where at least she'd have Lucas to help her. But she couldn't move. Something compelled her to stand and watch as Sam walked to the fireplace with its strange stone frieze. She wondered if the book could possibly say anything that was worth this fear, and humiliation.

As if he'd heard her thought, Sam turned back from the frieze to look at her. "That is, if you're certain that you want it?" he said.

"Why else would I have come here?" she spat back.

"Actually, I've been wondering that myself. Ancient texts tend to stir up more troubles than they solve. Besides, it's written in Aramaic. How do you mean to read it?"

Sophie pressed her lips together, unwilling to answer when he was so clearly mocking her. *Or is he?* A part of her had the feeling that she wasn't even real to him – just a minor character in his own drama, something for him to play off of until he managed to take what he wanted from her.

"Unless it isn't really you who wants it at all," he continued.

331

"This 'mission' wasn't your idea, was it? It was Lucifer's, and he used you because he couldn't get in here himself."

"He didn't!" Sophie cried.

Sam waved her protest aside. "I've known him longer than you have. He's terribly good at the lost boy act. We all had our talents…" He turned again to the frieze, and ran his finger over each stone in turn. "Lust, gluttony, greed," he said, "none of those. Not sloth, or wrath. Envy, perhaps – " He glanced at Sophie again, his finger hovering over the second to last stone, before it settled on the final one. "Pride. That's the one."

Wrapping his hand around the stone, he pulled, and it grated forward until it came free of the wall. He reached into the recess, his arm disappearing up to the elbow. After a moment he drew something out: a cylindrical bag of red cloth. He came back to the doorway and handed it to Sophie.

"The *Book of Sorrows*," he said, his tone and expression oddly circumspect. "The exact record of your revelation to Enoch."

Sophie looked at it, and then up at him, stupefied. "Why would you give this to me?" she asked.

He shrugged, and then smiled. "Because it really makes no difference whether you have it or not. I'll get your soul in the end."

Sophie clutched the bag to her chest, but she didn't run; not yet. Something in his words, in his expression, had wakened a premonition that she was missing something important in this exchange. "You sound very certain," she said.

He shrugged. "You rescinding your soul to me – that would be the ideal situation. But don't be tempted to think I don't have a backup plan."

Before Sophie could respond, she heard feet pounding up the stairs. She turned, expecting Lucas, but it was Michael who burst into the room, dressed in a kilt and holding a tarnished broadsword. Somehow, the sight of him frightened her more than anything she'd witnessed that night so far.

"You've overstepped your bounds, Azazel," he said in a stern, resonant voice. The Irish lilt was gone, replaced by a stronger version of the unfamiliar foreign accent she heard in Lucas and Sam's speech. Without turning to look at her, he said, "Sophia, get out."

"But – what – " she began, dazed.

"Out!" he bellowed, and she scurried. She took the stairs two at a time, ran through the sitting room and out into the night. Lucas was waiting for her at the bottom of the steps, his eyes wide and frightened.

"Sophie!" he cried when he saw her, leaping toward her.

"It's okay," she said, starting down the steps to the driveway, "I've got it – " And then she tripped. In a moment of horrific clarity, she seemed to watch herself fall. She tumbled to the ground, landing on her hands and knees.

There was a moment of perfect stillness, and then Lucas was rushing to her, "Are you alright?"

"Yes, yes," she said, pushing away his solicitous hands. "But the scroll…" She lifted the red bag from where it had fallen, and her heart dropped into her gut. She didn't even need to open it to know that the ancient paper inside had crumbled to a handful of dust.

CHAPTER 28

"I am an utter idiot," Sophie said, glaring at the pile of papyrus scraps lying on the table between herself and Lucas. It was late, and she was dressed in her pajamas. The adrenaline from her confrontation with Sam had long since drained out of her, leaving her limp and despondent.

"No, that would be me," Lucas answered, matching up two of the fragments on a glass plate with a pair of tweezers. "For agreeing to you going in there alone in the first place." He looked up, saw her chewing on her lip. "If it makes you feel any better," he said, "I think this thing would have crumbled as soon as we tried to open it, anyway. It's like an onion skin."

"Yes, but at least all of the pieces would be more or less in the right place. This is like some Aramaic jigsaw puzzle."

"It's a challenge."

"It's a bloody nightmare!"

"Don't worry," he said, brushing a strand of hair behind

her ear. "I'll put it back together – I've done this kind of thing before."

"You weren't working to a deadline before."

"We don't know that I am now."

"Suri more or less tells me to hurry up every time I dream of her."

"Yes, but 'hurry' means something different to an angel and a human." He placed another two fragments beside each other. "And of course, we're assuming that this scroll is actually the one we were looking for – which seems unlikely, given Azazel was so keen to hand it over."

Sophie had nothing to say to this, since she'd been wondering the same thing herself. Sam had no desire to help either one of them, so whatever was written on the scroll must either be bad news, or entirely useless. She didn't know which would be worse, and it raised a question she'd been trying not to consider. Now, though, she felt too exhausted to fight against bleak truths.

"Lucas…" she began.

"Sophie?" he answered, still intent on the paper scraps.

"You remember how you said you'll never age?"

"That's not really what I said."

"But you won't age physically."

He paused for a moment, and then looked up at her. "Okay. I've been waiting for this. And the answer is yes, Sophie, I will still love you when you're old and grey. Assuming it comes to that."

She smiled wanly. "Thank you for saying so, but that's

336

not quite where I was going." He remained silent, and so she continued, "I just can't help wondering why she – why I – did it. Became human, and came here. I mean, in the best-case scenario we'd have a few years together before we'd have to start hiding, and then, well, I'm mortal, aren't I? I mean, I'm going to die one day and leave you again, and then it really will be forever."

Lucas put down his tweezers and looked at her with stricken eyes. "Why are you saying these things?"

"Because they're true, and sooner or later we're going to have to think about them." She paused, passed a hand across her eyes, then began again. "All I'm trying to say is that I can't have done what I did simply for us to be together."

"Why not?" he asked, his voice leaden and his eyes painfully direct. "Wouldn't a few years together – more than a few, a whole human lifetime – be better than never being together again?"

"No," she said gently. He sat back, as if she'd pushed him. Sophie felt something twist painfully in her chest, but she made herself go on. "Don't misunderstand me, Lucas. If that's the best we can do, then I'll live and die happier than I ever thought I could. But I don't think it's going to be so simple, or so clean."

"Why? Have you remembered something?"

"No," she answered, "but I know myself. To do whatever I did for the sake of a few human years – it just isn't the way I think. It's too much like…like giving up." Because he was looking at her speculatively, which was better than hurt or anger, she continued, "I don't like to give up. But more to the point,

337

if a human life was all I stood to gain, I'd have done this long before now."

"Well then, why *do* you think you did it?"

"I think something changed. Maybe I learned something new about our situation. Obviously, I don't know what it was – but the point is, I didn't just default. I made a decision."

The speculation in Lucas's eyes had become a glimmer of hope. "Do you think...do you think you found a way to change all of this? I mean, for me to atone? For us to go home, and be together again?"

We can never go home, she thought, and then wondered why she was so certain that it was true. But she couldn't say it to Lucas. He wanted to believe that everything would be alright, and Sophie knew that if she really loved him, she'd let him.

So she said, "I'd like to think so."

He ran a hand down her cheek. "You should get some sleep."

"Do I look that bad?"

He shook his head, pushed his fingers into her hair. Despite her worry, their warmth soothed her. "You look beautiful. But you also look like you've had a very long day after a very long night."

"Okay," Sophie said. "I suppose I'm not much help here anyway..." She peered at the spiral staircase, but made no move to get up.

"Or I could leave this," Lucas said, "and come with you."

But Sophie shook her head. "No – you definitely need to keep working on it."

338

"Sleep here, then. On the settee. It's really very comfortable. Unless the light will keep you awake…"

"I don't think many things would keep me awake just now," she said, stifling a yawn as she moved to the sofa. Lucas turned off the overhead lights, leaving only the halogen reading-lamp angled over the table. He picked up a soft woolen blanket from the back of a chair, and covered her with it. He leaned down and kissed her.

"Thank you," she said.

"For kissing you?"

"For looking after me."

"Thank you for letting me." He kissed her again, and then he went back to the manuscript.

For a few minutes Sophie watched him working, placing and re-placing scraps of the scroll with methodical patience. In the unforgiving light his face was austere, reduced to stark planes and deep shadow, his hair a dark halo around it. He looked so much like the marble angel that it made Sophie wonder how many artists for how many years had been painting and sculpting the fallen, without realizing it. Still wondering, her eyes drifted shut.

*

The cemetery materialized immediately, as if it had been waiting there for the moment Sophie fell asleep. She was lying on the ground beneath the statue of Lucifer, still wearing the pajamas she'd gone to sleep in. Suri stood beside her, wearing a long, black, high-collared dress that looked either very old or very modern. Her ropes of hair were twisted into a knot. She looked off into the middle distance, chewing on the edge of her thumb.

Sophie sat up, and Suri caught the movement. "You're awake," she said, looking down at her with an anxious face.

"What's the matter?" Sophie asked.

"You went to Azazel," Suri said, her eyes direct and unblinking.

"How do you know that?"

"You promised to stay away from him," she said, the hurt and anger clear in her tone.

"No, I didn't," Sophie said wearily, standing up and brushing dry grass off of her clothes. Everything around her looked equally dead, like those last few days of autumn before winter sets in. The tree branches were bare and black, the flowers dry and shriveled, their seed-heads long since stripped bare. The air's incense smell was gone, replaced by something like the remains of a bonfire, doused by rain. "You said he's dangerous, and I agreed. But he had the manuscript I needed. There was no other way to get it. You should know that: you helped me hide it with him."

"Sophie, I promise you we never hid a manuscript with Azazel."

"Then why did he have it?"

"Are you certain that he did? You haven't read it, after all."

"I believe it's genuine."

"Either way, you've provoked him."

Sophie shrugged. "He didn't seem especially angry when I left. In fact, he gave me the scroll himself."

"Yes – and Michael gave him a bludgeoning in return. *Now* he's angry."

"Michael," Sophie muttered. "So that's how you know. I thought you said you and he didn't agree."

Suri passed a hand across her forehead. "It's not that simple. It never is, with us." She sighed. "The bottom line is, he's worried about you, and so am I."

"Why should you be?"

"Look, Sophie, hasn't it occurred to you that if Azazel was so eager to give the scroll to you, then even if it's genuine, it might be something you'd be better off leaving alone?"

"Of course it has. But I need to know the truth."

"The truth doesn't always set you free, Sophie. Sometimes it binds you, in ways that you'll regret forever." She was twisting her fingers together, tense and white. This disturbed Sophie more than any of her words: Suri had never struck her as a hand-wringer.

"But I need to know why I did it," she said, wondering why she had to try so hard to convince her friends of this. "Why I became human."

"Do you?" Suri asked. "Maybe it's better just to take what you have and be grateful for it."

Suddenly, Sophie was angry. "*Grateful?* That I had a whole

341

other life that's just been erased? That nobody will ever tell me the truth? Or that I'll grow up and get old and die while the man I love never changes? Sorry, but I don't really see much in any of that to be grateful for."

There was a long silence. Suri wouldn't meet her eye.

"I don't get it," Sophie said at last. "I mean, all of this time you've been prodding me to find out why I did whatever I did, and now you're trying to push me away from it. Why?"

Suri gave her an abject look, tinged with something that had never been there before: distrust. At last she answered, "Because I've realized that helping you may have been a mistake."

"What did Michael say to you?" Sophie asked, trying not to show how much those words had stung her.

Suri paused for so long, Sophie thought she didn't plan to answer. But then she said, "He told me to tell you to stop looking. To let time take its course."

"And you agree with him."

Suri's black eyes pleaded. "The alternative is just too dangerous."

"To whom? Or what?" Suri said nothing. "Are you trying to protect me, or something else? Is it the Balance again?"

"I think in this case, the two might be one and the same," Suri answered.

"I'm not an aeon anymore," Sophie said. "I'm human, and it's my prerogative to act like it."

"Meaning what?"

342

"Meaning, I don't care about the Balance. I only care about Lucas."

"I told Michael you'd say that," Suri said with soft regret.

"Well congratulations, you were right."

Suri looked at her for a long moment. Then she gave Sophie a smile that reminded her of the weird light that shines sometimes in the break between thunderclouds. "Alright," she said, her voice resigned. "If I can't stop you, then let's get it over with quickly."

She slipped a hand into a pocket hidden in the thick folds of her skirt, and drew something out. Something small enough to fit the palm of her hand. At first Sophie thought that it was some kind of paper construction, but when she leaned forward through the failing light, she saw that it was a fortune cookie.

"You must be joking," Sophie said.

Suri shook her head, smiling sadly. "It was you who gave it to me. I was meant to give it to you when you realized."

"Realized what?"

"Where you'd find the *Book of Sorrows*. To prove that it was the right answer."

"But I already found it – and destroyed it."

"Which is why I think I'm within my rights to tell you that there's another copy – though I'll probably be damned for it, anyway."

Hoping that Suri was just being melodramatic, Sophie asked, "Where is it?"

"Open the cookie."

Sophie broke it in half as Suri watched, and pulled out the slip of paper inside. On it was written: "…if God choose, I shall but love thee better after death."

"This isn't really very helpful," Sophie said.

"It's Elizabeth Barrett Browning. You know, 'How do I love thee? Let me count the ways…'"

"And still, not very helpful."

"I'm sorry, Sophie. That's the best I can do." Suri looked at her for a moment, as if she were contemplating grief. Then she hugged her tightly. Sophie felt a jolt at the contact, something like what she felt when Lucas touched her, except that while his touch sent her blood racing, Suri's seemed to flood her with calm. And so she was shocked to see tears on Suri's cheeks when she pulled away.

"Suri?" she asked uncertainly.

"Good-bye, Sophia," Suri said, her voice cracking. Then she turned and hurried away into the deepening dusk.

Sophie shivered, feeling at once utterly alone, and also as if she were being watched from every corner by hostile eyes. The wind soughing in the tree's bare branches seemed to whisper her name. She walked toward it until she stood almost against the trunk. She looked into the branches over her head, searching for anything vaguely scroll-shaped that might be hanging in them, but the branches were empty.

She turned then to sit down on the mausoleum, brushing dry leaves from its lid. As she did so, her finger snagged on something: a thorn from the rose bush that grew over the grave, now dry and brown. She sucked her finger as it began to bleed, but then, glancing down, she forgot all about it. She stared for a second, and then she reached down, ignoring the thorns, pulling the desiccated stems away.

In the place where the rose branches had been there was a symbol carved into the stone. A sigil: she was certain of it because, though it was quite different from Lucas's sigil, she'd seen it before, as a signature on the paintings in the Paris warehouse. She passed a hand over it, and felt little surprise when its twining lines shifted, rewriting themselves as her own name. She looked at the slip of paper from the fortune cookie, resting on the stone. The words swam up at her out of the gathering dark: *I shall but love thee better after death.*

Without pausing to think, Sophie put her fingers into the largest of the mausoleum's cracks and pulled. The stone crumbled like old clay. She pulled more and more of it away, working with both hands, tossing the rubble to the side. At last she could see inside the grave. There were no bones, nor any armor. All there was, was a roll of fibrous yellow paper, tied into a cylinder with a piece of faded blue ribbon.

With shaking hands, she took it out. She pulled off the ribbon, which blew away on the rising wind, and opened the scroll. At first the letters were as unintelligible as the sigil on the mausoleum's lid had been. This wasn't Aramaic, but some other language. Its shapes were similar to the sigil, as if they all belonged to the same alphabet.

Angelic script, her mind told her, and she knew that once,

345

she had known this language. She could feel the memory of it, just out of reach. She stared at the writing for a time, willing herself to understand. Then she remembered how easily the meaning of the symbol on the grave had come to her, when she hadn't been trying. She let her focus go slightly soft, her mind drift, and slowly, the script resolved into letters and words that she recognized.

"The Word and the Blessing of Enoch…" it began. Sophie sat down amidst the remains of her grave to read the rest.

CHAPTER 29

Sophie opened her eyes. Everything in the room looked exactly as it had when she'd closed them: Lucas at the table in the bright pool of light, the shadows gathered around its edges, making the room's other shapes indistinct. Everything was also utterly different, and would never be the same again. Sophie wanted to cry, but she stifled the urge. The one certainty left to her was that Lucas could never know what she'd just found out, and so she could do nothing that might make him suspicious.

Taking a deep breath to steady herself, she sat up. Lucas looked up at her with a radiant smile. The love that welled up in her in return was enough to break her heart. *Don't think about it,* she told herself, and made herself smile back.

"What time is it?" she asked.

"Late," Lucas said. "Or early, depending on your point of view."

"How far have you got?" she asked, getting up to look over his shoulder. He slipped an arm around her waist, pulled her close. She was relieved to see that he'd only managed to put together a few more pieces of the scroll. None of them were even half as big as the fragment in the library.

"Leave that," she said, turning her back on it to face him.

He looked at her in surprise. "I thought you were in a hurry to read it?"

She shook her head. "It doesn't seem quite so important anymore," she said. "I – I suppose I was just tired, before."

"Okay," he said, putting aside the tweezers and stretching his arms over his head. "I could do with a break anyway. Are you hungry?"

"No," Sophie said.

"Tired? I'll come with you if you want to sleep properly, upstairs."

"I don't want to sleep," Sophie said, although in fact she was weary as if she'd been running for the last few hours, instead of dreaming.

"I see," he said with a half-smile. He slid his hands up under her shirt, pulled her toward him, kissed her in the hollow of her belly. It was as if he'd touched a match to dry tinder. She melted into him, her blood raging, unable to think of anything but how to make him never stop touching her like that.

Except that it's impossible, some cruel, distant voice in her head whispered. The mad joy collapsed so suddenly into grief that she gasped, clutching at him as if she were drowning.

"I'm sorry," he said, looking up at her. Looking stricken,

though he didn't loosen his hold on her waist. "It's too fast, isn't it? I shouldn't have – "

"No!" Sophie said, sinking down onto his lap and wrapping her arms around him. She pressed her face into his neck. "Don't be sorry," she said. "It's all I want, but…" She tried to think of words that weren't a lie, and weren't the truth: that if she let herself have him the way that she wanted him, let herself feel a little bit of what they could never really be, it would destroy her. "It seems wrong," she said finally, "when Mairi is missing… when so many terrible things might be happening…"

They sat for a time in silence, Lucas stroking her hair, Sophie trying to think of something innocuous to occupy them until she got it together. After a moment she pushed back, looked at him. "Will you play for me? Your violin?"

He lifted his eyebrows. "Really?"

"Really," she said, thinking that listening to him play might distract her, at least for a little while.

"Alright," he said, standing up. "If you'll promise to play your harp for me sometime."

Sophie nodded. Lucas walked to a corner cupboard, opened one of its doors and took out a violin case. He brought it back to the coffee table and unsnapped the catch. Sophie watched absently as he took out the instrument, tuned it and tightened the bow. Then he looked at her. "Any requests?"

"Whatever it was you were playing that night," she said. "When we…met."

Lucas raised his eyebrows. "The Bach Chaconne? But that's so sad."

"Is it?" Sophie asked. "Sad" seemed an entirely inadequate word for the music she remembered as a dark, sweeping tide.

"He wrote it in memory of his first wife," Lucas said, fingering the strings. "She died while he was away on a trip. He didn't find out until he returned...the Chaconne was his response."

"You're right – that is sad." She thought back to that night, the way the music had pulled her from her dream. Pulled her to Lucas. "But it also seems to be more than that," she said at last. "Not just a lament – at least not from what I heard."

He gave her a curious look, but he said nothing else, only settled the violin beneath his chin and raised the bow. When he brought it down, it was with a violence Sophie hadn't anticipated. She flinched as if the chord had cut her, adrenaline winding her tight as one of the instrument's strings. She wondered then whether it had been a mistake after all to ask for this piece; but she had no choice now other than to listen to it.

And she was riveted. Absorbed by the music, the stark beauty of Lucas's face took on the otherworldly aspect of which she had seen flickers, but this time, it didn't fade. His eyes were fixed not on the strings but on something in the middle distance that Sophie couldn't even imagine. His fingers flew, the bow moved over the strings with an intensity that bordered on violence, as if he meant to wring from the instrument everything that it could give, to use it up. *This is why they say the devil plays the fiddle,* she thought, and then recoiled from it.

But she couldn't hide from the music's onslaught of emotion. She thought about the composer, pouring out his grief for his dead wife. Except that it went beyond grief, or even fury. It was as if he'd poured all of his pain into the instrument, forcing it to its mortal limits in an attempt to push them back, to make them rescind what they'd taken from him. She thought about Lucas, choosing this piece on that night before he knew that she'd returned to him. Had his own pain driven him to it? How many years had he grieved for her already? How would he bear the rest?

Stop it! She pushed the thoughts away, tried to exist only in the music, while it lasted. And yet, when the final notes shivered into silence, she found her cheeks streaming with tears.

"Not sad, eh?" Lucas asked, laying the violin aside and brushing the tears from her face.

"Not sad," Sophie said. "Something bigger. Cataclysmic. Except that's not what I mean at all…"

He smiled ruefully as he sat down beside her, and gathered her close. "Brahms once said something about that Chaconne – that on this one stave, for one small instrument, Bach had written 'a whole world of the deepest thoughts and most powerful feelings.'"

"That about covers it," Sophie said.

"He also said that if he'd thought of the piece himself, he'd have lost his mind."

351

Sophie had to laugh. "There's no one like the Romantics for melodrama."

But Lucas looked serious. Sophie had the feeling, as she seemed to so often with him, that he was reading far more in her face than she wanted him to. "Are you alright?" he asked.

"More or less," she said, swiping again at her eyes.

"Really?" he asked. "Because ever since you woke up, you've seemed different. Preoccupied. Did you have a bad dream?"

Don't think about it. If you do, you'll lose it. "I just need my daily dose of caffeine," she said, willing him to accept the evasion, whether or not he believed it.

"Do you want me to make coffee? Or do you want to sleep for a few more hours first?"

"Neither," she said, slipping her arms around his neck. "I want you to kiss me."

He smiled. "Easily done."

*

Sophie had the morning shift, and Lucas walked her to work. "What will you do all day?" she asked at the door of the pub.

He shrugged. "Sort bits of manuscript, I suppose."

Sophie fought down the instinct to protest, telling herself that he would never get far enough, soon enough, for it to make any difference. "Well…good luck with that."

"Thanks," he said, still looking closely at her, as if searching for something. Then, apparently giving up, he pulled her into his arms and kissed her. She looped her arms around his neck and kissed him back, fiercely. After a moment he pulled away. "Are you sure you have to go to work today?"

"If I call in sick again, Ruadhri will fire me."

"Let him," he said, tracing her hairline with tiny kisses. "You don't need the job. We'll lock ourselves in the tower, and not come out for anything. I have frozen pizza enough to last... well, until Christmas at least. After that, if we need funds, we can sell a book or two..."

Though he smiled, she could tell from the intensity of his eyes that he wasn't entirely kidding. She longed to agree with him, to turn around and go back to the tower room, to wrap him in her arms and never let him go. When she finally answered, she couldn't keep the tremor out of her voice.

"I have to keep the job, at least for the moment," she said. "Otherwise, my mother will be on the next train up here and then you'll *really* know what Hell looks like."

"How would she ever know?" he asked. "Go on – go inside now and tell Ruadhri you quit. I dare you." His eyes glimmered, his lips quirked upward.

She might have done it, if Ruadhri hadn't picked that moment to burst out the door, his face fixed in a foul expression. "Enough canoodling!" he said. "Sophie, I need you inside, *now.* Belial," he looked Lucas up and down grimly, and then shook his head. "Go make yourself useful, if that's possible."

Lucas saluted Ruadhri, with an ironic smile. "I'll pick you

up at the end of your shift," he said to Sophie, then kissed her once more, and turned back up the road.

Sighing, Sophie followed Ruadhri into the pub, and hung up her jacket. She'd expected a slew of breakfast customers to account for Ruadhri's mood, but when she came out of the kitchen and into the bar, she found only Michael, in his usual place, examining an enormous fry-up.

"Ah, young Sophie," he said as he speared a mushroom. He looked at her thoughtfully as he chewed, and then he said, "Come round here and have a cuppa with me. You look like you could use it."

Sophie glanced at the kitchen door, but Ruadhri appeared to have holed himself up in there. She could hear the radio loudly broadcasting some kind of sporting match. She came around the bar and sat down beside Michael, gratefully accepting the cup of tea he poured for her.

"Don't take this the wrong way," he said, starting on the sausages, "but you look like you haven't slept in weeks."

Sophie smiled regretfully. "At least you're honest."

"Please tell me that Lucifer isn't to blame?"

Sophie blushed and bit her lip, looking into her tea.

"Because I couldn't help but notice, you and he are on rather – ahem – cosy terms these days."

Sophie's blush deepened, but she said, "I promise, Lucas is a perfect gentleman."

Michael paused for another scrutiny, then he went back to

the fry-up. "That's difficult to believe," he said at last, "when he let you go into Azazel's house alone."

"He didn't have a choice," Sophie answered. "He couldn't go in himself, and we needed...well, you know all of that. At any rate, I'm fine."

"You don't look fine," he said softly.

"So you said. But there's only so much that make-up can do for a girl."

"That's not what I mean," he said. Abruptly, he pushed his plate aside and leaned toward her. "You found what you were looking for," he said.

She paused, but in the end there seemed little point in prevarication. "Yes."

"And you don't like what you learned."

She shook her head, afraid that if she tried to answer, she would break down.

"What *did* it say?" he asked, when it was clear that she wouldn't elaborate on her own.

"Do you honestly not know?" she asked in an unsteady voice.

"I told you I don't, and an angel can't lie. But perhaps, if you told me about it, I could offer assistance?"

Sophie studied him. His green eyes were warm, his face open, despite his serious expression. Still, it was easy enough to see in it the face of the angel who'd fought Lucas in her vision, at once brilliant and grimly intent. "I doubt it," she said.

"You don't trust me," he said with soft regret.

"I do trust you – to remain true to yourself. We've already had this conversation, Michael. You fought Lucas. You tore us apart because you thought what we felt for each other was wrong. How can you ask me to confide in you?"

Michael looked at her intently. "What if I told you that I've loved someone just as much as you love Lucifer? And that it was equally impossible for us to be together?"

Sophie blinked at him for a moment. "Are you joking?"

"That would be in very bad taste."

"Who was she? Another angel? A human?"

Michael shook his head. "It doesn't matter. Like I said, it was impossible – and that's why I fought Lucifer. The others judged him without any idea of what they were pronouncing on. I was the only one who knew exactly what I was doing to the two of you – and that there wasn't any choice."

Sophie studied him, and then passed a hand over her eyes. "Why are you telling me this?"

"Because I can see you need help," he answered, "and need it badly. And there really isn't anyone else qualified to give it."

Sophie knew, with bleak certainty, that he was right. She took a deep breath, then said, "Okay. But you have to promise not to tell anybody what I'm about to tell you. Especially not Lucas."

A flicker of some emotion crossed Michael's face then, so quickly that Sophie couldn't decipher it – or even be certain that she'd seen it at all. But there was surprise in his voice when he said, "I promise."

"Okay. I…Michael, I found the scroll. My revelations to Enoch." And suddenly the story was pouring out of her, as if Michael's solicitous eyes had pulled the stopper from the words she'd been holding in since she awakened from the past night's dream. But when she came to the scroll's actual message, she hesitated.

"I'm bound to keep my promises, Sophia," he said, "just as I'm bound to tell the truth. And if it reassures you, I can't use what you tell me to interfere with a human life. Not unless you ask me to."

Sophie looked at him a moment longer, and then she nodded. "A lot of it, frankly, I didn't understand. There were things about the Balance, and about something called the Well of Souls. Do you know what that is?"

"It's the place where human souls originate," Michael said, his eyes narrowed thoughtfully. "It's in the Garden – the aeons' realm – so I've never seen it."

"I can't tell you much, either," Sophie said. "The scroll seems to assume that whoever was reading it already knew the backstory. In fact, it was almost as if there should have been more to it…"

She trailed off, wondering for a moment about the possibility that the scroll had been incomplete. That there was some missing part that would make the rest bearable. But that was wishful thinking.

"Anyway, that's all really beside the point, which is that the Balance is degrading."

"We already knew that."

"Yes, but you know how you told me it was swinging all over the place? Well apparently that's not right. Not anymore, anyway. Now it's leaning steadily toward what the scroll calls the Deep. Which I'm guessing is a bad thing."

Michael smiled wryly. "A bit simplistic, but if you're on the side of humanity continuing to exist, then yes, it's a bad thing." He paused. "Did the scroll say why this is happening?"

"Apparently, the Well of Souls is being corrupted. It used to be that the souls that came out of it were neutral, and the choices they made in their lives determined whether they turned out good or evil. Now they start out unbalanced toward evil, so it's harder for them to end up good."

"Why?" Michael asked, clearly riveted now.

Sophie shook her head. "The only thing the scroll was clear on," she said, watching Michael intently, "was that it began when Lucifer fell."

Michael's expression was inscrutable as he considered this information, and then asked, "Does it say what we ought to do about it?"

"Send him back."

"Back to Heaven?"

"Right."

Michael shook his head. "Once an angel has fallen, there is no way back."

"Actually, there is," Sophie said. "Give him a pure soul. A human soul."

"That's not possible," Michael said, but he sounded as if he was trying to convince himself.

Sophie shrugged listlessly. "A lot of the fallen think that it is."

"How would you know that?"

There was an edge of condescension in his tone that made Sophie suddenly furious. "How would I know it?" she cried. "Because the results have been haunting me all of my life!" Michael looked blank, and she rolled her eyes. "Oh, please: don't try to tell me you haven't seen the Revenants."

"Revenants?"

"Those things that are left when one of the fallen steals a soul."

Michael's eyebrows drew together. "Of course I've seen them. But you shouldn't be able to."

She smiled balefully. "Why not? I made them."

"How on earth do you figure that?"

"Because I came up with the idea. It's right there in the *Book of Sorrows* – I laid out how I planned to go to earth as a human, and give my soul to Lucas. Obviously, some of the fallen got hold of the idea, and decided to experiment."

"Sophie – " he began.

"Don't," she interrupted dully. The anger had burned out as quickly as it had flared. "Whatever it is, it doesn't matter. Nothing will matter, if Lucas doesn't go back."

Michael sighed. "But Sophie, the very existence of the

Revenants ought to prove to you that this – exchange – doesn't work."

"No," she said. "It only proves that the fallen who've tried it weren't worthy."

"And Lucifer is?"

"Of course he is!"

"How so?"

"Because he would never try it."

"That's a bit of a conundrum, Sophie."

"Not really," she said. "You see, ever since Lucas told me what the Revenants were, I've been trying to figure out what it was about their souls that made the experiment fail. Were they the wrong souls? Not pure enough?" She looked up at him. The lines in his face were like chisel cuts in stone. "And then I read the scroll, and I realized I've been coming at it the wrong way. It wasn't the souls that were unworthy. It was the recipients."

"But if you could convince Lucifer to take a soul, then how would he be any different from the others who've done it?"

"Well, for one thing, he never should have fallen. The angels exiled him – not the Keeper."

Michael was staring at her, looking vaguely ill. "That may well be," he said at last, "but it's neither here nor there, if willingness to take a human soul would make him unworthy of it."

"No," Sophie argued, "it only means that the soul he takes must be willingly given."

She watched the realization dawning on his face, and then

the horror. "You can't possibly mean…" He trailed off. He couldn't say it.

But Sophie had long since accepted it. "That's exactly what I mean."

"Sophie, you can't!" he said, gripping her arms, his eyes suddenly wild.

"Of course I can," she answered calmly. "I told you I'd die for him, and I meant it."

Michael was shaking his head. "This is insane! He'll never let you do it!"

"The thing is, Michael," she said, disengaging his hands from her arms, "he won't have much choice. Or none that will seem any better. Because the other thing I learned from that scroll is that there's a time limit."

"What?"

"This little jaunt on earth as a human? It ends what I turn eighteen."

"You're sent back to the Garden?"

She smiled wryly. "Do you think I'd be allowed back in, after what I've done?" She shook her head. "On my eighteenth birthday, if I'm still alive, my soul – or whoever's soul it is that I have – will be released, and I'll cease to exist."

"You mean you'll die?"

"No, I mean I'll *cease to exist*. I turn to vapor, or foam on the sea, or whatever – the scroll didn't get specific. The point is, if my dying wish is for him to have my soul, he can't really refuse, can he?"

"Sophie, this can't be right…there has to be another way!"

Sophie looked at Michael for a long moment, and then she said, "I wish there were." She stood up as a group of walkers came in.

"Sophie, wait." She turned back to him. "Are you going to tell him?"

She paused. Until that moment, she hadn't known herself, but she was certain when she said, "Yes. But not yet. I have until June…" She trailed off, shook her head. "I've got to get back to work. But thank you, Michael."

"For what?" he asked bitterly.

"For listening."

CHAPTER 30

Although the pub was busy, the day seemed to drag on forever. Sophie spent it in a daze, waiting for it to be over. She was meant to finish at five, when Ailsa would take over. But by half past, she still hadn't arrived.

"Where is that girl?" Ruadhri grumbled, filling another pint as the queue behind the bar swelled with a new influx of hill walkers.

"I don't know," Sophie said, doling out soft drinks as fast as she could. "She was out last night. Maybe she took a nap and overslept." *Except that Sam was back early.* She tried not to look at the clock again.

"I've rung the house," Ruadhri complained. "Nobody answers."

"That's hardly surprising," Sophie told him, picking up a tea towel to wipe wet glasses. "It's a miracle that anyone ever hears that phone at all."

Ruadhri discharged another pint. "Is Belial at home?"

"I suppose so. Why?"

Ruadhri took the plates from her. "Go on and ring him. Ask him to drag that lassie's sorry arse out of bed and get her down here a.s.a.p. Unless you fancy another shift?"

Sophie picked up the receiver and took it into the kitchen, then dialed Lucas's number.

"Sophie? Are you alright?"

"Yes," she said, "but I'm worried about Ailsa. She hasn't showed up for work."

"I'll check her room and phone you back."

Sophie hung up, and finally gave in to the panic that had been building over the last hour. She was furious at herself for not checking on Ailsa last night when she came in. She'd been so preoccupied with the ruined manuscript that she hadn't thought of it. She wondered now why she'd been so ready to accept Sam's story that Ailsa wasn't well. It didn't matter that they'd fought: Ailsa was still her friend, and Sophie had let her down. She sat and waited miserably by the phone. Ten minutes later, it rang.

"Lucas?" she said.

"She's not here," he told her. "Her work clothes are folded on the bed, and it looks like her waterproofs are gone."

"It's been dry today," Sophie said. There was a long moment of silence, then she said what they were both thinking: "Sam never took her home, did he?"

"Stay there. I'll come get you. And don't worry – we'll find her."

But where? Sophie thought as she put the phone down. *In what state?* She pushed the thought back, though she couldn't quite stifle the image of a tall, ribbon-thin Revenant with long red hair.

Peering through the window in the swinging door, she saw Ruadhri still elbow-deep in pint glasses, his face fixed in a frown. There was no way that he'd let her go with a packed pub and no other help. Sophie turned back to the kitchen. She wrote him a quick note on a post-it, indicating that she knew where Ailsa was and had gone to get her, and stuck it to the door. Then she went to the coat room and pulled on her parka, just in time to see the approaching lights of Lucas's Land Rover.

It had begun to rain again. Sophie ducked quickly into the passenger seat. "Have you found out any more?" she asked, buckling herself in.

"No," Lucas answered, pulling away from the pub. "I tried phoning Pier House. No one answered – not that I expected it."

"Do you think that's where Ailsa is?"

"I think it's the obvious place to start." He turned the truck onto the road to the north shore – and then kept going, a full u-turn.

"What are you doing?" Sophie cried. "I thought we were going to Sam's!"

"*We* aren't going anywhere," Lucas said grimly. "I'm taking you home. I want you to wait in the tower until I get back. Lock the doors, and don't answer them for anyone – "

"Forget it," Sophie said. "There is no way I'm sitting at home while you go to face him."

"And there's no way I'm having a repeat of last night," he answered, in a stern tone she hadn't heard before.

"You can't tell me what to do, Lucas."

He looked over at her, his eyebrows drawn together, clearly ready to argue. Then he looked back at the road, and drove in silence for a few moments. "You're right," he said at last. "I can't. But I can ask you – beg you – to listen to me. Last night Azazel let you go, but that's only because it served his purpose."

"No," Sophie said, "he let me go because I wasn't any use to him."

"Why would you think that?"

"You said it yourself – he can't take my – " Sophie began, and then, realizing what she was about to say, fell abruptly silent. *He can't take my soul unless I give it willingly.* She had been so certain that he could never seduce her into such a thing, that she hadn't considered that it wasn't necessary. She didn't need to like Sam to be willing, or even to want to help him. She only needed to love someone over whom he had power.

The fragile floodgate she'd constructed against the terrible truths she'd uncovered the past night came crashing down around her, and she saw how he'd manipulated them all. If she didn't give up her soul to Sam, he would hurt Ailsa. And the worst part was, it would be for nothing: she'd be a Revenant, Lucas would still be stuck on earth, and even Sam wouldn't benefit, since he wasn't worthy of the soul she'd give him. Unless she could turn

366

his greed against him…and all at once, she saw a way that she might do it.

"Okay," she said.

"What?" Lucas asked.

"You're right. Take me home. I'll wait for you there."

Lucas was staring at her incredulously. "Seriously, just like that? You're not going to argue?"

She took a deep breath, tried to smile. "Let's face it: last night wasn't exactly a brilliant success. Besides, Ailsa will still be angry with me. We assume Sam is keeping her there against her will, but maybe she chose to stay. If it comes to talking her out of it, she's more likely to listen to you." The words sounded lame, even to her. She couldn't make herself come up with anything better.

In moments, they were pulling up in front of the tower. Lucas turned the car off and got out, then came around to open her door. *Focus*, she told herself. After years of pretending not to see the Revenants, she was an expert at hiding her feelings. This was only more of the same.

"Are you coming in?" she asked Lucas as he unlocked the tower door.

"Just to pick up a few things," he said, holding it for her.

Once inside, he started up the stairs, so quickly that she needed to run to keep up. In the sitting room, Lucas tossed his coat onto the sofa under the painting of the angel and the sea monster. He ran his hand under the right hand side of the frame, and the picture swung back, revealing a recess in the stone wall. Inside was a jumble of items, many of which looked like weapons. Sophie's guts twisted with foreboding.

"That looks serious," she said as he pulled off his top and picked up what looked like a heap of silver scales. It unfolded into a tunic made of metal links so fine, they flowed like satin.

"It is," he said, pulling it over his head. "It was a gift from Finbhearra."

"From who?"

"King of the *sith*. No one makes better armor – except maybe Azazel." Next, he pulled out something black and bulky.

"And that one's a gift from the local trolls?" she asked.

"No. From Interceptor."

"Is that some kind of underworld demigod?"

He smiled, pulling it on. "It's the company that makes flak jackets for the U.S. Army."

"And that?" she asked, pointing to the sword he was strapping to his back.

"Fragarach," he said, touching the mermaid hilt. "It was made by Lir, the sea god, for his son Manannan."

"Does that mean it's one of the Sacred Weapons?" she asked.

"You don't forget anything, do you?" Sophie shook her head, and Lucas reached into the alcove one more time, brought out something small and shining. It was the dagger, Carnwennan. Lucas held it toward her. "Keep it with you until I come back."

Sophie nodded mutely, clutching the dagger to her breast to hide how her hands were shaking. But Lucas saw it anyway.

"Sophie," he said softly, and folded her in his arms, "my

368

Sophia. Don't be afraid for me. God knows it's not the first time I've fought Azazel."

"It isn't?"

"Far from it."

"Who usually wins?"

He laughed wryly. "That depends who you ask."

"That isn't especially comforting."

"It'll be alright." He kissed her, and she clung to him, trying to tell him with the fierceness of it all of the things that she couldn't. "I love you," he said.

"And I love you," she answered softly. He gave her one long, clear look; and then he was gone.

*

The Land Rover's taillights winked out, swallowed by the darkness of the woods. Sophie ran upstairs. Upending her backpack on the bed, she hunted through it for the darkest, most rugged clothing she had. She chose a pair of heavy jeans, a warm black jumper and her walking boots. She stuck the dagger through her belt at the back, pulled on her jacket and put her head torch in the pocket. Finally, she pulled her long hair into a tight plait and tucked it into her jumper, then pulled a woolen hat over it.

She didn't go back downstairs. She didn't want to see the room that had become home to her, to shut its door behind her knowing that she might never come back. Instead, she let herself out the upper door and into the dark corridor with the arched windows. She followed it to the stairway, and then down to the entrance hall and out the front door.

Once outside, Sophie put on the head torch. She ran to the end of the house, to the outbuildings where the peacock had startled her on the morning she met Sam. She had never gotten as far as asking Lucas where his horses' gear was kept, but she guessed it had to be in one of the sheds. The first one was full of old farm machinery and dusty piles of lumber. The second, however, was divided into stalls. They were empty – apparently the horses lived outside – but at the far end of the stable she found a tack room with all of the bits and pieces she remembered from her riding days.

There were saddles and bridles of various sizes and shapes and states of decay. She had little idea how to go about choosing the right ones, so in the end she picked the set that looked the cleanest, figuring that it would have been used the most recently. She also picked up a head collar and lead rope. Then she went back outside, and started toward the paddock.

The ponies stood dozing nose-to-tail at the far corner of the field. Sophie set the heavy saddle down on one of the fence rails and hung the bridle beside it. Then she approached the ponies with the head collar. They looked at her curiously, not particularly alarmed, but also not too interested in moving. She sized them up as best she could, but there seemed to be little to distinguish one from the other – or, for that matter, from the *Each Uisge*.

Trying not to think of that, she approached the nearest of the ponies. It stood obediently as she buckled the head collar on, and after only a bit of coaxing, it followed her to the gate. She tied it up, and fumbled the tack onto it, hoping that it was a decent fit, and that she hadn't forgotten to buckle or tighten anything crucial. Then she untied the pony and led it through the gate.

She remembered enough about riding to be grateful that the pony stood quietly while she climbed up two rungs of the fence, and then hoisted herself onto its back. She settled herself, adjusted the stirrups, and then gave an experimental squeeze with her calves. The pony walked forward, and for the first time since Lucas had left, Sophie began to feel like everything might turn out alright.

She let the pony walk until they got to the woods, and then she nudged it again. It picked up a trot that rattled her bones, until she remembered how to rise to its rhythm. She was just beginning to wonder whether she dared ask it to go faster when something caught her eye – a faint, burnished dusting of light, far off among the trees. She jerked in surprise, and the horse shied, taking a few quick, skittering steps to the left.

It wasn't much of a spook, as far as spooks went, but it was enough to convince Sophie to keep her eyes fixed firmly on the road ahead. She concentrated on the faint pool of light from the head torch, on the steady clatter of the pony's hooves. She kept to the shoreline as she rode through the village, praying that nobody would be sitting outside the pub. But the village was quiet, the road deserted, and when Sophie turned up the side-road to Sam's place, she allowed herself a cautious sigh of relief.

The road was unpaved, rutted and muddy, and the pony took its time finding its way. It wasn't long before Sophie's muscles began to ache from the unfamiliar exercise. Still, she was glad of it, and of the need to concentrate. It kept her from thinking too hard about where she was going, or the fact that she had no idea how to proceed when she arrived. *One step at a time,* she told herself.

They climbed for what seemed like hours before the road finally leveled again, and the pony picked up its pace. Sophie couldn't say when she began to suspect that she wasn't alone, or even where the feeling came from. There was nothing to see, nothing to hear but the pony's footfalls and the ubiquitous drip, drip of sodden branches. Nevertheless, the feeling grew as she traveled, until she could think of nothing else. The pony seemed to have sensed something too. Its ears flickered back and forth, and the rhythm of its gait became uneven as it tried to speed up and Sophie fought to slow it down. Then, abruptly, it stopped. It stood stock still for a moment, its legs locked and its ears straight forward. She had only a moment to remember that this was a bad sign before its ears flattened and it reared.

Sophie was on the ground before she realized what had happened. By the time she got her breath back the pony had disappeared, running back the way they had come. Sophie stared after it in despair. She had no idea how far she still had to go, and she'd twisted her ankle when she fell. The head torch had also stopped working. But the immediate problem was whatever had spooked the pony.

She stood up shakily, reaching for the knife in her belt. She held it up. It cast the faint, icy, blue-green glow she remembered from the night she'd fought the *Cait Sìth*. She turned in a slow circle, looking for any aberration in the blackness surrounding her. Then she saw it: the same golden glow she'd seen in the woods near the village. It wasn't a Revenant. It wasn't anything she'd seen before. All she could think of was Lucas, running afoul of some trick of Sam's. Keeping to the trees, she crept toward the light.

Even when she was near enough to see it, it was difficult to make her eyes resolve what she was looking at; the light fuzzed the image. But as she watched, the horrific truth of it materialized. Two figures stood in that light, but only one of them cast it: Sam was glowing, faintly golden. In his arms he held a woman, wearing a torn red jacket, her long, blonde hair darkened by rain.

She seemed to be fighting him, but weakly, as if Sophie had come in at the very end of their struggle. After a moment she stopped, and hung limp in Sam's arms. He lowered his mouth to hers. Sophie plunged forward, but the dark underbrush slowed her. By the time she reached them, Mairi's face was grey, while Sam's had begun to blaze brilliantly, more beautiful and terrible than anything Sophie had ever seen. Then he flung Mairi's limp body aside, and shot off into the woods.

Sophie stood in the sudden darkness, shuddering and trying

to catch her breath. She couldn't make her mind work properly. Thoughts and emotions spun and slid, so that she couldn't decide what to do first, which way to run. She couldn't even recall which direction Sam had gone when he disappeared.

And then she felt a presence behind her. She turned to find a Revenant a few meters away – the one that had once been a girl called Jenny MacCrae. Sophie was surprised by her own lack of fear as it approached her. Now, as then, it came with its arms outstretched, the withered flesh hanging off of them like rags. This time, though, Sophie stood her ground, clutching Carnwennan in both hands. She swallowed hard, preparing herself for it to reach again for her face.

Instead, it passed her by, stopping instead by the body of Mairi MacIvor. It stood looking down at the girl's still form, and though there wasn't enough left of its face to register expressions, Sophie could feel the sadness coming off of it in waves.

After a few moments it looked up at Sophie again. She waited, barely breathing. Then the creature opened its mouth and a word emerged, no louder than a sigh: "Please…"

"You can speak?" Sophie whispered, as its face smeared in and out of focus. The Revenant nodded. "What – what do you want?"

"She wakes," it sighed, looking down again at Mairi's body. Sophie followed the Revenant's eyes, and to her horror, she saw that the dead girl had begun to emit a cold light of her own. Her splayed limbs twitched as if touched with an electric current; her eyes opened, staring blankly up at the face above her. The Revenant reached down, took the hand Mairi raised, and helped her to her feet. The girl stood swaying, her eyes disoriented. Though she was still whole, her movements were jerky, mechanical, not remotely human. She was horrifying in a way that the tattered one could never be. Sophie backed away.

"No," said Jenny's Revenant, pulling Mairi along as she followed her. "Help her."

"I don't know how," Sophie said, her voice louder now, though still tremulous. "I wish I did." She was surprised at the conviction with which she said it, and the pity that welled in her for these lost creatures whose hell she'd unwittingly orchestrated.

The Revenant said nothing, only hovered there, its eyes imploring her to understand. "I – I'm sorry," Sophie said. "I wish I could help you, but I have to go."

The Revenant reached toward her again. Instinctively she drew back, but the creature didn't touch her. One bony finger came to rest on the blade of the knife, which Sophie held before her still, glowing like a beacon.

"Here," it said, once again bringing its hands toward its chest.

It took Sophie several moments to accept what the creature seemed to be saying. "You want me to *stab* you?" she asked then, with disbelief. The Revenant continued to look at her calmly, and nodded once. "I can't!" Sophie cried. "I just couldn't…and – and anyway, it won't work…"

Or would it? She'd never tried to kill one; she'd never even considered it. On one hand, it seemed strange that there would still be so many of them wandering around, if it was so simple to kill them. Why would the angels who'd made them leave the evidence behind? Then again, they might have lacked the means. The dagger wasn't just any knife, after all. It was a Sacred Weapon. It was capable of killing a demon or an angel – why not a Revenant?

And then she had an appalling thought: what if the reason they'd been following her all her life wasn't to frighten or torment her, but that she had the ability to end their suffering? What if the ancient warrior in her room that night hadn't meant to threaten her with its knife at all, but only to implore her to free him with it, as this Revenant now did? It all made a perverse kind of sense.

She looked from the knife to the Revenants, appalled. But when she thought of all the years she'd spent running from their kind, when perhaps all they'd ever wanted was release, she knew that she couldn't refuse. Sophie raised the knife. If there'd ever been any question of the Revenant's intent, it faded when the creature tore away the remnants of its clothing, baring its chest to her almost eagerly. Its eyes rested on her. In the light of the head torch they looked sad – and human. Drawing her arm back, Sophie drove the knife into the center of the Revenant's chest, as hard as she could. For a moment its eyes seemed to widen, in wonder or pain, she had no idea. Then it collapsed. What had been its body disintegrated into a pile of rag and bone.

Sophie turned to Mairi then. This was infinitely harder, because she still looked human; because there had been a chance to save her, and Sophie had missed it. "I'm sorry," Sophie said, "for what happened to you. I'm sorry I didn't stop him." Mairi looked at her with vacant eyes. But as she watched, two tears formed in their corners, and spilled down her cheeks.

"Okay," Sophie said. She raised the knife, shut her eyes, and drove it into the Revenant's breast. Its light vanished, leaving Sophie in darkness. Just as she began to panic, her head torch flickered back to life.

Sophie stood for a few long minutes, staring at the remains of the girls Sam had killed. She wanted to cover them, to bury them, but she had neither the means nor the time; not if she wanted a chance to save Ailsa.

"I hope you're at peace," she said, wiping the blade clean on her jeans, and then sticking it back into her belt. Then she turned toward the road, and ran.

CHAPTER 31

She didn't run for long. Her twisted ankle hurt, and the shoulder the demon had raked had begun to throb. The road seemed endless, compressed as it was to the frail circle of light cast by her head torch. She began to feel that she was walking in an endless loop, continually passing the same damp block of forest. Occasionally, she thought she caught flickers of movement far off in the woods, lit by a spectral glow. None was near enough for her to be certain that it was a Revenant, but for the first time in her life, she felt no dread at the prospect of meeting one. She preferred not to consider whether this was because she'd learned they meant her no harm, or that she had the power to kill them.

At last, the road began to incline downward. She passed the spot where Lucas had parked the Land Rover the night before, and then the woods ended. She stood looking down the grassy slope, tumbling to the sea. The moon was full, the clouds thin enough that its light turned the bay to pewter. The dock stretched into it like a charcoal line on paper, the sailboat a dark, shark-like shape at its end.

A long shadow of Sam's house stretched across the yard, its proportions warped and nightmarish. The windows were dark, but it was still the obvious place to begin. Sophie's dagger began to glow again as she descended the hill. Holding it in front of her, she made a slow circumnavigation of the house, peering in what windows she could reach, but all was still and silent, the rooms apparently empty. Heart in her throat, she tried the front door. It was locked. If Ailsa was in there, there wasn't much Sophie could do about it alone.

As she stood wondering where to go next, the wind lapsed for a moment. In the sudden silence, she heard the faint clash of metal on metal. It came from somewhere above her. Sophie turned and looked up at the dark ridge of the hill she'd just descended. At first she saw nothing, but as she scanned the skyline she caught a flicker of light far out on the headland, by the ruined castle. She watched, and this time there was no mistaking it: a flash of gold and red showed for a few moments, flame-like in an empty window, before dying back again.

Gritting her teeth against the pain in her ankle, she took off in the direction of the ruin. Nearer the headland, the hill was forested again, and it seemed to Sophie that she thrashed through the trees for hours, all the time terrified that she would arrive too late. But when she finally broke free of the forest, the lights still swirled and blazed, the red and the gold now distinct.

Sophie climbed the rest of the way up the hill and then

stopped, flattening herself on the damp ground just below its crest. Parting the grass and bracken, she looked toward the ruin. She could see now that the light came from the angels themselves, illuminating what had once been the castle courtyard. Sam's was the same brilliant gold that had flooded him after he took Mairi's soul; Lucas's was red as heart's blood.

But it wasn't only the light that made Sophie pause. In the same way that the moonlight turned Sam's house to something menacing and larger than itself, the angels' light seemed to expand them beyond the human selves Sophie had come to know. As they fought, they looked both ethereal and elemental, too big and bright for their ordinary, earthly surroundings.

They attacked each other with a horrifying brutality, crashing together with a sound like shattering stone, swords meeting in showers of sparks. They flew apart again, danced and whirled so fast that they dissolved momentarily to blurs of light. It seemed to Sophie that every blow one of them landed must be the one that finished the other. Yet they seemed hardly to feel them, as if they were impervious to each other's weapons as the stones around them. Neither of them faltered or stumbled, and gradually, as she grew accustomed to the scope and violence of the duel, Sophie realized that very little was actually happening. They were too well matched.

She dipped back below the ridge, trying to think of what to do next. It was clear enough that Ailsa wasn't up here with them. But if she wasn't in the house either, then where was she? Sophie looked down the hill once again, wishing she'd thought to find out more of the lay of the land when she'd still had time. Ailsa could be anywhere: a hidden cave, a forgotten outbuilding, or any number of islands or crevices along the lonely coast.

And yet, Sam needed her, and needed her close, if he meant to use her as a bargaining piece. So why wasn't she in the house, or the ruined castle? The only thing Sophie could think was that he'd decided it was too risky. Ailsa might have found a way to escape from there, or someone might have remembered that she'd been with Sam last night and come looking for her. Sam had to have hidden her in a place that no one would think to look, but would also be easily accessible. Somewhere that involved waterproofs.

And then, she knew. With one last glance at the warring angels, Sophie turned and plunged back down the hill. Descending was far quicker than climbing had been. Her ankle had begun to feel better, and she was making good time until she came to a patch of scree. She'd stepped onto it before she realized what it was. The stones slid and rolled, pulling more and more along with them as they descended. With a leap Sophie was free of the rockslide, but the damage was done. Scree poured down the hillside like a slow, intractable tide, its roar drowning out everything else.

They won't have heard it, she told herself. *They* can't *have heard it*... But nevertheless she ran, slipping and sliding in the damp grass and bracken. She'd almost reached the beach when there was a flash of gold light beside her, and then Sam was

381

standing there, his sword on his shoulder and his eyes bright as day above a supercilious smile.

"Why, Sophia. Lovely of you to drop by."

"Where is Lucas?" she demanded.

"That's very rude, when I'm standing right here, at least as likely a prospect as – "

"Where is he?"

Sam waved a hand toward the heights. "Where I left him."

"Why are you doing this?" Sophie cried, trembling with rage.

"If you're only going to waste my time with rhetorical questions – " he began, turning to walk away from her.

Sophie plunged forward, half-aware that she had begun to emit a glow of her own: a clear, brilliant blue. She grabbed Sam's shoulder, full of a rage like nothing she'd ever felt, and whipped him around as if he weighed nothing. "Answer me!" she demanded.

"Why?" he asked, but she heard a slight waver in his voice, saw a flicker of uncertainty in his pale eyes as he took in the blue light, the sudden strength.

"Because it's *my* soul you want," she said. "You had no cause to drag Ailsa and Lucas into this, never mind that poor girl, Mairi."

Sam's smile softened, turned almost tender as he plucked her hand off of his shoulder. Despite the strength she'd gained with the blue glow, he was still stronger than she was. "Sweet Mairi. I hoped you'd find her."

"I *saw* it, Sam!" Sophie snarled. "I saw the whole thing – and I don't think even you could convince anyone that that was a willing sacrifice!"

Sam shook his head, still smiling. "You don't understand at all, do you? But then it's just like Lucifer not to tell you."

"Tell me what?"

"It's your soul I *need,*" he said, as if speaking to a child. "But as for wanting, any of them will do." He stepped toward her, and though she wanted to run, she couldn't make her limbs obey her. He reached out, ran a finger down her cheek. An electric jolt went through her, terrifying but also, in some incomprehensible way, exhilarating. "Feel that? It's a hit, Sophia. A rush more potent than any human drug. I may not get where I want to go with a stolen soul, but they do help to pass the time."

With a cry, Sophie raised her dagger. Again, she saw the flicker of uncertainty in Sam's eyes. But then he reached out and caught her hand. "Think about it: do you really want to kill me before you find out what I've done with your friend?"

"Sophie, run!"

Her eyes cut to the shadows behind Sam. Lucas was standing there, no longer glowing, though his sword was drawn. His eyes locked on Sophie, full of despair and anger – and resignation. Sam let her go, turning to lunge at Lucas. Sophie stayed long enough to see him parry the lunge, and then she ran.

The pier was longer than it had looked from the house, stretching far out into the dark water, as if it had been built to accommodate a boat much larger than the one tied up at its end.

Sophie knew that if she was right about Ailsa's whereabouts, then it was only a matter of time before the two angels followed her. As if in confirmation, a few meters shy of the boat a flash of light whizzed past her, and then the deck of the boat was jerking, as if hit by a storm wave.

Sophie ducked behind one of the pilings, peering out to get her bearings. She didn't know much about boats, but she was aware that the entrance to a yacht was somewhere at the back end. Lucas and Sam were fighting now at the front. If Lucas could keep Sam engaged, she might just be able to get to Ailsa before they realized it.

Sophie looked at the sky. The moon was growing hazy beneath a scrim of fog, and heavier clouds were drifting in from the north. She hadn't thought that she would ever wish for rain, but she was wishing for it now. She waited what seemed interminably until one of the clouds finally eclipsed the moon. Then she came out of her hiding place and crept along the dock to the end.

The boat wasn't tied flush to the dock, and it rocked with Sam and Lucas's shifting weight. The gap was wide between the pier and the deck, but when the boat tipped toward the dock, it was just near enough for her to jump. She stole a final glance at the two angels. Lucas was glowing again with blood-coloured light, his sword blazing like a sunset. Despite his golden glow, Sam's sword was blacker than the water or the sky, like a sliver cut out of the night onto a starless void beyond. For a moment the two blades met, sliding along each other in a shower of white sparks. Sophie took a deep breath, and leapt.

It was a perfect, beautiful jump, timed exactly so that she landed on the boat's deck just as it rolled toward her. As soon as she landed, though, Sophie knew that she'd made a grave mistake. Sam and Lucas stumbled, losing their footing as the deck heeled too far over with Sophie's weight.

They looked up at the same moment. Sam reached her first, with a catlike leap. But it was Lucas who broke the silence, saying, "Sophie – I thought I told you to run!"

The hurt in his tone, the sense of betrayal, made the words terrible. Sophie couldn't think about that, though; she couldn't allow it to distract her. She let out a breath that felt as if she'd been holding it since she woke from her dream the night before. Then she said the words she'd hoped she wouldn't have to:

"I had to come, Lucas. He'd never let her go otherwise."

"You think you can convince him to hand Ailsa over?" he asked incredulously. His voice was rough, and Sophie couldn't tell whether it was with fear or exhaustion or anger. Of course, it hardly mattered – he would be angry with her soon enough. She wished there was a way to explain, to save him the pain, but she couldn't risk any kind of signal. For her plan to work, Sam had to believe that she truly meant to sacrifice herself for Ailsa.

"I know I can," she said.

"How?"

"I'll give him what he wants," she said, allowing her voice to wobble as if with uncertainty and fear.

"Have you gone mad?" Lucas cried, taking hold of her arms as if to shake her.

"No," Sam said, resting his sword on his shoulder and giving her a thoughtful look. "I believe she's finally seen sense. After all," he turned to Lucas, "you're going to have to kill me to get me to give up Ailsa, and let's face it, you've been failing quite spectacularly to do that for several thousand years. So," he said, holding out his hand to Sophie, "shall we?"

"Let her go, first," she answered.

"Sophie!" Lucas cried, anguished.

Sam sighed as if Lucas were a tiresome and slow-witted child. " Sophia is about to make a very noble sacrifice, Morningstar," he said, with an ironic emphasis on the name. "You could at least let her do it with dignity."

"She isn't sacrificing anything to you as long as I'm alive!" Lucas spat back.

Sam smiled. "The thing is, it isn't really up to you. She's decided; you lose. Bad luck, Morningstar. But no hard feelings, right?"

Lucas raised his sword in two hands and swung with murderous strength. Faster than Sophie's eyes could follow, Sam reached out and caught the blade in one gauntleted hand. Blade and gauntlet ground together: the perfect stalemate.Sam looked at Lucas. "You know, even if you win, you won't save the girl. If I die, she dies. I made sure of that."

"You're lying," Lucas said.

"Do you really want to gamble with her life? Think of the

remorse…how it would eat away at both of you," he gestured to Sophie, "until you couldn't stand the sight of each other."

His tone was gleeful. Sophie had never felt such perfect hatred as she felt then. "Drop your sword, Lucas," she said in a strange, tight voice.

"Sophie?" he said, looking at her as if he didn't know her.

Please, just do it! "I can't let her die, Lucas," she said, her voice shaking in earnest now.

"And you'd join the walking dead to save her?" he cried. "This is mad! Ailsa made her decision – you shouldn't be the one to pay for it!"

"I deserve to pay for it. She wouldn't be in this situation if it weren't for me."

"How on earth do you figure that?"

"Stealing souls was my idea."

"What?"

Sophie took a deep, steadying breath, then said, "I read the scroll, Lucas."

"But it's in pieces – "

"There was another one. In Suri's cemetery."

Understanding was dawning on his face. Slowly, he lowered the sword, as Sam's face twisted into a smirk. "You read it last night. That's why you've been so strange today. Why didn't you tell me?"

But it was Sam who answered, "I imagine she wanted to break it to you gently."

"Sam!" Sophie hissed, glaring at him.

"Why would you need to be gentle?" Lucas asked her, his voice like two stones grating together. It was enough to break her heart.

Focus, Sophie. "That doesn't matter right now."

"Oh, but it does!" Sam said, smirking. "It's the worm at the core of this whole pathetic drama. Do you want to tell him, Sophia, or should I?"

"Please, Sam, don't do this," she said.

Sam rolled his eyes, then turned to Lucas and said, "You see, you don't just flout the laws of the Balance and live happily ever after. You pay for it – with about," he cocked his head, looked her up and down, "eight stone of flesh? Eh, Sophia?"

She couldn't answer him. She couldn't even look at him. Her eyes were riveted on Lucas's face – at the first cracks of despair surfacing there. She couldn't fine a suitable answer amidst her crumbling plans.

"In fact," Sam continued, "I'd say eighteen years was a generous trade. We *are* talking about turning spirit into flesh, after all."

"Is this true, Sophie?" Lucas asked tremulously. "You'll only live for eighteen years?"

"It's true," she said softly. She reached a trembling hand toward him. The ragged cloud parted for a moment, torn by the rising wind. The sudden moonlight illuminated Lucas's face. It seemed to have turned to stone. He didn't take her hand. Slowly, she let it fall.

"When were you planning to tell me this?" he asked tonelessly, at last.

"When I had to," she answered.

"And so you've just accepted it?"

"What else can I do?" Sophie asked, anguished.

Lucas was silent for several long moments, looking out to sea. Then he turned back to her. "This doesn't make sense," he said . "You told me that you wouldn't have traded away your existence for a whole human lifetime. Eighteen years makes even less sense."

Sophie looked away. She had been hoping he wouldn't remember that.

"Oh, go on," Sam said, "tell him."

"Will you shut up!" she cried.

"There's more?" Lucas asked.

Sam shook his head, rolled his eyes. "Honestly, if someone planned to die for *me*, I'd want to know about it. I mean, I can't really think of a better way to say 'I love you.' Flowers, chocolates, nothing really measures up – "

"Die for me?" Lucas interrupted sharply.

"Really, Morningstar, you're slow," Sam sighed. "She came down here to give you her soul. Her redeemable, *human* soul. So that you could go back to Heaven."

"*What?*"

Sam smiled. "If it weren't so clichéd, it would be rather sweet. Too bad it was all for nothing."

"It's not for nothing," Sophie said stonily, "it's for Ailsa. You let her go, or you get nothing from me."

Sam studied her for a moment, and then he smiled, swinging his sword in a black arc, then resting its point on the deck. "Alright. But first, Lucifer, your weapon." He held out his free hand.

"You must be joking," Lucas said.

"I'm hardly going to turn my back on the two of you without some kind of collateral."

Lucas's hand tightened on the hilt of his sword. He glared at Sam. Sophie put a hand on his arm. "Lucas, please, just do it." She willed him to hear in her voice that she knew what she was doing – knew it better than he did. He looked at her for a long moment. She couldn't tell whether he understood; she couldn't tell if he loved or hated her. But reluctantly, he handed the sword to Sam.

"Thank you," Sam said, and tossed the sword into the water, where it gleamed brightly for a moment before it sank out of sight.

"Sam!" Sophie cried.

"Oh, don't get your knickers in a twist. It'll be easy enough for him to get it back when all this is over – *if* everyone behaves." He gave her a pointed look. Sophie shut up. "Good. Now, I'll get the girl. And just to be clear, if either of you takes one step from where you're standing, she dies." He turned and walked back the way Sophie had come, and then disappeared down a hatch to the boat's interior.

As soon as he was gone, Lucas turned to Sophie, his face wild in the flickering moonlight. "Run, Sophie," he said in a low voice.

"And let Ailsa die?"

"Yes," he said with cold certainty. "I don't believe a word of that scroll, and nothing is more important than keeping your soul from Azazel."

"I know that."

"You do?" he asked, brought up short by the unexpected words.

"I also know what I'm doing." Sophie took Carnwennan out of her belt and fed it up her sleeve, as Lucas watched, bewildered. She paused, looking behind her. There was movement at the hatchway again. "There's no time to explain. Just play along with me. Please."

"Sophie – "

Sam was walking back toward them now, pushing Ailsa in front of him. "Lucas, *please!*" she whispered.

He gave her a grim look, but he nodded curtly. A moment later, Sam shoved Ailsa in front of them. Her eyes were wild, her hair bedraggled, her mouth and hands bound. "Oh, Ailsa," Sophie said, reaching toward her. Ailsa began to cry. She turned her head aside, as if to hide the tears from Sophie, revealing a long, dark gash in her right cheek.

"Untie her," Sophie told Sam.

He smiled. "What do you take me for?"

"I take you for a lying bastard who'll go back on his word

the minute he gets what he wants. You already disarmed Lucas. Now let her go, or the deal is off."

Sam looked at Sophie for a moment, irritation flaring in his eyes. Then he said to Ailsa, "Scream, and I'll finish you," and he cut her bindings with his black-bladed sword. She gasped as he pulled the duct tape from her mouth, then choked on a sob.

"Now give her your car keys," Sophie said.

"I think not," Sam laughed incredulously.

"Right," Sophie said, "let's go, Lucas." Sophie made to push past Sam, but he put out a hand and stopped her. "Fine. Car keys." He offered them to Ailsa.

"Sophie?" Ailsa asked. "What is this all about?"

"You can drive, right?" Sophie asked.

"Yes, but – "

"No buts," she interrupted. "You didn't listen to me before. Please listen now." Ailsa took the keys in trembling hands. "Go straight home," Sophie said. "Lock the doors, and don't let anyone in until Lucas comes for you."

"But what about you?"

"I can't leave Lucas," Sophie said. "Please, Ailsa…"

Ailsa gave her a frightened look, and then she ran, leaping off the boat and onto the pier and heading toward shore. Sophie watched her until the clouds closed over the moon again, and the darkness swallowed her. At the same moment, Sophie heard a strangled cry, abruptly bitten off. She whirled to find Sam standing behind Lucas with his shoulders in a vice-grip, the blade of his sword against Lucas's throat.

"Kneel, Morningstar," he said with cold glee.

"Let him go!" Sophie cried. "Let him go or I'll – "

"What?" Sam asked, looking up at her. It seemed the black had eclipsed the blue and white in his eyes: they were like a skull's empty sockets. "You have nothing left to bargain with. So you'd better do exactly as I say, or I'll run him through." As if to punctuate the point, he ripped off Lucas's flack jacket. "Now," he said to him, "kneel."

Sophie's eyes came to rest on Lucas's. They were sad and hopeless. Slowly – carefully, because of the blade pressed against this throat – he knelt. Laughing softly, Sam came around to look down at him, tracing the point of his sword around Lucas's neck until it rested in the hollow of his throat. A fine line of blood sprang up in its wake, and ran down Lucas's neck. It seemed to crawl forever, like ink against his moon-bleached skin.

"You have no idea how long I've wanted to do this."

Sophie stared at Lucas in mute misery. She knew that she'd misjudged Sam as badly as she had the jump onto the boat's deck. And Lucas looked back, his expression slack, as if he'd given up. All at once he lurched to the side, then swayed as if trying to regain his balance, pressing the sword's point more deeply into his flesh. He fumbled for the deck with shaking hands, as if to keep himself from falling.

"What have you done to him?" Sophie cried, starting toward Lucas. Suddenly the tip of the black sword was poised on her own breast. She stopped.

"Qeres," Sam said.

"What?"

"Poison," Lucas gasped.

"Ancient Egyptian," Sam added, "and one of the few that works on angels. Don't worry, it won't kill him," he told Sophie. "It'll only paralyze him for a while. He'll be perfectly conscious, and able to fully appreciate your generous act."

"Where…did you get…" Lucas tried, and then slumped onto the deck.

"You wouldn't believe me if I told you," Sam said, prodding him with the toe of one black boot. Lucas gave him a murderous look, but that was all; the poison had clearly taken effect. "At any rate, we're running out of time. No doubt the redheaded bitch will make straight for the pub, and round up a rescue party. So: Sophia." He lowered the sword, offered Sophie his hand. She looked at it as if it were contaminated.

"The stakes haven't changed," he said coldly, when he realized that she wasn't going to take it, "only the playing pieces. Either you give me your soul, or I'll run him through."

"What's to stop you running him through once I have it?"

He shrugged. "You'll have to take my word for it."

Slowly, Sophie reached out her hand. Sam took it and jerked her toward him, then dropped his sword to pull her against him. The moon flickered in and out of the ragged cloud, making his smile a leer. She looked up at him with utter loathing; and then she looked away.

"Good," he said. "Probably better that way."

She felt his breath against her cheek. He kissed her there, let his lips trail to her throat. Sophie shuddered, trying to keep calm, to keep her mind on the dagger in her sleeve. And then his lips were on hers, sucking hungrily in a parody of a kiss. She felt the panic of being too far underwater when the breath runs out; of something at the core of her resisting, pulling against him.

Knife! her mind screamed at her. She slipped her right hand down his chest, weakly, as if she were losing strength. At the same time she used her left arm to shift the dagger upward, toward it. Now she really was weakening, the night fading into an absolute blackness crowding the corners of her vision. Summoning what strength she had left, she shoved hard against Sam, pushing herself away from him.

He hadn't been expecting it, and he stumbled. He held onto her left arm, his black-gloved hand circling it like a vice. But her right one was free. She shook the dagger downward and grasped its hilt. It glowed brighter than she'd ever seen it, though at the same time she realized that her own glow had faded, and her unnatural strength with it. She wasted no time, slashing upward at Sam's throat. She felt the blade catch on flesh, but not long enough or deeply enough to have done any real damage.

Sam roared, swiped at her arm with his own. His hand connected with her wrist like a brick; she knew that it was broken even before the pain blossomed. The dagger fell from her powerless fingers, skittered across the deck and out of reach. Sophie fell to her knees, scrabbling for the sword Sam had dropped, but he was faster. He swept it up with terrible grace, lifted it with the point aimed at Lucas's heart.

"No!" Sophie cried through the screaming pain. "If you do it I won't – "

Sam drove the sword downward with a brutal strength. Rather than drive through Lucas's chest, though, it turned aside with a whine of metal sliding on metal. Sam ripped through Lucas's shirt with the point of the sword. The fabric fell away, revealing the chain mail, glowing faintly.

"Faery armor," Sam spat. Then he lifted the sword again, and slashed Lucas's neck.

Sophie screamed and stumbled toward him, crying words she didn't hear. She clutched at his shoulders, squeezed them as if squeezing could stop the blood pouring from his throat. He looked at her, his eyes already dimming, his lips trying to form words he couldn't sound. Sophie leaned down, smoothed his hair back with hands soaked in his blood.

"Take it," she sobbed. "Take my soul, now, before it's too late." She leaned down and pressed her lips to his, tasting the ferric tang of blood. But though he kissed her back, there was none of the strange, sucking pull she'd felt when Sam had kissed her a moment before. *Take it!* she willed him, even as she was certain that he wouldn't.

Shock had driven Sam from her mind. Now he grabbed her good arm, dragged her off of Lucas and tossed her aside. Then he lifted Lucas, as easily as if he'd been a rag doll, and heaved him over the side of the boat, into the sea. Sophie pushed herself to her feet, her mind full of the single thought that she must follow him.

She was half way there when something caught her injured arm. The bright, hot pain brought her to her knees. Sam dragged her upright again, pulled her roughly against him. She stared at him for an uncomprehending moment, and then she said, "You – you can't. If I'm unwilling, it won't work – "

"I don't care," he said, taking her face between his hands and leaning toward her.

And Sophie found that suddenly, neither did she. What did it matter, after all, what happened to her? Lucas was dead, she would be dead within a year. She didn't want to be a Revenant, but at least she knew now how to kill one. When Sam was done she would pick up the dagger and finish it.

Sophie stopped struggling. Once again she felt his lips connect with hers, felt the tugging at the core of her. She looked at the sky with its tearing cloud and flickers of stars. The moon must have found a clear space somewhere, she thought blearily, because the whole world seemed to glow with its blue-white light.

Except that it was too blue to be moonlight; too steady and bright. *Maybe it's because I'm dying,* she thought dreamily, watching the sky spinning beyond Sam's shoulder. And then, suddenly, it was gone, replaced by a face from a nightmare: the Revenant she'd come to think of as the warrior.

As Sophie watched, a hand came up beside the head, no more than gristle and bone, knotted into a fist around the gold rings that had once adorned its wrist. It came down like a hammer on the back of Sam's head. He whirled in surprise, and Sophie collapsed on the deck. She lay for a moment, unable to move, barely able to breathe. She watched, half-focused, as a horde of Revenants swarmed onto the boat, some from the pier, some clambering up from the water below. Sam stared at them too, obviously stunned. He began to fight when the first of them closed its hands around his arms, but they were tenacious, clinging like crabs as he shook them, until there were so many of them that he could no longer lift his limbs.

The warrior lurched toward Sophie then. She felt a faint crawling of the old fear, but grief and pain distanced her from it. She made no attempt to pull away from the Revenant as he stopped in front of her, holding something out. It took her several long moments to make sense of it: it was the dagger, Carnwennan. Slowly, numbly, she reached for it with her good hand. As her fingers closed over it, the Revenant said, "Kill… him…our sire…"

Finally, Sophie's beleaguered mind processed the obvious: "He made you?" she whispered. "All of you?" There was a chorus of whispered assent, barely distinguishable from the wind in the rigging. "And killing him will…?"

"Release," the warrior sighed.

Sophie drew a deep breath, turned to Sam. The Revenants had pulled off his coat and his armor, leaving his chest bare. He glared at her – a baleful, furious look – but she found that despite everything, she didn't hate him. It was as if Sam's sword had severed everything vital in her at the moment it pierced Lucas's throat, and now she could feel nothing at all.

But she did know her duty. She raised the knife. Her eyes settled indifferently on Sam's. Then she drove it into him, where she guessed his heart would be. It seemed she'd guessed correctly, because he went limp in the Revenants' arms, his eyes rolling back into his head. There was a sound like a long, deep sigh, and then the Revenants collapsed too: some falling as whole bodies, others as heaps of bone, and a few very ancient ones into piles of dust that dispersed quickly on the wind.

Sophie gazed for a moment at the hideous scene in front of her, but rather than disgust, she felt a hopeless kind of peace. Peace, and utter weariness. She still held the dagger in her hand, dark with Sam's blood. Slowly, she wiped it on her sleeve, until it was clean and shining faintly again. Her legs gave out abruptly, and she fell to her knees on the deck, amidst the remains of the Revenants. She opened her own coat, and set the point of her knife just to the left of her breastbone. She took a deep breath, praying for the strength to finish it. *One, two –*

"Sophie!" A girl's voice, screaming. The world swam in front of her eyes. She felt vaguely angry. Now she would have to muster the strength all over again. She swayed, fell into momentary darkness. When she opened her eyes again, she was looking up into Ailsa's tear-stained face. She heard voices shouting all around her, saw flashing lights.

"Oh, God, Sophie, I'm sorry!" Ailsa wept. "I'm so, so sorry!"

And Sophie's one clear thought before she blacked out was, *So am I.*

EPILOGUE

Two men stood in the lashing sleet on the heights of the promontory, with the sea crashing hundreds of feet below. Far out on the wild water, a boat battled toward the mainland, looking fragile as a toy.

"It *is* fragile as a toy," said the younger man, pushing a strand of long, black hair back from his face.

"You can't do that down here, Theletos," Michael said. "The humans don't like having their minds read – not without permission, anyway." He glanced at the younger man. "Neither do I."

"Apologies," Theletos said, neither looking nor sounding remotely apologetic. He watched the boat with narrowed eyes, his fine features set in an intense, if unreadable expression.

"I still think you shouldn't have let her leave," Michael said. "At least not without finding out whether or not she remembers you."

Theletos frowned, narrowed his bright blue eyes at the boat.

"It would've done no good. She has no capacity right now for anything but grief."

"You can't know that."

"Of course I can. I know her better than anyone ever has, or ever will."

Michael flushed, frowning, but said nothing.

"It doesn't matter, anyway. It's no longer your worry."

"What?" Michael demanded.

"I'm here to relieve you of your duty." Seeing Michael's shock, he frowned. "Come on – you can't be surprised, after everything that's happened."

Michael flushed with anger. "I suppose it's *my* fault she managed to kill both the dark *sith* and the demon I sent, before they could kill Lucifer?"

"No," Theletos said evenly, "but it's your fault that she came within moments of killing herself."

Michael blanched. "That was a fluke. She was never meant to be a part of that fight. I had it on good authority that she was safe at home – "

"Don't bother, Michael. You know it isn't my decision."

"She's still alive," he said defiantly. "And Lucifer's dead. All's as it should be."

Theletos smiled sadly. "Nothing is as it should be."

Michael gave him a long look, which Theletos met and held. "He can't have survived that fight," Michael said after a moment, but it came out as a question rather than a statement.

"Then where is his body?"

"Perhaps a current took it, or a sinkhole – "

"We found Azazel's easily enough."

"But the poison, the blood loss – it's impossible!"

"Very little is impossible, Michael – particularly when Sophia is involved."

Michael looked down at the boat, which was rounding the point. The clouds tore open for a moment then, and the water that had been silver was suddenly, blindingly blue. All of the defiance was gone from his voice when he spoke again: "What will we do?"

"*We* will do nothing. *I* will follow her, and bring her back, as I was sent to do."

"It won't be easy. Not if she finds out that Lucifer lives."

Theletos smiled again humorlessly. "Then you'd better start praying she doesn't find out."

The next pages contain the opening of Riven, the exciting sequel to Bound, coming summer 2012. For more information and the book trailer, go to www.sarahbryant.net

PROLOGUE

She couldn't stop crying, though she couldn't remember what she was crying for. She only knew that something had been taken from her, something so vital that she didn't think she could ever be whole again. And though a part of her wished that she could remember what her tears were for, another part of her knew she couldn't bear that memory.

But she did remember weeping like this once before, for years beyond count. She remembered a bottomless pool filled with her tears. But that had been in the Garden she would no longer enter. Here, her tears ran down her face, like a human's, and like those mortal tears, they disappeared into the long, indigo grass, leaving no trace.

Sometimes one or two of the angels came to try to comfort her. There was one with ropes of white hair and a silvery aura, who smiled and spoke about dancing. There was another with an aura of fire, and green eyes bright as gems, who spoke of inevitability and sacrifice. There were others, too, who came less frequently. All of them talked as if her silence were a vessel they were determined to fill.

But the one who came oftenest never spoke at all. He had black hair, black eyes, but an aura like a summer sunset. Sometimes he came with books, and sat by her silently, reading. Sometimes he brought musical instruments, and played them with a skill that told her he'd practised them, not just relied on his innate ability. Sometimes he brought little gifts – a shell of a heartbreaking blue, a handful of pure white sand, a speckled feather. Things from the place she dared not remember. She left them where he laid them, at her feet.

On the day he finally spoke to her, though, he didn't place his gift with the others. Instead, he knelt in front of her and offered her something on the palm of his hand. It was a tiny, cut-glass bottle with a silver stopper.

"I thought that this might help you," he said. His voice was musical, but then every angel's voice was musical, just as their faces were always beautiful.

Nevertheless, she looked at him more closely than she'd looked at the others. There was something about him that set him apart from them. Maybe the sympathy in his dark eyes. Maybe the kindness in the turn of his mouth. Or perhaps it was the fact that he would sit in her silence for as long as it took her to break it, because, somehow, she knew this was his intention.

And so, surprising herself and, apparently, him, she answered, "What is it?"

"A lachrymatory. A bottle for your tears." It was the shape

of a tear itself. He touched the stopper. "The tears evaporate slowly, through the cork. They say that when the bottle is dry, the grief will be healed."

"Who says this?"

"The humans. They made it."

Hesitantly, she took the bottle from his hand. As her fingertips brushed his palm, a warmth passed into them and spread through her, as if he really were wrapped in a summer sunset. Her cheeks flamed. Raising a hand to them, she realized that they were dry. She looked at him in amazement.

"What is your name?" she asked.

"Lucifer," he answered.

"Light-bringer," she said softly, nodding. Then, "Thank you. But it seems I don't need the bottle after all." She offered it back to him.

"No," he said. "It's yours." He reached out and closed her fingers around it, and then, boldly, his own gold-brown ones around them. The surge that went through her then made a shadow of the first. The whole world seemed lit by his brightness.

But as she began to smile, the light faded. Lucifer's hand dropped from hers as black clouds rolled across the sky, and then they were no longer sitting on an indigo hill, but on the pitching deck of a boat on a nighttime sea. Lucifer's face greyed, and then melted, his form dissolving even as she reached for him, turning to liquid beneath her hands, which rolled away as she scrabbled to contain it. She shrieked his name into the howling wind, but the last glowing drops escaped her fingers,

merging into the opaque water that rescinded nothing but the
cracked shadow of her own face.

CHAPTER 1

She was not shrieking when she woke. She wasn't even crying. But a low, involuntary noise came from deep inside her, as it did every time she woke from a dream of him, to relive the loss all over again.

Nothing in Sophie's life before Lucas had prepared her for that loss. His death didn't just devastate her, it consumed her, so that she didn't know where grief ended and she began. It turned her days to a dull, protracted ache, her nights to the horror of dreaming of him, or the equal horror when she didn't. She truly didn't know which was worse: the cold reality of another night without him, or awakening from a sweet dream to an aftershock of that first, sickening thud of realization that she would never see him again.

Her only consolation then was how little time she had left to bear it. When she'd first learned that she would cease to exist on her eighteenth birthday, Sophie had been devastated. Now, a mere month later, it was almost a comfort. Of course, no one but

Michael knew about it. No one knew about the dreams, either; not even her mother, whom, more often than not, she woke to find standing over her bed, awakened by the keening, her eyes frightened and helpless.

Guilty as she felt for making her mother suffer, Sophie refused to talk about what had happened, allowing her parents to believe the story Michael had told them when they came to take her home from Ardnasheen. It was the same story he'd told to the police and the papers and the hospital that set her broken wrist. That she and her friends Ailsa and Lucas had all run afoul of a well-integrated sociopath, and she'd narrowly escaped becoming his victim. That Lucas had saved her life, but tragically drowned, along with the criminal, in doing so. That unlike Sam's, his body hadn't been found, and likely never would be. Not in that fathomless black water, full of fast currents and deep crevices.

Everyone believed his story, even Ailsa. Michael had cleaned up her recollection of that terrible night before anyone could question her, along with the blood and the remains of the Revenants. But when he'd turned to Sophie to do the same, she had fought him until he backed down. Every memory she had of Lucas was precious, and she meant to keep them all – even the painful ones.

"You can never talk about it," Michael had said to her, when he realized that he'd lost the argument. "You can never tell anyone what really happened."

"I'm not stupid, Michael," she'd said bitterly.

His eyes had been like an old dog's: sad and pleading. "Think about it, Sophie. It will be a terrible burden. I could take the pain away."

"You mean, make me forget."

"I mean, you don't have to suffer."

Her answer to that had been a withering look. She could see that he was worried, though he needn't have been. She could never have talked about what had happened that night, even if anyone would have believed it.

As it was, though, there was no parallel for her grief, and no outlet. She spent both day and night curled in her bed, eating only when forced to, pinned between merciless pain and the inability to cry, believing that nothing could ever be worse than living every day without Lucas. That was, until her parents threatened her with the hospital.

With her childhood bout of therapy still fresh in her mind, Sophie got up, got dressed and began to act out her "recovery". She had her hair cut into a bob that

hung just shy of her shoulders, because her mother assured her a new look would help her move on. She hid her dangerous thinness under layers of clothes. She even pretended to be enthusiastic when her mother suggested a move to Edinburgh, where the Art College had offered her a temporary teaching post after a lecturer had left unexpectedly.

"But I thought you hated Scotland," Sophie said, not wanting to alert her mother to her own dread of returning there.

Though Edinburgh was worlds away from Ardnasheen, it still felt too close for comfort.

"I hated living on a sheep farm in the middle of nowhere," Anna answered, putting a sandwich Sophie hadn't asked for down in front of her. "But Edinburgh is different. Tiny compared to London, of course, but still a city. And the art college is first rate. It's an honor to be asked."

Sophie picked at the sandwich, feeling as if her stomach were full of stones. "But what will I do there?"

"Get a job," her mother answered, with a canny look in her blue eyes and a steely practicality in her tone that told Sophie more than she would ever say aloud about the real reason for the move. "You could have a look at the university, too. Or take some music lessons – Edinburgh's a mecca for *clarsach* players."

Sophie said nothing to this. She hadn't touched her harp since Lucas died. She didn't think she ever would again. But to say so would only spark another argument. Besides, she could tell that her mother didn't really want to talk about university or music. She wanted to talk about the thing she hadn't yet said.

"Please just say what you mean, Mum," Sophie said dully.

She expected her mother to protest, to pretend Sophie hadn't guessed she had a motive. Instead, taking a deep breath, she answered, "It's time you put what happened behind you. Re-engaged with life."

Re-engage with life. It was impossible on so many levels that Sophie had the urge to laugh. Looking up at her mother, though, she knew that this would lead right into hospital. "Okay," she said, and went back to picking at the food she couldn't possibly swallow.

*

A few weeks later, lying in her old bed in the new flat in Morningside, Sophie had to admit that her mother had been partly successful in her first goal, if not her second. She hadn't had a dream since they'd arrived in Edinburgh – or none she'd remembered. Nor had she woken to find her mother standing over her, and slowly, as the days passed, her mother began to lose her hunted look. More to the point, she backed off a bit in her attempts at forcing food and sympathy onto Sophie.

And, as her mother had suggested, she got a job. She didn't particularly want one, but when she saw how desperately her mother wanted to believe that it would help her, she put in an application at a coffee shop and accepted the job they offered. She reasoned that it would at least make one of them feel better, and since she was going to be miserable anyway, it didn't much matter where she went about it.

On her first day of work, Sophie got up at six. The café didn't open until nine, but she always woke early now, even when she didn't dream. She left her bed and padded into the kitchen, cringing as her bare feet came into contact with the cold linoleum, and turned on the kettle with a hand only recently liberated of its plaster cast. When the water boiled, she filled a mug with it, and then folded her hands around it. She didn't want a drink, only the warmth of the hot porcelain.

As she held the mug, she gazed blankly out the window. The flat was on the top floor, and the view from the kitchen was an uninspiring montage of rusting downpipes, grizzled flowerboxes and soot-stained chimneys. Sophie stared at it until the water in the cup was lukewarm. Then she put the cup down on the worktop and went into the lounge.

She opened the curtains covering the big bay window, carefully avoiding her harp case which lay underneath. Anna had set up her easel in the window's flood of light, and was already at work on a blue-toned cityscape. Sophie thought she recognized a section of the Royal Mile, though she didn't know the city well enough yet to be certain.

It was definitely Edinburgh, though. Not the colourful, bustling Edinburgh of Festival brochures, but the late-autumn version, where the pubs' hanging baskets were full of weeds and papery brown leaves, and the grass in the parks bent and silvered with a heavy mist that never seemed quite cold enough to turn to frost, under a sky in shades of gray. *Bereft*, Sophie thought, and wrapped her arms more tightly around herself, trying not to feel the ruts and ridges of her starving body.

Abruptly, she turned from the window. She would go for a walk, to fill the time until the café opened. She pulled on clothes and boots, then an old waxed jacket of her mother's. She walked down the four flights of stairs, let herself out into the chill grey morning and then turned south, away from the city center.

414

She was going to the Braid Hermitage. She'd walked past its entrance with her mother several times. Though they'd never ventured inside, something about the dark tangle of woods so close to the city had pulled at her. The streets were quiet as she approached it, aside from a few early dog-walkers. By the time she reached the gate by the old Toll House, though, she was alone.

She paused to look at the little stone house. It was the kind of place she might have wanted to live one day, if things had been different: old enough to be interesting, small enough not to be intimidating. There was no sign of life in the house, now, though, and the garden was a tangle of long yellow grass and overgrown bushes.

A flicker of movement and colour at the back of the house caught Sophie's eye. She pushed through the creaking gate, onto the path that led into the reserve. At the center of the back garden she found what she was looking for. It was a small tree – a Hawthorn, she thought, though without leaves or flowers, it was difficult to tell. By the look of its gnarled and twisted trunk, it was very old. It was covered in bright strips of cloth tied to its twigs and branches, so that the tree seemed alive with multicoloured butterflies. A string of little silver bells hung from one of the lower branches, tinkling softly when it moved in the breeze.

The tree was beautiful, but there was also something strange about it, as if it belonged to another place or time. *Bells ward against faeries*. Sophie shivered, remembering the similar string of bells at Niall Aiken's cottage in Ardnasheen. Niall Aiken, who had become another of Sam's victims. Crossing her arms over her chest, Sophie looked around. At this time of the morning, a London park would have been populated with runners and dog-walkers. Except for one set of footprints in the mud of the track, however, she might have been the last person on earth.

Sophie stood looking at the path disappearing into the tangle of winter branches. For the first time since Lucas died, Sophie felt afraid. *What for?* she asked herself. No Revenants had appeared to her since the night on the boat, and at any rate, that night had proved that they weren't to be feared. As for human threats, there was little left for her to lose.

Shaking off her hesitation, Sophie began walking briskly up the path. The burn ran sluggishly beside it, smelling vaguely chemical, as all city streams seemed to do. A couple of mallards approached hopefully when they saw her, and then went back to picking at the stream bed for food when they realized she had none to offer. Other, smaller birds flitted among the bare branches, but there was something subdued about their movements and even their chatter, as if nothing could quite penetrate the early winter hush.

The footprints petered out at a shallow spot in the stream, across from a large stone house that Sophie thought must be the Hermitage that the park was named for. She stopped, looking around. There was still no sign of anyone but herself on the path. The silence felt thick, the bare trees and dark, glossy stands of rhododendron watchful. *You're being stupid,* Sophie told herself. *There's nothing here.*

And so what if there is? a smaller, deeper part of her wondered. What, after all, did it matter if one of Lucas's *sìth* appeared and swallowed her whole? She'd failed to save him, and saving him had been the purpose of her human life. Everything else was killing time.

Sophie looked down the muddy bank of the burn, daring something to emerge from the water. She saw nothing but a dead white moth, spiraling in an eddy. And then, something else. A flicker of movement that didn't belong. She climbed carefully down to the water's edge and peered into the shallow pool. A rusting ring from a pull-tab can glinted dimly among the pebbles. Fine green weed drifted in the current, anchored to a white stone.

Or did it? There was something slightly off about its movement, as if it were out of time with the flow of the water. And then, between one blink and the next, the stone became a face, the weed a spill of green hair fanning around it, bound with a filigree band of silver, studded with pearls. It was a beautiful face, but also terrifying, for although its features resembled a woman's, there was nothing human about it. The pallid skin was tinged blue-green, the cheekbones too sharp and the cheeks too hollow, the eyes golden and feral, with a cat's pointed pupils.

As Sophie watched, the water woman smiled with predatory glee and reached toward her with a pale, long-fingered hand. Sophie fell back with a cry as the tips of the woman's fingers breached the surface of the stream, thin and pale as bones. She

417

tried to push herself to her feet, but they slid on the slimy mud of the bank. She turned, engulfed now by terror, and grasped at the stones and exposed roots in the bank, dragging herself upward. Something cold and wet and strong as a vice closed around her ankle. She cried out again and kicked hard against whatever held her, and it let her go.

Sophie didn't pause to see whether she was followed. She scrambled up the rest of the bank, turned back the way she had come – and ran hard into something. She stumbled back, yelling again as she felt hands close over her shoulders. It took her several moments to realize that it wasn't any monster that had grabbed her, but a young man of about her own age.

A young man, she saw as she recovered from her initial shock, who belonged in a fashion photograph, or on the cover of the edgier type of romantic novel. He had fine-boned Eastern features, long black hair indifferently tied back with what looked like a loop of electrical cable, and the bluest eyes Sophie had ever seen. He was dressed in a jumbled collection of clothes: several shirts layered under a bobbled lime-green jumper, paint-spattered jeans held up by a red necktie threaded through the belt-loops, scuffed combat boots, and a black parka. He was asking her something.

"Pardon?"

"I said, are you hurt? Did you fall?" His accent was soft lowland Scots, cut with something more foreign, possibly Asian.

"No. It was…I mean, I was…" *What, Sophie? Seeing scary green-haired women in the water? Being chased by monsters?*

418

She drew a shuddering breath. "I thought I saw something down there," she said, pointing toward the bank she'd just scaled. "Something…bad."

He raised his eyebrows, but he turned toward the stream. He started toward it.

"I don't think you should go down there," Sophie said.

The young man only smiled, and disappeared over the edge of the bank. He was gone long enough that Sophie began to wonder whether he, too had fallen afoul of the woman in the water. Just as she took a step forward to look, though, he reappeared.

"I didn't see anything," he said, looking at her curiously as he dusted his hands on his trousers. They, too were paint-stained, the nails filthy.

Sophie wondered if she was losing her mind. She wondered if the man waiting for her to answer was as much a figment of her imagination as the green-haired woman had been. Because she had to have been. No other explanation made sense, least of all that she was real. Water horses in secluded Highland ponds were one thing; *sìth* in polluted city streams were quite another. Or so she wanted to believe.

Pushing that thought away, along with any doubts about the young man's reality, Sophie said, "I'm sorry. I thought that I saw something in the water, and then when I went to look I slipped, and caught my foot on the way back up, and my imagination got going…you know, with the woods and being by myself and all…"

She knew that she wasn't convincing him, even before she looked up to see his half-smile. "Look, thank you for coming to my rescue," she said, trying to sound calm and collected, "but really, I'm fine. Anyway, I've got to go. I'm expected at work…" She was already walking away, but the man didn't move. He just stood watching her with that same, strangely knowing expression on his face. "So…well…good-bye," she finished.

"Very well," he said as she began to walk away.

Very well? she thought. *Who talks like that?* Except, of course, she'd known someone who did.

"I'll see you soon," he added. And though it was only a throwaway expression, something told her that wasn't how he'd meant it.

About the Author

Sarah Bryant was born and raised in Maine and Massachusetts, before attending Brown University to study English and American literature. After that she moved to the UK to do a masters in writing, where she met and married her Scottish husband. After fifteen years in southern Scotland, Sarah and family have moved to the wilds of Washington state, USA, to the horse farm she's always dreamed of. *Bound* is her fifth novel for Snowbooks, and her first for young adults.